Pure

Pure

TIMOTHY MO

TURNAROUND
BOOKS

PURE

First published in Great Britain in 2012 by
TURNAROUND BOOKS
Unit 3 Olympia Trading Estate, Coburg Road, London, N22 6TZ

www.turnaround-uk.com

Copyright © Timothy Mo 2012

British Cataloguing in Publication Data

A CIP catalogue record for this book is available from the British Library.

ISBN 9781873262795

Typeset in Dante MT by Palimpsest Book Production Limited,
Falkirk, Stirlingshire

Printed and bound by CPI Group (UK) Ltd, Croydon, CR0 4YY

B.H.H
Let him come hither

This fiction is a distillation. About places and personages, dates and dialects, its principals have not always been exigent. None have any but an ideal existence in their own lucubrations.

Contents

PART ONE

Transformer

The ink of the scholar is more holy than the blood of the martyr.
– Hadith

The ancestral Jewish terms for it were, first, *Tum-tum*, dating perhaps from the Babylonian captivity. Sometimes the word was *andreygenes*, obviously of Alexandrian, Hellenistic origin – the two sexes merged in one erotic and perverse darkness. Mixtures of archaism and modernity were especially appealing to Ravelstein, who could not be contained in modernity and overflowed all the ages.
– Saul Bellow, *Ravelstein*

No one believes unless they have first doubted.
– Abu Hamid al-Ghazzali of Baghdad d. IIII, author of *The Incoherence of the Philosophers*, answered by Averroes in *The Incoherence of The Incoherence*.

A mutt like me.
– Barack Obama

Time like an ever-rolling stream
Bears all its sons away
They fly forgotten as a dream
Dies at the opening day.
– Isaac Watts 1674-1748

I

Snooky

Call me a Believer with a Blackberry, the Mohammedan with the Mac. Did I seek the destiny that follows? Was it my desire?

Did I cocoa. Was it heck.

But.

Something happened during my walk on the mild side. The hatch slammed and through it I shot, erect and natty as Saddam in his overcoat and coiled necktie, except for the mother of all drops I would dress myself in a seething ball-gown and would find on my lips not the kalima but some onomatopoeic Chinese imprecation.

I have never added up to what I wanted. The sum of me has never equalled my hopes. Whether I added to the store of self or subtracted from the principal, the result was equally unsatisfactory. For hours I would stand before the mirror, striving to look more female to my own regard: eyes larger, lips fuller, cheekbones more delicate. As soon as the mirage of femininity started to shimmer from the transparent depths of the glass, it would disappear. Giving up the forlorn struggle, I would then endeavour to look less mascu-line: absence of bristle, smaller ears, softer eyelashes. That never worked, either, and I would flounce away in tears which, did I but know it, gave additional lustre to my orbs. I wanted to be Miss World and I found myself serving a life sentence in a male body. I discovered myself as quite the wrong character in a story I never wanted to hear.

A pair of early memories for you. The nasty one first, so that the honeyed will be the one that lingers. Paw, my father, in company with my half-brother, Adi the thug, shaking me furiously by my meagre 12-year-old shoulders and shouting, "You are not mine, you cannot be mine! Whose are you?", then cutting off my long hair with a pair of earthy garden-shears. That still awakens me with the scalding dream-tears wet on my cheeks, so let me pass to the sweetest of remembrances: the little girl who came into the group of boys at school, took my seven-year-old hand, removed me from the game of football where no one had chosen me for their team, and led me to the skipping-rope and the song emphasised by the clapping hands. Oh, the happiness, oh, the belonging, oh, the joy. That girl was Jefri's younger sister.

I wouldn't want you to think I was miserable the whole time. Quite often, it was a throbless pain, like the cosmic anguish the tweedy philosopher knows in his study, the while he puffs contentedly on his pipe. I made sure I had a smile on my face. I looked prettier that way; it was better than make-up. Siam was the Land of Smiles – make that the Land of Wiles. It helped that I liked what I put in my mouth – incandescent green papaya salad topped by black field-crab, chased by a prophylactic squirt of breath-freshener. Oh, yah, and, of course, dicks both hooded and circumcised. I ate wonderfully well – that I knew after four years of daily insult to the palate overseas. I had plenty of sex. I had plenty of sunshine. We Asians like being Asians, Siamese being Siamese, Malays being Malays, Viets being Viets. But a warning. Scratch us, there's a snarling xenophobe behind the smile.

Personally – will you believe me – I've never truly hated outsiders. Not just because I was a non-belonger myself. Not just because of the gender issue. What mellowed me, what cosmopolitanised me, was Cinema. The movies were my joy, that and the whole pop culture. Contemporary, I mean. The Age of Aquarius is as lost as the Upper Cretaceous; punk is passé; hip-hop is history.

I had my columns in the *Siam New Sentinel*; you might have seen them. Professor Ainsley B. once told me *sotto voce* in my ear when he awarded me my prize that my film reviews could have appeared in the *Los Angeles Herald Examiner* or *The New York Times* without appearing out of place. I waited in vain for him to repeat this in his public panegyric into the microphone, but never mind.

Of course, to earn my crust I had to write subtitles for kung fu flicks and the local horror movies, supply the lines for the dubbing on the Japanese and European arthouse stuff, as well as write the jingles for cigarette and deodorant ads that preceded the movies in the malls of the capital. The commercials paid the best. Sometime they worked out as little screenplays, which were a labour of love. What I learned with the Taiwan and Hong Kong crap was that direct, literal translation was always lame and halting, while the bold and apparently discordant rendering into everyday idiom worked a treat. So, there'd be a group of woefuls in sheeny Ming or Ching drag with topknots or pigtails as appropriate, standing outside a blind-walled, courtyarded mansion or 15th century lantern-hung inn, reeling from some twist or other of the screenwriter's imagination (as well they might), usually the assassination of their teacher or the abduction of his daughter. "Eiyah!" or "Aiya!" was the exclamation of surprise and horror, preceding lines that my predecessors had rendered typically as "Eiyah! Landlord Chow's evil cohorts have kidnapped Mei Mei. I will have their intestines for suspenders." I would translate the "Eiyah!" as "Fuck me dead!" So, in my hands, it would go something like, "Bugger me backwards over a barge-pole! Those slimy mothers have nabbed teacher's kid. Let's cut their ghoolies off and fry them in boiling oil!" It was farcical, but it taught me a serious lesson on the way – you could pull anything, however weird, into your particular orbit and make it, if not normal, at least banal.

I am not a native speaker but I have an affinity for the English language. Once I heard an African say, "The English language is a harlot – she will go with anyone who cares to use her." (Me, I figured that just made her one of my Gang). What she was more like to me was the Fairy Godmother, finding me a ragged Cinderella without make-up, crying in the kitchen. She waved her wand but, alack and alas, midnight came all too soon. Yah, just thinking in English always made me calm down. It predisposed me to compromise and rationality, made me find nuance and ambiguity. Of course, I started like every other ungifted Siamese idiot with stuff like, "Him have cold same-same you before but now already sneeze littun-bit only." But as with anything – tennis, ballet, rhythmic gymnastics: oh, to prance twinkle-toed with swirling ribbon and whirling hoop! – I who had the talent soon left everyone at the starting-line behind, even though for a long time my accent dogged me like a *soi* cur, made my *farang* friends, even Avril, wince. Maybe it was my grating Tranny voice but, more, my lazy Thai tongue. You spoke Siamese without one but the *farang* needed the tongue to speak English, like you needed a jack to change a car-wheel. In the end to switch cultures or change languages was easier than converting from Fahrenheit to Celsius. When I spoke English I was an aristo, when I spoke native languages I was same-same everyone. No, worse and weaker than them.

I had high taste in cinema, low taste in literature. I always detested Hollywood, except for *The Wizard of Oz, Dr Strangelove, Some Like it Hot*, and, mebbe, *Shane*. In particular, I despised the works of Mr Steven M. Spielberg, the Jew whose middle initial is Mediocrity.

What do I like? All of Kurosawa, Satyajit Ray, Pontecorvo, Pasolini, Truffaut, Godard, Buñuel, Fellini, the early black and white Polanski, and the Bergman of *The Seventh Seal*. I could chuckle at Hitchcock's campness and admire his technique at the same time; laugh at old British stuff, *Carry On* films, Ealing comedies, the twists and turns English could take, the Cockney rhyming slangs. But the classics bore me. So Shakespeare and Beethoven send me to sleep; it's always a race between unconsciousness and appreciation where the former is destined to triumph. I can savour some antique stuff out of context. I liked Nietzsche's theme music to *Space Odyssey 2001*. I like science fiction. I read and re-read the stories of Borges, the blind Argentinian whose tales are serpentine but also fast and decisive as a sidewinder. I adore Japanese anime and manga. When I see them on the rack, I still pick up Betty and Veronica comics – with my black mane, I always identified with Ronnie.

Yet sometimes, just sometimes, I felt the classic English stir within me. Rather, it was words that came through me – despite myself – like I was a medium or a Ouija board. You could say it was the spirit or genius of the language, all its dead writers, coming through my mouth and brain like ectoplasm, or green, gooey Nickelodeon slime, something alien and repellent to trite, modern me but having its irresistible way. Still, there existed a limit to what the great thinkers of the past could tell me. I appreciated the form in which their thoughts were cast but the content was beyond me. Their experience was not relevant to mine. That was the reality as opposed to the piety.

Yah, but Hollywood . . . well, Hollywood, I felt, had failed America, itself, and also us, the outside world. It was founded by Jews, you know. All the major studios were Jew-run, Jew-owned. Mayer, Goldwyn. They had backgrounds in dry goods retail in

New York before opening the early live entertainment halls and then starting their historic move to California. They were outsiders and they still possessed that mercy the outsider is prepared to extend to those even worse off. The lynch-mob in a Western is simply the pogrom in Stetsons. Maybe they'd have found a place in their hearts for the poor ladyboy. In the early Westerns rarely is the hero the Lawman; rather the Outlaw, the Outsider, the saddle-tramp, the Wandering Jew but armed and, um, in chaps. The Western was ostensibly the quintessential, the most undiluted American genre but in reality the most adulterated, the most adaptive, the most eclectic, the foreignest. There was the spaghetti Western of the Seventies but even before that, at the grand buffet of American cinema, there had been the Sashimi Western – *Seven Samurai* and *Yojimbo* become vehicles for Brynner and Eastwood. And why stop there? They even sent poor Kurosawa into the future and Outer Space with *Star Wars* – the quarrelling robots, the fugitive Princess, all anticipated in *The Hidden Fortress*. (Yah, sorry to recycle the start of my prizewinning review, but I was so proud of it).

I once wrote a satirical screenplay (you figure out who the satire is on).

FARSI FORCE FIVE

or

IRANIAN NAVY SEALS (INS)

EXT. – DUNES. NIGHT

A pair of Iranian Navy Seals clad in desert ghilly suits and checked turbans lie in the sand with infra-red binoculars to their eyes. They are armed with Dragunov sniper rifles, fitted with bulky Starscopes, AK-74 assault rifles, a PKM light machine-gun, RPG-7 rocket launchers, and Makarov pistols. Thousands of stars glitter in the constellations overhead, matching the lights from an American armoured column encamped below in a winding wadi. Another trio of diehards join them, sprawling in the sand.

ALI (Team Leader)
Yo, Raghead!

HUSSEIN
Hey, Sand Nigger!
(They Hi-Five).

KUBLA
Yo!

TARIK
Present!

MUSLIM
Hoo-hah!

ALI
Fedayeen, lock 'n load.

TARIK
Roger that, Fellow Believer.

ALI
Clock your four. Three bad guys coming your way.

A trio of US Marines, smoking cigarettes and carrying rolls of toilet paper, trudge up the sand-hill. One clutches the seat of his pants, the other his abdomen.

HUSSEIN
Dude, ice those Infidels.

The first glimmers of a rosy dawn become discernible in the East. The thick, black stubble on all the Iranian Navy Seals' faces is apparent. An open box of Turkish Delight lies in the sand, next to a gagged sheep in red cami-knickers.

TARIK
I have a visual on the Impious. Switching to optical from infra-red.

MUSLIM
Wind half-value 2 knots ESE. Range . . . Frick . . . laser's screwed.

ALI
Use the reticles.

KUBLA
Yeah, bro'. Shoot them fuckin' hereticals in the reticles.

TARIK
Roger. Range to target 700 metres. Temperature 29 degrees.
Barometric Pressure 1010 millibars. Humidity unchanged. Check,
check. Adjusting windage two minutes of angle.

MUSLIM
The kafirs have stopped. They're squatting. Don't take deflection.

TARIK
Shall I make the shot?

ALI
On my three.

*At this critical juncture the whine of the turbo engine of an Abrams
tank drowns their whispered conversation. The monster can be seen
throwing up huge plumes of sand, pink as the Turkish Delight in the
fingers of the dawn.*

ALI
Wait, wait. No, no, no.

TARIK
Take the Unbelievers out?

*A huge boom! and the long brass cartridge case of the Czarist-era
Mosin-Nagant 7.62x54R round used in the Dragunov spins high into the
air, glittering in the roseate rays of the virgin desert day.*

ALI
You idiot! I said "No! No! No!" Not "Go! Go! Go!"

KUBLA
Hey, man! Now I know why we always say "Negative!" instead
of "No!"

ALI
Take the fuckin' shot!

MUSLIM
He was short, line was correct.

TARIK
Adjusting elevation dial one click.

*Another huge boom! The three American Marines, now seen to be two
black, one white, who had been crouched down – in fear – and also in
line – are thrown backwards into the air.*

MUSLIM
One shot, three hits.

ALI
In the Name of God!

HUSSEIN
Alhumdulillah!

TARIK
Peace be upon their heads. Not.

HUSSEIN
Hit, hit, hit. Yay, Mujaheedin. Three Christians sent to Jehovah.

*ALI runs into the open, firing long bursts from the box-fed LMG. An
entire company of 100 Marines rushing from their tents, carrying rolls
of toilet paper and M-4 carbines, are sent bowling over in sprays of
sand. An American Apache attack helicopter flies towards him, spewing*

flames from its 2-inch rocket pod and chain-gun. An A-10 fixed-wing tankbuster swoops from his right. The long, whirring thunder from its fixed, nose-offset 30mm Gatling gun sounds like a giant wind-up toy. The spent casings from its depleted uranium rounds pock the dunes like the rain they have never known. ALI's shorter burst makes the Apache disintegrate into a huge orange fireball. It explodes in the air and again on impact. FX. The face of its hook-nosed pilot, the name BERNSTEIN clearly painted on his helmet, contorts in fear as the electronic aiming monocle drops from his eye. HUSSEIN fires a single shot from his Makarov pistol at the A-10 as it zooms past at 500 knots and 700 feet altitude. The pilot slumps in his titanium-armoured tub. The jet crashes into the dunes, one of its tail-mounted engines breaking off and spinning 100 feet into the air before MUSLIM fires the RPG at it, causing it to smash into 1001 silver splinters and shards, pink in the glare of the rising sun.

TARIK
Eat your fuckin' heart out, Chuck Norris!

ALI
Nice work, team! Now let's go kick some more Judaeo-Christian ass!

KUBLA
Ee-hah!

(They speed into the distance in a commandeered US Humvee to the strains of 24 Hours from Tulsa. Montage of Gene Pitney singing, super-imposed over now orange ball of desert sun).

I HAVE TWO STUFFED toys in my room, one is Minnie Mouse and one is Daisy Duck, both in high heels and mini-skirts. Snooky has taken the liberty of decapitating both of them. On their necks I have mounted rubber balls and on those balls pasted photos of the faces of Mr Sylvester Stallone and Mr Steven Seagal. I hate violence, I really do, the pathetic, patriotic pornography of Hollywood. It was always an easy target for collage. I used to do lots of them, many featuring the younger Bush in a pixie hat. They went like hotcakes in Khao San Road.

It was Avril who put it to me that Hollywood actors – in fact, everyone, cinematographers, FX, sound, sparks, editors – are much, much better than the vehicles they appear in. But the films themselves cannot be more artistic or more intelligent or they wouldn't make their money back. The Hollywood movie isn't the equivalent of a mediocre novel or even gonzo journalism; it is rather the thick book laid up in piles at airport bookstores come to lumbering life-in-death.

Avril was one of my best friends. Out of foreigners and out of women – born women, I mean – she was the very best. It was just horribly ironic she had a name I could never say properly. Every time I mustered tongue against recalcitrant palate, *Av-ree-yoo* would come limping out my mouth. At one time she had been Dean and Journalism Instructor at one of the biggest English language schools in Bangkok. I'd met her first when she was working in a financial boiler-room with 37 other *farangs*, cold-calling her product an inch this side of the law. It was actually disreputable me who'd made Avril respectable by getting her part-time restaurant reviewing on a give-away advertisement sheet. She'd parleyed this into "media experience" and from there moved into "education" and then back again into print journalism but higher up the food-chain. Yah, yah, she retaliated by calling me a "bottom-browser", what else? Originally, she'd replied to the self-serrated tear-off stickers I'd posted to lamp-posts in Asoke, offering personal Thai conversational classes for all levels, just after I'd arrived job-less in the capital. In our first lesson I taught her the Siamese for ice-cream (*Ice-a-Karee*). Yah, the Thai language loves euphony and abhors final consonants. This was followed by *Is-a-Lam* and *Is-a-Lat*. You guessed the first. The last means "freedom".

"Oh, what a coincidence," said Avril, with the formality and politeness of our early acquaintance. "Doesn't Islam mean 'submission' in Arabic?"

I complimented her on her general knowledge and in my inno-cence thought the first class had gone very well. I mean, come on; she'd never forget those first three words, even if she was reeling with shock at the spectacle her teacher presented.

However, "Oh, boy, were you ever disappointed when I showed," she had the nerve to accuse me, when we knew each other slightly better. "You were hoping for a hunk, weren't you?"

Our friendship would be cemented 13 months later by a three-day trip up-country to Chiang Mai where one of Avril's teachers would expire in circumstances far more exasperating than the norm (say, of a heart-attack, drunk, on top of a pre-pubescent Cambodian girl). This teacher, alternatively Paul or Paula, had been a *katoey farang*; yah, an American post-op Trannie. She'd been stabbed by her Thai b-f who'd gone on to strangle himself with the very effective ligature electric flex makes, if you're ever thinking of shuffling off this mortal, uh, coil: it doesn't suffocate you uncomfortably but bites into the carotid and jugular, cutting off oxygen supply to the brain and putting you outta your misery in seconds. It was my little set's preferred method. Wish I'd known when I'd staged my juvenile bid back home; then I wouldn't be carrying those scars on my wrists. Yah, suicide – the *katoey*'s barmitzvah. A ladyboy was never alone. A *katoey* had two constant companions: Su and Ana, suicide and anorexia. Ana was closer at hand, more demanding. Su was a beckoning vision in the distance, enticing, alluring. I did my best to stay away from the bitch but sometimes she closed the distance before you knew it.

Avril's misery and mine lasted longer. I set up the cremation for Paula and her lover at the *wat*, not mentioning I wasn't a Buddhist, and even cleavered the ritual coconut and splattered its juice on the faces of the cadavers. I was permitted to stand not too far from the monks; I counted nearly as a guy, even with my hefty aura of Chanel *No 19* or *Shalimar,* not to mention my tartan miniskirt. Avril couldn't get within ten feet of the monks, especially the young ones doing the religious equivalent of National Service.

"Thanks, Hon," she said afterwards. "I don't know what I would have done without you."

"You're darn right," I said. "What in hell's name were you thinking of, hiring her? An A-list weirdo." (Paula had tried to top herself three times before the Thai guy had done it for her – like mine, the old scars had been visible on the wrists of her corpse, except with her three chevrons she had been a sergeant and I had just been a corporal).

"I cannot believe my ears, Snooky. How can you of all people be so self-righteous?"

"Just because I'm a Tranny doesn't mean I'm a fruit cake. We're not all the same behind the lip gloss, you know. I'm not a fricking freak-show. I'm your friend – Snooky."

She squeezed my hand and that was that. We were great girl-friends.

I've never been with a girl – some in my set had – but once Avril and I kissed at Hogmanay. She was drunk, I was high on ice. Her tongue flicked into my mouth. She exclaimed, "You kiss like a girl, not a guy."

"How do you know? Got a dykey past?"

"Because I've kissed guys, nitwit."

I was good company for Avril. She had a lousy social life. I'd be out with her when the *farang* men, so far from merely ignoring her, would insult her. Oafish comments made well within what they knew was earshot. With Isarn prostitutes coming outta the wain-scotting, Avril was their chance to get revenge on every Caucasian woman who'd rejected them back home. "We're the ones with the power here, you old cunt," one of the more lucid said to her in the basement bar of a five-star off Silom. "Here we do the choosing, here we're the chicks." As I was about to grab this most appropriate opportunity to retort, Avril elbowed me in the solar plexus with a panache a kickboxer would have envied. Like all the Siamese, I loathed the *farang* men in Bangkok. Well, I'll make an exception for the ones who admired me. I thought the other guys the most selfish, ignorant losers anywhere. There was another occasion when I seri-ously thought of pepper-spraying a *farang* who was rude to her at the taxi-rank – knowing every Siamese in the vicinity would turn out with bottles and sticks to help me. But Avril once again got her arm in the way and said, "Hey, hey, you're a kinda weird knight in shining white armour." The third time it happened, I realised Avril didn't need back-up. A drunk reeled up behind her while she was ordering her takeaway *latte*. With a leer she couldn't see, he asked, "Sucked any good cocks lately?" Without turning round, she answered levelly, "No, I can't say I have, but I bet you did." She didn't demolish the guy; she vapourised him. At the peril of the brimming paper cups, I threw my arms around her outside.

The day I told her she reminded me of Sally Bowles in *Cabaret* but in turn of the millennium Bangkok, not Hitler's Berlin, she positively glowed. What I meant was, she reminded me of Liza Minnelli: short hair, pixie face. She was lovely but ridiculously conscious of her big legs. I sometimes thought she put up with me because she admired my slim ones so much. Anyway, that's Avril. She's the only person I told about the diagnosis shortly before I had to leave for the South.

She was my escort when I went to get the prize – best arts critic writing in English language medium as non-native speaker (SE Asian region), sponsored by an Australian Bank. I got US $8,000, not Australian. Judges were Professor Ainsley B., the chain-smoking 6ft 7ins tall Professor Emeritus at Arteneum with a 4ft 10 ins Filipina in tow, young enough to be not just his daughter but his fricking grand-daughter and Saoul Bello, a completely different kind of Filipino. Thereafter, I liked to say his name quickly as in that case people might get the impression I had won the plaudits of the famous Jewish author of *Herzog the Rain King*. This would have given the left-wing Dr Bello fits, as he had made his name from zealous anti-Americanism and, by extension, firm anti-Zionism.

I passed this happy thought on to Avril, who hissed back, "Henderson, you idiot! The author never thought of his character as anything other than Henderson! And Bellow was a closet Canadian!"

"Oopsie!"

Dr. Evelyn B., Professor Ainsley's brother, a gossipy queen with a sexual appetite even heftier than his hetero twin's, had winked at me before the announcement and indiscreetly told me I'd won. He got a scolding from Ainsley and a black look from the bank's representative but, thanks to his congenital inability to keep a secret, I was able to get an extra dab of lip gloss on and feign an even greater degree of surprise than I would have done before I went on to give what Avril told me was an utterly inappropriate impersonation of Meryl Streep getting the Oscar.

I forgot Evelyn quickly. I mean, camp is to Tranny as cocoon is to butterfly. However, not only would we meet again one day but we would – how can Snooky put it? – play correspondingly important parts in each other's lives.

Anyhow, those days of preview, premiere, prize-giving, press conference, photo call, pre-prandial cocktails, unspoiled by unpleasant premonitions, are long past. They were my golden age, my private Renaissance, the sheen long since dulled into the mere patina of recollection. Of course, nostalgia does deceive. I wouldn't want you to think everyday involved haute couture, catwalks, disco openings, free lunch with the septuagenarian male restaurant critic ("I handed the Dragon Fruit to my colleague who, with her long nails, was far better equipped to peel it than I"), or me being thrown screaming into the deep end of a hotel swimming-pool and losing the top half of my bikini to no very grave scandal as I had chosen to remain flat – and, of course, as infertile – as the Isarn plateau.

To be honest, here's how seven out of ten days went: wake-up at noon, masturbate, re-draft review, drugs, chatroom, Rubik cube, paint nails, masturbate, drugs, read emails, third draft, check Do-Ann's latest on-line porn movie, doze, fourth draft, drugs, strip nails and enamel again, fifth draft, write, drugs, Rubik cube, nails. I took Nubain and amphetamine. If you surmise the meth induces repetitive behaviour, yah, you're right, you're right. I injected the opiate and smoked the meth. Once a month I'd drop an E before I went dancing. I kicked the habits some time ago, of course. Would I be so forthcoming? It was safer to get the ampoules of Nubain on prescription from a tame doctor, or, to put it more precisely, to have the prescription form handy to explain the black market vials I could get for US$3. It's synthetic, not from a plant like cocaine or morphine, which must be why it's so cheap. I only started on it as a downer for the amphetamine while I was in Manila. You can't sleep after meth; you're an ice zombie. You can't eat a morsel, either. That's why they gave it to Liza Minnelli's mother, Judy Garland. Actually, though neither drug can be said to be addictive in the physical sense, the meth you smoke is more of a pull than the injectable opiate. Nubain isn't at all addictive, not like heroin or crack. Three, four times a week was all I needed. But, I confess, I confess, I'd have the flame under the meth four or five times daily.

Oh, what a joyous ritual it always was! You needed two half-inch wide strips of aluminium foil. The easiest (and safest) form to carry them was as the wrappers for sticks of our local blueberry chewing-gum. You soaked a pair of foils in a glass of water, peeled off the wet, adhering tissue-backing as gently as if it was the membrane of a dick, and you were ready. One strip was to roll around something like a diary pencil or a drinking-straw for the tooter, the other was to fold into a long V-shaped run as the pipe which held the drug. The cheapest cigarette lighter acted as a heater. Remove the flame-guard and fold a tiny chimney of rolled foil to focus the flame. In order to ignite the gas you would have to hold the flue to another source of flame as the sparker would have gone with the flame-guard. Like everyone else, I kept a thin yellow Buddha candle alight for this purpose.

The knack was to make the meth hot enough to melt but not so hot it caught fire. Both the red *yah bah,* or *Mad Mix,* pills from Burma and the crystal meth splinters that did, indeed, resemble pulverised ice behaved at the end exactly the same, though their presentation was so different. The methamphetamine both contained melted into caramel, this liquid sledged merrily down the foil, the meth sublimated into smooth, sumptuous, albino clouds and you sucked up, the neophyte quickly for fear of losing it to the atmosphere, the habitué in a slow, steady pull into the lungs.

Why did a smart, well-educated chick like Snooky do it? Well, it was like being picked up by a giant trapeze or swing and whirled 600 feet in the air in a rush of utter joy. That lasted a few all-too-short seconds but afterwards not only was your mind fresher and clearer than it had ever been (since your last hit, silly) but the entire skin of your body was a giant, delicious organ of sensation. When you were high, a touch from Frankenstein's monster or Quasimodo could make you swoon with the lasciviousness a meth-less caress from the beloved never could. Even as your partner breached your sphincter (or you hers) you had freeloaded the portals of bliss.

The red pills were cut with caffeine to 30 per cent strength (there was a green double-strength pill as well), while the more expensive ice would be 99 per cent virgin. But so what? The billowing fumes were exactly the same, without the acridity of cigarette smoke, only a slight chemical singe to it if you'd overheated. I can hear the crack and pop of the crystals in my mind even now. I'd get about 13 hits out of a retail sachet of ice, again the size of a fingernail, the same but less potent from the red pill which was exactly the diameter of a drinking straw (in which they were transported with the ends stapled and heat-sealed off). Funny thing was, the residue, the *"Kee"* or crap as we called it, what you scraped off the spiral folds of the uncoiled tooter and smoked again, using the former pipe as a tooter this time, was a lot stronger than the virgin, unspoiled chemical – meth *refritos,* I guess.

Nubain I used to think of as Protestant, compared to the Catholicism – the charismatic Mexican Catholicism – of the meth. It was between you and the transfiguring drug. No candle, no glittering receptacle, no incense clouds. Unlike that other injectable, heroin, no heating in a spoon with the holiest water available. You stuck the needle in the ampoule, pulled out the plunger of the syringe, and shot up. Fastidiously, I wiped my skin with alcohol first. There would be the coolness of evaporation, followed by the heat of the hit; the quick sting of the needle, then the fluffiness of no pain. Nevertheless, to watch, it was a clinical, unglamorous process. Even Ritchie or Tarantino's cameraman could have made nothing out of it. In the vein of the forearm would leave brown tracks with time, even with the horizontal laddering of thin razor scars I'd inflicted on myself in my teens, not to mention the suicide stripes. Instead I'd shoot up into the chunky, thick purple cicatrix I had concealed deep in the web of my thumb and forefinger. You'd never know. I thought of it as my spider-hole, my Warhol. Talking of Tuan Andy, I remember the scene from *Chelsea Girls* where Brigid Berlin, a pal of his favourite actress, the svelte Nico, who was the beautiful other I imagined myself to be, administered herself a shot of I don't know what, smack or distilled water, straight into her big, fat butt through the denim of her blue jeans. Never seen anything like it. Made you feel sorry for the needle.

In those days I was whippet-thin, with a good complexion and glossy hair. The oestrogen pill (no, I didn't smoke it) made the face just as lustrous and smooth as it did my mane as beneficent side-effects of its real purpose which was to puff the little I had on my chest, widen my hips and rounden my arms. All of which it reliably did. Funnily enough, it didn't blur the shape of the leg, as it did with the arm, which none of us wanted anyway. The male knee, honey, is incomparably superior to the female as an aesthetic object. My thighs were long, slim, athletic without being overly so; my calves elegant as Dietrich's had been. Our legs, my legs, looked better than any born gals. Poor Avril. What no drug on earth could do was give us dainty feet or tiny pinkies. The pedal extremities – allow me this – remained galumphing. Pedicure just made it the more obvious. I do, however, recall the time when – in a lustful reverie of cascading dopamine – I got a hard-on staring at my own shiny toe-nails.

I confessed proudly to Avril, "I guess you could say that's the depths of perversion."

"No," she retorted, "the height of narcissism."

I could never have come back from that but in any case we were leaving the newspaper office on the slim canal boat and I was slammed back into my seat as we roared off at water-ski speed to disembark three miles and six minutes later with ruined hair-dos and glazed eyes. Good as a fairground-ride but nothing to beat the meth high.

I figure if I could choose a place and time, as opposed to body, where I could have lived it wouldn't have been, say, the Athens of Plato, the Medina of the Prophet, or the Florence or Rome of Leonardo and Michaelangelo, but New York in the late 1960s and early 1970s. Of course, it's vanished, so it might as well be Neverland. I wasn't born until 198- and then into quite the wrong corporeal and social circumstances. I was 6ft tall with size 10 feet. I guess just as some animals are more equal than others, so some *katoeys* are more female than others. There was quite a range from Miss Gay World aka Miss Queen, lovely pre- and post-op Trannies, indistinguishable from beautiful female film stars, except for their voices (the long gowns hid the huge shoes) to thugs in drag so hairy, redoubtable, and grizzled, Snooky wondered why the fags bothered.

I fell in between. Maybe if I wasn't good-looking enough to have been one of the starlets at Tuan Andy's factory, I could have been a cheerleader for the New Wave; I could have been an acolyte of Morrissey's, a disciple of Warhol, an intimate of Edie, a confidante of Ultraviolet. Oh, the times we could have had! Oh, the high old times! And for me the High Priest would not be Warhol himself but Mr Lou Reed. I wrote a five-page appreciation of the Velvet Underground for the 1066 Lifestyle magazine – the one I recommended Avril to: they took her articles but never paid her – so I can refer you to that in depth. Suffice it to say here that the game of spot-the-influence on all of later pop, that is to say punk, grunge, post-punk, house, rap, too, can be played for ever. It's all in the Underground; they were way, way ahead of their day and they've never dated since. It's as fresh as the day (or night) it was first jammed.

In another sense, it has never dated, as well. Most of them, musicians and camp-followers, groupies, girl-friends and fag-hags, died young or young-ish. They had short, beautiful lives. That's what Snooky would choose; yah, that's what Snooky has. I've got a poster in my room; it dominates it, actually. Better, the poster has a room to flaunt itself in. It's a B & W pic of Candy Darling on the bed upon which she was to die, aged 28, wearing a blonde wig, maybe because of the chemo. They say she got the blood cancer because of the hormones she was ingesting by the fistful but maybe that's urban legend like the hair-dye and Jackie Kennedy's brain tumour. About that I don't know, but I can say she was born James Slattery but then M2F, girl, just like me. Joe Campbell was the one they called the Sugar Plum Fairy. They are all immortalised in *Walk on the Wild Side*. I must play that 22 times a day on my pod or my phone. I had the entire album – a title to conjure with, too – as what they called an LP on black vinyl digitally remastered at great expense and then, fuck it, peer to peer came along. I figure I shouldn't begrudge my surviving idols their paltry royalty, anyhow.

I didn't need to pay royalties to Princess Diana and the other Sloane Rangers for my favoured affirmative *"Yah!"* I picked it up from, I think, the gossip column in *Vanity Fair*, not an English mag as you might expect, and I swear I heard the Princess's lady-in-waiting saying it once when a CNN news crew was eavesdropping. Its languor suits a tall person, assent graciously dropped, y'know, from a height. Besides in Siamese, the more proletarian or American "Yeah!" is the homonym for "terrible" or "atrocious", so you'd be quite likely to get a knee in the face for merely giving your assent.

Well, Snooky better tell you about the life she had rather than the one she wanted. I actually know what Little Joe and his side-kicks, never losing their heads even while they were giving it, felt like. You know, escaping the restrictions of their small towns and big families, and finding their new selves in the anonymity of the great city. That hadn't changed in 30 years and across continents when I made the same jump. Truth to tell, it was probably harder for them. Asians are easier-going, more tolerant. I used to hear Avril complaining how conformist we were, which was true enough about us in the bunch, but, when it came to individual people, we cut them more slack. And then when it came to TVs, shit, there were many more of us here. Siam, Singapore, and the Philippines must hold three-quarters of the ladyboys in the world. Put at its crudest – yah, depend on me to do that – I was much less likely to be kicked to death on a Bangkok street than on the New York subway. In fact, we were more likely to be doing the kicking than the straights. TVs, at least Asian TVs, are mostly tall. Nine out of ten will be. No one in my group was under 5-11, except for Air

Fun. We were an impressive sight, lemme tell you. When we strolled through the street-market a ripple of excitement or visible shock-wave of cupidity amongst the vendors preceded us. We had so much more buying-power than mere girls. Big smiles wreathed the faces of the female vendors, eager anticipations we rarely disappointed. Lipstick tubes, mascara boxes, unguent pots, perfume sprays, jars of face-whitener and tubes of armpit-blancher, eyeliner, nail varnish, rainbow palettes of face powder, sparkling glitter blush-on, were snatched up by us with joyful shrieks. One seller dealt only in large-sized female shoes, another only in gowns for a giantess. We were only too ready to pay hard cash. The haggling which characterised the secretaries' and shopgirls' dealing with stall-owners was unknown to us.

The group I hung out with in my first days in the city were a lot rougher than the models and promotion queens whose number I was to crash months later. There were 11 in this outfit.

THE GANG
or
THE OUTLAWS

1. *Do-Ann*, meaning *Moon* or *Month*. So-named after the monthlies she could not have.
2. *Air Fun*. Her name meant *Apple*. She was the shortest, 5-9, and did her hair in a pageboy.
3. *Poo*, which doesn't mean what you think, but signifies *Crab*.
4. *Goong* or *Prawn*.
5. and 6. *Lek* and *Noi*, or *Tich* and *Tiny*. They were the biggest among us, 6-3 and 6-1.
7. *Mew*, meaning *Milk* as said in a Siamese accent. She'd changed it from the more vulgar *Nom*, which could mean Tits as well as Milk.
8. *Chompoo*, meaning *Pink*, not shit-chewer.
9. *Om* or *BJ* – onomatopoeic. So-named because she never gave them. For a *katoey* this was as rare as a vampire who didn't drink Type B.
10. *Wow* (as in the exclamation of surprise) meaning *Kite*. To fly a kite meant masturbate.
11. *Cartoon* – self-explanatory.

Like I say, Tich was a 6ft 3ins amphetamine pusher (the Mad Mix *yah bah* pills adulterated with caffeine, not the uncut ice). Poo and Goong specialised in shoplifting at big department stores. Being the skinniest and most feminine of us, they could fool some male store detectives. Into the fitting-room in a loose, long dress and out with multi-layers of French blouses and Billabong shorts underneath. Milk and Tiny were the deftest pickpockets, followed by Om and Wow. We others would just provide distraction and cover for them, grabbing some poor *farang*'s or Jap's balls, sticking our tongues down his throat without any preamble at all, while Milk and Tiny divested their victim of his wallet, phone and, quite often, wristwatch as well. Very late at night it might degenerate into the next best thing to a frank mugging. Never pick a fight with us. It's a mistake to think we're defenceless. When push comes to shove, we're men with a man's strength; maybe wiry rather than bulky but that's always better in a bundle. Did you ever see the *katoey* kickboxer, Noon? Or catch the movie about her life? I gave it a rave in the *New Sentinel*. Divine and deadly in the same mouthful. She said she never knew whether to kiss her opponents when they were reeling or elbow them in the face. Do-Ann certainly knew what was required. I've seen her, shining in her blush-glitter like the moon she was named after, make many a burly *farang* see the stars that surround her by night when she wound up a big one to the temple or behind the ear, assisted by a falsetto warcry and the brassknuckles she carried in her purse. Effete but redoubtable, no?

I had the bad fortune to be present at one such affray – not at all my choice of social event even in my delinquent late teens – when a huge, simply enormous, black guy who'd already banged out Tich's front teeth and sent the silicone fishbone in Pinkie's septum deviating East-West instead of North-South showed signs of continuing belligerence from the kerb where he'd been neatly tap-tripped. Most of us had pepper spray but the novelty in town in those far-off days was an electrical stungun disguised as a cell-phone. We'd already stymied more than one snapping *soi* dog. The devices made a nasty rasping (not unlike Do-Ann's voice) as they powered up and then a blue halo jumped across the horns of the terminals with an intimidating snap. I grabbed it from Air Fun. It was clear she was longing, just longing, to test it on a human subject. (Siamese people consider blacks very nearly human). I held it an inch from his eye and recited as if it was the Gettysburg Address: "This is a MK II Brandenburg Taser, the most powerful hand-held, non-lethal weapon in the world. If your idea of a good time is lying totally paralysed but perfectly conscious on the pavement while a six foot *katoey* with an eight-inch dick stands over you, then go ahead, get up and fight. What's it gonna be, punk? Do you feel lucky? Well, do you? Make my night."

Of course, he chose discretion as the better part of valour. As we left, Prawn, who hadn't understood a word but comprehended 100 per cent of the tone and gist as if it had been Dirty Harry reciting the lines, said reproachfully to me, "Big Sista, you know what you are? A macho ladyboy, that's what, *tea ruck*." She was speaking ruefully – I'd had her without benison of latex or KY right up the ass the previous week and the silver piercings in my navel had cut her crack and coccyx.

Now, uh, that brings me to my next point. Only one of us in the group had, at that stage, proceeded to ultimate recourses. The surgeon's knife. Gender re-assignment. I heard Tangier used to be the place in Candy Darling's day but no longer. Bangkok and, especially, Phuket were the places. Foreign *katoeys* swelled the hospitals' revenues, as if there weren't enough home grown re-assignees. We weren't really a criminal bunch or, to put it more truthfully, our hearts weren't in the commission of our misdeeds. It was to get together the $3,000 for Poo's man-made vagina, a prospect as long in the planning, and eventually, as under-utilised in its first months, despite the ploy of a cheap tariff for similar market reasons, as the Bangkok subway system. A little tinkering with busts, noses, Adam's apples and what-have-you (or what-have-you-not) didn't count. Me, like I said, I was flat as a boy. Guys liked it more. In fact, it had dawned on me one dawn in Pattaya Beach Road that guys liked my penis a lot as well. "I have everything, why you not taking me?" was the wail of many a rejected post-op transformee. The guys, you know, didn't want a mutilated man. They wanted chicks with dicks. In my experience, they couldn't wait to get their lips round it, these paragons of hirsute heterosexuality. From my own point of view, I didn't wanna be parted from my cock. I was unique in this, I think, but I loved the unbearable tingling in the eggs when I was being butt-fucked. Didn't happen every time and was usually from being long-dicked by a Caucasian – tickling the prostate way up there – but it was not a sensation I readily wanted to lose. Oh, it was lovely.

After work, whether mugging or compensated orgy, we'd relax the same way, slurping soup noodles at rickety tin tables on the pavement, our long legs jutting out from the tiny stools designed for the standard-sized Siamese heteros who looked down on us morally and over whom we towered physically.

DO I NEED to say that these were the joys of metropolitan existence? Up country had been worse than a wet day in Christian purgatory. With the exception of my Paw, though, most of my family had been OK. Fathers are famously troublesome about *katoey* sons and mine was no exception. Education was all about earning more money. I should have been an attorney or worked in a bank. My Mare (please pronounce as female horse) and Paw would have settled for businessman, as long as I was a straight. A family guy, right, with a house and lot and 4.7 children, sitting in the back seat of a Corolla, purchased on collateralised bank loan. What they got – and what they would much rather not have seen – was a near six foot TV with a rhinoplasty and artistic aspirations in a foreign language that were unlikely to prove revenue-generating. After the time he'd cut my hair with the garden-shears, Paw did once raise his hand to me. I was 15, tall as I am now but much skinnier, even without the meth habit. I'd said something sassy back after he'd told me to take the red paint off my toenails and, for the sake of the good name of Pattani Muslims, to walk like a man. The hand went back but he didn't strike. Mare knew much better than to try to interfere on my behalf. It would only have made things hotter for me. Paw just flicked up my hair where I kept it behind my ears, concealed against the time I'd perambulate not in *sarong* but tight, belted shorts with my "girl" friends. I understood his dismay. I just wish he understood mine. I was gonna have a very tough time at 17 with the army conscription. His best friend had a son who was a kickboxing regional youth champion. Paw would have settled for a weekend soccer player. What I did was shriek when I leapt for a volley-ball, not that I had to go that far for it, given my height. I played on the girls team when I could, e.g. when it was not strict competition where the other team could cry foul. Yah, Snooky was an iron lady years before the movie *Iron Ladies* was ever released. Paw wouldn't let me wear the girls' uniform of long black pleated skirt and short-sleeved white blouse and thick belt to school, though I always walked with the females down the leafy, red-earth lane. Despite the strife with Paw, those were days of innocence, me as Eve in the Garden. Twenty years back, schools weren't segregated. Girls would wear the veil; girls wouldn't wear the veil. Muslim boys invariably chose to wear the white skullcap and, under duress, so did I. With her tresses underneath it, Snooky looked like a badminton shuttlecock. Buddhist boys were bare-headed but you could still be friends with them.

THE MOST popular boy in the school, however, was indeed a Muslim. Jefri was a natural leader. Even at 12 the charisma shone through; at 15 it was gonna be already blinding. He had this – he could make you feel – even me, the of no account ladyboy in the making – as if you were the only person in the world who mattered to him at that moment. To run a marathon, I suppose, you need a good heart and lungs. To manipulate people, that is to lead them, you needed what Jefri and virtually every other con man and statesman in the world had – the gift of mute flattery. Worked like a dream every time, even when the mark had an inkling. At the end of classes at school No 7 (painted ten feet large on every building surface in case you might forget) he'd be at the centre of his little group by the hot biscuit vendor's cart, little coins of sweetness that melted on the tongue. He was the captain of the *sepak takraw* trio, even if he wasn't necessarily the best at kicking the perforated wicker ball. His Paw had a job in Kuwait that only let him come back every five years but the family lived very comfortably on the remittance.

At that time Jefri didn't yet have even the wispiest vestige of facial hair that could be called a goatee but he'd been born with the typical round, small Muslim face that I, for instance, lacked. By comparison I was equine and, once you got to know me, as neurotic as one of the Sultan of Brunei's polo horses. But Jefri was even nice to me. *"Diman a?"* he'd call. "Stay. Now we are a complement." I liked that, the equableness of the acknowledgment, the lack of criticism, exclusion. It was like saying, "Be one of them," in Arabic which, come to think of it, in my case was an enjoinment to all and sundry to enrol as Females of the Second Category.

Jefri's niceness to me was extra-refined niceness, the sugar icing on the cake, because apart from Paw everyone was nice to me. We were a tolerant people, then. Adulterers went unstoned; thieves retained their hands; and whatever fate was reserved for TVs in Saudi or Afghanistan was unknown in Pattani. (Credit where credit is due, Snooky would like to acknowledge that the Ayatollah Khomeini, though a follower of Caliph Ali, never proscribed the Persian Transgenders). At that time the leaders of the local smuggling syndicates held more sway than our imams. It was an innocent trade with plenty of money in it – bringing cigarettes up on the train from Malaysia. Jefri's brothers were big wheels in the traffic. They weren't as nice as he was; in fact, an evil-aspected pair as bad as my brother Adi. When they came by, we all made sure we smiled like the sun had just come out after a downpour. This was the opposite of a, I think it was Fellini, memoir where the kids in an Italian hilltown hissed the green-visaged villain in a festive pantomime. At that time, at that stage in life, we didn't resist harm; we propitiated it. Jefri's face would grow serious; sometimes they'd take him with them, for him to rejoin us in half an hour or the next day. We could never tell which it was gonna be. However sombre Jefri looked on leaving, there was never a trace of sheepishness on his return. The circumstances of his departure were expunged; the slate was wiped clean. It was his turn to grin. I dunno. Can I compare it to going to the bathroom to answer a weightier call of nature after a morning glass of black *kopi o* and a fried roti? It was polite and mature not to remark on it, part of everyday life which was not worth highlighting. You knew something feral had been done, leaving an evil stink behind long after the doer had gone but no one was gonna write an ode to it.

Girls and boys liked Jefri impartially. When he came back he usually had money and he'd buy the bowel-loosening roti all round, banana or pineapple if you so desired, and maybe a green, red, and white sago and coconut milk *es cendol* to wash it down.

There was a time when Jefri did not show the next morning. Or the one after. Word spread. Crossing back from Malaysia into Siam, he'd fallen off the roof of the train. That's the high sanctuary they usually clambered to, through the window slats of the compartment, when the customs gendarmerie made a swoop. Hauling his zip-up sack, striped like Joseph's jacket, after him, Jefri had slipped. There'd been a rain shower. Fortunately, the train was going slowly and he landed in the forgiving mulch of a paddy field but he'd still twisted his ankle. Ever afterwards he had a limp. I remember the day well as it was the time (1) I gave my first head and (2) I saw the classic movie of our Siamese South, *Papillons 'n Posies*, the first of dozens of times. Both were *al fresco* experiences: the BJ to a share-taxi driver in the bamboo thicket of the town's largest traffic roundabout and the movie projected against the wall of our school playground. Up to then I'd only cuddled with a few classmates, pecked them on the cheek, and squashed my lurid, popsicle-stained tongue into one shocked lad's ear. When Jefri hobbled into view there was a mass, chattering flight of the girls over to him, with me bringing up the rear and the boys behind me in turn.

"It's OK," he said. "Just a sprain. I'll be OK in a week." Which he was, but we still fêted him as if he was being brave about losing an entire leg. The point was we were all sure he'd have been as stoic about this as he proved in coping with his minor injury, so we might as well have the fun of making a hero outta him. Anwar, another juvenile smuggler, had broken his hip and arm falling off the roof of the train two weeks previously but attracted no sympathy at all. There are the loved and the glorified in their penumbra of luck and light and then there are the rest of us. Everything they say and do is noteworthy, their comments taken up and repeated for admiration and emulation where another's of equal merit would be ignored or even condemned.

Five weeks later Jefri was bouncing out on the *takraw* court as if the ankle was brand new, enjoying the rapt attention of the spectators and failing to connect with the rattan ball no more nor less times than previously. He was 16. I was 14. In objective terms of life lived, damage done, errors made, it seems like someone else's lifetime ago, an older person's from a bygone age. In subjective terms, it is also like yesterday. Which is the truer?

Jefri's brothers were men, with families and children. The two younger daughters of the oldest were already in or nearing their early teens, old enough not to be wearing colourful clothes anymore. I'd glimpse them speeding around on a Honda Cub, their beige headscarves flapping. Little demon speed queens that they were, they still meticulously addressed Jefri, a mere couple of years older than they, with respect as Uncle. They were nice little girls. It wasn't their fault their fathers were pigs.

I haven't mentioned my half-brother much, have I? My alter ego, my evil twin, my id. No, that would make more of him than he deserved, the thug, the simple, uncomplicated thug. Adi was Paw's second son by his other wife, the one he'd left behind in Riau, the archipelagic Indonesian province a 45 minute ferry ride off Singapore. Adi was just a 45 minute ride from undiagnosed autism. He never behaved like a brother to me. I tried to be sisterly, only to be rebuffed by a wall of glowering silence. Only once did he speak of me after I had attained the age of 12 and it was to say in answer to a stranger's query and in front of all and sundry, "I have no siblings. There was a brother but he died." That was meant to be me, the one who died. It was worse than a physical slap in the chops, done in public; family was that important to us. Mare, my mother, not his, he greeted. With Paw he was respectful; he needed to be, he had no financial resources of his own. Riau was famous for being the home of the best, the most correct, the most original Malay. He would speak, usually of vulgar or material things, in his 100 per cent unadulterated, aboriginal, and excellent *bahasa melayu*. It did little to dignify the subjects but everyone else admired it. The fact that he didn't wear Malay attire but favoured the off-duty wardrobe of the Singapore hoodlum – Hawaian shirt, blue cloth bomber-jacket with epaulettes, white shoes – seemed to cause people to admire his accent the more, like a jewel offset by an eccentric setting. Close-set eyes, flat nose with hairs sprouting outta the nostrils to the sunlight, the worst teeth in the world, and a two inch nail on the left pinkie finger completed the outward ensemble.

I wanted to hint he wasn't Paw's son at all, his mother an adulterous whore but I lacked the guts: no fragrant gang of primpers yet, no stun gun in my knickers. It was no secret Adi pushed stronger stuff than cigarettes. *Da da* they called it over the border. As yet I was a virgin where this was concerned. I only started the shooting-up and the smoking at college.

Jefri could be friendly with anybody. I didn't hold his civility or cordiality to Adi against him. Rather, I admired him for it in the way one might watch someone bring a fierce dog to heel.

We both got to leave at the same time. Jefri to study Chemical Engineering in Jakarta and then KL, me to pursue languages in Manila. There was a Sultanate programme, a network of Islamic scholarships overseas, mostly in Indonesia. It was very difficult, almost impossible, for a Muslim to get into a Siamese university. There were literally a handful in any of them – average of five students out of thousands. I have no idea how I got selected. I did feel smarter and quicker than the others in class but my grades were quite ordinary. Teacher said, "Everything is in the hands of Allah, so there is a reason. But I have never been more surprised." Maybe they chose the oddball because it would be difficult to imagine anywhere more un-Islamic than where I went, short of a piggery. I often wonder if that's how I came to the attention of the Look Khreung – off the scholarship list, rather than through my journalism. If you studied abroad the Siamese authorities assumed you'd been radicalised and I have to record that this was a workable assumption. Still, the vast majority of Siamese going to the Philippines were Buddhist, taking medical studies, usually ophthalmology. At university in Manila and later, during my compulsory half semester at the Muslim State University of Mindanao, they told me I'd scored high on the IQ test and well on the English language paper, a subject formally unstudied by us at home. I had picked it up by myself, from television and from the back of the cereal boxes smuggled in from Malaysia. If, like Hal the deranged computer gone rogue in *Space Odyssey*, I am ever stripped back layer by sophisticated layer to my lowest beginnings, I would probably recite nutritional values, calories, and vitamin contents. Some tricks and habits I took into English from Siamese, like checking into an immaculate new five-star hotel with scuffed luggage. Most obviously, I cannot stop calling myself Snooky instead of "I". That's because the Siamese like to refer to themselves in the third person instead of the first. If you have the misfortune to be called Monkey, you will tell your friend, "Monkey feels hot, he'd like to go in."

So, let me replay my opening remarks: *Snooky has never added up to what she wanted. The sum of her has never equalled her hopes. Whether she added to the store of self or subtracted from the principal, the result was equally unsatisfactory. For hours Snooky would stand before the mirror, striving to look more female to her own regard: eyes larger, lips fuller, cheekbones more delicate. As soon as the mirage of femininity started to shimmer from the transparent depths of the glass, it would disappear. Giving up the forlorn struggle, she would then endeavour to look less masculine: absence of bristle, smaller ears, softer eyelashes. That never worked, either, and she would flounce away in tears which, did she but know it, gave additional lustre to her orbs. She wanted to be Miss World and Snooky found herself serving a life sentence in a male body.*

Another quaint habit of written, this time, not spoken, Siamese, is to run everything together without any punctuation whatsoever.

Nospacesbetweenwordssentencesparagraphsetceverythingjust runontogetherlikethis.

Yah, nice, isn't it? Not.

Avril had been forced to flee the classroom in her teaching days, hysterical with laughter, in order to save the face of the Level Four student whose essay on Friendship had begun: "Friendship better than enemyship. Friendship have colddrink and sunshade enemyshiphavebigguns and angrysailor killyou."

One reason I liked to refer to myself in the third person was because it did not antagonise Paw. Gender differentiation in English takes place in the third person – he or she. I, the first person, is for everyone. It's the other way round in Siamese. There's one word for I that a girl uses – *Chan* – and another for a man – *Pom*. The word for he or she is the same; it's unisex: *"Cow"*. When I called myself *"Chan"*, Paw would grind his teeth in vexation.

I'm sure he was glad to get rid of me. What did he think? I was coming back as virile and striated as Rambo? Mare cried. I cried. I was ashamed I was glad to be leaving her.

Manila was so pleasant I will abstain from extolling her sunsets, her seafront boulevard, her cosy cafés, her discos and her noble and ancient ruins, and let you take it as foregone. In any case my paradise might be your hell. Even the dismal weeks down south in Mindanao in the Muslim University only counter-pointed the exuberant celebration of life that was Manila. Above all, there were the Filipinos, the sweetest people. And for the first time I mingled extensively with my own kind – *bakla*, *bayot*, as *katoeys* were called – and they were called. Funny, it hadn't been in my own country, where we were not exactly short on the ground. I got advancement and great marks, more than I merited really, for the Manila college was run by and for a mafia of gay professors and gay priests. Oh, girl, it was nearly as good as making it to New York. My nickname – all Filipinos have to have one in their gaggle, their *barkada* – was Snooky. At home I was – wait for it – Ahmed. Who wants to be fricking Ahmed? I had taught the Filipinos the Thai word for "fun", *sanook*, and from it they gave me my beautiful new name, Snooky, fit for popsong or cartoon. The nickname was bestowed on me at the end of one of the best evenings of my life when, in a gold sequined sheath, exalted by a full strength tab of E and an Oxycontin to smooth me out, I'd mimed on the college stage to a rapt audience my second-fave song of all time *I'm your Lady and You are my Ma-a-a-an*, followed by *One Moment in Time* and as encore and finale – in a falsetto as squeaky as Frankie's – Frankie Valli's *Walk like a Man, Talk like a Man*.

It wasn't so much the college literature curriculum that put the finishing gloss on my command of vernacular English. Ainsley and Evelyn B. were to be scathing about "the grim Philippine diploma grind". (Snooky wondered why they'd stayed so long in the RP until the reason dawned on her). No, it was my part-time job in the Call Centre, dealing with irate British and Australian owners of faulty Italian washing-machines and dish-washers. (Let Snooky give you an unsolicited tip: always buy US-made appliances, not European; Maytags never break down). She developed a Filipino accent, Tagalog rather than Ilokano, the better to fit in. "Hair-Low-Oh! Dis is Snooky! How may I help you, serr/mum?" I would trill melodiously into the head-set, while I winked, stuck my tongue out, and made masturbatory gestures in thin air to my laughing *bakla* sister whose furious client I could hear shouting through both her own phones and mine. We'd stagger out at 4 a.m., smoke the ice that was known there as *shabu*, and do BJs for free on any passing *guwapo*.

Of course, working on my student visa was flagrantly illegal. My experience of two foreign bureaucracies the one in Manila and the Siamese administrative apparatus imposed on us Muslims in the South – was this: the Filipinos were personally friendly but the system was a gridlock. The experience was of doing backstroke in syrup. In my home South the administration was equally bribe-prone and inefficient – dramatically worsening in the early years of the millennium – but the Siamese officials were personally frigid and sour to the point of hostility. The experience was one of swimming in a chilli-laden fish-sauce straight from the fridge: you shed tears of frustration.

Nevertheless, doing the crawl in the sticky stuff, four years in the Philippines flashed by like four weeks in Pattani. I crossed swords, just once, with the Dean of Discipline. (He was a bitter hetero passed over for promotion). This one was prepared to allow me a girl's uniform blouse with trousers but not a skirt. I forgot his brusque, un-Filipino dismissal in two minutes. I never once went home. And if I never was to attend the Thai Oxford and Cambridge, the Siamese twins of Yale and Harvard, which were Chulalakorn and Thammasat, so what? My English was the better for it. I never spoke a word of Malay or Siamese between 2000 and 2004. You can't learn a living language from books only and certainly not from the copywriters for Messrs Kelloggs. At my *despedida* party I broke down, smudged my mascara and wept floods as I said farewell to my Christian friends, these tears far more unaffected than the ones I had shed for Mare.

Snooky can't say anyone came to much. Girlie Lebumfacil (who was even camper than his name) ended up as quite a successful gown designer.

For my part, while on campus, I had done a little bit, er very littun-bit, of student journalism. No, Snooky is being modest. Actually, she was a glutton for as many assignments as she could get; she wrote a whole half-issue on the films of Lino Brocka, the gay prize-winning Pilipino director who would meet his end, like so many, on a motorbike. Well, really, it was a car, but, yah, darling, motorbike sounds so much better. Jimmy Dean's PR should have done something about that. On the strength of the student journalism, back in Bangkok, I wangled some work from 1066, a giveaway listings magazine run by a very handsome blond *farang*. I had got off the Philippine Airlines jet and failed to catch the Hualamphong express train down South (couldn't face Smallville again, even as Supergirl). Not much money from the good-looking *farang* but great interest and minimal glory. Next I wrote programme notes for a newly opened Arthouse Cinema and concert/lecture hall complex owned by the NY-returned scion of a Siamese billionaire brewing family. A year and a half later I got a job on a real newspaper. I wrote horoscopes for the *New Sentinel*. In Thai a *More Do* is a fortune-teller (literal translation "Doctor Look"). I made my saucy predictions more like Doctor Hook and the column – *Anna Court, your More Do who Does More* – was a hit from day one. Then the film critic, an old American soak, was too drunk one Monday to go to a preview and I stood in and then became the fixture. It was a lot more money and a whole bundle of prestige and glory – in the eyes of the cultured, anyhow. My ambitions were small but I'd made it.

★   ★   ★

SO HERE'S HOW I fell through the flap in the floor of my newly constructed world and on down into the pit.

One night – or, more accurately, morning, as it was 3 a.m. – came a tiny knock on my door, more a scratch. We were having a *yah bah* orgy. Meth smoke jetted out the nostrils of Mew and Wow. They looked like bison in wigs, respiring on a cold prairie morning. Yellow candle wax had congealed on the floor like so much saffron semen. Indeed there was also white semen, from Goong, who had already ejaculated and soon to issue from Noi who was jerking herself off with Mew's dick in her mouth. Like I said, meth made you incredibly horny, whilst also giving 90 per cent of guys what was known as "crystal dick" or the droop. At least five hours of impotence which not even 100mg of sildenafil could put right. Snooky can say with her hand on her heart that all she was doing was lying on her stomach, soles of her bare feet waving a saucy semaphore in the air, painting her finger-nails for the seventh time, while she watched with half an eye a crude local movie with minimal technical values, involving a pair of very young Isarn peasant girls and a bisexual Bangkok pimp. It was a cultural come-down for the DVD player which usually played Pasolini, at the very least.

Silver foil glinted where it had been promiscuously thrown to the floor. It was, Snooky flatters herself, a scene worthy of the cave of shadows in *The 120 Days of Sodom*; it would be hard to imagine a more incriminating or dissolute spectacle. Certainly the police who came smashing through the door I incautiously opened a quarter of an inch looked as startled as the bevy of TVs lying on the floor with tooter or dick in their mouths. They were all waving their guns, the Keystone Kops I mean, as if they were arresting the most dangerous kind of armed criminals. I knew bad acting when I saw it but was too stoned then to ponder why. "Is that a gun or are you just pleased to see me, *tea ruck*?" I asked and for reply got a revolver butt smashed on the bridge of my nosejob. Eiyah, three times over! Oh God, I was blinded immediately by the flood of tears and disabled a few seconds later by the pain.

All chaos broke out. Tich headed for the washroom to dump her pills. (Fifteen of them counted as dealing and meant a death sentence). Cartoon, who for some reason was naked except for a pair of satin bunny ears, tried to jump off the balcony on to the corrugated iron roofs 20 feet below but only succeeded in snagging herself in the lines of my washing. Crab, extricating her, handed me a pair of my own frilly apricot Triumph panties to stem the gore pouring out my hooter but even as I squeaked my thank-you *"Kha!"* found I had the presence of mind to use a no less slinky but black pair. We girls, y'know, use those on our blood days. Do-Ann was actually brave enough to shove off one tightly uniformed thug who had an evil grin on his square-jawed mug the whole time he had Prawn in a head chancery but got thrown down and given a good kicking by the sergeant and sergeant-major. The others, lacking Do-Ann's forlorn gallantry – we'd seen it so many times on kerbside or in department store holding-room – huddled together in the centre of the room and shrieked a quasi-choral dismay.

"I hate fags," said the senior NCO, heel of palm on his gun-butt, as he administered Do-Ann a few final shrewd kicks in her thin ribs.

At that moment my eyes cleared completely and through the door ajar saw on the darkened landing the janitor and behind her every apartment door crowded with onlookers. In the first split-second I saw her complicity and then the angry flush as she read my mind. Why? I mouthed but with my panties to my face the old hag couldn't see. Shit, I had tipped her retard adult son every Monday when he brought the polythene vat of potable water up the cracked stone flights to my door; exchanged greetings with her as I passed her glassed domain by the main entrance.

The cops handcuffed all of us – highly unnecessary, no one was stupid enough to run from Bangkok's Finest. They took us down the stairs to where an open-sided Toyota utility with facing benches awaited us, indistinguishable from any other two-row bus. Each landing of the dingy apartment block had been like a theatre encore. Despite the fear, and worse than that, the apprehension, there was part of us fags which lapped up the spotlight. Anti-climax descended once seated in the pick-up. The driver, not a policeman, or at least not in uniform, drove us very fast through the back streets and then even faster along the 2-lane tollway.

We found ourselves in the courtyard of one of the capital's main police stations. Raucous jokes followed us on our progress to the booking-room. Do-Ann, whose hair this month was dyed scarlet and not blue, attracted shouts of, *"Daeng,* is your asshole red like a baboon's?" but was bold enough to answer back. She primped and pouted in the wall-length mirror of the interview-room, knowing perfectly well it was 2-way with the duty commander scrutinising us on the other side. She said, "It's gonna be 20 thou each and I don't mind throwing in a blow-job. I'll kneel if that's the price to walk." She actually used the English slang for fellate rather than the Siamese, which – as you already know – is "Om", with its overtones of mantra and the quiet enjoyment of a puerile popsicle.

The door by the side of the mirror opened. Feisty though she was, Do-Ann hastily took her seat. No less than a police Lt.-Col emerged. Dyed (black, of course) hair pomaded down and with not too much paunch straining at the tight shirt-buttons, he looked relatively cherubic and certainly youthful for the rank. We were too experienced to draw much encouragement from this. Going up the police ranks from the gorillas on the street to the generals at the apex, they got more civilised, which is to say innocuous-looking, the higher they rose. But appearances were deceptive. The cherubs were definitely deeper-dyed in evil than the *shaitanes*. The fact that they were always in a good mood and smiling and the sergeants were in a bad and always scowling only made them the scarier. It meant their designs had been consummated.

"OK, throw the shit out. This one stays," he said. A bald translation does not do justice to the contempt in his words. I would have had trouble captioning it for the flicks. To the word "This" he had added the suffix *-tua*, used for animals instead of the classifier *-khon* used for human beings. My friends left me without a word or look.

All the cops, too, vacated through the same door, while the Lt.-Col retired to his inner sanctum. I was left solitary as a hermit to reflect on my special fate. After half an hour, with eyes demurely downcast, but covertly regarding the mirror all the while, for the first time in my life I found my appearance ridiculous, from my too-long hair to my false eye-lashes. The usual one minute mirror check-out, OK occasionally prolonged to ten in vainer moments, only tended to fortify my self-esteem. It wasn't the circumstances of being in the precinct house now, it was just the self-scrutiny went on too long, like the way ears or toes look funny if you stare at them too long, only this time it was my whole body. I wondered if they found me as ludicrous as I found myself. Of course they did; ten times more.

The door by the glass opened again. It was a different officer, so high-ranking he wasn't troubling with uniform and, *tea ruck,* honey, he no way looked cherubic. Thin-lipped, disdainful, he resembled a gay hanging-judge. Without warning he cracked the sharp edge of a metal ruler over my knuckles and, quick as a boxer, got in a second slice which smashed my nails before I could get my hands in my lap. Over the chair backwards I fell, pulled by my tresses, and then a kick knocked out two perfectly healthy front teeth. There was the sound of precisely placed boot heels approaching me, prone on the floor. Crying and moaning, I saw he was still wearing official issue patent-leather boots with metal moons on the inside heel to make an accompanying click to salutes. What I got were stamps – or stomps, I should have rendered them for Westerns. I tried to think of Clint Eastwood in *High Plains Drifter* and *Coogan's Bluff* – until my tormentor started to punish my spine and I got frightened of becoming paralysed. I was too scared for crying now. It stopped. Boot clicks went to the door. I stayed fetal. Shit, could Snooky ever have used an ampoule of Nubain. I heard no door open, no boots on the floor, but a different voice spoke to me. It was a soft voice, emollient, you know, like balm. Unspeakably kind and understanding. It was that, despite the evidence of my senses, which made me think the speaker had not been in the room before. No one who spoke to me like that could have been privy to the brutality that had gone on in there. Surely. Snooky believed in the speaker more than she did her own ears.

"It's OK, Snooky," he said. "I'm not going to hurt you. You can get up. Do." It was English spoken by a Siamese who had studied abroad; the accent was much better than mine. I opened tear-blurred eyes and saw brown Weejuns, a hint of sky-blue sock, and nicely pressed chinos. And he was a Look Kreung, a half child, a Eurasian. Handsome as a movie star. He tut-tutted over my bleeding nails but somehow seemed to be missing the gory horror that was my mouth. My incisors lay on the floor. He handed me a tissue and gestured to me to pick them up. I understood there were limits to anyone's selflessness and compassion. He wasn't picking them up for me because he was frightened I had HIV. I didn't blame him. I would have been chary of a *katoey's* blood. He pressed the intercom and asked for milk in Thai. *Nom.*

I said, "She's gone home already." Gallows humour.

He replied, "So she has. You can, too, soon if . . ."

The milk came, cop-borne, steaming in a glass. He sent it back. A glass of cold came. He told me to drop my teeth, complete with the long, grisly roots, into the milk. The expression of brutal impassivity on the cop's face flickered infinitesimally, signalling now he really had seen it all.

"You can try getting them re-implanted," said the Look Kreung. "Sometimes they take again."

And mostly they don't, Snooky thought.

"So, Khun Snooky," said the Look Khreung, "I think you are looking at a long stretch. Minimum 20 years. Absolute minimum."

"Snooky thinks it would be just three," I quavered. In fact, I lisped with my swollen tongue and no teeth to push it against.

"It might have been if it was simple possession. But you ladies had 15 pills there. Quite a stash. That's considered dealing and I'm sorry to say . . . well, theoretically – very theoretically – the judge would be within his rights to hand you down a death sentence." He left that hanging in the air. "But, of course, that probably won't happen. Just 30 years at the worst. Why, you'd only be 56 when you got out."

I began almost to wish I was getting a standard police beating from someone stupid.

"But then you might not have to go to jail at all. Not if you can help us."

Oh, shit, was I ever ready to help them. The witch who'd set me up, she was into fencing stolen DVD players, even dealt a handful of pills a week herself. She deserved all she got. Outside Hollywood disco was the guy who sold us E; I'd give him up as well. He wasn't above overcharging us double when supply was scarce and sometimes his stuff was so weak it didn't work at all. I remembered staring at everyone's glum faces when what we'd popped failed to lift us at the 45 minutes mark, which meant it wasn't going to in 45 hours. And, Lek, the motorcycle taxi-driver, who'd simply pocketed my 600 Baht and told me his "agent" had been nabbed. "There's a coupla motorbike guys at Soi Melika, Rachada, who, like, you know, on the side . . ."

Look Khreung's boyish features creased in disbelief as much as distaste. "Do I look like Khun Moo the Nark? I just need to check something. I'll be back before you know it."

"Wait first . . ."

I was left on my own. The solitude was much worse with him gone. After five minutes the door opened again. My smile, much like a seven-year-old's I should imagine – give or take half a pint of gore – died on my face. Two paunchy cops, twirling billy-clubs by the short handle of the L, regarded me with professional objectivity.

"Not so lovable now, *chai mai*?" said the stouter of the two.

"I've seen worse on a rainy Saturday afternoon in an up-country brothel, boss," said his sidekick.

"Well, let's make it Sunday," said the first and without further ado he pivoted and slammed the short end of the stick into my stomach. I couldn't even cry out. I found myself on all fours, faintly surprised the blood could still flow from my mouth. They played *takraw* a bit, with me as ball, and were talking about whether to shove the long end or the short end of the club into me ("Trouble is, she might like it, boss,") when I saw Weejuns.

"That's enough for now," said the Look Khreung. "Sit it back in the chair."

After they'd closed the door, he said, "Don't worry, you'll get your breath back. You won't asphyxiate, though that tends to happen a lot here."

When he spoke again it was in the Southern language, quite incomprehensible if you were a speaker of standard Bangkok Siamese.

"What do you know of Abdullah K., also known to his friends as Jefri?"

I was so surprised I stopped being frightened.

The next question came while I was still doubled up and hadn't been able to answer the first yet. "When did you last see your half-brother?"

Altogether I must have spent four or five hours closeted with the Look Khreung. At one point there came a knock. Quite a senior officer, a Major I think, came in. He made a respectful *wai* (or should I say a *why*) with his hands – the gesture that resembled Christian prayer or the start of the breast-stroke swimming style – and asked, "The Lt.-Colonel sends his compliments and wants to know if you'd be using the room much longer. *Khrap*."

"Tell him I'll use it as long as I fucking want. *Khrap phom*."

I kept talking and talking. The Look Khreung wanted to know everything about me and my past, particularly about the most boring parts of my life and the least interesting of the people who had so far figured in it. Snooky had striven to forget Jala and Pattani in everything she did and thought. Now it reached out and grabbed her, like a hand thrust from grave-spoil at the end of a horror movie. But I was only too happy to keep the flow of info coming. I verily babbled. I didn't want him leaving the room again, though I wasn't so stupid it hadn't dawned on me that he was the most ruthless person in the station.

Every now and then he'd backtrack, catch me out in inconsistencies that weren't actually contradictory at all if you knew the full picture. Like why I said I had only met Jefri for the first time after the school grade of Matayom 3 when I had also related that he had been a year ahead of me in the earlier Pratom grades. I explained, very quickly in a great sprinkling of blood, that I had glimpsed Jefri from afar at play with his pals during break when I was six but had only spoken to him in Mor 4 when I was 13.

My father's trips to Aceh and Riau and to Medan and KL were duly noted. And my religious beliefs?

Luke-warm at best, I explained.

Did I believe in God? In some kind of Supreme Being?

Yes, I did. In the former.

And was this the God of Muslims? Allah? Did I consider myself in the last resort a Muslim, however unworthy or weak?

And now I asked a question, feeling I wasn't gonna get hit for my presumption, even by proxy. "Are you a Muslim yourself?"

"No."

"Then let me explain."

I hadn't thought about this kind of thing in years; it had been quite irrelevant to the life of liberation I had tried to lead. "It's part of who I am, even as I fight to reject that identity and make a new one. I can't lose it. It's not really about religion for me, it's a sense of where I came from and heaven knows Snooky needs that. It's belonging."

"So you feel at one with other Muslims?"

"You're mixing me in with a whole bunch of people I don't belong with . . ."

"You just said you want to belong."

"Yes, but people," (I was careful not to say "you"), "say 'Muslim'. That is a word that encompasses all kinds and types of people.

They don't say 'Christian' and define you just by that. I mean Christians – there's the American insane fringe, the ones who think God made the world in a week and gays will burn in hellfire for eternity; then there's Mother Teresa; oh, and, of course, Jesus himself, he was the sweetest guy; and then there's the ones, like me, who hardly believe at all but go to church for a white wedding or buy chocolate eggs for the kids once a year, and there are the priests who abuse children and steal the church ornaments, and then there's Father Lankester Merrin in *The Exorcist*. There are all kinds and conditions of Christian and it's the same for us. Not everyone is a hostage-taker, a cutter-off of heads, or a suicide bomber . . ." I stopped. "Sorry." I didn't want the goons coming in again to punish me for my eloquence.

"On the contrary. You couldn't have sung a more pleasing song." I thought of the opening riffs of *Walk on the Wild Side*. That's how my day had begun. What he'd got from me was the failing lament on the sax which ended it.

"OK, then, Khun Snooky. I could take you off and show you a place where bad things happen to bad people. You've never heard Arabic spoken so quickly as it's spoken there. I really ought to do that so you can see what happens to people who let us down, but I don't think I need to do that. Go and see a dentist. It's six a.m. now, not long."

"*Kha*," said I.

"Go on, then. You may go."

I hesitated.

"It's OK. Everything's on a different footing now."

"You mean Snooky doesn't get kicked?"

"Ah-ha-ha-ha, that would be the least of your troubles, a simple kicking. Just don't forget what could happen. But you and I, that's not something that's going to occur between us; we're really on a higher plane. And you can forget any possibility of a drugs charge. That's history."

"And my friends?"

"You don't have friends now, not a single one in the world. Just me."

I went out into the street, half-expecting the others to be waiting for me, at least feisty Do-Ann. There was no one.

2

Victor

The Venerable Victor Veridian, Archdeacon Emeritus, Fellow in Modern History and Senior Tutor, Brecon College, Oxford

Quite why Brecon should have attracted the patronage of so many Oriental despots and their modern descendant, the dictator, eludes my best understanding. We came, almost in a fit of absence of mind, to specialise in the education of their progeny. Wadham did entertain the son of the Asian strongman Ferdinand Marcos and a few others of greater or lesser notoriety, this little tradition perhaps started by their late Warden, Maurice Bowra, who was actually born in China. Many years after that, St John's was adorned by the very bright Abhisit Vejjajiva (known at Eton as "Veggie"), who would one day become Leader of his Thai Majesty's Loyal Opposition. But at Brecon we admitted the spoiled brats one after the other. As any Admissions Tutor could tell you, Wadham, St John's, Balliol, and ourselves, are all in the same group of Colleges for awards and entrance, so it is entirely possible we acted as wicket-keeper to all the odd balls bouncing in from the East. Certainly at Brecon we had over after over of the little blighters. The most preposterous little pipsqueak of them all was the Sultan-in-waiting of Bengorra. Never did a stroke of work. Turned up to the Commem with two London harlots in tow. I put it to him that he needed to improve his mind, if not his behaviour, so that he might the better serve his people. "But, Victor," he said. "My brother is an absolute monarch and so shall I be. We don't serve the people. They serve us." Oh, yes, Princes, Sultans, Field Marshals, Emirs, Amirs, Generals, Kings, Prime Ministers (that was an unholy inversion of democracy for the wicked to relish), Emperors, and why stop there? Divinities, too. Thrones, Dominations, Princedoms, Virtues, Powers. Paradise forfeit but pursedoms secured for the Bursar. The whole new quadrangle and Library were built with this kind of subvention. It was all grist to my mill, of course. I wouldn't want anyone to think I was holier-than-thou. It's a cliché of the craft that one works with what one finds, one comes to the laudable end through means so frequently unsavoury that lesser souls come to doubt the worthiness of their own cause. I can say I never did.

The Saint is conventionally seen as a rather ethereal creature. Francis of Assisi feeding birds by hand. Poppycock. He'd have wrung their necks if God had required it. Saints, Richard always said, are ruthless folk. They'll turn your comfortable life upside down, destroy you and your family without compunction in a Higher Name. They use people and throw them aside; chew them up live and spit the dead fibre out. You wouldn't, Dick said, want a saint for a friend. Heaven forfend. He was thinking of Anselm, of course, but it could be any number of them. Becket, to my mind, was no kind of a chum to Henry II and I speak as a priest, though far from a turbulent one. The only turmoil I have known has been of the inner kind, a long time ago, of course, and whatever little I have suffered has not been the long, dark night of the soul which tempers the saintly mettle. Actually, I wouldn't breathe it publicly, but part of me admired ancient Morgan for saying he'd always rather betray his country than his friend. Boy-friend, the old sodomite meant, of course. I'd reverse the terms of the argument and say I'd forgive my best friend for selling me down the river if it was for Queen and Country.

The Cold War has been succeeded by a quite intemperate conflict. You knew where you were with Ivan. Like us, he pursued the rational path of material self-interest. With would-be saints and prophets, you've got no idea what's going to jump out of the woodwork. To paraphrase Wilde, the unpredictable in pursuit of the uncontemplatable. The *revanche de Dieu* would have occurred without any contribution from our part, meaning the West gener-ally. It had its own context. What we did was nurture a snake in our bosoms, or, to put it less emotively, we created a fifth column out of nothing on our own sweet tods. I refer to the mass immi-gration into the United Kingdom of the Urdu-speaking populations of the northerly parts of the subcontinent. In fact, mostly into the Kingdom's own Northern heartlands.

If I can add my tuppence worth to the debate, it occurs to me that on neither side was there anything volitional about the process.

The receiving society would rather not admit the strangers at its gate, unless necessity drove. Those crossing the estranging sea would rather not leave the loved faces around the familiar hearth, unless the need was even more dire. And in both these cases the necessities were economic imperatives. Our own economy was chronically short of labour, in particular skilled labour, in the decade after the War. Skilled labour was not forthcoming from the subject populations of the old Empire but in any case the buses needed conductors (Padraíg would make the roads they lumbered along) and the assembly belts still required the human hand, whatever its colour. It has often occurred to me that it would have been better in the long run to have accepted less economic growth 50 years ago, or even a contraction, and to have a happier, more stable, more homogeneous society today. I think the Anglican Congregation would have become less of an irrelevance.

I am not a bigot, I am not a racist. I recall talking to my dear friend Matthew Lumumba at the ABC. I was unwise enough to refer to "your people", meaning black people. "My people, Victor?" he retorted. "My people are a bloody nightmare."

The immigration from the Antilles was, in retrospect, comparatively benign in its social consequences. It created a lumpen class in the absolute Marxian sense – and unfortunately a visible one, identifiable by skin pigmentation which, as has been observed, is a poor genetic marker. The influx from East and West Pakistan was infinitely more fraught with consequence. The wisest, most anguished words I ever heard on the subject were from a Cassandra at the Traveller's, ex-ICS and Ch Ch, who said, "We could have told you these people don't integrate. We could have told you their resentment turns to hysteria. We could have told you that half a century ago." Sage, rueful nods from his friends. An unfashionable, probably incorrect as they say now, opinion but one worth taking on board. The chap I feel sorriest for is Honeyford, the Bradford Headmaster, who pointed to the dangers of the multi-cultural society in a time when it was distinctly unfashionable to do so. Of course, the liberal-left hounded him out of his job. He was merely correct – not that being right should be considered a virtue. What Forster said, though he was a King's man, I find the quintessence of the Oxford method, and what I have always striven to teach, "It's not important to be right, it doesn't matter at all if you're wrong. Only keep an open mind." The education I gave my young men did not supply answers to their questions so much as inspire them to ask a further round of questions, the solutions to which either lay within themselves or could never be supplied at all. The kind of education which offers answers of attractive certainty can be found at Ampleforth or Qom, not at Brecon.

I enjoyed my conversations with Teddy for 30 years, though those conversations have only acquired semi-professional point in the last decade. Nobody could have personified the open mind more than Teddy. He was the most brilliant undergraduate of his day. *Literae Humaniores* had never known anything like him. The transformation, metamorphosis really, into Arabist seemed wilful at the time. Now it appears as a masterstroke of prescience. What was once an intricate, esoteric, and pointless study (as the contemplation of beauty usually is) became a skeleton key to the unlocking of a rare stasis in the modern world. I asked him if he had foreseen any of this at 23 when he had come to the fork in his life. Teddy-like, he didn't so much change the subject as come up with what seemed at the time a complete *non-sequitur*. "The worst of all monsters," he declared, "is the Asiatic mind inveigled by the demons of the West."

"Surely the other way around?" I ventured.

Teddy shook his big head. He looked a bit like Frankenstein's monster himself with his long hair and he did shamble as he took his bulk around in those battered carpet-slippers he wore for the gout. "David," this was his colleague in the Department of Oriental Studies, the late Reader in Chinese, "says the worst civil war of all time was the Tai Ping rebellion. Hardly anyone's heard of it, but 20 million died."

"Well, I have," I replied. "Can't come up with the exact date but mid-19th . . ."

"It was a common or garden peasant insurrection," said Teddy severely, "made uniquely slaughterous by the half-baked notions Protestant missionaries put in the head of its leader. He thought he was the Second Son of God – and we all know what that leads to."

"Well, don't look at us."

"Mao Tse Tung," said Teddy, undaunted as usual by my flippancy. "Look what he did with Marx. He was worse than Lenin and Stalin combined. Pol Pot and his Missis – they were Sorbonne-trained. She was a Shakespeare scholar . . ."

"Lady Macbeth, presumably. But you can't hold us responsible for what people do with our cultural baggage train."

"I'm glad you can call Christianity baggage, Victor." Rumour, possibly unfounded, was that Teddy had converted and made the hajj himself.

"You know perfectly well I was referring to Herren Marx and Engels."

"And then when we stick our fingers in the pie and give it a good stir ourselves, preparatory to our taking a hefty slice of it . . ."

We'd been down this road many times before. "I admit that when nation-states move it's usually in their own material self-interest but sometimes it chimes with the moral thing to do."

"A self-serving cloak. Look what we've done to the Middle East. I was in Baghdad in the 1950s . . ."

"Yes, Teddy."

"The frightening thing about you and your chums, Victor . . ."

"Clients, Teddy."

"The frightening thing about you and your masters is not that you're stupid or wicked. It's that you're clever and decent."

"Well, thanks for that."

"Then again, high intelligence is no impediment to bungling incompetence. And we all know what the path to hell is paved with."

These were old salutations and rejoinders in our debate. It wasn't over, not by a long chalk, when Teddy passed. I'd prepared his obit for *The Times* years before. I wouldn't be surprised if he'd prepared mine as well, so as usual he'll be enjoying the last word.

"Oh, look, Victor, there's one of those wretched rats crossing the Rector's Lawn again."

"Where? Oh, yes, that's their usual run, by the lead drain-pipe with the coat-of-arms. Pass me the De Lisle. No, not there. I transferred it from the Burmese chest to the Badjao child's burial jar."

Teddy wasn't exactly a hypocrite but he liked to provoke me sometimes for the sheer enjoyment of wallowing in liberal dismay. This was most blatant with the firearm. He was about as effectual as Watson trying to prevent Holmes from taking potshots with the saloon pistol in Mrs Hudson's rooms.

"For God's sake, Victor. You're going to kill an undergraduate one day."

"Cull one, would be the word. The cartridge box, if you would. That's still in the teak chest."

Phut! Went the fat-barrelled, ermine-lined little carbine, quieter than a cough in Conclave and a splendid relic of spliced Anglo-American mechanism from SOE days. As usual I missed – "Drat!" I exclaimed – but sent the rodent scurrying. On the rare days I scored a hit, it would simply disintegrate but I would also say "Drat!" as an alibi.

"It beggars belief that an ordinand in the C of E should possess such a thing, let alone be proficient in its use."

"I know an Australian Monsignor who can field-strip the Owen gun blindfold. Mind you, it's only got about three moving parts."

"Just like Father, Son, and Holy Ghost. There's a wonderful party trick for the next Synod."

I was barred, by the way, from Teddy's student do's. I was in good company; Bill Deakin, Vivian Green, and dear old George were also *persona non grata* at his At Homes. Teddy himself was Laudian Professor of Classical Arabic but he spoke very fluently modern colloquial Arabic in the way of an Iraqi and would very decently have over Middle Eastern and Malayan students from all over the university to his rooms overlooking St. Giles. Lebanese, Egyptian, Iraqi, of course, Jordanian, Yemeni, but oddly enough never any Saudis. Teddy was always good enough to stand bail for their various peccadilloes before the bench – off the top of my head: hashish, shoplifting, public nuisance against south window of Marks and Sparks in the Cornmarket, grievous bodily harm, drunk and disorderly. Teddy said the last – the most innocent to me – was what they'd get into hot water for, if it was bruited back home. I have to record the vast majority were law-abiding and usually engineers and post-graduates, unlike the undergraduate and underperforming sons of despots I was mentioning earlier who tended to read soft courses like English or PPE. As I say, Teddy wouldn't tolerate any of my fishing-trips to his parties. That was his word for it. I called it "talent-spotting".

A lot of rot is talked about this. Such as the broaching phrase, "Do you wish to serve your Country?" (Which, of course, could only apply to the sons of Albion). You'd have been laughed out of court in a previous age, let alone this for uttering sentiments like that. I mean, it was in its way as useful a phrase, both euphemistic and unmistakable, as "Hello, sailor!" But you had to be very careful whom you approached. A rebuff would have been a terrible thing, a reflection on one's own judgment which, nevertheless, one would be honour-bound to report. In cases of doubt I liaised with George. George was an economist (the modern witchcraft) but a canny Scot. He'd been elected Fellow of St. Joseph's at the precocious age of 23, shortly after the War. We'd usually agree to err on the side of discretion. Most of our recruitments were Europe-bound which, as I have said, was the emphasis of the day. But also Pakistan, India, Indonesia.

Funnily enough, in those days – meaning up to the mid-1990s – the FO had dreadful relations with the Indians and good ones with the Pakistanis. The former had a chip on the shoulder about the Empire which the latter lacked. Bhutto, the democrat, was by all accounts a greasy crook. His daughter, Benazir, was an improvement on the father and President of the Oxford Union in her time. Zia, the hang 'em high, flog 'em hard, moustached general, an apparently unlovable dictator, who had old man Bhutto judicially murdered, was liked and esteemed by everyone who personally met him, including the *Grauniad*-readers in our own Embassy. He was as straight as a die, kept his hands out of the till, spoke the truth, and stood by his word. He was universally regretted by his acquaintance. To this day, no one knows who brought his plane down but the Pakistani ISI would make Byzantium look like the Methodist Conference chaired by dear old Donald Soper. George and I stuck a few shrewdly placed pins into the Indian juggernaut and into the West Pakistanis as well. At one time I was absolutely positive that they were going to incinerate each other. One of my Indians definitely ended up as a double-agent but he didn't start off that way, so it was outside George's and my purlieu. A good pick of ours, though, was an Indian who was an absolute firebrand at the Union but – so we were told – proved a very steady and reliable source over the years.

I never discounted anybody for what I would call youthful zeal. You could have belonged to the IMG or SLL and I wouldn't rule you out on that basis alone. With very few exceptions, I did find the Indian politicians an ungrateful and sticky-fingered bunch. We sold them the Jaguar about which the Pakis kicked up an unholy fuss, largely unexplicated by our own press. The significance of the Jaguar was that it was the simplest, cheapest aircraft that could deliver a nuclear bomb at low-level and get away. In those far-off, innocent days no one thought of the one-way suicide run.

Going further east, Asia was thoroughly infiltrated by the KGB. Derek Davies, an extremely likable Taff (and in the FO – in Vietnam – before he became a journalist, which we all know is the standard euphemism for spy) had the wizard wheeze of exposing every single one of their embassy plants, amounting to some 30 agents, in his *Far Eastern Economic Review*. He ran their mugshots, to boot! Davies was a Cambridge man but I had given a few tutorials at Oxford to his taller predecessor and erstwhile superior, Dick Wilson, in whom I found kindred spirit. Davies had a run-in with the Singaporean government in the 1970s over his magazine's publication of what they termed official economic secrets. The bigger secret which the Singaporeans were kind enough to keep for a long while, even at the height of the spat, was that Derek kept a mistress in Singapore! The Singaporean Special Branch needed very little instruction from us; we could have learned a thing or two from them. Our own SE Asia station was situated there for a very good reason. Next door, as it were, the Malaysians were a good deal less efficient but very tough with their own religious fanatics. Many of them had to run for their lives to Indonesia where, thank God, they did not attract a large following, though still very dangerous. Brunei, with its oil, would have been a rich prize for the Indonesian generals but a squadron of Harriers and a battalion of Gurkhas formed our thin red line.

When I was still green, I was instrumental in placing a young chap who rejoiced in the soubriquet "Merde" Mahler into a position in one of the great Asian banks and he started by working for the local branch there. Or was it KL? My memory is quite shocking these days. I can't say Mahler was a lot of use. He acquired deep cover by marrying a Muslim (he was kind enough to inform me he was already circumcised), but cover for what? He never supplied any intelligence worth speaking of but made himself a fortune along the way, on his own account, with commodity speculation. SIS and, before them, SOE had long-standing ties with the house, going right back to the days of Peter Fleming and the Brothers Beswick, so I'm sure they forgave us for dropping Merde on them from a great height. After the elapse of more than half a century – beyond a generalised feeling of disappointment among his masters

– there appear to have been no deleterious consequences as a result of my poor judgment of character and I feel both the nation and Veridian have escaped unscathed. In semi-retirement now, Mahler appears to have re-located himself to somewhere called Mae Hong Son or is it Langkawi? (Remind me never to go there).

With Siam, as I could never stop calling it, we did have, if you forgive me, ties. George's nephew had been a beak at Eton before he became celebrated as the next bright young dramatist and he said to me, "At any given moment, Uncle Victor, there'll be any number of Thais at Eton. Including, but not necessarily, royals. It's been going on for years." I refrained from telling him, as it's still theoretically covered by the Official Secrets Act, if that's not too arch of me, that I used to knock back tumblers of Glenmorangie with a Siamese Prince in the Café Royal during the blackout. Not to mention being serenaded on the piano at the seaside by a King's daughter, the while I sipped luke-warm Earl Grey from the saucer – that being totally unclassified.

SE Asia as a whole was a part of the world that went to sleep after 1975 and we forgot about it, only sending duffers like Mahler. Marx was correct in observing that history repeats itself, the first time as tragedy, the second as farce. When I think of the likes of David Smiley and Xan Fielding, who trod the boards of the SE Asian theatre for a Scene or Two and had me, for a start, completely over-awed, and then summon up the long-shanked, stooping, red-haired personage of their successor Merde (he was six feet five inches tall), I'd laugh – if I could. Well, it's started to wake up with a vengeance and what we have out there coping is our Fourth XI, playing on a very sticky wicket.

On a larger somnolence now ending, Teddy said to me, all credit to him, I can date it exactly, it was June 1968, the year all seven of my Brecon boys took Firsts:

"We're on the brink of a great convulsion in the world, Victor. Listen to me, please. The Muslim world has been in one of its states of suspended animation for centuries, since the time of the Sublime Porte. Now it's showing the first signs of stirring from its torpor. It's people possessed by an idea, Victor, by a faith, not actuated in the first instance by their own material interest. You can't negotiate treaties with a force like this and you can't obliterate an abstraction in a mushroom cloud like you can something as potent even as a nationalism. They'll turn our world upside down, wait and see. Then it'll all go back to sleep again for half a millennium."

Well, I admit I didn't take him as seriously as I should have done but I did find a parallel in my own pond. The pendulum beat of history, swinging from one extreme to the other, was a rhythm also felt in the study of history, in historiography. As a young historian of the 17th Century, I and my peers reacted against the constitutional and narrative school of the Victorian, Gardiner. We tried to explain the English Civil War in terms of social and economic forces. Well, all of us but Veronica. Thus we tried to understand the Puritan divines, Cromwell, the Levellers, sects like the Diggers with their refrain, "When Adam delved and Eve span/ Who was then the gentleman?" But in the end we all came to see, even the one-time Communist, Christopher Hill, that the Puritans were not fighting for economic interests under the cloak of theology. They were, indeed, fighting for religious principles and we have to take their utterances at face value. After all, men were prepared to be burned to death at the stake for their beliefs 100 years earlier. It wasn't actually as difficult as Teddy thought for me to comprehend the notion of religious fanaticism, though I personally was steeped in the agnostic values of a state church.

I have no personal experience of the Middle East and I have to say most of Teddy's anecdotes related to the digs he'd been on in the 1930s in Syria and Iraq. He had actually met Lawrence, T.E. that is, at All Souls when he, the unhobbled undergraduate Teddy, held a Brackenbury at Balliol. Apparently, Lawrence's idea of giving a dinner party was to heap a pile of tins on the floor, spam, bully beef, beans, and provide his guests with can-openers and spoons. On encountering mild words of remonstrance, not from Teddy, Lawrence was good enough to warm the contents of the tins by first steeping them, unopened, in hot water. Teddy said there were scars on Lawrence's back, observable during a swimming party on the Cherwell, but he personally thought the scene with the Turkish Bey in *Seven Pillars* to be an invention. We actually opened his inscribed copy of the limited edition (there was also one of *Revolt in the Desert*, I noticed) and subjected the episode to our joint forensic scrutiny.

I should say several generations of collective wisdom/scepticism were brought to bear during this close textual analysis and it was an opinion arrived at independently but synchronously by two very different temperaments that the only sentence which rang true was when T.E. wrote of his physical inability to offer initial resistance and escape, once apprehended by the rude Anatolian soldiery. He remarks, "I cursed my littleness." And, of course, though lantern-jawed as Desperate Dan, he stood somewhat under five feet six inches.

Teddy reckoned it was a composite mosaic of experiences, some pleasant, some unpleasant, some sought, some very much unsought, which he sublimated in his own "factitious" history, while I opined that it referred to a single traumatic experience, perhaps from his schooldays, which he thus catharticised and romanticised as being in the larger cause of British interests and pan-Arab nationalisms. What I didn't mention to Teddy was that something I understood only too well was Lawrence's lifelong sense of being the outsider, of being looked down upon. Although his father was a baronet, Lawrence himself was born on the sinister and distaff side, so maybe I had more than one thing in common with the Great Man. I found out about my illegitimacy when I was 16 but I can't say it exactly scarred me.

Teddy agreed that my interpretation certainly echoed the earlier and more notorious sentence where he wrote of friends entwined in embraces in the hot sand which were the "sensual coefficient" of the whole undertaking. Teddy believed he was tormented by guilt over his betrayal of the Arabs, at the Conference table and before, and that he never recovered from this classic schizophrenia of the double agent. What we both agreed was not in doubt was that he was both a very complex and a very great man. John's portrait of him in the robes of a Sheikh of Mecca is surely one of the most romantic in the great tradition of British portraiture. Teddy said he had never understood why we had sided with the Jewish state rather than the Arabs when the whole spirit of the public-schooled British Empire-builders had been inimical to the sickly stews of the cities. Their bond had been with the nomad in his wilderness and with the hardy love which was not that which cossetted the family. I pointed out that we owed a massive financial debt to the Americans from the war and that the Jewish lobby dominated banking, print media, television, publishing, the stock-market, the entertainment industry, and hence politics in the US.

I also added that the public schoolboys won the British Empire but the administration of it, once gained, was the work of grammar schoolboys.

Teddy had a long-running feud with a couple of Harvard academics – Jews, of course – whom he regarded as little more than ignorant zealots with a souped-up sociological vocabulary. Teddy was also the first to admit that the diamantine Jewish intellect was the superior intellect. These chaps were paste. He did prize and esteem Isaac Deutscher, the Polish Trotskyist in exile in Hampstead, who wrote a book of essays entitled *The Non-Jewish Jew* and celebrated his acceptance into the CP as a young man by singing the Internationale and eating a salami sandwich over the grave of his rabbi grandfather. I liked Deutscher a little less but had to borrow ten bob from his wife Tamara when I was pickpocketed in Great Russell Street, leaving the British Museum Reading Room. She stood me a glass of lemon tea, too, at the Patisserie Calorie. One of Teddy's maxims, and why he respected Deutscher so much, was never, ever, to see anything from one's own vantage-point or self-interest. This enabled him to arrive at his verdict that the state of Israel was an insoluble conundrum for the would-be peace-brokers. "It's not a question of Right vs Wrong," Teddy said. "Like the Second World War. And it's not a question of Wrong vs Wrong like . . ."

"Saddam vs the Mullahs," I suggested slyly.

"Do hold your tongue, Victor. I'm not rising to the bait. Why it's impossible to broker is that it's Right vs Right. From the Zionist perspective: Might has been proved to be Right. No one lifted a finger for European Jewry before or during the war. We could have bombed the yards and lines to Auschwitz. In the event, we never diverted any of Bomber Command's resources to the task, not even a squadron of Mosquitoes which could have done the trick. So they know they can kick the poor Palestinians from here to Kingdom Come. In any event, if we're talking about ethics, the world owes the Jews a homeland. Then the passage of time has merely confirmed the rightness of their stewardship. The generations of Jewish children born in Israel and the occupied territories regard it as their home and birthright; it's as profoundly theirs as it is the Palestinians'. Look what they've made of it – mile after mile of market gardens, green peppers and mangoes growing in profusion in what would have been scrub or thorns if left to the Arabs.

Development, prosperity, even with an economy worse distorted by the defence budget than Hitler's. Then from the Palestinian viewpoint: their land was stolen from them by the hordes of arriving Jews. What was not taken by outright violence was obtained by chicanery and legalism. How can you produce title to land your forebears have lived on for centuries before there was such a thing as a registry? They've every right to their outrage. And if the Jews object to their methods, holy moly, the Stern gang wrote the book on post-war terrorism. Remember Dennis Anstruther? He was blown to pieces at the King David Hotel."

I knew Teddy only in middle life, he ten years my senior, when we had already launched upon careers, his profane one far more distinguished than my vocation. I think I'd just returned to Oxford from Durham when we met at Felix's rooms in Hertford, which would have placed me in my 44th year. Dennis Anstruther I had known as an undergraduate – we were Magdalen men, Demys in our respective years. He had got a congratulatory First and placed extremely highly in the FO exam. He had been my dearest friend, along with his wife-never-to-be Lillian. I loved Dennis Anstruther as much as I have loved any human being and Teddy would probably not have mentioned him had he known.

Teddy and I were known throughout the university as a fine old pair of eccentrics. He with his locks and slippers and myself in my pink beret and leather trousers. I acquired the latter much as the British Empire is said to have been gained. When I dismounted from my motorbike (a real thumper, much better than Aircraftman Shaw's Brough, and one of the most powerful that BSA ever made) outside Schools one day, I forgot to remove my leathers before I got to the lecture-room, although I had remembered to don the gown. I found the leathers to be sturdy and comfortable, answering to a need and also apparently the vagaries of the fashion cycle, continuing to wear them long after the royalties, flooding in yearly, generated by *Erasmus to Locke*, had bought me the Bristol. And the Lotus. And the flat above Kipling's on the Embankment. And the cottage at Great Tew. And poor Lillian's annuity. I should think textbooks somewhat more remunerative than pornography.

Sometimes people got the wrong impression. I don't know why, although I was supposed to look a little like the short-story writer Angus Wilson, as was proved by a comic misunderstanding in the

Reading Room. For example, dear Howard Colvin, whom I would occasionally accompany on his motorbike excursions to ruined monasteries and abbeys, never attracted impertinent animadversions at all, although he did keep a wife to counterbalance the motor-biker's overalls. I put it to him that we should do our best to avoid T.E. Lawrence's fate and he replied in his mild voice that could deliver a payload as deadly as a Jaguar's, "What a glorious way to go. I'm deeply flattered, Victor." Howard's mildness was never proof against what he called "reckless attribution", e.g. every stairwell in every mansion in Britain accredited to Adams and every fireplace to Holland, but when off his patch he could be awe-inspiringly cavalier himself, as when he stated that Offa's Dyke (the purpose of which is unknown) was "clearly a barrier to the cattle-rustling endemic on the Welsh Marches from prehistoric to Anglo-Saxon times." His method was the well-known one of excluding the impossible and ending up with the truth, however improbable. So, the great ditch did not meet the criteria of the usual human purposes for construction works, to wit (1) shelter (2) irrigation or drainage (3) memorial or funerary (4) religious (5) military or fortification. You, therefore, had to look for particular circumstances. Cattle had been raised there since time immemorial and they could not travel uphill, whereas the ditch and slope would offer no impediment to human passage.

I could wish the Bodleian had offered impediment to our passage. Howard was famed, justly, for his skill at briskly unfurling the fragile medieval manuscripts and pipe rolls that might take less expert fingers fully five minutes to open. One day three of us were showing a visiting Ivy League mediaevalist round Duke Humfrey's when a very distinguished (and now dead) former holder of the Chichele chair decided he, too, would take the robust Colvin approach to a priceless 13th century parchment. The brittle, and, as I say, extremely valuable thing, simply disintegrated into six or seven pieces before our horrified eyes. No repair was possible. Howard stuffed the pieces back into a place not their own, while the culprit kept a somewhat embarrassed *cave* for him. Then all of us, with a combined age of nearly three centuries, scarpered like guilty schoolboys.

I met Howard during the war when he occupied an obscure niche in Intelligence way below his capabilities but which enabled him to get round to many a noble pile before the Luftwaffe blitzed it. He'd scored a glorious coup in Malta in 1942 when analysing aerial photographs (for which his research expertise in ancient architecture was supposed to have trained him). It was again a wonderful illustration of the combination of abstruse and original thinking with practical commonsense on which both scholarship and Intelligence appraisal are founded. Howard worked out (1) that the spidery white lines on the photos, taken at a safe hour for the unarmed planes, were dew-laden telegraph wires which vanished as the sun rose and (2) these lines of communication would not be wasted on civilian purposes but would lead directly to the HQ of General Kesselring.

Bombers were duly despatched. Howard said to me that his quiet ratiocinations had led to a maelstrom of flame and metal that resulted in the deaths of many estimable young men who were probably not Nazis at all but that he believed he had only done his duty and he, too, had been fair game for the bombs that the Stukas and Heinkels had dropped by the ton on Valetta Harbour. Howard added the real hazard was the shrapnel falling from our own AA, long after the Germans had flown away. (He wasn't being flippant, either). I'd already lost a bit of my foot, a finger and half from the left hand, and gained the bar on the MC when I met Howard and had been long seconded from first the Sherwood Foresters and then Popski's to SOE. (I've hated sand ever since, whether the beach in Pembrokeshire or George's spaniel's sanitary-pit). Perhaps the wound was a blessing. I might well have died young with Keith and all the others and, unlike him, never contributed anything at all to the world. I think the only time I ever felt proud of the Military Cross was when it shut that frightful harridan Thatcher up at the time I refused to assist at the Falklands thanksgiving.

I am not dodging an inference, by the way. Whatever my inclinations might have been, I sublimated them in my work, scholarly rather than curial. Gibbon – who would have flattened lightweights like little Bernard Levin or Gore Vidal in the joust – poured scorn on those ancient religious who had submitted to voluntary castration to, as he put it, "disarm the tempter". Well, I'd signed my weapons to SALT level talks and never used them. A life of near-celibacy has not been a major problem. For those who would not, or could not, credit this, it says more about them than it does about me. The last time, and I went off at half-cock as it were, was in a baths in Japan. I had accompanied George there, staying a week by myself while he went to talk to some of our Cousins in Guam, or was it Okinawa?

Then we returned on a RAF VC-10 via Hong Kong, Singapore, and Gan. In the Crown Colony George introduced me to a huge, jolly Australian journalist, who was bluff charm itself except for the circumstance that he would persist in addressing me as Archdeacon. It was like being in Trollope. *He* ended up in one of young Alec's more successful novels. Middle-aged Alec, I should say, though to me Alec will always be the 13-year old fag with the precocious vocabulary that so impressed his young history teacher, just into Holy Orders himself. More my cup of tea was meeting Charles Pincher again, after a lapse of more than a quarter century. He had left the Crown Colony and was now Professor of Imperial and Maritime History at an Ivy League and author, to boot, of some very informative books on the Portuguese and Dutch empires. He was good enough to laugh when I said they combined the sobriety of the monograph with the ebullience of Masefield. Charles had been a prisoner of the Japanese and a very young Intelligence Major (weren't we all!) with fingers in Operation Remorse, just after the War, when our paths last crossed. He was still married, I was pleased to hear, to the strikingly attractive and intelligent American gel he'd left his wife for at the commencement of hostilities (international, not marital). Had my inclinations lain that way, I'd have been off like a shot, too.

We didn't say anything to each other but I knew the Professor and Major (at Sandhurst a decade before me), but mild in manner as his surname was pugnacious, had headed up British Intelligence in the Colony just after the War, more or less as a satrapy, and still had the ear of the same potentates as I did. Despite having remade his nest over the pond, he was quite scathing about the monstrous US Consulate In Hong Kong, just a gigantic listening-box on springs, really. Charles told me they closely monitored all the traffic from China, including any navy intercepts they could get on the side. Typical of Cousin Jonathan – reliance upon technology to the detriment of the thousand tiny, real voices that cancel out each other's errors and biases and give you the truest of pictures. Human assets are what it's all about; the electronic eavesdropping is essentially passive. Bill Hayes, who was the most extraordinarily well-read scientist, bridging Snow's Two Cultures in his own spry, slight person and overlooked for the big prizes because of his complete lack of pomp and circumstance – molecular biology was his field – always said the Americans thought you solved a problem by chucking money at it. I remember the consternation in the SCR when Bill remarked that most of his scientific colleagues had read their Dickens and Milton and could recognise a Beethoven symphony when they heard it but that we non-scientists weren't just ignorant of science but revelled in our ignorance as if it was a badge of honour. Why, most professors of history or literature didn't even know the Laws of Thermodynamics! You could just see everyone with their sherry-glasses trembling in their hands, resolving to look them up the moment dinner was over. I can still remember entropy on the strength of that rebuke. Of course, the flaunting of erudition for its own sake is merely the higher vulgarity. Quoting *terza rima* in a private letter or a public exam paper, for instance. At one level you could say the index of a society's civilisation – that is to say, its accrued scientific knowledge and artistic attainments – varies inversely as to the number of tattooed or pierced people within it. That would certainly tell you where the citizens of 15th century Florence and the tribes of the Amazon Basin find themselves on the scale. I hardly knew where to look when a gel from LMH turned up for an out-college tutorial, scholar-begowned but with a stud through her nostrils and blue hieroglyphics on her knuckles. Then again a pretentious literary *jeu d'esprit* will deck itself out with an excess of quotations or a plethora of epigraphs that are merely intellectual tattoos.

Where was I? False economies. Yes, to be brutal, when it comes to spying people will always be cheaper and more effective than the latest gadget but these folk have to be picked, planted, nurtured, and harvested. ("Yes," Teddy once snapped, "and shat upon, too.") It takes time, a long time, to put them in the ground and the best ones won't want to work for you, at first. Now this is the real skill, recruiting and handling, manipulating and coercing men and women to such a point that in the end not only do they do what you bid but they think that is what they wanted themselves all along. A certain confusion has to be actively sought.

What one should be completely clear about is that there should never be physical brutality of any kind – without good reason. Not even a slap. I said I wasn't choosy about methods but that is something I would never countenance, a cuff round the ear as bad in principle as electric shocks. What we dished out to the Germans we rumbled was as a love-tap compared to the tricks the Gestapo got up to. You mustn't forget who you are and what you stand for. They talk about a multi-drug regimen being the most effective for illness and so an interrogation or a turning should be multi-pronged. The carrot will only appeal to the venal or the weak, the stick may only reinforce the strong-willed in their recalcitrance. The stick applied (metaphorically, of course) and the carrot dangled are far more effective when used simultaneously in tandem. Threaten to expose a peccadillo or, in extremity, issue a threat to injure a loved one (never actually to be carried out) and the strongest will cave in. Best is to apprehend the mark in some folly, weakness, or crime and threaten to expose it. If he co-operates the slate will be wiped blank, quite clean. You can have a bag of guineas or you can see your son go to prison – the gold glisters all the more alluringly for the alternative. One needs a small stick and a large, orange carrot. One must also not leave the asset who has been turned with his (or her) self-esteem totally violated. If someone feels worthless, they will indeed behave in a worthless way. If, say, someone happens to be a physical coward who fears a harsh interrogation, he should not be excused a certain degree of physical discomfort but nothing amounting to a frank chastisement. He should be given just enough, it could be a very small amount, of cold, sleeplessness, or hunger to the point where he has not yet broken. Then all mistreatment stops. This way the asset feels he has heroically resisted, will co-operate without feeling he has betrayed his cause or friends, and will be that much better an asset.

I am proud of my country and the things for which it stands. This is a distinctly unfashionable sentiment. We lost the Empire and with it a role. Our new one is to play second fiddle to the young American imperium. Give or take a dent to the old Lion's pride, the new empire is still our cub. Its values are our values. We should stand behind those beliefs – but not with such utter subservience to the Americans that familiarity breeds contempt. Oldfield had completely the wrong end of the stick there. Ancient empires lose faith in themselves and this, as much as economic or military decline, secures their slow demise. Age after age their tragic empires rise, as Bax's words to one of my favourite hymns begin. The best lack all conviction and the worst are full of a terrible certainty. What Yeats wrote is as true now as it ever was. There is a tide of barbarism and ignorance, a very revelling in obtuseness, that threatens to drown all the achievements of rationality. The barrier against this is Christian belief, always tempered with reason. I cannot believe lock, stock, and barrel in all the praeternatural aspects of Christianity: the virgin birth, the Resurrection, in any other than a metaphorical sense. Nor can I believe in the miracles, performance of which are the prerequisites for beatitude and canon-isation, without a very large pinch of salt. Belief itself is the miracle. I myself doubt but the doubts make my faith the stronger after I vanquish them. Faith in the miracle of Christian love for your Fellow Man, whatever he does to you. And I believe the civilisation of which I am a product is superior to that which seeks to destroy it. I should perhaps try to end on this note of affirmation but I still retain some sense of philosophical integrity. So I must record Teddy, sitting on the triumphal chariot, whispering into not the Imperial but the Presidential ear his "Memento mori!"

I put it to Teddy that far from being ashamed of ourselves, we should feel a sombre pride, that when faced with incoherent hysteria we should speak calmly and clearly (rather than with the stutter of liberal guilt). Teddy's face darkened. "It sounds awfully like a polite and contemporary version of the White Man's Burden. You're saying one culture is superior to another when it's merely different."

I replied, "Difference, by its mere existence, predicates superiority or inferiority in the quality in which there is variation. There are certain absolutes which run across civilisations – kindness is better than cruelty, the starving should be fed, the drowning saved. People have the right to be free of torture or arbitrary imprisonment. Our civilisation excels at these. It isn't perfect, there are black spots, but, as Churchill said, democracy is the worst of all political systems – except for the others."

"Well, Victor, I know you regard me as the woolliest of *Guardian*-readers but, in fact, I'm not actually that enthralled by *demos*. Have you noticed that democracies throw up mediocre leaders as the rule rather than the exception? I mean the Americans are in love with stupid presidents. Look how popular that cretin Reagan was. Yet dictators are never mediocre people; they can't be, or they wouldn't have got where they are."

"So what are you saying, Teddy? Do you really want to live under an Indonesian or Syrian despotism instead?"

"Of course I don't but, when you're dealing with them, remember that you reach the absolute through a chain of relatives and variables. You can't analyse Arab societies using concepts like nationalism or democracy. They're foreign imports. Even nationalism is a non-indigenous notion, though Nasser tried to create it and exploit it and so have the Iranians (non-Arabs, by the way, old chap) for similar reasons. Tribalism is a valid local phenomenon, I'm sorry to say."

"And what I'm saying is we aren't perfect and nor are we going to stay the best pragmatic choice, Teddy. But at this given moment in the human saga we provide prosperity and immunity from abuse to our populations to a degree unparalleled in history. The concept of chivalry, for instance, is unknown in Asian cultures. *Pace* Maurice, it's the product of very specific historical circumstances – a meld of Christian meekness and the pagan Teutonic warrior ethos. I don't say it myself but the American military eggheads would say it makes us not only braver but better. Is that relative enough for you?"

"Dear God, Victor! You appal me, even by your own dreadful standards! Where do I even begin? Look, you can't cherry-pick from a culture. The worst aspects of a civilisation are simply the obverse, the Janus-face of the best. We live in a culture of cold personal relations. Those you regard as our inferiors – hold on, I've let you have your say, you're behaving like an Arab in the bazaar yourself now! – come from warm cultures. We subordinate personal relations to an abstract and impersonal code of honour. For them personal, and clan, relations are paramount. So, yes, they're predisposed to nepotism, patronage, vendetta, corruption, a very loose sense of communal as opposed to familial responsibility, but you and I wouldn't be shunted off to die in the old folks' home as will be our fate in this perfectly evolved society of yours in the very near future."

Actually poor Teddy spoke prophetically there. Certainly of himself. Likely of me. "The shame is," he continued, "that the exchanges between us . . . Sohrab and Rustum, I mean, not you and me . . . are at such a superficial level. You wouldn't represent the whole of America by a group of bigots in sheets holding burning, fiery crosses and a noose but that's just what the West does with Muslims: the Koran and the Kalashnikov. Groups like al-Qaeda and Jemaah Islamiyah and the Brotherhood and the Abu Sayyaf, they're just the Islamic Ku Klux Klan. They're not representative at all."

"I'm not so sure about that, Teddy. I think they're legends and heroes to the Muhammadan masses. Zarqawi and Bin Laden are the Islamic Robin Hoods, living in caves and deserts rather than the glen and equipped with Russian firearms, instead of a bodkin at the business end of a yard of goose-fletched willow."

"You're talking about the lowest human instincts, about the *schadenfreude* we all fight in ourselves."

"Some of us fight it less than others. Some not at all. Taking up your very astute comments on misrepresenting a culture, why do the mullahs think we loathe our contemporary tripe any less than they do? I mean the culture of sensation, of instant gratification, of the death of thought? Sex in between the ice lollies? You talk of the creation of Frankenstein's monsters in the East through the imperfect assimilation of Christ or Marx but I'd almost rather have that than the bland froth off the top of Western Civilisation that blows to all four corners of the globe now as cultural spume."

"Couldn't agree more, O, Venerable One!"

"I can only be grateful you are not addressing me as the Venomous Bede today. Without being the old relic, we do have more to offer to the world than psychedelic drugs and promiscuity. You take the most recent layer of a civilisation, without the anchor its tradition and accrued learning provides, and you're at the mercy of every temporary current, prevailing wind, fad, and impostor. Waugh cottoned on to that early – what did his obit say: the taproot of tradition without which every dear thing withers? Yes, God knows where you'll end up. Far from shore and stark raving mad."

"So what's your prescription? A jar of quince jam?"

"Do unto others as you would be done by. Learn from the great who have gone before you. Be sceptical of the quick and easy fix."

"Very good, Victor. But we can't populate the world with saints or even the young men you've taught."

"Oh, saints, Teddy, saints. The patience of the saint is as short as the life expectancy of the martyr."

3

Snooky

Couldn't get my teeth and nose fixed straightaway. It was still too early. I travelled on an empty bus. In my *soi* the dogs barked at me and then a couple of the motorcycle drivers nudged each other. The dogs, I think, smelled my crusting blood. At this point Snooky started to feel real sorry for herself. Not because of the mongrels but the other dumb brutes. I kept my face expressionless. Quite easy. It hurt if the muscles expressed emotion. Once in my room, I surrendered to my feelings. Sitting on the hard bed (soft gave me backache by the morning), I noticed a bruise on my instep. How had I got that? I didn't recollect the third-degree included being stamped on while standing. Perhaps it had happened while being loaded on to the pick-up. Nothing in my room had been touched. In fact, the remnants of our pot-session still cluttered the floor. Of course, by this time the Buddha candles had gone out. I made it to the bathroom. In the mirror I beheld a tragic clown. My mascara had run with my tears, blackening my cheeks and leaving a comic trail, while the gore had caked into rouge patches. My split left eyebrow, which again I did not remember being struck, had swollen to the point where it was plump as labia, pouting to emphasise the gash. My nose, my gun-butt-brutalised nose, my 20,000 baht nose, did indeed resemble a red ball and my rubber lips needed no swathe of lipstick to emphasise their unnatural size. Gingerly, I parted them to inspect my teeth, or lack of them, and, of course, the only way to do that was with the muscles that make a sickly smile. I groaned. It was a horror, my grisly gums, the loose sumps.

On cue the phone rang; the landline, I mean. I knew who it was. The Gang only used mobiles.

"Hallo, Snooky," said the Look Khreung. "*Sabai dee mai?* Are you well?"

"Yes," I replied in English, the deadness, the despondency in my voice, its awful acquiescence, startling me but also ringing familiarly. It sounded like a line from a movie, rendered by one of the great method actors, but not a macho one.

"Good. In that case, delay your trip to the dentist."

"What?"

"Some evidence of facial damage makes your conversion to the cause look all the more plausible."

"No! No! You said I could get them re-implanted if I was quick enough." I patted the teeth in their milk-bath, encased in the elastic band-nipped bag, for all the world like a sticky Siamese dessert.

"Well, that's 50-50 anyway. Save yourself the expense."

"I thought you guys would pay."

"You thought wrong."

"*My die*. No can do," I wailed. "My face, my face."

"Pull yourself together," said the Look Khreung, with absolutely no sympathy in a voice gone steely.

"They all know what a coward Snooky is," I said. "They see me banged up like this and they'll figure out I caved in like a cissy straightaway."

Down the phone came a cluck of disgust; then he hung up. I washed my face, took an oxycontin and went to Do-Ann's dentist, Rut-dah (her name meant big baby eyes, though over the mask they were more like Dracula's). One tooth, incredibly, was to take. The other fell out six hours later. Even more incredibly, I felt horny that evening. Do-Ann wanted to take advantage of the gap in my teeth but I pointed out the blood. Instead she had me in my booty, inserting her glorious thin dick the while I depressed the plunger of the Nubain-loaded hypodermic, delivering the entire delicious contents straight into my first and second toe webs. (Yah, we did it from the front). That night I slept.

I'd always had problems with Carpal Tunnel Syndrome. Probably more from texting than typing on the laptop. Possessing the thin nest wrists, I was vain enough to set them off with all manner of bangles and bracelets. Anyhow, I awoke with the telltale pins and needles and paralysis in my right hand, and knew I would have to wear the metal and elastic splint day and night for a week – the Gang always said it was a device for giving up masturbation. I wore it as I SMS-ed Avril. The Mac, the reliable, rock-steady Mac, dispenser of porn and recorder of my profoundest cinematic thoughts, was running a tad slowly and erratically. If it had been a Windows-clone I'd have said it had malware but Macs don't get any in the wild. Sometimes I thought it acted like a reflection of the health or otherwise of my own mind, or, to use its own terms, the mirror-site of Snooky's own psyche.

I phoned Avril, the kindest, most reliable, not to say, feminine, person I knew. She agreed to meet me the next day at our favourite Starbucks. I hoped the CTS splint would be an alibi for the state of my face.

"Jesus, what happened?" Avril asked with a concern that brought tears to my eyes.

"Car crash," I answered. "Serves me right for not wearing a seat-belt like you said. Better get used to condoms, too."

"Oh, God, and your nice teeth, too, sweetie. Who was the idiot driving? Tich?"

Avril had never met my set but I had regaled her with their exploits so often she knew them as well as the cast of *Cheers* or *Friends*. Noi used to drive while Do-Ann in the back gave people the finger. For some reason, four *katoeys* walking – though risible to the vulgar – had nothing like the comic impact of four TV's driving themselves in a car. You work it out. Maybe you think the same. If so, kindly elucidate to Snooky.

"Yah. The reckless bitch," I said. "We're lucky to be alive."

"Oh, sweetie, how awful for you."

My face felt dead, immobile, but the bruised muscles must still have had some honest play in them beyond my volition because Avril looked sharply at me. "Are you levelling with me, honey? Was it gay-bashers?"

"How could it be?" I answered with a glibness that gratified me. "I'm a woman."

"Yeah, and the Dalai Lama's a Roman Catholic."

"Is this what they call tough love, Avril?"

"Take it how you want, Superstar."

"Don't I always. Hey, does my eyebrow look like pussy lips?"

"Now you mention it . . . you're going to have to make do with it as your only one."

"Yah, and blood comes out of it, too." Then I cried and cried. Avril sat tight, just passing the kleenex. She knew a display of sympathy would only prolong things, had probably provoked it.

After a while she handed me the complimentary newspapers. "Seen the opposition today?"

There were several English language papers in town. I tried to avoid the *Bangkok Post*. Their reviewer, Kong Khian Keng, a Southerner and a Muslim like myself, but married, was so far ahead of me in the game it wasn't funny. He hadn't had the benefit of my time in Manila but was a far better stylist than I would be if they gave me ten years at Harvard. How anybody who had never left Siam in his life could write as beautifully as that was a mystery. The guy who wrote for *The Country*, an organ with a distinct Indian twang because of its Sikh subs, was a scowling, hot-tempered Chinaman who despised me so much he had never addressed a word to me in three years at the preview theatre. I always felt he was gonna pop me one in the chops just as a duty to manliness. His pen name was Hanuman, after the Indian Monkey God, but I thought of him as Hangman.

"Spare me," I said.

"Nope. No quarter today. Kong's brilliant as usual."

"Yeah, King Kong. Fuck him. I'm green with envy."

"You have your moments, too, sweetie. We'll go to the bookstore and have a giggle after coffee, that always cheers you up." Avril was referring to a standard pastime of ours which involved picking out a book at random from the shelf of vanity-published local expat "writers" and reading out a para, any paragraph. Their misconstructions, infelicities, and frank paroxysms of incorrect grammar could reduce us to helpless hysterics within seconds and never failed to produce at least a superior grin. The impassive Siamese store staff were used to seeing Avril and me clutching each other, falling round their aisles, fighting for possession of the lurid volume the other was holding at arm's reach.

She did warn me once that whilst I could write standard English better than any of the bums and no hopers on the shelf, as a non native speaker my ear for the vernacular wouldn't be the same as theirs and I should feel free to approach her, my pupil, for clarification in case I became the victim of some terrible practical misapprehension.

"You mean in case I come a copper?"

"Cropper," she said severely. "You see? It's Cockney."

"You think I didn't say that as a joke?" I riposted, flicking out my long, sinful tongue. I left it out a fraction too long. Avril stuck the loose barcode from the book-jacket on to it. I was still sputtering on the pavement outside when Avril said, "Don't worry on my behalf, darling. It's not transmitted through saliva."

She had once claimed the brilliant expression about an acerbic NY theatre critic "leaving no turn unstoned" as her own while working for her student mag in Montreal but her native Quebec honesty had shown through a week later. (Before she compounded the transgression by claiming that while a sub she'd come up with the headline Me No Leica for an unfavourable review of the theatre play *I am a Camera,* which was later filmed as *Cabaret*). She was a treasure-trove of industry gossip. Now she started talking about Rock Hudson, Burt Lancaster, and the other stealth queens of the Fifties, which were favourite topics as you might imagine. Avril's aunt had worked as a publicist in LA not to big stars but to other lesser lights in the entertainment firmament who were still known, at least to me, after the passage of half a century. If that isn't a kind of immortality, I don't know what is. Ages ago Avril had told me Lancaster was a cross-dresser. Avril's aunt while a student at Notre Dame had been recruited to work in the vacation as a waitress at a party not in Hollywood but at Aspen, Colorado, and had been offended when instructed in advance not to gawp at the stars arriving. I had understood her feelings – everyone wants to be thought cool already. Half-way through the party Burt had made his entrance, biceps and pectorals bursting through his little black dress and eyelids turquoise with mascara. Well, Avril's Aunt had gawped. No honorarium for her.

I couldn't match this level of anecdote but contributed the story of how Poo, playing a pre-op bit part in a blue movie, had appeared to partner a famous, unambiguously hetero, local movie idol. He'd no idea his solo scenes, taken in the same hotel room as the real antics would play, might be spliced into 20 minutes of depravity enacted by Noi and Co.

"What was he doing?" Avril asked.

"Oh, yah, usual stuff, talking head. The director got him to lean forward and he stuck a cigarette in his mouth. That was like a fruitful template."

After Avril got over that one, she capped me with a story she swore was simple truth from one of our Sports subs, Ray, who'd previously toiled on the desk of a provincial newspaper in a university town in England which I will call the Pernell Post. Nothing much happened sports-wise in the small towns and villages of the shire, though the city did have a football team of its own. Bored out of their minds, the lads on the sports desk decided to invent not one imaginary soccer team but an entire non-existent league. "You've got to see," Avril pointed out very reasonably, "that they couldn't play against themselves; they needed opposition and you couldn't have them playing league teams that actually existed – the cat would have been out of the bag at once."

The practical jokers began cautiously with three lines, buried deep in the paper. Then the story grew with a momentum of its own until it arrived with a fanfare that dismayed its perpetrators on the front page. A fictitious team from the tiny village of Steeple Phennelton, so tiny you'd never find it on a map, became the giant-slayers of the league. Gradually, they ran up an unbeaten record, with a string of victories marred only by a single goal-less draw. The sportswriters excelled themselves in their atmospheric previews (even taking the pains to get some of their predictions wrong), while their dramatic reports of extra time goals and penalties attained a vividness never otherwise achieved in the humdrum accounts of real matches (just gangs of yokels hacking round a sodden piece of leather in the goo).

One day the editor came into the newsroom from behind his frosted glass preserve – a dramatic, old-fashioned entrance, impossible to replicate in our open-plan Bangkok office – waving the galleys of his own organ in excitement and demanding a feature on the team, interviews, photographs (of which, strangely, there had been none hitherto). "I can't think why you haven't thought of it before," he rebuked the Features Editor. "It's the best sports, no, best human interest story we've had for years, since the 98-year-old rescued the 70-year olds from the blaze at the Care Home." Usually, Avril told me, the front page would be reserved for photos of giant, prize-winning marrows, which were a kind of ground vegetable grown in temperate climes. This didn't seem so odd to me as back home photographs of giant, bubble-car-sized groupers caught in the South China Sea occupied just such a prominent position in our own local rag. The flabbergasted fish could wear, with their gaping mouths, very human expressions of dismay.

"So what happened?" I asked Avril. Were there presentations of plates and silver cups that were entirely rigged? Or did they just terminate the league there and then? No, said Avril, they phased it out slowly over a period of months. To kill the whole farce off suddenly would have excited suspicion that was not there. They made Steeple Phennelton lose 3-0 in their next match and draw against the worst team in the league in their subsequent fixture. Saturday by Saturday the fortunes of the Steeple Phennelton XI waned into mediocrity, admittedly without any huge defeats but only occasionally cossetted by minor victories. Their star strikers were transferred, their most prolific goal-scorer was crippled by injuries their grizzled physio could not conjure away with his magic effleurage and tapotements, the goalie got a detached retina in a game of tennis, the staunch and steady full-backs retired, as did that great and reliable helmsman, the captain. The big reports became a matter of a few paragraphs and then, finally, the whole League vanished into the oblivion from which it had been born.

"Didn't the bosses ever find out?" I asked. "The editor, the proprietor?"

"No," said Avril. "To this day, decades later, it's a secret – apart from the people like me that Ray and his pals told. It had to be. It would have been not just a firing offence but something that would have stopped the perps from ever being hired again. Yeah, Bigmouth, don't get ideas. Don't you ever dare write about it!"

"Who me?" I asked with big, innocent eyes, hand on the valley of the heart between the twin peaks of my falsies.

"Yeah, you, you little plagiarist. You're not above going through our trash-baskets for good lines."

"Please, Avril, please. Not plagiarist. Parodist. Inverter. Homage-payer. Satirist."

"Actually, the whole thing's so English, you know, Snooky. They love this kind of pranking. I mean not just the louts but the upper-classes, too. The rich call it a spoof, the working-classes call it a 'wind-up'."

"Don't tell me Canucks never fool around in those long winters of yours. Don't you guys have a word for it?"

"Two. *Un vilain tour.* OK, it's three."

"Spell."

Avril obliged.

"Like it, like it. But not as much as *nostalgie de la poo*."

"*Boue*, idiot. You know, Snooky . . ."

"What?"

"No. It's OK."

"Come on. Didn't you once say people should be shot for tanta-lising like this and then clamming up?"

"OK. Why are Thai people such fucking liars?"

"What?"

"Come on, you know damn well what I mean."

"Well, depends. Could be to be polite and avoid mutual embar-rassment and hurting feelings."

"Yeah, I heard that 100 times. But it can be damn malicious and when money comes into it, it's downright dishonest. I'm not insulting you about the cash you've borrowed from me, baby."

"And that I've never paid back. Well, we're a very money-minded, mercenary people, Avril. It's the Chinese in us. And, yah, we are sneaky sometimes, I admit it. Not just to *farang* but ourselves as well. I guess we don't respect truth as much as you guys do. I mean, intrinsically. It's not something that's solid for us, it's not such a big deal."

"I swear to God people give me the wrong street directions just for the fun of it."

As Snooky, too, had in her unregenerate past been part of just this unstated conspiracy, handing the hapless *farang* down the line in completely the wrong direction, relishing the joke the more for the fact of her fellow misdirectors being unknown to her, and she to the subsequent conspirators, she confined herself to saying: "Could be your shaky Thai."

"You mean I can't hear the difference between 'far' and 'near'? *Klai* and *Klai*?"

"It's your *farang* ear. They do sound similar but one is said lower and more emphatic."

"Look, Snooky, any folk whose word for far is an exact homo-phone for the word for near – except you say it in a loud voice – cannot be said to be reliable mentors or to have a strong grasp on where they find themselves. Hey, baby, you're smiling again!"

"Ow! *Jep!*" I exclaimed as I laughed. But it was true. An hour with Avril had been worth two aspirins and half an E.

"Yah," I said, "OK – just for Avril's ears only: Thai people hate foreigners and love money."

"That's not exactly a secret."

Before we left, I drew up a long vocabulary list of Siamese words for Avril on three paper napkins. And I did use homonyms, meaningful, comic homonyms to help her remember. A selection:

1. *Pie Nigh?* Where are you going? (The commonest Siamese greeting, not really interested in the answer). *Pie Do Way.* Let's go (and have it off) together. (Interested in the answer).
2. *Keen Cow.* (Eat. The national sport).
3. *Tea ruck.* Darling. Honey. (I've been using the expression promiscuously but you haven't understood till now).
4. *My pen wry.* It doesn't matter. You're welcome. *De nada.* I don't give a fuck.
5. *My me.* There isn't/aren't any/doesn't have.
6. *Me my?* Are there any?
7. *He.* Vagina. (Yah, I know, it should have been called a *"she"*).
8. *Men.* Stinky (They do tend to be, much more so than us women).
9. *Man Now.* Lime. (We both agreed we'd like one, with or without a gin and tonic, right away).
10. *Die my?* Can I? May I?
11. *My die.* Not possible. Not allowed.
12. *Choke Dee.* Good Luck.

"OK, *tea ruck. Snooky my me he, my pen wry,*" said Avril as she departed.

THAT WAS the last amusing part of the day. At 9 a.m. next morning my landline rang. It was like a private hotline to Satan. Only creditors or officialdom rang on that. The good stuff was usually SMS, like Avril's, received earlier at 8.33 a.m.

Her text had read: HEY GIRL, CHANCE TO GET THE BROWLINE TATTOOED.

(Snooky had replied: WITH SOFTBALL WELTS TO MATCH THE BAT FLYING OUTTA MY BUTTCRACK – which tattoo had been an excess of early Metro days).

The Look Khreung said down the crackly line, "11 a.m. outside

Planet Hollywood, Siam Square." The line went dead. I waited, then heard the janitoress hanging up downstairs. Uh-huh.

Snooky spent a leisurely 20 minutes taking off her make-up to show her black eye, cut cheek, sutured eyebrow, and flattened nose to best advantage. He wanted us to look inconspicuous in a night-life zone deserted by day. Fuck him. By the time I finished, it was too late to take the BTS skytrain and arrive on time. We all hated the station escalators, anyway. As your particular stair rose from the bustling purgatory of street-level Bangkok to the tranquil paradise of the platform, sniggers from behind would alert you to the ignominy of all and sundry at the rear seeing your carefully tucked-away dick and balls bulging over your butt-fold.

I beckoned a motorbike and sat pillion – side-saddle, of course – in high-heeled wedgies with my leather mini-skirt pulled low to expose the cord-thin gusset of thong panties trapped in my bum-crack. When the motorbike taxis weren't dealing dope, they were police informers. Their numbered waistcoats cost a fortune – so did your fare. The drivers were licensed to a single home *soi* and had to make the return trip passenger-less. I figured the Look Khreung would not like me arriving with a witness who might see his face. I figured also, if I was killed in an accident on the way, that would shaft his plans, too. Talk about cutting off your broken nose to spite your own battered face. That was deep in Snooky, too, and she knew it. Well, we went at the speed of fright, zooming like a witch on her broomstick over everyone's head on the elevated road and zipping even faster when underneath as the pillars flashed by like Star Trek constellations at warp-speed in hyper-drive. It wasn't just the 90 mph parts of the trip that made it the fastest transport in town. When cars were stalled in a jam two miles long, you glided past along the side or down the middle – it really was like travelling in an invisible dimension. I arrived alive, on time. The horrendous casualty rate amongst motorcyclists did not include professional drivers. As Do-Ann once said, with a twinkle in her eye, if you do something every day you get good at it, and quick to the finish.

The Look Khreung appeared from nowhere as I was pulling the blue plastic banknote from my purse. "OK, Lek," he said to the driver, "Go." At the dismayed expression on my face, he said, "What? It's free, isn't it? Not like your teeth." He led me through the maze of jewellery and clothing stalls in one building – couldn't help scanning the paste and gilt, Snooky is an unreformable shop-aholic – and across the road into the neighbouring mall through glass swing-doors, before exiting through another set of doors and returning to the first building. We did this a few times before finding ourselves at a table in a deserted juice-bar. He told me I would be going up-country, by train. At least it wasn't the coach. I would return to the haunts of my childhood – a good word; it referred to a living death – and do absolutely nothing for a protracted period. "That'll be easy," I responded bitterly. "There isn't anything to do." I should wait for people, including my half-brother and Jefri (whom he kept calling "Abdullah") to come to me. I should not take the initiative. "Not as the usual *modus operandi* anyway," the Look Khreung said. He opened his mouth, but I grimaced, letting him know I understood the expression at the cost of creating a twinge in my cheek.

"Yes, I keep forgetting your attainments," he said. "Very impressive, really, considering you had none of my advantages. I can safely say your crap's no worse than the *farang* hacks."

This stung Snooky's vanity enough for her to inquire, "Where did you learn your Latin, then?"

"Oh, antique sort of place. Near Liz's suburban villa, not quite in the country but by the river, don't you know. Nowhere that would let in the likes of you, even by the backdoor. You prefer the backdoor, don't you?"

I began to tremble; it wasn't anger, it wasn't really fear. But he intimidated the shit out of me, his arrogant address. He had no pity in him. *Songsang* was the word, an important one in the Siamese emotional vocabulary (it was not an extensive book). He gave me a cover story. "Keep it simple, don't embellish things the way you people like to do. The truth is always easiest to stick to, except where we obviously can't divulge it. Say you got beaten up by the police, which I'm afraid is true. Any suggestions? Come on, we don't want to find your body in the rubber grove in the morning."

I hesitated. "They made me eat pork?"

"Oh, yes. Why didn't we do that? A nice raw Chiang Mai sausage for you."

Snooky gagged a little. I wasn't the most religious person in the world. Ingesting alcohol and semen gave me no qualms but the flesh of the pig, pink and cloven . . . uh.

"Any other suggestions to keep you in line?"

I hoped my silence did not appear sullen.

We moved on to what they regarded as high value. There was a particular religious school and its head they were interested in. Jefri was connected. A chain of sweet and sour soup restaurants in Northern Malaysia held the key to another plot. I couldn't stop snickering. "I don't blame you," said the Look Khreung, "but that's the form of their overt organisation."

"Well, there's always the American Mafia and pizza parlours," I said.

"I'll send you an order for take-out. We'll communicate, like this. I've got a special little box of tricks for you. No one'll know what it is; you'll feel like James Bond. Actually, perhaps you won't. More like Pussy fucking Galore." He gave me the address and password for an email account and told me it was the electronic equivalent of the dead letter-box. It wouldn't be a tree trunk or a garbage bin. I would be too far away from any normal haunts for this to work. The email programme itself was within a website dedicated to the study of Hittite cuneiform script and was for purported professors of etymology to leave academic comment and correspond with each other. Unless you had a de-scrambler in your computer, you would only see fabricated emails conducting highly technical linguistic disputes about proto-Indo-European Subject-Object-Verb word-order and the temperature at which clay tablets might have been baked. Or, indeed, half-baked. These overlay the real messages. Further, I would not click on SEND but press SAVE DRAFT. I would also get requests – "Don't think of them as orders, you're the one on the ground." – left in the DRAFTS Folder, not INBOX. However, the notional recipient's address was Vice Versa with Blind Carbon Copy to someone known as LK-Floreat 50-50. I thought through the implications of it. "Is someone trying to be funny at Snooky's expense?" I asked.

"It did occur to me. In fact, it actually has a significance to me, Floreat and 50-50, that it won't to you. Maybe you can guess the last."

"Oh. It's you! Half and Half."

"Ha, ha. Ho, ho. Now shut up and listen for a change. I can have your face re-arranged even more radically, if you'd find that amusing."

"Please, don't, sir."

"Vice Versa is a *farang*. He does not have the extreme good fortune to find himself resident in this country like ourselves. He may be in America in Harvard, he may be in Australia, he may be in Wales or Scotland, New Zealand, or Hong Fucking Kong. I may even be lying to you. He may be a Singaporean. He may not exist at all except as a figment of my own imagination. For practical purposes, he could also be living one mile away from you and, such is the miracle of modern technology, the correspondence would feel exactly the same. I will tell you one thing about him – he is much older and cleverer than me but not as smart as me. That's to say, wise about a piece of shit like you. But I'm always there in the background, so don't get ideas. I targeted you, so our local procedure is that I cannot run you. I think it's stupid, but there you are. Let's call it the Petchabun Protocol or the Ayuttayah Axiom. Your case has been contracted, outsourced. Plausible deniability is all the rage these days. Actually, if you knew, you'd be honoured."

I kept my fancies to myself for the term of the briefing. His parting gift was a Taser stunner, disguised as an eyeliner pencil, which he didn't seem at all worried I'd test on him. I think he knew what a wreck he'd made of me.

But not so much of one I couldn't party a few last times with LES GIRLS, as Avril called them in her texts. I could never work out if the first word was the French definite article in its plural number or an abbreviation for lesbian. The Look Khreung had expressly warned me against consorting with old cronies in former haunts but, what the hell, *my pen wry*, if we went off the beaten track we usually followed, nobody would know. I guess in me was much more of Filipino fecklessness and Thai-take-the-hindmost than I liked to think. In any case the Look Khreung was hardly going to summarily execute what he now called an asset (I kept to myself any word play on this). The real danger, which gave me already butterflies in my stomach, lay when I got home down south.

As instructed, I attended the tiny mosque in my *soi*, green-minareted and crenellated like a Disney palace, right opposite the

7-11 (known as a Sewen, where I bought my candles and lighters). I'd never been in there (the mosque, the mosque) in all my months in the capital. Just passing by, I had always felt it was where torpor, an intangible essence, had been able to assume the qualities of an aroma. I put up my long hair behind my malleable ears, the same way I'd done at school, wore jeans and unisex rubber flip-flops in fashionable but androgynous black. Thus I gained entry to the non-curtained, male, bearded part, barefoot, abluted, and at odds. Who the fuck was Snooky? The butterfly wriggling back into the baggy brown cocoon?

Weekends, I knew what I was: the party-girl, screaming Princess Snooky. Friday prayers saw the end to sobriety. I would duck out the mosque into the Sewen, get some cigarettes, then flee up the dim *soi*, past the hot soy-milk cart, the barbecue barrow, the durian vendors, the snake-fish roaster, and into my little block. I'd primp, pout, pencil a max of 15 mins, dash out (only once getting my calf scorched by a bike exhaust), pick up a tiny bottle of Red Bull in the same Sewen (they never recognised me in my drag the second time I came in) and catch the last Hua Hin bound coach. Yup, just to be on the safe side I'd got Les Girls to change our playground. The latter coastal resort was an extra two and a half hours on the bus, in the opposite direction from our usual jaunts due East, and perhaps a little staid for the likes of us since the King had his palace on the hill. To go there and do what we did on his nether strand was like blowing a raspberry at God, likely to be accomplished with impunity but theoretically calamitous. We rode ponies on the beach, like falsetto cowboys, but without a disapproving audience it was only half the fun. Half-way through the evening, Noi said, *"Thee nee mai sanuk, nar beua mark,"* which I mentally sub-titled as, "Hey, this place sucks." None of us had wanted to cast extra blight on the proceedings but Noi always had the gift of saying the unsayable, as when looking at the new haemorrhoids around Air Fun's sphincter, caused by over-enthusiastic congress with a humungously-endowed Nigerian, she had remarked, "Put tomato sauce on those and it would be Italian."

We all nodded gloomily.

"Sorry, sistas," I said. "My stoopid idea." To my disappointment, no one tried to gainsay me. Here were we stuck in hermetic Hua Hin, thanks to Snooky. "OK, girls," I suggested, "let's go up the road to Cha Am. There's a new disco there, according to my news-paper." This brightened Les Girls up considerably. They were very proud of me and set great store by the rag's recommendations. I was the only one who could write English, so the accomplishment of reading reviews was akin to deciphering runes or envisioning the future in frog guts. We set off six in a *tuk-tuk*, with me thinking of frying-pans and fires. To my surprise, most of fashionable Bangkok was milling around the car-park and entrance. I turned my head sideways so that my hair fell across my face. It wasn't so much on account of my battered face as I never liked being seen with the Outlaws by my respectable glitterati friends. There were limits to their bohemianism. Avril had used that French expression *nostalgie de la boue* to explain my attachment to characters and haunts I should have outgrown. As usual, no one was very keen to let us in and Do-Ann's offer to perform a kneeling oblation on one of the bouncers having been received with less enthusiasm than she might have hoped, we were reconciled to making nuisances of ourselves in the open air when I heard a, "Hey, if it isn't Snooky herself!" It was Dag Olsen, the manager of a five star in Wireless Road, to whose new lobster bar, serving the crustaceans of Newfoundland rather than the Gulf of Thailand, I had accompanied our elderly restaurant critic. One of his former local trainees now managed this gleaming new palace of sound. In less than a minute – far quicker than Do-Ann's tenderest ministrations on the most eager of subjects – we were inside.

As you shall see, this piece of good luck was about as favourable as getting the last stand-by seat on an airliner doomed to crash. At the time I received the awed congratulations of my friends with what I hoped was charming modesty. *My pen wry*, sistas.

I have to admit it was a pretty hot scene. I was wise to the attempts of new discos to win themselves a name by creating huge lines outside when there was actually no one inside but this place throbbed like a giant heart. Its theme was Outer Space but on the line of the Jetsons rather than cosmology, with jet-propelled busboys and busgirls equipped with anti-gravity packs, refuelling the customers with lurid drinks. They were wearing roller-blades, but the concept worked. And, fuck me dead, our order-taker was a *katoey* like us. "Equal opportunity employer," I said drily but of course not one of my dear friends understood. It turned out the drinks were on the house which did my stock no end of good. I resigned myself to enjoying the prestige of sponsor rather than wit.

"You think they got the E supply sorted out yet?" Prawn enquired. "That's the trouble with soft openings."

"Get some *yah bah*, if they don't," Noi said, "we'll eat it, if we can't smoke it in the water-closet. The vanilla tastes nice anyway. I don't like the look of the inside security."

"Sista," I said, aghast, "don't you ever learn?"

"It's outta town, girl," Noi remonstrated. "No problems."

"Snooky doesn't think wrong," Do-Ann said grimly. "I don't like the look of the security guard either."

"Have we had a run-in with him before?" Prawn peered through the darkness.

"No," said Do-Ann, "he's cute. I'd remember him if we had."

"What, you were looking up at his face from your knees?"

We all had a good giggle. Fun evening already. We knew how to amuse ourselves in the dullest times. The strobes and lasers came on. So did the strains of Lou Reed. I think Dag must have told them to put *Walk on the Wild Side* on for me. It was an oldie and a bit slow for contemporary dancing but Les Girls had acquired the knack of swinging slowly to it. Here, with our tresses, we'd look like jiving Wookies. Do-Ann and Cartoon were first up to the floor. I followed indulgently in the rear, as I was the one who had the strange whims.

Snooky took a deep breath. Taking stock of life – where you've been, where you're headed, who and what you are – is, like the inception of a revolution, normally accomplished in tranquillity: the library, the john. The decibels level attained by a good modern sound system – as this sure was – makes a discotheque dance floor an odd choice of place to start such a review. But for Snooky it was both home and a hermit's eyrie. I might as well have been half-way up the Himalayas to Tibet or in the rocky fastnesses of the Empty Quarter. I was safe from temptation and distraction. I mean, no one comes up and starts a conversation in that din. I closed my eyes and opened them.

I saw it but I didn't hear it. Two flashes at the rear of the hall. There was a flurry of movement, as vigorous but more purposeful than what was happening on the dance floor. But it was a scene from a silent movie. There was no soundtrack to help interpret what it was. Then a great press of bodies – all towards the exit. Oh, demeaning, demeaning; something so natively Asian about it. It could be Filipinos; it could be Cantonese; it could be Malays; and it could be us, the Siamese. And then da meaning did hit Snooky. My heart came into my mouth, not the most alien object that had ever been in it. A fricking disco fire. One of our famous blazes. What a humiliating way to go. We were all done for. We'd be found, charred as neglected BBQ chooks, curled up like fumigated cockroaches on our backs. I wailed. The deafening music came off, the lights went on.

Near the back of the disco a man stood over another, whose hands were held up. Another lay on the floor. The standing guy had a pistol. Around the prone man was a whole lake of blood. The armed man fired. All the life went out of the imploring victim, like a switch had been turned. The bang was enormous – not like the movies at all. It made me realise how powerful the music had been. Two men went towards the guy with the gun. He shot at them, too. Screams. One fell, hurt, the other dived for cover. You could see the difference. Everyone else took a leaf out of his book and hit the floor. Me, too, gawping, foolish, recidivist Snooky. I found Do-Ann, the dear thing, down there – as it were – already. She was normally so foolhardy but had obviously learned the difference between pluck and idiocy. Her eyes gaped under the fake eyelashes. Do-Ann was dead.

I looked again at the armed man. He was laughing, still brandishing the pistol. Now he put it in his waistband. *"Dee chai!"* I heard him cackle. "Heppy! Heppy!" Reverse the word order and it meant good or noble. That was the Siamese, I thought bitterly. His friends were treating him with greater consideration than the consideration – admittedly extreme – you would extend an armed lunatic with plenty more in the clip. Then I recognised him. Suchon N-. *Ma Bah Chon.* Mad Dog Chon. The son of the most dangerous political godfather in Northern Thailand. The guy was notorious for pulling shit like this. He passed within ten feet of me on the way out, still laughing. The disco bouncers made way. One of the thugs *wai*-ed him. Mad Dog ignored him but one of his own bodyguards politely *wai*-ed back, setting off a whole chain reaction of polite *wais* between the two groups.

I felt Do-Ann's pulse to be sure. Her wrists were a man's thick wrists; she'd always been envious of mine. No pulse detectable at all. Cartoon crawled to me, followed by the rest of the Outlaws. I shook my head at the unspoken question. "She's gone." Noi began to cry, unaffected feminine tears. Wow's crying was horrible – like a donkey braying: raucous, charmless. I could see why people hated *katoeys*.

But not enough to shoot us. Do-Ann had been hit by a stray bullet or one that had passed through the body of the first guy Mad Dog Chon had shot in an altercation over seats. And the guy he'd shot – sure enough of himself to push Chon in the dark – had been a police captain. Nowhere near high-ranking enough to challenge Mad Dog's Paw.

Under the full glare of the disco's lights Mad Dog had been seen, smoking pistol in hand, by about 300 people. Not one of them ever bore witness against him. Not even us, Do-Ann's grieving friends.

We sat on the coach the next morning, with what seemed a lot of trendy Bangkok. Rich Bangkok, of course, went home by Mercedes. The dudes in the seats immediately behind us thought it a foregone conclusion that Mad Dog would get off scot-free. "Mad Dog'll probably have to lie low for a while," said one. "Maybe go abroad to Singapore or KL, like the last time, then come back when it's all died down. He can say he thought he was entering a firing range which had background music, not a disco."

"No way," said his pal, "it's a test of the Old Man's power. He can't look weak or the other country politicians won't respect him. They've got to bold it out. Strong Heart, big brod."

"Right on," corroborated a third from the aisle seat across me. "Mad Dog's just the kid and the Big Wolf has gotta be seen to protect his cub. If he can't do that, he can't protect no one and all the rag, tag and bobtail'll desert him."

"Was there someone else hit, I heard?"

"Just some fucking fag, they said."

"Good riddance, the shit. They should put open season on them."

Sniggers all round. I knew they'd clocked us, though we'd practically been cowering down in our seats. At the comfort stop, we made sure we made water together and left the lonely bathroom in unison. No one gets left behind. Do-Ann herself would have lingered with purposeful insouciance, maybe have got us all into a fight by now. We'd already split the contents of her handbag between us – her two budget phones and the smartphone, her amphetamine stash, spare change, perfume spray, lipsticks, blueberry chewing gum (only bought for the foil), and a wad of 500 baht bills. I sat out the remaining hours to Bangkok, thinking of her naked on the tray, the cock and balls she'd hated so much in life destined to go with her to the pyre, the scrotum already bloated with the gas of decomposition to the size of a grapefruit. We'd phoned her real sister and left it at that. We were too scared to get involved. Before the Southern Bus Terminal, with the river still to cross, we split up. I felt too ashamed to look the others in the eye.

Our friendships survived the police bust, just. But this was too much for the sorority. Our band was jinxed. I knew they were offering donations at the Buddhist temple, buying charms and medals and necklaces and amulets, changing their SIMs to more auspicious numbers and losing contacts in the process.

But the Look Khreung hadn't lost contact with me. Snooky should be so lucky. He told me I needed to spend more time opposite the 7-11, meaning the mosque. That was the way he put it. He told me he was delaying my return to the South for a few days more. "In the interests of your own safety, Snooky. We need you more plausible. And no more R and R with the other perverts. You must be stupid if you think I don't know all you're up to."

I had been hoping against hope that I could continue my reviews for the paper. It wasn't so much a crutch for my apology of a life. It was the entire justification for my existence. The fantasies I saw on the flat, silver screen and then my lonely ponderings thereon were far more intense and real to me than my tedious round of actualities (as were the erotic, *yah bah*-induced reveries that could last half a day – oh, that world of delicious shadows!) But my new master would have none of my old mistress (was that Muse a *katoey*, too?) The Look Khreung said I had to "tender my formal resignation".

The Arts Editor was stunned. She was nearly 70, one of those high-class old Siamese who had been born in America (as the monarch had been) but all the more nationalistic for that. I don't think she'd enjoyed her time at Sarah Lawrence in the 1950s. What wouldn't I have given for that. The time, the place, an all-girls university. She'd admitted to me that in those days – not just in her set – nobody had ever heard of Warhola. Talk about history unfolding all around you unaware. Anyway, she was so shocked by my quitting she conducted our whole conversation in Siamese. "Is it money, Khun Snooky? We can pay a little more." She used the word *neatnoi*, strongly accenting the first stress as one tended to do when (a) on the subject of lucre (b) slightly embarrassed. I could imagine her as a teenager in a twinset and plaid skirt at Lawrence, saying, "Neat!" I assured her money was not the issue, while mentally kicking myself for not wheedling more out of the owners when it had plainly been on the table. She was worried I might be crossing to take Hangman's slot. I suddenly realised that she saw me as young, cool, trendy. Maybe even glamorous. After I remained adamant, she lost her temper with me and reminded me how I'd got my big chance with them. This was too much. It was insupportable for me to keep the act up. I cried. She consoled me. "Going back up-country? Family, isn't it? We'll take a locum, keep the place open for you to come back for six months. It's nothing. It's nothing." What they couldn't do was have me write from hundreds of miles away down South – with it being email, as the Look Khreung had pointed out, what was the difference? – or preview the movies from the net. She said in English, her last words on the subject, "We need to keep it real, Khun Snooky."

I got quite ill after this. Nervous stress, I thought. Psychosomatic illness. Who wouldn't be after what Snooky had gone through. I snuffled as I thought about it. The fucking Look Khreung, riding me like an ever-present shoulder-imp. My dear friend gunned down in front of me. Poor Snooky. I was better off dead (well, maybe not quite). The prayers made me feel better. I knew the words and gestures from childhood, of course. It was reassuring to go through them; the ablutions, the prayers, the open hands, the prostrations. I went five times a day now. Once the Imam nodded at me. I was surprised he'd noticed. I thought I was quite nondescript during my appearances there. "You are thin," another worshipper said to me as I fumbled for my shoes. "Eat rice," he exhorted. "Take care of yourself. There are few of us here." He meant Bangkok, of course, not at our particular place of worship. At the 7-11 I bought a tetrapak of rose-hip juice and a litre of chocolate milk (0% Fat). The till-girl re-arranged her sultry North-Eastern features to give me a dazzling smile. "No Red Bull tonight?"

"Just the fruit juice and the milk, little sis," I said. She and her co-cashier both snickered. The word for milk and breasts, as you know, is pretty well the same. And, as you also know, I had no tits. As the electronic door tone sounded behind me, I reflected I had been much less anonymous, not to say androgynous, than I supposed. They had put 7 and 11 together and duly come up with 18. Maybe Lou Reed's corner convenience store knew who he was, too.

The early nights, the hi-protein and vitamin diet didn't seem to be working. I was getting more run-down, not less. My skin itched; I sweated. In the morning would be the damp outline of my body on the sheet, as if it had been the Shroud of Turin. My neck and my armpits swelled. Getting the picture? At last I burst out in a rash which ran in a belt half-way across my torso. The vesicles blistered, then crusted. I knew what it was. Shingles. The half-brother of herpes. We had a euphonious name for this derangement of the nerves: isoog-isai. Trouble was, I'd had it before. You were only meant to get it the once, as the echo, as it were, of childhood chicken-pox.

Dr Cheuan was a young woman. Her steroid injections had worked wonders with my yah bah allergies, what Americans called "speed bumps" on the skin. Most people get them on the chest and back. I used to get mine on the face – oh, woe – and shins.

"It's unusual, Khun Snooky," she said, "twice is definitely not usual. We can run tests . . ." She was a nice girl from a rich Hokkien family but she was not making the usual eye contact. She had not failed to do so after swabbing the pus of the gonococcus from my sphincter.

"AIDS?" I said. That was what everyone thought of us. There was no hurry to get to the Sentinel's water-fountain after me.

"HIV, you mean," she said, severely as she could.

"Very correct, but as far as Snooky is concerned, the distinction is academic."

"Well, we can run that one and a couple of other tests, too. My cousin's just joined haematology in Bangkok Nursing. I'll see if we can't shave a few satang off the bill . . ."

"Oh, thanks so much, Pinky," I said a lot more warmly, addressing her by her familiar name.

"Oh, it's nothing. It's only blood-work. A CBC, maybe a DR-70.

Dengue, Treponema, Hodgkins, myoblastic, we'll run it all through. You'll find it's just anaemia and late nights."

As you can see, short of her being my personal gynaecologist, she was the perfect MD for me.

A few days after our consultation, I was going out, in blouse and shorts, to buy some polythene bags of red-curried mutton from the friendly vendor to eat in my room when the pavement came up to meet my face. I was under the impression I was standing with my palms outstretched to prevent something fast, invisible, and powerful – I don't know, maybe, a meteor or a motorbike taxi – from collision, with me. I had no sense of shock or pain. Then I discovered myself to be flat out, horizontal on the pavement, with outstretched hands having saved my face from impact. There was a fine sprinkling on the pavement – not red curry, but blood spraying from my nose every time I breathed. Now I felt the shock of the blow. It had come from behind. The relatively innocuous fall itself had caused the nose-bleed. I got a kick in the ribs. I knew the vital thing – I had to get up. Staying down, I would get kicked to death. We are a kicking folk – Siamese boxing bags, *takraw* balls, soccer balls, people's balls, and heads. I got a helping hand, which was a preliminary to a full-blooded slap in the chops. A voice hissed in my ear, "He says you should thank him. See? Saved you time and money. No point getting anything fixed when you had this to come. Think of the bruises as cover when you get down South with all the other pigs."

Next moment the hand released me and the same voice was grunting in pain. He had been struck by the Muslim well-wisher, from opposite the Sewen, come to my aid, the one who'd told me to eat more. My acquaintance was holding a clothier's metal ruler. His simple, good face had only one expression on it – concern for me. I pushed him away. I didn't want him hurt. My assailant had the cropped head of a bonze or a soldier. A bike came for him. I grabbed the trowel of a roast chestnut vendor, poured the steaming charcoal down his shirt, and ran. Behind me I heard roars of agony and fury. They were as gratifying as they were intimidating. Turning left at the end of my little lane, I raced down the main *soi*, screaming as genteelly as I could, just missing a kid on his push bike and an old woman laden with market vegetables. "Going for a dump?" someone asked cheerfully. (I think it was a brat heading into the computer gaming café). Frankly I had, at least consciously, no idea where I was bound; I just desired to put space between myself and revenge. A sanctuary appeared before me, crenellated, bulbous. I shot into the mosque, only just remembering to kick off my wedgies, but then finding my breathless way barred by one of the Imam's new assistants from Narathiwat.

"Join the other ladies behind the curtain, Older Sister," he said politely, not looking directly at me. Giggles from behind the drape, broad grins from the men. Never say we lack a sense of humour in even the most solemn circumstances. I was glad enough to get behind the curtain. Outside there was kerfuffle. But not too much. I heard the voice of the Imam himself: soothing, polite, dissuading. I had never heard him speak standard Bangkok Siamese, only Arabic and Southern dialect. The motorbike thundered off. I knew they dared not make a ruckus inside a Bangkok mosque – as authoritatively frowned on as running round a gasoline pump-station with a blazing torch. Tutting mildly, Imam showed me out by a backdoor. Yah, Snooky had been saved by kith and kin.

My phone rang an hour later. The Look Khreung said, "What a hot heart you are. Collect your ticket at Hualamphong tomorrow. You've got the fan coach. My office still smells of burnt meat. If you fuck up, he'll be the one I assign to your arse."

Half an hour later, it rang again. I told myself under any circumstances not to be a wise-ass. But it was Dr Cheuan. She said, "Khun Snooky, I have a result. Are you sitting down?"

PART TWO

The Caliphate

1. Snooky
2. Shaykh
3. Snooky
4a. Umar 4b. Snooky 4c. Shaykh
5. Snooky

Borges also employed two very unusual literary forms: the literary forgery and the review of an imaginary work.
– Wikipedia

I am He Whom I love and He Whom I love is I.
– Al-Junayd

O Sohrab, wherefore wilt thou rush on death?
Be governed: quit the Tartar host, and come
To Iran, and be as my son to me,
And fight beneath my banner till I die.
There are no youths in Iran brave as thou.
– Matthew Arnold, *Sohrab and Rustum*

The Filipino is worth dying for.
– Ninoy Aquino, 500 peso note,
Republic of the Philippines

We are destroying the real and building up the fake.
– Wen Jiabao

I Yam what I Yam and I Duz What I Duz.
– Popeye

In these my pages I shall describe things as I saw them, things as I heard them, so that my book will be an accurate record, free from fabrication. You who read my lines may do so in trusting confidence, because in them is naught but verity.
– Marco Polo, *De Mirabilibus Mundi*

In my 25 years experience, governments lie to each other. That's how business is done.
– Robert Gates

Snooky

Where we were, we had it both ways. Silly, Snooky's being serious. She means, we had the advantages of town and country, *kota* and *kampong*. These two irreconcilables were merged in our situation. We were encircled by our own magic forest, protected by its monsters and ogres, but within 20 minutes scooter-ride of the North-South highway between Chumphon and Hat Yai and, hence, the facilities, such as they were, of the nearest town. Shaykh himself confessed to an inherent distrust of cities. For him, the urban spelled corruption, adulteration, complexity of a specious kind. Temptation, he said, and defilement, were not things that happened to the modern Muslim in the Garden. These wolves fell upon him in the town. The defence lay in simplicity.

Yah, where we found ourselves was pristineness itself. But Snooky has to admit she found it anything but peaceful or relaxing. If she failed Shaykh, there would be neither excuse nor exoneration on grounds of an unpropitious locale. You were expected to win, playing at home or away. What Shaykh offered instead was wholeness. That was his personal gift to Snooky. Others came to him already as homogenes. Simple souls. Sometimes Snooky envied them. What Shaykh did was put her two cloven halves together into something composing critical mass. She shall always thank him for it: for pulling the lever and firing the bolt of lightning into her brain that gave her life – like a cut bloom all the more precious for its transience – where before there had only been the stupor of a daydream.

The scene of these operations was beautiful, distinctly beautiful, even for a citygirl like Snooky. Let her imagine it from the air as it must have looked to God. Our buildings would appear as so many chocolates nestling in an intricately filled box, or as jewels in a filigree setting, the texture of the palm-frond and corrugated iron roofs complementing and contrasting, the former comprising housing and the more substantial latter public-buildings, but all settled in their contrasting smoothness and roughnesses amid the plump arborage. Banyans we had, yah, and frangipani, the first a social tree, the tree of community, with its exposed roots growing from above, from the branches into the ground, rather than vice versa, sombre-hued, giving an aura mostly of brown but sustaining encounter and gossip in its shade and amid its crooked vantages and snaky seating, while the more beautiful and powerfully fragrant frangipani with its rubbery white flowers – so many giant shut-tlecocks – was actually the tree of death, of cemeteries and morbid contemplations. The zephyrs in this Garden of Innocence murmured, like Snooky's old visitor Khun Su, that Life was plain and utilitarian but that Death was a glamorous perfume. Yah, we, the students, wore virgin whites every day but the ragged lines of washing, in back of the trees, that provided decency and decorum of attire were nothing less than a sleazy eyesore.

For Snooky banyans were Chinese and then secondarily Siamese – not at all Muslim or Malay – with the colourful ribbons and tassels the Buddhist villagers liked to loop and trail around the venerable growth. Frangipani was more Islamic, more Malay, though its leaves were dollar-green and the blooms, with their fragile yellow filament, waxy-pale as Chinese skin and not banyan-dusky. When I put it to Shaykh, months later, he resolved my difficulties in the way he always did: devastatingly simple but subtle, too, so that I was left perplexed as to why I had tormented myself so. "But, Ahmed," he said. "Both trees are very Islamic trees. God did not gift either to the *kafirs*." Sure, you don't have to tell me it was kind of a fricking stupid exchange but part of Shaykh's sophistication was fearlessness of the inane. It was perilous to underestimate him on the basis of his slight Malay vocabulary and occasionally shaky English grammar. These were his parting words, uttered with a smile that contained no mockery: "The banyan resembling a diagram of the Decision Tree. Isn't it, Ahmed?"

We were an old *pondok* school brought up to speed by him. We didn't just have a hall for learning Holy Koran by rote and practising our Arabic and *Jawi* script. No, we also had a laboratory, a library, an observatory, a cyber-room, a batik factory, a gamalan room for the Javanese orchestra, a badminton court, a metal workshop, an infirmary, and a tiny botanical garden. As a contrast to this public plenitude, our student dormitories were flimsy and mean. Without discipline they could have become sordid quite quickly. This was not the case with our teachers whose rooms, though appropriately simple, were both commodious and lofty-ceilinged. Here was a message to the young and impressionable. The very lay-out of the joint was a proclamation that there existed strength in numbers and in fervour power, but that hierarchy was primary. Yah, personally, Snooky could never work out whether Shaykh was a progressive traditionalist or a conservative revolutionary.

In our school everything went like clockwork, always just so. It led me to think that Shaykh had been there a long time, like the spectacular karst formations on the other side of the valley that rose sharp as the crests on a dinosaur's back. In fact, Shaykh had been at the *pondok* only two and a half years. In that time he had transformed a sleepy provincial institution into a living instrument that quivered for the proof.

Over our heads rose the chant, always the chant. The recitations were led by Shaykh's assistants, only rarely by himself, when, however, the pupils and acolytes would reach a very crescendo of calling and swaying. As with any school, the lowest classes comprised the youngest or the very stupid. Our particular curriculum began, but did not end, with the Koran. The aim, easily achieved, was for us all to be able to recite it by heart. At the time Snooky arrived, she already mostly could. Couldn't tell you too much what it signified, of course. To remedy this we learned the holy language, Arabic, itself. I liked it for the age-old reason that I liked my teacher, much as math proved do-able back in high school because the instructor had been a kind and gracious old Chinese lady. Haji Hassan was the mildest, most scholarly of fellows. Not a priest but still a haji twice over, and certainly an Alim, a learned Muslim, or *kyia* as we called it in our dialect, he wore the kind of frameless spectacles on a cord known as pince-nez. The big buck teeth and quivering lip below failed to sabotage but rather enhanced the pince-nez, making him look like a learned and benign rabbit. The haji, I think, desperately wanted the lenses to make him look severe but instead the glasses' precariousness conferred upon him an air of permanent vulnerability.

This was the reverse of Shaykh who strove to appear indulgence itself but at his most benign was merely spine-chilling rather than outright paralytically scary. Haji Hassan was Acehnese but the graduate of a very famous Cairo university where he had learned his Arabic in the company of students from all around the world and – it was rumoured – had joined the Brotherhood. In Aceh it was said he had managed the Islamic Bank but he discouraged allusion to this. He saw himself as an Arabic scholar, not the next worst thing to an outright usurer.

"Come, come, Arabic is easy," he would exhort us. "With God's help, it is only difficult if you choose to make it so." And: "The Holy Language is for all Muslims, not just for those lucky enough to be born into it."

At this, I had to bite my tongue. But he was alerted straightaway. "Ahmed doubts you, Haji!" squealed a 13-year-old peasant boy.

"Yes, Ahmed?" The pince-nez flashed under the strip-lighting.

I shook my head. What was I thinking of? Extolling as a parallel my affinity for the language of the Great Shaitane?

"Not sharing your valuable Bangkok insights today?"

Sycophantic laughter from the village boys who comprised most of the class.

"God Willing, Ahmed is here to learn, Haji," Snooky said. "Please enlighten me, Haji. God has chosen the honest *bumiputra* to be the receptacles of Wisdom, not the wily urbanites." As a wily urbanite, I was putting into practice one of Shaykh's most useful precepts. "Modesty," he liked to say, "is a virtue. Humility a weapon."

It certainly disarmed Haji Hassan, who contented himself with the mild rebuke, "Neither Imam Umar nor myself are *bumis*, though God has a special love for the sons of the soil. I rely on Him."

I should add now that the major mortification for Snooky in the *pondok* so far – but as nothing compared to the future taste of Tariq's own medicine – was being called by her birth name of Ahmed. Could there be a fricking uncooler appellation?

On our curriculum Koran and Arabic were followed by study of the Commentaries on the Holy Book and then study, not less but more exhaustive, of the Commentaries on the Commentaries. Not to mention the Commentaries on the Commentaries on the Commentaries. It was all impeccably scholarly but made Snooky think of Phil Spector. Snooky admired the integrity of the reasoning but it was also kinda arid and austere for her. More to her taste, as a Borges-lover, were the stories whose proper name she will tell you later.

Imam Umar, who had been holding the fort, till Shaykh's return, as our *Tok Guru*, was even older than Haji Hassan and half-blind with a milky cataract which made him all the more alive to the quirks and foibles of his fellow man. He'd stand there monitoring our trite activities with his dead, opaque eyes and a face bright with curiosity and glee. This was quite often in the misfortunes of others but he was also prepared to delight in the good luck of acquaintances, especially where he had a material look-in. His coffee-brown complexion set off the snowiness of his beard as if the latter was a cameo carving on shell but his nacreous orbs glowed in that dark face like the eyes of an alien, albeit a sociable one. His chronic, high-pitched giggle was a constant in the garden, often enough at moments that would have been regarded as inappropriate, coming from us pupils, as a cellphone's ringtone in a concert hall.

But Snooky is getting ahead of herself.

It was only after I had been at the *pondok* some weeks that I was told to report to a different class instead of Haji Hassan's Koranic study. This was Shaykh's special private class, where I was to find my old friend Jefri.

I had not seen him since a few weeks after I had arrived from the North and met him in our town at his sister's house.

My bruises and contusions had still been on my face at that time, black, blue, and red, like the passport entry stamps and visa waivers they proved to be. From an objective point of view, I could not fault the Look Khreung's craft. I just hoped there would be no need for exit stamps once the black eyes had faded.

I had been staying with Jefri's brother-in-law and his older sister, rather than with Mare. To his sister, the same one who had led me by hand to the girls' games at school all those years ago, I was a walking, breathing martyrdom in progress. We two girls had a good old-fashioned cry together. Then she glimpsed a glorious opportunity. She was, of course, unable to use cosmetics herself. Her younger sister, too, was way past the permissible age when young Gulf girls, say, went abroad in the streets with their cheeks and lips colourful as clowns and with their earrings and necklaces jingling like wind-chimes. But me! There were no proscriptions on my face. She called her friends over. They went to work. I felt like Snow White, only with the Seven Dwarves in headscarves. By the time Jefri arrived in town from the *pondok*, my horrific facial injuries were legend in the town, my speedy recovery due to the beneficence of God and not least to the ministering skills of the sisterhood.

I told Jefri I had been victimised for no reason, coming out the little Mosque in Bangkok, trusting this would correspond with the reality if he ever checked it out, garbled as true stories – except *hadith*, there I've used the word – do get in the course of enthusiastic transmission.

I told Jefri I was sick of the Bangkok life, of the injustices Muslims suffered not just there but apparently everywhere, of my feeling I had come to a crossroads in my life, of my desire to do good, to play on the *takraw* court and to fall there if necessary, rather than just sit on the sidelines doing nothing. As I spoke, my voice had a real tinge of bitterness. I surprised myself with my genuineness. Of course, it wasn't just inspired technical acting in the School of Method (had Brando got himself beaten up to play Terry Malloy?) I genuinely was pissed. Only what I was pissed about was losing my charmed, my arty, my metropolitan existence. The sporting metaphor might have done me good with Jefri. He considered; smiled that smile, at once confident and deprecating; and made no promises at all. He left on his motor-bike to return to the *pondok* without a backward look.

His sisters were crying. I said, "*My pen wry.* You will see him again soon." The older one said, "That's the first time we've seen Jefri for two years." I could say nothing. The younger sister said, "It was the time studying abroad. Town was too small for him after that." The older one said with sad pride, "*We* were too limited for him after that. And he became zealous there. To Jefri we are lax, lax and lazy."

The younger smiled wanly. They were both still loyal to their strange new brother: "It's boring for him to be awake in a dimly lit room in which everyone else is snoring." I was impressed she could speak figuratively.

"I hope my own snores didn't wake you up," I said lightly and we all laughed the local laugh which is to tragedy as kryptonite is to Superman.

A few days later, I was hauling my stripey zip-up bag out the bowels of the coach as it shuddered on the main highway, while two boys on release from Haji Hassan's class waited for me astride two popping, parping old motorbikes. Jefri's text had said, "Come to us," that was all. One boy drove me. The other waited, looked both ways, followed, halted, drove back a little to the highway, and hid in a banana grove surveying the road, before roaring past us again. They might have been brigands astride camels. The red earth track to Shaykh and the *pondok* was six kilometres and six centuries long.

At the *pondok* there was no such thing as a school captain but, had there been one, it would once again have been Jefri. The qualities that had predisposed people in his favour in the town also operated here in the forest. That was one thing that hadn't changed. I drew consolation from this. Not much, but some. Being Ahmed, I needed all I could get.

As I said, about six weeks after my arrival, I was summoned from Haji Hassan's class and taken to what was called the Maproom, or the class of high-flyers personally taught by Shaykh. At the time I had arrived he had been away. It was whispered he had been to Mecca, to Sudan, to Chechnya, furthering the Jihad. There were all kinds of stories about Shaykh. Some said he had been a nuclear scientist, others a chess grandmaster, or a tutor to the Saudi royals and the Sultan of Brunei, and also a champion at the game of squash where he had defeated Jehangir Khan. It was related that outside Kandahar he had killed a Soviet Major-General in hand-to-hand combat and routed in public disputation in Jerusalem the Cardinal in charge of the Catholic Church's Index. The safe consensus was that wherever he was from, he had come from a wealthy family but had turned his back on comfort and corruption.

Jefri introduced me to the others in the Maproom, some Sumatran illegals, two Malaysians, but mostly Jawi speaking Thai Southerners like ourselves. I was, by then, a little faint of heart. I regretted being plucked out of Haji Hassan's classes. I had never been nondescript in all my life but it had suited me to be so in the *pondok*. Deep down, I dreamed of wriggling outta this nightmare fix into which I had been stupid enough to get myself, either by supplying a surfeit of information to my controllers or, even better, a slew of lies.

On the rare occasions when something pleasant has happened in my life, it has always been a surprise. Not once was it predictable. When it's expected, that's when things go rancid on you. Jefri's friends came round me. The smiles were genuine. "This is your home now," "Be one of us, Ahmed," "Yes, we are your family," "Ask anything, my brother."

I have only ever wanted to be accepted. My difference recognised, then me accepted. Tears pricked my eyes, but there was no mascara on them now to run. As I blinked them away I became aware of a change in the room, too much to call it a stir or commotion. I was no longer the centre of attention and I never liked that.

Before important personages we Southerners tended not to prostrate ourselves, like the Northerners. Maybe it was the feeling that one should only humble oneself thus before Allah. It was even in me, this rebellious instinct. With the Northerners, if a Royal passed by, within seconds it could start to look like the carnage on some ancient battlefield, bodies mown down by chariots everywhere. I found the Philippine gesture of taking an elder's knuckles and placing them gently on one's forehead to be far less demeaning, less extorted, and therefore more touching. I cannot say Jefri's group littered the ground prone but they were certainly in a form of vertical *rigor mortis*, waiting for instructions from the zombie-master.

A very tall man was silhouetted quite black in the doorway against the blazing sun. Ford or John Carpenter couldn't have asked for better back-lighting. He was so tall, I thought my sentimental tear drops were magnifying him. I blinked rapidly just to check and found the normally ultra-cool Jefri shaking his head in horror at me. He had thought I was batting my eyelids at the Master! A hoarse, very high-pitched voice said, "But please show more consideration to our new arrival. Welcome Ahmed. Peace be upon your head." And these were the first words Shaykh directly addressed to me, as I stammered back, "Upon your head peace."

He was well over six feet tall, nearer 6ft 6ins than 6ft 3ins, slim, with the darkest face made blacker by such white as had developed in his beard, which was long and square as a buzzard's tail. On his close-cropped head, perhaps as a tribute to his adopted people, he wore the little Malay hat and over a long white robe what I later discovered to be a Soviet army jacket in winter camouflage with the padding removed. This was obviously trophy, rather than the homage of the hat. At night he'd prefer the comfort of a red and white checked shawl. He walked with the aid of a slender, silver handled ebony cane, which picked up the flecking in the beard and both the solid black of the hat and the reflective sunglasses that protected the failing eyes. I got used to seeing the perfect miniaturised image of myself, as I did not want to appear, in his impermeable lenses. Bar Lord Vader, it is safe to say he was the single most arresting personage I had ever seen, on or off screen, in my entire life.

Behind Shaykh, his prosthetic hand not unlike the claw of the pubic louse I had seen under the low power field of Doctor Cheuan's microscope, followed the unlikely figure of Haji Tariq. Stocky, short-legged where his master was all elegant extension, he appeared both brutally strong and also at the extreme of etiolation, potent in the way of a poison: pale as a corpse, his eye-patch like a punctuation point on an otherwise empty page. As with all eye-patches, it was the elastic garter which conferred the bravado, while the patch itself was invalidism.

Snooky did, in the initial pinprick of shock, before the anodynes of habituation and second nature dulled reflection, ask herself why so many of these guys, meaning the heroes and martyrs, spiritual and material, of the holy war, should look like they had just been sent from central casting. Few of them were as nondescript as discretion dictated they should have been, wherever in the world you encountered them. If Snooky had to manufacture a spectre to spook the great American public she could do no better than the Hellfire-martyred Sheikh Ahmed Yassin of Hamas, sitting in his wheelchair, with his pale, blind eyes rolling under his floppy head cloth and his wheezy falsetto calling imprecations upon the Great Satan. How can Snooky put it? Scheherazade meets Peter Sellers.

Yassin's condition was the result of a childhood accident but part of the answer was that many other warriors of the Jihad had actually fought in the physical war, principally in the mountains of Afghanistan, but also in our own jungles and those of Ambon and Mindanao as well, and paid a price. The pious and the brave would be the first to pay it. Where the enemy enjoyed such superiority on the battlefields, and in the air of the angels, most would simply be blown to pieces. Those who lived to tell their tale, and inspire those who would follow, would indeed be maimed and mutilated but wear the disfigurement with pride. Plus, of course, they wanted to scare the fuck outta the rest of us. They didn't get a medal; instead, they lost something, like a hand, a foot, a leg, an eye. And what Shaykh would ask of poor Snooky was to lose something even larger, her soul.

The room was big and airy: so were the ideas. Apart from the green-board there were only three teaching-aids, all cartographic: two maps of China and South East Asia and a huge globe on Mercator's projection. You needed these to appreciate the symmetry and beauty of Shaykh's dream. Even I, with education, and the ability to visualise in the mind, still find it hard. For some of the country boys in the class who were completely innocent of geography – you could have told them the world was flat, if Shaykh had corroborated it – the feat would have been impossible. And now it is Snooky's task to explain to you without any visual aid at all.

The dream of Shaykh and his co-conspirators – I call it that, but for them it was merely Plan A – was to establish a pan-Islamic republic or theocracy across all the existing national frontiers of South East Asia. As Shaykh explained, this had nothing of greed in it. It was not expansionist; it was not exploitative. It was a resto-ration and a restitution. It was not old-fashioned imperialism or a modern Jewish land-grab. He said the war to reclaim the lands stolen from the Palestinians by the Jews was the concern of every good Muslim but that the military might of the Jews was such that it would, God willing, only be won after a struggle of decades or even centuries.

But the Muslim Magic Kingdom in South East Asia could be won far more quickly; it was a realistic prospect, not the mirage which shimmers only to recede before truly desperate men. At the centre of this Magic Kingdom of our very own was . . . the unlikely kernel of Singapore. Singapore, presently a Chinese rat-hole, would one day, God willing, be our Islamic Camelot, Singha Pura, City of the Lion – the Islamic Lion-to-be – situated on the equator, the line which belted the world's navel. Our median point would also be the centre of the world geographically and culturally. Shaykh used a felt marker-pen, screwed into a homely geometry compass, a trite instrument of the classroom enlisted now, like ourselves, into his great cause, to describe a perfect circle around Singapore.

The North – or top to us as we looked at it – took in Aceh (which was Haji Hassan's part of the world), Malaya, Penang (that other Chinese mousehole), Southern Siam, of course, where we discovered ourselves, Cambodia with its Cham Muslims, Borneo – both Indonesian and Malaysian – the Southern Philippines comprising Mindanao, then down to the Celebes Sea, Sulawesi island, Java, Sumatra, Aceh again. We looked at it, stunned as Cortes might have been. It could have been cut out and put on as a *peci* or *songkok*, or as a toupé, on the top of the world if the North Pole had been scalped from it. But that was not Shaykh's own way of looking at it. He told us to think of the magic circle as a mighty whirlpool, a Muslim maelstrom sucking everything good into it and whirling out everything bad.

At first Snooky ventured to think differently. Snooky thought city thoughts, satirical thoughts; she thought thoughts at all: it was Neverland, with the *pondok* students as the Lost Boys and Tariq swooping on us like Captain Hook, with perhaps guess-who auditioning as Tinker Bell and the clock ticking against her.

Shaykh smiled dazzlingly at me. The man had the whitest teeth. His calm, his blandness, his abnormal lack of intensity, belied the fact that in achieving his goal he proposed to violate the territorial sovereignties of half a dozen expensively armed Kingdoms, Sultanates, and Republics. Behind him Haji Tariq showed his betel-ravaged teeth and gums. With the eye-patch and the spitting – lime and areca, though, not a tobacco quid – he could indeed have been a Hollywood pirate. All he needed was the parrot or a monkey. When he spoke, you realised he himself was both parrot and monkey.

"The Caliphate," he said.

WE WERE, of course, not alone. It was best to think of ourselves as wasps or soldier-ants, or even termites, in separate hives and nests, some of us completely unconscious of the other colonies' existences but all working to the same goal at the bidding of our Kings, Queens, Amirs, Sultans, and Sheikhs who lorded it in their own individual cell and enjoyed communication with their peers. There had to be a Queen Bee or King Sting, right? Snooky knew we had accessories, accomplices, co-conspirators but there had to be somebody directing and co-ordinating everything. The body, even of a spider, has to have a brain or it will work to no purpose;

there would just be the wild and reflexive spasms of a palsy. The question was – to Snooky, not the others – how high up in the chain was our own Shaykh? Who did he take instructions from? Were we the only ones he led? Was he a minor chieftain in the enterprise of South East Asian Jihad, a bit player, a character actor, a minor star, or actually the leading man? I knew, without being told, Snooky was just one of the extras. (At the time I didn't think of stuntman). I so much wanted him to be a great Jihadist, or more correctly Mujahid, but I wasn't sure even where he was from. I did know the leadership of Jemaah Islamiyah was in Indonesia. Lots of them were in fact Malaysians but peninsular Malaya was too hot for them and they'd crossed the Straits for what was a more vociferous but much safer life in Java.

If Snooky thought about Shaykh, he'd been smart, heading in the opposite direction, North rather than South. I thought of a bunch of Hollywood outlaws, the James gang, maybe Butch Cassidy, dividing the bags from a train or bank hold-up and heading off in separate directions to elude the pursuing posse. What might have been Shaykh's mishap or bad luck or wrong turning was his students' immoderate good fortune. He was too good for us, too grand. No one needed telling that. We knew – in the words of the time-honoured greeting – he could never be one of them.

I took the greatest care not to give my controllers the smallest hint of our leader's stature or his exceptionalness. At first this was to ensure my release from their employ at the earliest possible moment; later, of course, to protect the man I grew to love and admire. I encoded the information into my device. Despite the Look Khreung's words at our final meeting, I wasn't sure who it was going to or where. It could all have been a load of disinformation issuing from his mouth.

With me I had my battered old Mac for alibi. It was a sacrificial defence, to be relinquished straightaway upon challenge. Its virgin white lid – to be lifted as gingerly as that of the thronged Western toilet of a Burger King or McDonald's on a public holiday – was by now smeared all over with irremovable black finger-smudges. To Snooky's surprise, it would never be confiscated. And then there was the real communicator the Look Khreung had given me – a volume of Malay scholarship that concealed a C-driveless unit, run on a Linux derivative with a sphinx-like firewall and automatic scrambling and encyphering. The low-power chip was an antique from the '80s but there was a whopping 8GB of temporary memory. What looked like decorative shards were tiny solar panels. The motherboard and cards were sewn into the leather cover. In short, it was the way the *shia* bomb will one day be delivered: in the diplomatic bag, not the cone of a missile. As a final touch, there were two screens: one in the mirror of my compact which was indeed rapidly confiscated and another head-up display in a pair of spectacles. As myopia was an affliction common amongst young and old in the *pondok* they were not looked at, or through, twice.

Snooky thought of herself not as 007 but 000, the Siamese for the former being *Soon Soon Jet* and the latter *Soon Soon Soon*. She did think she might be dead soon. It occurred to her that the device's purpose was as a self-destruct skull-shatterer of the type implanted in brains in Hollywood SF. She could have safely and efficiently communicated by a variety of traditional means. I mean, why, for fuck's sake, not the famous dead letter box? They coulda stirred themselves to make a collection every two months. This was a way of controlling her with the threat of exposure.

The cyber-room of our little Eden was run by Tuan Anwar and his assistants, Brother Idi and Brother Jefri (not my Jefri). Let me call him Jefri 2. We called Anwar "Tuan" – somewhere between Esquire and Lord but more reverential than simple Sir – even though he was a young man of about my own age. He'd studied Business Management in Jakarta and then Robotics in KL and the mild and silly geek really was a kind of genius. Anwar came from the real sticks, a tiny island *kampong* to the south-west. He'd hardly left his school campus in Java, spending most of his time in the fluorescent twilight of lab and workshop but, like my own Jefri and so many others, he could no longer return to the different darkness of the sunlit *kampong*. "Finished for me there, Brother," he said with a grin. The old life, the old Anwar, were destroyed but the new one was still in the throes of making. After a few weeks at the *pondok*, I had to take on board that behind the smiles, under the devotion, Snooky wasn't the only one with an ID and location crisis.

The first time I went to the cyber-hut Anwar and Brother Idi were putting up a new website with a video of a Humvee getting blown to smithereens to the strains of North African melodies. By himself, Brother Jefri 2 was playing what looked like Warcraft rather than Counterstrike (there were certain unspoken perquisites to the job).

Sometimes, unknown to my controller, I didn't use the device they'd given me. I'd take a huge risk and use one of Jefri 2 and Idi's machines. In a way it was actually less dangerous. There was a greater risk of being caught but the punishment would be less severe, e.g. not death as it would be for having 007's gadgets in one's possession. I had a (heterosexual) porn site in another window ready to be called up as instant alibi on F9. I figured something compromising would be more plausible and end speculation rapidly. All Haji Tariq wanted to do was bawl you out and give you a whipping for this kind of misdemeanour – certainly much preferable to being beheaded and actually likely to improve, rather than defile, Snooky's moral reputation. What I didn't want was someone clicking through steps and menus in their mind and coming up with Fatal Error Traitor. On the same principle, I set up a mailfetcher under Post Office Protocol 3 to forward mails from all my old sites to a new umbrella address. I never bothered to open a single communication from the Gang but I was kinda hurt Avril gave up so quickly. Yah, call Snooky sentimental.

For the present, and on the other more important email site I shared with my controllers, I made sure I had reams of commonplaces and pieties preceding and following a very small kernel of consequence (only slightly more consequential than the commonplaces). However, for present purposes, I shall redact this verbal smokescreen. I was to refer to myself throughout the correspondence as Ludorum and my contact, as I related, would be Vice Versa. Sometimes I would Carbon Copy in the Look Khreung. Thus:

TO: VICE VERSA
SUBJECT: EAST OF EDEN
DATE: 8/6/200-
FROM: LUDORUM
YOUR DRAFT HAS BEEN SAVED

In the name of Allah, most lenient, most merciful, Lord of the Worlds.
Ludorum finds himself in a very beautiful situation, as he related before. It is like the Garden of Eden, as known by First Prophet

Adam. Ludorum informs you there are many teachers, none really outstanding from the others, but he regrets he cannot attach jpegs for your perusal as he does not have a camera and this would anyway attract attention even if he had one (a camera). Today a Teacher said the wisest words. 1. "Islam is religion of tolerance. 2. Islam is religion of reason." These are wonderful counsel which we should all take to heart. I see no signs of religious extremism in the *pondok* nor are there any attempts to brainwash the students made upon them. Of terrorism and conspiracies I see no sign. Only here is Holy Koran study and study of Islamic thinkers (may Allah be well pleased with them!) whom you would not know. We play badminton. Chinese the best at this but, God willing, Malays also excellent. Ludorum has been here nearly three months and can report nothing of interest to Vice Versa. Ludorum asks V.V. to let him go.

TO: LUDORUM
CC: LK-FLOREAT-50/50
BCC: À VOUS
SUBJECT: VIX SATIS
DATE: 9/6/200-
FROM: VICE VERSA
YOUR DRAFT HAS BEEN SAVED

I have received your very unsatisfactory communication of yesterday and am now bound to issue you a stern warning. You are plainly not taking your duties seriously. This is one thing. It is quite another to play the giddy ass. I have acquainted myself with your newspaper scribblings and the tone and vocabulary of your communications to us does not accord with the style and sentiment of the former. One might be termed *la nouvelle vague*, the other the stagnant village pond. I am therefore impelled to draw but two conclusions: either you are poking fun at us or the person communicating with us is not the person who was originally recruited for this duty and you are, therefore, an impostor. Either way, I can predict the consequences would be nothing less than dire for you. My disinterested advice is to be yourself and evince all sincerity in your dealings with us.

P.S. You are not writing *The Commentary on the Gallic Wars*. There is no need to communicate in the third person. I require a detailed account of the training at the school, particularly military training, a summary of the background of the teachers and a description of their physical characteristics. We understand the principal is from the subcontinent and may be a Pakistani or Afghan. Also a word-by-word account of their pronouncements and comments: e.g. "Islam is (the) religion of reason" will not suffice as a report. I appreciate you may as yet, while a newcomer, not safely take photographs but a sketch-map of the grounds and an indication of the purpose of each building would be helpful. In future, you may find it useful to enumerate your paragraphs.

TO: VICE VERSA
CC: LK-FLOREAT-50/50
SUBJECT: APOLOGY
DATE: 11/6/200-
FROM: LUDORUM
YOUR DRAFT HAS BEEN SAVED

I humbly apologise for displeasing you with my previous reports and will do better in future. I am now 100% certain you are not the person who forced me into this and also sure that you are not the avatar of someone Siamese. I can detect some British-isms in your letter, a couple of which I do not fully understand, although I see from context a dizzy donkey is someone who is trying to goof off on you. Please be assured I have no intention of disrespecting you.

To supply you with the information you request (BTW a sketch cannot be attached without a scanner) :

1. There are 87 of us in the *pondok*. Most of us are boarders and of these 90 per cent are local Samsam people who can speak their own dialect and Southern Thai and Bahasa Malay as well. A handful are Sumatrans and Javanese. There are two Filipinos from Mindanao. Only 10 or 15 come from peninsular Malaya and are the youngest, aged between nine- and 11-years-old. We have little to do with them and they hardly participate in our activities. It would be safe to assume they might be cover for any clandestine activities. They could also be used as human shields in the event of a military raid. So, please, do not even contemplate such action.

2. I have not been here long enough to have proven myself to the teachers or my fellow pupils, even to the one from my hometown

whom I knew as Jefri and you by another name. With respect, are you sure you are not mistaken in his identity? The Jefri I know is a quiet and peaceful boy. Consequently I have not been fully initiated into the group or the strategy or intentions of its leaders.

3. Our teachers are relatively uninspiring, without a single exceptional or charismatic individual more distinctive than the others. The Head is a short, fat man with a froth of short, white curls for a beard. I think of him as the Milk Sheikh to myself but dare not divulge this impertinence to my fellow students who would assuredly report me. Perhaps he may be a Yemeni or a Libyan. Certainly he is not from this area. He is not from Pakistan or Afghanistan, as you inform me. There are three or four other teachers, two of whom have completed the pilgrimage to Mecca, one of whom is of African appearance and rarely leaves his room. He is known as Imam Idi. They are all quite young men.

4. I now have pleasure in recounting to you some of the homilies of our teachers. Please do not think I am trying to insult you or that the opinions are necessarily my own. I am a microphone. These are a selection from those voiced by our head teacher. They might sound severe but his bark is worse than his bite:

(a) The Crusaders call us ignorant fanatics. Did we ever burn people alive for disagreeing with us or for maintaining that the earth goes round the sun and not the other way round? Or for saying the globe is not flat? I tell you, we were modern when they were barbarians steeped in their own ignorance.

(b) They call us intolerant! Four hundred years ago in Spain, while they were still burning their heretics at the stake and massacring Jews, we protected the Jews! Muslims, the Moors, protected Jews from the tortures of the Inquisition! Can you believe that? That was our goodness, our generosity which they repay with their tortures now of water and electricity!

(c) Do not be fooled by this so-called vaunted technological superiority of the Crusaders. We are their equals. They confuse and weaken themselves with this . . . this Arts nonsenses. That is to pollute and smear the glass of Science we look through and with which we master the world God gave to Muslims. It is not we who are backward but them. Muslim explorers and travellers like Ibn Bautista knew all the parts of the world when the Christians could not travel ten miles from their muddy and insanitary villages. Long,

long ago we were already inventing when they were in the dark ages. Medicine, algebra, philosophy, libraries. Seven hundred years ago Muslims had the best medicines and the most advanced weapons. It was a Muslim engineer, may God be well-pleased with him, who invented the crankshaft, who invented gears. And without that their tanks would not run! They stole our knowledge!

(d) The sun is mighty beyond imagination. The flames at its edge which seem like frills on a shawl, are millions of miles long. But it cannot burn here on earth, in this world of men. Not unless its rays are gathered by tiny, brittle fragments of glass. God is the sun and you young men are the broken shards.

5. As I related before, most of our classes centre on learning Holy Koran by heart and studying the *hadith* and Commentaries of the Golden Age. We also learn Arabic. *Hadith* are the relations delivered to us through time about the doings of God's Messenger. Koran takes precedence over *hadith* in terms of authority but as stories the *hadith* have an appeal that scholarship does not. Example of famous *hadith* – there are thousands – would be *hadith* of the Pen and Paper and *hadith* of the Prayers.

Hadith of the Pen and Paper, for instance, is narrated about the time Muhammad – may peace be upon his head – fell ill and wished to make his will and leave guidance. He asked his Followers for writing requisites and they refused to supply these, saying all that was necessary was in Holy Koran already and even a great Prophet like the Messenger of God – peace be upon his head – could not supplant this. Muhammad – peace be upon his head – was merely testing his Followers and was glad. He made a full recovery.

Hadith of the Occasions to Pray relates to the dream the Prophet – pbuh – had when Allah told him the Faithful were to pray 50 times daily. In his kindness the Messenger of God – pbuh – found this too onerous and prayed God to reduce the burden, which he did by half to 25 times daily. Again and then again the Prophet – pbuh – returned to request mercy and eventually by a process of halving on every request for leniency the Faithful were left with five times of prayer a day. Muhammad – pbuh – would have returned to God even then but felt embarrassment and shame for so importuning Allah.

Each *hadith* begins: So-and-so Narrates that he heard or saw the Messenger of God – pbuh – do or say such-and-such. These narrations are passed down the generations through a chain or relay of transmitters, thus So-and-So Narrates that he heard So-and-So say of the Prophet that he had it from So-and-So who had it from a Follower of Muhammad that he was present when . . .

There exists a whole science of sifting and grading of *hadith*, their reliability, the strength and temper of the individual links in the great chain of transmission which results in the classification of the Narratives as 1. authentic 2. weak 3. fabricated.

A *hadith* is more likely to be accepted as true if it came from a single ultra-reliable source, such as a near relative of the Prophet – pbuh – namely his daughter, wife, or nephew. If this is not possible it will help if it comes through a network of trustworthy narrators who have been recounting the episode simultaneously but separated by geographical distance. In this way collusion in a fabrication would be rendered far less likely in a time before electronic communications.

6. We do have a library. It comprises mostly religious texts. Your report of a chemistry laboratory is not correct, or at least it became defunct before my arrival. I have not asked questions about things before my time here. As you must appreciate, this would arouse suspicion but I need to inform you that it is an even more delicate matter here as, generally speaking, Asian people, and particularly the class who have chosen to be here, are not at all interested in the specifics of what happened before their time. It does not concern them personally. We are a practical people, fixed in the concrete and the present. My foreign friends have liked me to enlighten them about these things in the past, so I am emboldened to speak in this way to you.

7. As with the laboratory, we do not have a model farm. I presume this means a smallholding and not a venture run on perfect textbook agronomic principles. Bearing this in mind, I do not see how or why we would wish to stockpile large quantities of chemical fertiliser, as opposed to natural. Given our share of natural calamities, principally the flooding that affects the Hat Yai area every year, such a toy farm would go broke in no time at all.

8. There are indeed "special classes" taken by the head teacher. These mostly involve mental strengthening exercises of a non-religious kind and, for a favoured few, some discourse of a mathematical nature.

I am glad my last report met with your "qualified approval", although I am not sure what Beta Double Minus means. As to your comment that our *pondok* teachers are trying to overtake the West scientifically while looking into the rearview mirror instead of through the windscreen – ha-ha. Well said.

I also accept your comment about me being "clearly bohemian by predilection but pedantic in nature." I think you must be, or have been, a professional writer. Yes, you have never met me but this is perceptive. I cannot, for instance, stop looking at people's feet in public, particularly on public transport, and counting their toes to make sure there are ten, no more and no less. This is not really a fetish, so much as minor obsessive-compulsive disorder to go – you might say – with gender disorder. In a country where people tend not to wear socks or closed shoes this gives me plenty of scope.

Where was I? Ah, yes, sir, less well said are your remarks about my attempts to educate you as to *hadith*. I did not realise you had a friend who was an Arabic scholar. Let me guess – he was an Egyptian, perhaps? However, I have to tell you that I was not, as you put it, trying to "pad out" my communication with non-essentials. I thought it would help you understand the *pondok*. For you to refer to authentic, weak, and fabricated *hadith* as a kind of "triage of likelihoods, with truth always being the first casualty of war" is not at all funny. It verges on blasphemy. Rebuke me, if you have to, but do not insult me or my religion. President Bush clearly says the West is not at War with Islam as such but only against Terrorism.

When you tell me that the Hadith of the Pen and Paper is also known to the *Shia* as The Hadith of the Calamitous Thursday, since they claim Muhammad – pbuh – was about to nominate his nephew Caliph Ali, the *shia* martyr-to-be, as his legitimate successor but found the stationery to do so was out of stock – well, you tell me something I did not remember. I agree with you that, as you put it, this relation must be "of unimpeachable veracity" since the rival sects both cite it, though with "radically different intent". There are bitter disputes as to the other stories and narratives which I find as arid as you surely will.

I do not understand what you mean when you talk about the "different geological and educational strata" in the language of my communications to you and their incompatability. I alone have written the emails. Nor was my mentioning of the science of verifying *hadith* meant to be a sarcastic reference to the value of my own information to you.

I admit my remarks about my companions living in a thoughtless present are contradicted by my remarks about the *hadith* and by our Principal's glorying in the great Muslim scientists and philosophers of the past. But this contradiction is only the sort of inconsistency picked up as a debating point. I am giving you a true and accurate picture. For instance, would it surprise you to hear that our Principal finds the Hadith of the Prayers to be weak as he calculates the division by halves from 50 to five to be erroneous?

The leaders of the *pondok* are not fools and you would be making a huge mistake to proceed on this assumption.

My last word is that it was not "El" Badawi, as you spell it, but Al-Bukhari who collected most of the *hadith* in the medieval times as you call them. I believe you must be thinking of the Mujahid who provided the huge quantity of explosives for the attack on the *USS Cole* in Yemen, who escaped captivity twice, and is still a free man. I dare to tell you I envy him.

Now I will answer your new questions briefly and then will not communicate for a few weeks unless necessary.

(1) I have seen no signs of weapons here. There is certainly no firing-range and you have been misinformed as to this. Some of the young Malaysian boys have slingshots made from strips of tyre inner tubes and jackfruit branches which they use for hunting birds. It was, strangely enough, my friend Jefri who made the catapults for them but by this I do not wish you to think of him as our "armourer", as your friend puts it. Strangely enough, I can tell you I do actually know what a Kalashnikov assault rifle looks like and also an M-16 or M-4. I had to research various kinds of weapons for a screenplay I once wrote.

(2) There are no unarmed combat classes given here. It would not be karate, still less kung fu as we hate the Chinese, or judo, if there were such class, but the native Malay *pencak silat*.

(3) The mental strengthening classes I mentioned mostly involve increasing the memory. So we will be shown many objects on a table for five seconds and then have to write down as many as we can remember. We also have resistance to interrogation classes where we are deprived of sleep, blindfolded, told we will be burned but have ice put on us instead. I fainted when this was done to me and, in fact, developed a red rash similar to a scald. We are taught to give limited information and to remain consistent at all costs. Consistency is the key. This is quite funny as you caught me out in inconsistency. Our training is defensive rather than offensive in nature as one can be arrested by the police, soldiers, or unknown para-militaries at any time here in the South. We do play sports. Of these, individual sports are discouraged, particularly excellence in them. Thus badminton and table-tennis are played as doubles. There is also an ancient village game where we link hands and form a chain against an opposing team. Both teams eventually join hands and merge.

Also, when I first came here, I was told to fall backwards from a platform in a frangipani tree about six metres from the ground. I was very frightened as there was only hard earth (it was still the end of the dry season, as you will appreciate if you are in this country). I feared I would break my back. However, I feared the teachers more and knew it was a crucial test. I threw myself backwards and fell into a sheet of canvas held by my fellow students who had crept up as my back was turned. They embraced and congratulated me but the Head Teacher scolded me for shrieking in such a high-pitched voice as I fell and scaring such birds as had not fallen to the slingshots. (The young boys are very expert with them). I think the teachers were not too angry as most of them were fighting not to laugh.

(4) Once we went into the town to a coffee-shop. Do not think Starbucks. It has an open front with no door but a sliding metal screen, a bare concrete floor, steam rising from the noodle vat, and permanently wet formica-tabletops. Our teacher had a Masaman chicken and peanut curry with two *roti* and then *kopi o*. We had none. "Ah," he said in surprise, "you are in need of refreshment." He bade us collect all the glasses from the vacated tables, which were in a disgusting mess, as was the floor. Then he poured the dregs of the coffee which made not one but three full glasses. He then used his cigarette-lighter – this particular teacher smokes clove cigarettes from Sumatra – to heat the sides of the glasses until the cold coffee

steamed and bubbled. He invited us to taste and when I burned my fingers, said, "With the spoon, my silly son." He then inquired of us what it tasted like and we answered, "Praise God, sweeter than usual," (which was because the sugar settles to the bottom of the glass even when well-stirred). He answered, "God has use even for the dregs when they join together. When heated by faith, they are no longer contaminated by the germs of the previous user."

In conclusion, please allow me sufficient time before my next report as I do not want to arouse the curiosity of those around me. (And, let me add, Malays are indeed a curious race and cannot keep secrets for long. Someone standing, reading a personal letter from home, can expect to have three of his fellows reading over his shoulder and passing comment in no time at all).

I trust my frank speaking has not offended.

With this apology I sign off until my next communication.

OUR SOUTH HAD BEEN in flames long before Shaykh ever arrived. It is true to say that he poured petrol on the fire with gusto but he did not change the path of the conflagration. The blaze he set with our aid did not act as a fire-break or cause the orange tongues to jump higher or further. He would never have claimed that. It would have been akin to blasphemy, arrogation of the Power of God. It was the wind, Divine Wind, which would stop it in its tracks or spread it. And even if it appeared extinguished, like a dangerous brush fire, it could re-ignite at any moment for it smouldered on, not concealed in pockets and hollows of terrain, but hidden in the hearts of men.

The government in Bangkok was in denial about us, whilst still ferociously repressing us, the officially non-existent. They resembled someone seen from a distance lashing out viciously with a stick at thin air, appearing insane, but in fact attempting to swat hornets, the unswatable. The Bangkok spin was that bombs, assassinations, murders of teachers, arson, raids on police-boxes, were the work of bandits and smugglers, not secessionists and zealots. For their part, the Malaysians gave Shaykh and the leaders of the other Mujaheedin neither help nor sanctuary. The last thing they wanted was what the Muslims of Siam desired: to be incorporated into Malaya.

Of course that was the last thing Shaykh wanted either. He didn't want to fight for a half-way house to the Caliphate, a compromise. He didn't want us incorporated into a prosperous, stable, inert Malaysia. I think that for him the road and the caravan were everything, not the final destination. That was an anti-climax he would always dread.

JEFRI CAME FOR ME at 4.45 a.m. The first clouds of the Indian monsoon towered over us. At nights there had been the boom and crack of unproductive thunders. Not a drop had reached the prostrate fields.

"It is time," Jefri said. His face was a mask of perfect seriousness, neither grim nor exultant. "Come."

HAT YAI WAS bracing itself for the annual floods when we arrived in comparative style on its outskirts in an air-conditioned Korean people-carrier. Grey two-storey breeze-block terraces and tenements made up the town. It was one of the nearest big places to the Malaysian border and its main industry was servicing the frustrated Chinamen who crossed the frontier to get their rocks off in the town's massage parlours or brothels. Illegal casinos plied their trade as discreetly as the brothels and beer-gardens were blatant. It was Tombstone – the week before they telegraphed the brothers Earp – and Snooky was there to watch and learn.

Shaykh was not gonna rain fire and brimstone on this modern reconstruction of Gomorrah. The instrument of his chastisement would be a mere motorcycle bomb: a rickety Honda sent to the forensic graveyard by the cheapest of Finnish cellphones. This kind of act was about as unique in our parts as the ubiquitous papaya tree which, regardless of season, sprouted everywhere. There had been so many ring-detonated bombs that the Bangkok government had tried to control and register every Subscriber Identification Module in Siam before stalling at the complexity and pointlessness of the task. Just buy a SIM with a false ID, preferably not shouting "God is Great!" as you counted out your Baht 300. It wasn't the acme in bombings but I figured you had to start somewhere. What was different about our device was where we were gonna put it. We would set it off inside the tiled lobby of a brothel, more like a lounge than a garage, where everyone was in the habit of leaving their scooters and motorbikes. Usually, the massage parlours (palaces was more the word; they were the most opulent and elegant buildings in the municipality) didn't get bombed. You had to figure it was bad for business. Their pay-offs would help finance independence and yet more Jihad.

But Shaykh would have none of it. He meant to cauterise to the root, excise the growth even it if was a minor one. Even gold melted in the fire of Shaykh's wrath.

Jefri was team leader. He and other of Shaykh's most trusted students had staked out and reconnoitred the quarter previously – that was why we had computers and cameras in the *pondok* at all (or, to be accurate, expensive phones with high-def lenses as they lent themselves better to surreptitious picture-taking). We picked up the bike in the back streets. These were as full of tiny two-seat beauty parlours and doll-house bike garages as the main thoroughfares were with the gilded bath-houses. Jefri had me ride pillion with him, then dropped me short. I was to keep lookout but, of course, they also didn't fully trust me on my first run and put a back-up on me. The others came up on foot and passed me by without a look. One of the few cool guys, Iskander, stayed on the opposite side of the road from me, eating a popsicle outside a 7 11 with great flair. Jefri returned on foot. I ad-libbed. I went into the Seven, came out with a vial of Bird's Nest Elixir and a tubby miniature flask of Red Bull, both of which I knocked back like Shane did his sarsaparilla before I followed the others. Snooky thought she was petrified. Snooky thought she was enjoying herself.

To divorce a woman under Sharia, you say *Talak, talak, talak.* Well, I was confused, I was confused, I was confused. We sauntered off on our separate ways, not looking like we were connected with each other at all. I never set eyes on our detonator, Inginir, who was equipped with a phone provided by our computer nerd, Jefri 2. However, I certainly heard the connection. Considering it was just over a key of malleable grey explosive with ball-bearings, it was a heck of an impressive blast. I was 14 minutes and just under a mile away but I saw a glass window shiver like transparent gelatin. There was silence for five or six seconds. We had been told not to keep walking when the bang came but to stop and walk back in its direction with everyone else.

Neither our Muslim brothers and sisters nor our Buddhist foes failed Shaykh and Haji Tariq in their predictability. Out their shops and apartment rooms they poured. It was like splashing water on an ant nest. In the distance I could hear screams. From the people in the street next to me I heard only comments of eager interest. A thrill pulsed in them to become participants, hopefully in safety, rather than just bystanders. Where had it gone off? Maybe the cinema; certainly not the vegetable market. Perhaps by the park or the Indian café. No one mentioned the pink light area. After a while we heard a siren. Then a bloodied man appeared at the top of the street. He was a Muslim. Clutching his arm, he assured everyone he passed over and over, "Thanks be to God, I am alright," and "God willing, my injuries are slight."

Iskander answered him in heartfelt tones, "Yes, I praise Allah indeed. God is Great, my friend."

I kept walking, quite swiftly. Iskander and a Javanese junior looked at me with some consternation from the other side of the street. I increased my pace. When I looked back they were no longer with me. I was very near the scene of the bombing. I could smell smoke. I was retracing Jefri's steps now, not my own, as I had not gone this far before. I saw the brothel for the first time. The damage to the flimsy breezeblock and plaster rendering was severe. The galvanised iron roof had been blown off. Six or seven motorbikes had been hurled from where they were parked into the street. Jefri's Honda was recognisable only as the most damaged.

One pink, fluorescent striplight hung awry from a brothel six doors away. A long-legged girl with one shoe on sat under it, her hands over her ears. Scorched bundles of rags lay higgledy-piggledy outside the nearer houses. I knew what they were. I discerned the beginnings of something horrible . . . then Jefri's hand was on my shoulder. "Cool, bro', keep it cool," he said. For the benefit of anyone hearing, he was speaking standard Siamese, not our dialect. He steered me away through what was now a crowd, growing by the moment.

Our way was blocked. "He's gonna throw up," said Jefri, using the very onomatopoeic Siamese word for vomit, and a path opened for us as the Red Sea had formed into walls for the Jew, Moses. Jefri patted my shoulder kindly, even though his hand was clamped to my elbow. I felt I was being rescued from drowning.

Back at the van, Haji Tariq was not so kind. He bitch-slapped me on the back of the head twice as we drove off. The others were

not with us but at the bus station, on their way to different desti-
nations further south, or across the country to Satun on the West
Coast. It would be three days before everyone was back at the *pondok*.

It might be thought that Shaykh had acted recklessly in sending
so many of us but he had been prudence itself. He had a timetable
to work to and he wanted us to garner experience quickly. The
first exploit outside our neighbourhood was the safest time to do
it when there was least attention.

This he did not explain to us in so many words but it was implicit
in the words of congratulation and exhortation at what I can only
describe as a debrief lubricated by prayer. These were held in the
room that housed the globe and maps and were somewhat less
fervent than those of our departure. Now Shaykh was able to
explain the significance of the target, of the abominations brought
by the fornicators from over the border. He said this was the opening
shot in our campaign, in what would probably be a lifetime war.
He said we should not think of it as revenge. Revenge was for
small, frightened men and it was negative and limited. The trouble
with revenge, he said, was that it ended where it began. Ours
was a productive violence that would lead to the creation of the
Caliphate. We used violence as a midwife.

Someone raised their hand. He was disturbed – this sounded
like what Communists had said many years ago. His Uncle had
been sympathetic to them. Shaykh said the Communists had
been godless but they had been clean. And their problem was they
had been insufficiently ruthless. The Christian Bible had this state-
ment in it: "Vengeance is mine, saith the Lord." This, said Shaykh,
was not as true as the circumstance that Mercy and Compassion
were the prerogative of Allah. Men had no business showing leniency. It was a divine attribute. To show clemency was, therefore,
blasphemous. He looked round the room. The interpolator with
the Marxist uncle had his eyes cast down, as well he might.

Shaykh said, "One of us let his Brothers down, or nearly did, if
Jefri had not stopped him." His terrible eye fixed upon me. "Stand."

I felt faint. A horrible nausea came upon me. I feared I would
vomit, for real this time, pollute devoted ground and defile the
neutral airs with my stench.

"He knows who he is. Stand."

I clambered to my feet. Then I did pass out. I heard the whomf!

of my head striking the teak. I came to a few seconds later. Jefri 2 was palpitating my cheek. Idi fanned me with a native, grass – i.e. non-Chinese – fan.

"Pick up his prayer beads," growled Haji Tariq. For a moment I wondered if he meant to have me garrotted with them. "But what is this?" he suddenly screamed in a very high-pitched voice. My blood ran cold. I knew my life wasn't a cop-drama so I wasn't exactly wearing the wire, as in *Prince of the City*, but I feared my dishevelment had revealed some horrendous, compromising evidence. It had. But not what I had thought.

"A tattoo!" screamed Haji Tariq, whose expression of sincere rage, as opposed to bass stage truculence, was in the high registers. Shaykh was suddenly over me, taking a personal, as opposed to objective, interest, and blocking the light by doing so. What the Haji had seen was the comparatively neutral, coin-sized pineapple tattooed below my navel. Now he was flinging the layers of my clothing aside, rucking up my gown, pulling down my modesty drawers. He rolled me over on to my stomach. Don't smile. I always preferred it from the front, actually, like a woman. Rectal massage plus inter-crural friction.

Haji Tariq yelled in perfect horror. Shaykh shouted, "Shaitane, now we have you!" They were looking at the tattoo just over my butt crack – the bat flying outta the cave. I have omitted to mention before – no point in being vulgar for the sake of being vulgar – the Siamese motto that was above it, like the ornamental lintel on a gate. I had originally commissioned, *"Beware! No one gets out alive!"* but Do-Ann had bribed the tattooist – working with a bamboo spike and a hammer, not a needle-gun – to do a dotted arrow and *"Insert penis here."*

Shaykh roared with rage. "You have desecrated the temple of your body! You have vandalised the property of God! No good Muslim is with a tattoo!"

There were some stifled gigglings. Shaykh was about to round on the culprits when Imam Umar whispered a translation of the characters into his ear. Shaykh, I could see with my left (facial) cheek to the floor, turned grey. Like, the blood left his dark face.

"Bring me a switch," he roared.

I heard one of the Indonesian boys whisper to another, "I think Brother Ahmed is a *waria*."

"Tell me something I don't know," his friend replied.

The cane arrived. Haji Tariq looked expectantly at Shaykh. Tariq was the disciplinarian; I think he was sorry that at the *pondok* there were no hands to cut off or adulterers to stone. Certainly the more scholarly but spiteful Imam Umar was. "No," said Shaykh. From my prone position, he rose above me like the Petronas Towers. Oh, God be thanked, I thought: commutation from the quarter where only mercilessness was to be expected.

"That's too good for this wretch," Shaykh said. "And it is only a punishment, not a cure. Bring acid. It is in the truck battery." I'd seen the faces of minor wives who'd been disfigured by the sulphuric that jealous major wives had paid to have flung on them. It melted the hair, too. Now it was me who called out loud, a wail of direst dismay. I could feel the ripple of sanctimonious glee going through the onlookers. Shaykh's rage was sincere, unalloyed. It was the crowd I held in contempt. I feared Shaykh but I could not despise him. Never in a million years.

I could hear the arrival of the acid-bearers. The klutzes had staggered back, bearing the whole heavy battery instead of decanting the sulphuric acid into glasses on the spot. They obeyed the letter of their instruction and, besides, were frightened to keep Shaykh waiting. It reminded me of the occasion Mare had taken the entire contents of my sister's amoebic stool, urine and all, to the appalled doctor in a gravid plastic bag instead of a tiny specimen in a bottle.

"Outside," barked Haji Tariq, in command of his tonal register again. "They'll ruin the floor, boss."

"How long?" Shaykh asked Idi, who hesitated.

"Not Malay time," barked the Haji. "Give exact estimate."

"Um. Fifteen minutes," said Idi. "Er, God Willing. We have to be careful of our eyes."

"Alright," said Shaykh. "We have to make a public example. Assemble everyone in the garden."

"What about his nose?" Haji Tariq asked. "That looks like a new nose to me. That's *haram*, too."

Shaykh examined it. "No, it's just broken, Haji."

"You're lucky," said Haji Tariq. "I'd a mind to cut it off."

"Take the table out," said Shaykh.

"And bring rope," added Haji.

"I need to go to the bathroom," Snooky groaned.

"No," said Haji Tariq.

"I'm, I'm . . . going to soil myself."

"I can smell it," said one of the Malay juniors with the *kampong's* lack of inhibition.

"Get the filthy dog out!" bellowed Haji Tariq. "Now!"

A surprisingly large crowd of volunteers hustled me out to the ablutions block. One or two dealt me light cuffs on the back but were instantly stopped by Jefri.

"Please, Jefri," I begged, "can I get clean briefs from my cupboard? I've already had a little accident."

He nodded. He looked troubled by my plight – my whole plight, I mean. At my bedside I grabbed a whole pile of laundered clothes. In them was my stash: *yah bah* pills, syringe, opiate ampoules. The tiny pills were easy to conceal in quantity; the ampoules weren't, except in the butt. Yah, OK. I haven't been honest with you, right? Contrary to assertion, I had been continuing in that vein. Sorry. But then imagine being me. How can you turn off a habit like switching off an appliance? I did try to cut it down, honestly. And at the *pondok* it wasn't that easy to get privacy, so I was well down on my city consumption. But, yah, Snooky had been high as a kite in Hat Yai.

In the bathroom block I shot up into my toe web. Two of my precious ampoules, but I figured I needed the double dose. I hid the syringe behind a loose brick I knew about.

"Ready?"

Jefri and his cohorts marched me out. He whispered in my ear, "Take it easy, Bro'. Try not to yell. I'd dilute the acid but that would just prolong the agony." I squeezed his hand. Girl, *tea ruck*, I was walking on soft, fluffy clouds.

At the table, one of the juniors was grimacing in pain. He'd splashed the tiniest drop on his eyelid. Even rinsing immediately, he would have to wear an eye-patch for a month and then sunglasses for two more after that. A small price to pay to look like an Afghan Mujahid.

Shaykh fixed me with his gaze but his words were for all. "We will cleanse Ahmed of his defilement in a spirit of brotherhood, not of chastisement. But this presents us all an opportunity to learn. He has merely pricked the surface of his skin with blue ink.

This is nothing. Belief is an invisible tattoo that the Mujaheedin wear, that unites us all. It is, God willing, indelible by men." He nodded to Haji Tariq who then began dripping the acid on to me. The evil oil took a while to react. I smelt it first, then I heard sizzling.

"Careful it doesn't trickle beyond the back," I heard Jefri say.

"Just the writing only," Shaykh said. "Leave the bird. We will not cause unnecessary suffering." He looked at my face. I was astounded. Through the warmth and fluffiness of the opiate, I saw awe and admiration in his eyes. My Shaykh looking at me like that. I took his hand. I showered kisses on it. Oh, my beloved mentor. He did not pull away with disgust. In Jefri's eyes I saw the look, too, as he personally helped the juniors wipe me down. Jefri whispered to me as I was hurried, face-down, on a stretcher to the infirmary. "I am proud of you, Ahmed. You did so well. Now use your courage for a cause, our cause." And then, "Do you believe, Ahmed? Do you really believe? I fear you do not. You must try harder."

And I answered in a whisper as intense as his, "Yes, Jefri, I will."

"We must get above our weaknesses, Ahmed, like you. We must strive to get better, we must get high above our bodies' pain."

Later, Shaykh came to see me. He told me I was forgiven, that in the Christian Bible there was the prodigal son who was loved more. "Be less complex, Ahmed," he enjoined me. "Have a simple, biddable heart. You will find happiness and fulfilment there."

YOU ARE WONDERING what I look like now, in the *pondok*. I look a sight. I cried when I cut my tresses in the city. And I cried again with chagrin in the *pondok* when I discovered that, of course, the one thing that was permitted there was hair of shoulder-length. I could have kept most of it. Instead I found myself with the crew-cut of the youngest students. I wore a skull-cap, not the Malay *songkok*, but dressed in a long white gown like everyone else. As a member of the Maproom, I got issued leather slippers instead of the rubber flip-flops of the juniors. But what I could never, ever reconcile myself to was . . . my fricking beard.

It had been Haji Tariq's doing. I hated him more for this than for the scars at the base of my spine months later. I'd been popping oestrogen pills like peanuts since my mid-teens. They had obviously built up in my system. When I stopped taking them – I only smuggled in the covert essentials, nubain and speed – to my pleasant surprise, I found I still did not have to shave. I'd never been lasered on my whiskers like Do-Ann had. I was frightened of the sting after I'd had warts on my sphincter zapped off with a laser by Dr Cheuan.

That did not escape the attention of Haji Tariq. Beards were as much the order of the day for those of mature years as prayer-beads or a *songkok*. Only the pre-pubescent were excused them. Even the most hairless kind of Sam-Sam like Jefri sprouted a few billy-goat hairs on the chin to approximate the Saudi goatee. As for Haji Hassan's and Inginir's, these lacked all conviction but Haji Tariq's black bush could have scrubbed frying-pans. (I am reminded of the song British troops sang about Hitler, Goering, Himmler, and poor old Goebbels, to the tune of the theme from *Bridge on the River Kwai* – a river upon whose floating discos the Gang and I jived many a time). But when the Haji looked at me what he saw was someone whose follicles weren't trying at all. It was no use protesting, "Haji Tariq, it's not my fault. It's beyond my control. God made me that way."

Haji Tariq just growled, "God made Muslims with beards, like he made the tiger with stripes." I refrained from countering that there was such a thing as a white tiger. Haji was quite capable of having me whitewashed by the juniors – that was the basic way his mind worked. I needn't have troubled. A few days later he was waiting for me outside the refectory. The Haji's idea of fun was never mine but the smug grin on his face told me something special was amiss. He opened his palm like a golden falcon was gonna fly out of it. Two big green capsules lay there. "Before food, Ahmed. You may help them down with water, not coffee."

"What are they they, Haji?" I wondered if they were suicide pills – not issued in the resistance to interrogation class.

"God willing, testosterone. For making your beard, may God be pleased with it."

"Oh, no, Haji. Please, no."

"Please, yes."

I swallowed them miserably (no problem – I inhibited my gag reflex years ago) but not as miserably as I did on succeeding days when it became apparent that the fricking things were working all too well. That wasn't the half of it. I sprouted whiskers in profusion, easily exceeding Jefri's sparse chin quorum. But I got them on the chest and much, much worse, in the nose and ears, to boot. And then, as I gained hair in undesired places, that on the crown of my head began falling out.

On my morning pillow the incontrovertible evidence lay strewn. A moulting gorilla might have been sleeping there. Soon I noticed the accelerating thinness on the top of my head. As Snooky grew hairier, she ascended in the favours of Haji Tariq and, indirectly, Shaykh. Once, the Haji pinched my cheek jovially as he handed the pills to me and I smiled a wan and subservient smile. As he departed for his *halal* delights, I stamped my foot in vexation and punched a tree. As I nursed my hand, the realisation came to me: this, too, was the testosterone talking.

I had an unwanted visit a month or so after our overland to Hat Yai. Not menstruation, not whiskers. It was my thug half-brother. He'd come with Jefri's two brothers. Jefri did his best to look pleased. As he was a good person but a lousy actor it was painful to watch. This infamous trio had travelled from our hometown together. That immediately put me on my guard. What scheme had they hatched? It wouldn't be anything clever but it would certainly be to everybody else's disadvantage. It turned out the tedium of the journey was simply too much for the half-wits left to their own devices; so they had pooled resources. Even tackling the cheapest Malay or Siamese newspaper was beyond Paw's sorry progeny. Adi used to say my mother was a whore who had lain with other men as his real brother could not possibly be a *katoey*. For my part I preferred this notion to the thought that the sadistic oaf could be my blood-relative.

At first he didn't recognise me. It was only the dislike in my eyes which alerted him. "You," he exclaimed incredulously.

"Be very careful what you say to me here," I answered. "There are all my brothers around me and this is my home."

I saw the resentment flicker in him like a flame. He was about to attempt a rejoinder when the oldest of Jefri's brothers said, "Of course, we are all brothers here, come in the spirit of brotherly love. Eh, younger Bro'?"

Jefri smiled the dazzling smile he gave when he was so embarrassed he wished a hole would open up in the earth and swallow him. "Come on," he said, "we have iced water for your refreshment."

My so-called sibling had come about Paw's money when he died. By the depressed standards of our South, Paw was counted as affluent. At least, he was wealthy for someone who was not of pure Chinese descent. In fact, because of his appearance and for alighting from his ancient white German saloon, someone in Hat Yai had once shouted a standard greeting in Malay at him, "Chinese pig, go back to China!" Paw had an ironic turn of phrase sometimes. Maybe I got it from the old man. He said to Mare, "I am deeply flattered," before calling to the heckler, "Be one of them." (He was smart and left it at that; didn't want the car vandalised while we were shopping). Because of Mare, I thought of myself as Muslim but Southern Thai rather than Malay, while Jefri, for instance, considered himself Malay.

Maybe it was the Thai part of Snooky which knew about Paw's various businesses: the rented-out houses, the little durian orchard, the cashew plantation, the tailor-shop. But what Adi wanted to know about were bank accounts in Malaysia or Singapore, or land Paw might have in Medan or Meri. Also to dig about for the terms of any will. He was eager that it should be *sharia*. That way females, my sisters for instance, didn't get a look in. Only the men like, um, ourselves would inherit, Adi pointed out. It was a bit easier for him to say this, looking at the bearded me.

"Is that false. You know, glued on?" he asked

"I am sorry to say, it's not," I replied.

"God is Great," he choked.

Jefri's brothers returned with him. "Suits you," the eldest said. I did not rise to the bait.

"So think about what I have said," Adi exhorted me, as if we'd been talking about something elevated or to my material advantage. I knew perfectly well he was out to screw my sisters, Mare, and me.

At this moment Haji Tariq and milky-orbed, cataract-ridden Imam Umar, with a pair of good eyes between them, passed by. "In the name of the Merciful, who are you?" the Haji asked brusquely. As Adi stammered a reply, Imam Umar said kindly, "We discourage visits, even from close relatives."

"So, say your say and then be about your business," Haji Tariq added.

It dawned on me for the first time that they made a very effective good cop/bad cop tandem. As Jefri's brothers watched them go in awe, Adi said incredulously, "Those are your teachers?"

"Well, they certainly have nothing to learn from us," I replied. "Yes, they are our imams. But above them, there is Shaykh whom even they fear."

"A sheikh? From Arabia?"

"That's just our name for him. He indulges us in this."

Jefri smiled. "Yes, as Ahmed says, he allows it, but not much else."

On impulse, I said, "Get Iskander to take a photo of your brothers on his phone. A separate one of Adi, too. A little memento. No, not you. Just them. Hey, what black faces! Smile, guys, smile! Watch the Birdie!"

After they had gone, I said to Jefri, "Don't tell me, your talk was about crime and money, wasn't it."

He laughed.

THE FACT THAT Shaykh and Haji Tariq were outsiders was of no practical consequence. They never went short of local knowledge or cover. Haji Hassan for his part had left Aceh so long ago – he'd still been in his teens when he departed for Cairo – that he was more Malay than the Malaysians and as Siamese as the Siamese. The local students and Imam Umar, who'd passed most of his long adult life in the locality, supplied all the native detail required. And, as usual, the devil was in those details.

What you have to understand about our South is how dirt-poor everyone had been kept for the last 90 years by the corruption of the Siamese. Nothing good ever came to us. Our brothers hated the very sight of a uniform: whether it was the olive of the police, the brown of a school-mistress, or the saffron of a monk. We had nothing, nix, in common with the Buddhist North. (Of course, that was just the very reason Snooky had chosen to spend her sentient life in the capital). We looked different, we dressed different, we ate different, we spoke different. We were the only part of the Kingdom that, years ago, had ever come near anything approaching regicide. Mujaheedin had shot down

Princess Vibhavadi in her helicopter when she had diverted to pick up two wounded Border police near Surat Thani. That had been a loss for everyone. The Princess had been kind and she had been clever. Snooky read the novel she had written when she was only 18 and was always sad there were to be no more. Yah, that's what humanitarianism got you in our parts. This in a country where there still existed a crime of *lèse majesté*, where you did prison-time, as if the day of D'Artagnan had veritably returned, for breathing the teeny-weeniest, itsy-bitsiest *soupçon* – as Avril put it – of anything unfavourable or critical about the monarchy. Shooting down a helicopter was certainly an act of criticism. The lesson was clear: to the *juwae,* or young resistance fighters, nothing and no one was inviolable. For us, the Kingdom itself was violable.

These were the big issues of the past that could still reach out and affect you, like the pull of the moon was responsible for the rise and fall of the tides, even if it seemed counter to commonsense, even if your feeble senses couldn't feel the force, even if the mighty waves could.

Still, Jefri, Iskander, and I seemed a long way distant from palaces and treaties and invasions as we stood silent in the moonbeams throwing long shadows in a lonely rubber-grove. You couldn't, believe me, get more local than that. The worst of the rains were nearly over. Rats and snakes reduced to swimming for their survival during the floods found themselves snug again in their holes and boles. A five metre king cobra had taken refuge in the Observatory before Tariq had neck-forked and bagged it. And here we three were out, hunting for prey. We were not after exotic species, outlanders, but local vermin. Haji Tariq had called them that, with lip curling in beard. "These are the worst kind of *kafir*," he had said. "Have no qualms at all. But this time you will see the faces of those you send to their fate. And this is Shaykh's test for you. Do not fail it."

The test had taken us half-way across the isthmus of Kra, not by magic carpet or Hyundai, but by non-aircon bus with plenty of small town changes. One thing I can safely say: Jefri had kept us well-hydrated. I lost count of the Cokes and Vitamilks he bought us. He was paymaster and quartermaster both of our little enterprise. Iskander and I didn't have a *satang* in our pockets. This was a condition Iskander had known all his life, so it didn't worry him but it freaked me out. It meant I was totally dependent on Jefri to get me back, which was the whole idea. I had to stick to him like the messy white latex which trickled down the slim rubber trees into the receiving cups. The fricking stuff virtually glowed in the dark and, yes, you already surmise what it made me think of. Jefri had made contact with a Chinese guy at a big rest stop, hours ago, and received a bolt of cloth from him. As he unrolled it in the light of the moon, it revealed three glinting parangs and a matt hand-gun.

"Don't look so nervous," Jefri exhorted me. "I'll be the one holding the gun and it's easy to use. You and Iskander have the parangs."

"That's what worries me, Jefri, " I replied. "How come it's a Chinese guy giving it to us?"

"No surprise," Iskander said. "Those Chinks would sell their grandmas if the price was right."

"You don't think wrong," I said, "so let's hope he doesn't sell us out, too."

Jefri decided this conversation was headed in the wrong direction. "We are in the hands of Allah," he said. "We tread in the path of his Martyrs and fear nothing." This wasn't an original line. Imam Umar was forever coming out with it.

"In the name of God," intoned Iskander, as I hastily followed suit. Iskander still had his iPod wires dangling round his neck. The techies in the *pondok* got cut the most slack. Having contraband like that would have got a whipping for a junior. Of all the brothers he was the coolest; ace at mending anything mechanical, motorbikes, fans, you name it, and the most laid-back, too. He'd hardly said a word the whole trip, the scratching we heard in his earbuds a whole realm of bass to him.

"OK, careful with the parangs," Jefri said. "They've been whetted razor-sharp." Irrepressible Iskander made to shave Jefri's flimsy three chin hairs. Oblivious to the dangerous jape, Jefri was busy loading the gun, which was a revolver. "Look," he said, "if anything happens to me, pull the rod out, tip the gun sideways and the chamber will fall out, and put the bullets in their, er, holes, whatchamacallit, like eggs in a box and push the rod back in. No safety-catch. Just pull the trigger. Cock the hammer back first, if you want for accuracy, so that the pistol doesn't wobble, but you don't have to do it."

"Yah," I said. "Just like if we had foreskins, you don't have to pull it back before you piss, but it's recommended for the Buddhists."

There was a total silence after I had delivered myself of this. Just total non-acknowledgement. No rebuke, no embarrassment, just a complete non-registering. This was what always happened after vulgarity (nearly always from Snooky) in the *pondok*. Dirty jokes, smut, couldn't find a place there. "Yah, sorry, Jefri," I said. "Seen the movies. I can load a gun." Actually, Snooky wasn't imagining John Wayne or Henry Fonda twirling a shiny .45. Unwanted visions of her childhood self in a sarong, legs held wide, being circumcised, floated before her.

Iskander said, "I've fired them thousands of times on video games. It's exactly the same as a real gun. Haji Tariq was amazed how good I was when we practised in the hills."

"God is Great," said Snooky, again unreproached.

The fact that I found myself lying in thorns a little later while the other two had soft grasses was not, I am sure, my punishment. Jefri wasn't small-minded. We lay still for three hours. Snooky didn't care. She'd have stayed there three days if that was the price of nothing happening.

Along the earth track came four figures. I thought they were women carrying rifles. I was prepared for that, too. A little later I could see they were Buddhist monks with staves. As they came up a slight slope towards us, Jefri fired. I felt it was too far off, although I'm the last one to be accusing steady Jefri of losing his nerve. I now know it was the first time for him as well as us. Anyhow, he did hit one of the monks but high, in the shoulder that was bare. The monk dropped his staff. I could see he was very young, prob-ably a 17-year-old doing his novitiate, the Buddhist barmitzvah. The older monk was fumbling in his robe.

I distinctly heard the click as the hammer of Jefri's gun fell on what proved to be a dud round. The older monk pulled out a pistol and blazed away at us as fast as he could. It was obviously a much better weapon than the Chinaman had given Jefri. At least a dozen shots came our way in under five seconds, smacking and whirring through the trees.

"Shit!" shouted Iskander, "Run, Bro', run!" Myself, I needed no encouragement and was legging it through the shadows before Iskander had finished his words. I heard a single shot, obviously Jefri retaliating, then a continuation of the fusillade, then silence. Jefri appeared through the rubber trees, walking and methodically re-loading.

"Got him, Bro'?" Iskander asked breathlessly.

Jefri shook his head. "Let's get to the road."

The two bikes were waiting. "Toughest monk I ever saw," Iskander said. Jefri and I began to giggle, like uncontrollably, worse than marijuana snickers. Our pick-ups – one feels that to earn the title of "extraction team" one arrives by whirlybird – wore helmets, probably not to comply with the law. I never found out who they had been.

We roared off, Jefri and Snooky on the same bike. Some distance before the highway we shot across a line of men laden with giant versions of the same kind of striped zip-up bag I'd used to carry my original effects to the *pondok*. They panicked, a couple of them dropping their heavy burdens. Then a big gun-shot, much louder than the pistols earlier, followed by the sound of someone clacking a shotgun slide.

Our drivers revved their throttles. Going over a bump my balls, my Haji Tariq-enlarged testicles, banged verily into my abdomen. But we weren't fast enough to avoid a second shot. This time I heard Iskander yelp. We got to the highway but just whizzed over it into the oil palm plantation on the other side. I felt even at this witching hour it would have been better to have checked and looked for a truck coming. Motorcyclists and their machines ended up squashed under those road-trains. I'd see it once a month, at least, back home.

The palms, a regulation metre from each other, stretched literally for miles into the distance like the serried ranks of the Chinese terracotta army. Jefri forced our guy to stop. He examined Iskander's shoulder. It looked like he'd been hit by just two or three pellets. "You're gonna be OK, Bro'," he reassured him.

Iskander didn't answer, "If God so wills." No, he replied in the Thai way, "Hey, it's nothing, Big Bro'. *My pen wry, pee.*" Tough kid.

Jefri said, "That's the spirit. Show the same heart as Ahmed did with the acid." I put my face into the driver's shoulder in case it betrayed me. Quite a nice, hard, man's shoulder. We got going again. Two men dashed behind a palm. We skidded to a halt, then wheeled round the next palm. It was like trying to catch a cat. We had the speed and power but they had the agility, and the obstructing trees favoured them. Eventually our inhuman engines wore down their stamina.

Jefri pointed his revolver at them. "What are you?" he demanded in Bangkok Siamese.

"The same as you," one of them gasped.

"No, you're not," Iskander said grimly in Jawi.

"Yes, we are," the other insisted, in the way Siamese persist in an untruth when the cat's out of the bag. Snooky believes the expression is cognitive dissonance. Jefri yanked the Buddhist amulet off the plantation-worker's neck. "We are not idolators," Jefri said. "We believe in the One and True God." I could see he was trying to make himself angry but he just sounded despondent. The men were poor, poorer than Jefri and Iskander, their feet and hands dirty and calloused.

"On your knees. Look away." Jefri gestured with the revolver. He nodded to Iskander who produced his parang from nowhere. I'd dropped mine long ago. The parang looked new, magical, in the gleam of the moonlight; not the scuffed and homely implement of toil it actually was. Of course, the worn wooden handle was concealed in Iskander's palm. Even as it flashed, I was in denial.

The wind of the blow ruffled the hair of the taller worker but no more than that. Iskander had missed. Maybe he'd closed his eyes like I used to when I served the Birdie in badminton with a dainty squeak.

Thinking back on it now, Iskander had probably chosen the taller of the two kneeling men – the one not wearing the amulet – as being the easier to chop, like stick-swiping the flower that reaches conveniently to waist-height. Anyhow, that was it for the unfortunate labourers. If they'd had any doubt what Jefri had in mind for them, it was dispelled now.

With a gurgle of panic, the amulet-wearer leaped to his feet and vanished into the dark lines. He'd had a better view of the missed blow than the intended victim. It has to be admitted the amulet might have brought him luck. His companion was scarcely less slow but, just as one insect a fraction faster than its competitor will survive for millions of years after the other is extinct (with its evolutionary tendency, not a comparison I would make to Imam Umar later), Jefri hit him in the leg with his reflex shot.

The labourer limped two and a half steps, then fell into a palm. Iskander had jumped at the report and uttered a vulgar expletive which I will again translate as, "Shit!" He'd been looking for his iPod which he'd dislodged with his vigorous but inaccurate swing.

Jefri raised his hand again, then lowered it. He and Iskander grabbed the wounded man by the waist and tried to pull him down but in order to stay standing the fellow was embracing the palm like it was his mother. They brought him down after a surprisingly even tussle – the weight of two against one and that one wounded: but then he had the strength of terror. The Buddhist was burbling frantically in Northern Thai, even in normal times a melting, birdy tongue but now a very slew of pleas.

Snooky put her fingers in her ears. She closed her eyes. I used to do it with horror movies in the preview theatre – even the crude local zombie flicks got to me. When I'm about to faint I smell metal in my nose. I got it now. In the dirt my fingers tangled with thin cable. Trip-wire to a Claymore mine? No. It was the headphones of Iskander's music-player which led ineluctably to the pod itself.

"Ahmed? I hit you?" Jefri asked with concern. His shirt was drenched with blood. Their victim had stopped screaming while I was passed out. In his dark hands Iskander had something more the size of a football than a *takraw* ball.

"Put it in the fronds," Jefri said. "It needs to be intact when they see it. Don't want animals getting to it."

I retched drily. Nothing came up but a little white phlegm. Probably the remains of the bus-station tetrapak of soy milk. I straightened up. "I found your iPod, Iskander," I said, dropping the set into his wet hand from such a cautious height that he nearly lost it again.

"Oh, wow, thanks a million, Ahmed," he said with real gratitude. "Don't know what I'd do if I lost it. Don't tell the Imams."

SHAYKH WAS FURIOUS. Silly Snooky, she'd been expecting praise and commendation all round. But Shaykh's face was taut with rage. I just seemed to jinx things even when it wasn't my direct fault.

"Exactly who do you think you are?" he asked. "Terrorists?" Iskander looked at me, then back to Shaykh, then at Haji Tariq behind him. Shaykh was having a bad eye day and resorting to extra large dark lenses which gave him the look of The Fly. Haji T. fiddled with his prosthesis. He seemed ill at ease as he always did when he secretly disagreed with Shaykh but had to present a united front. Haji Hassan polished his pince-nez, while Imam Umar metaphorically hugged himself in glee to see us in hot water.

Iskander said, "Well, er, yes, Shaykh, we are terrorists, we are Mujaheedin."

"No!" shouted Shaykh. "What do you think I am? The Old Man of the Mountain sending out his Assassins? Did I drug you on hashish? Did I tell you to murder everyone you saw?"

Iskander looked despondently at me.

"I am speaking to you, not him," said Shaykh, suddenly cold and in control of himself.

"I don't understand," Jefri said, and his humility and ingenuousness disarmed Shaykh in the way it would never have done with our other teachers. Imam Umar scowled at Jefri. I think Iskander had been looking for me to support him in the invention of a falsehood, to say whatever it was the incomprehensible Shaykh wanted to hear.

Shaykh said, "You were to kill the monks, not some poor farmworker. It was carefully chosen as an easier mission for you to learn from."

"But he was a *kafir*, Shaykh," Iskander protested.

"Can you kill every infidel in the world? Would God want you to? No. Can you convert them? God willing, yes. We are not waging Jihad against the people. We are waging our holy war against the agents and symbols of our oppression: police, teachers, monks, civil servants, soldiers. This was pointless, this was savage."

"But, Shaykh, the other Mujaheedin and *juwae* are killing villagers and rubber-tappers every day."

"Not us," said Shaykh, emphasising each word. "Actions like yours do not bring the Caliphate closer, they push it beyond reach."

"Now I understand," said Jefri. "Maybe one day in the Caliphate, if God so wills, we will have to rule these people as they rule us now. Then they will be more easily governed if their memories are not as bitter as our own. Maybe they can even become as us."

"Then I have not wasted my time," said Shaykh. "You may go."

"What?" shrieked Imam Umar. "No punishment? Just words of scolding?"

Shaykh reflected. "For a week only eat white things," he said. "Cleanse yourselves."

"Shaykh?" said Iskander. Jefri pulled his sleeve. We should go while the going was good. As we escaped into the maze of the banyan, Iskander said despondently, "Rice. White rice all week. Rice porridge – that's no joke – if we're lucky."

But Jefri answered, "Filleted fish, chicken breast, soya milk, biscuits, peeled bananas, yogurt, bread rolls and cheese . . ."

Iskander's eyes widened as an idea hit him. "Vanilla ice-cream!" he shouted. We hugged each other. Just then Haji Tariq caught us up. It wasn't to heap infliction but to advise. "Shoot dead first, then decapitate," he said. "That way they can't run or dodge. Dead men cannot duck. The head-cutting is not a particular punishment for the individual. It's a warning to others."

I can say my thoughts were no longer of virgin vanilla ice-cream. They were of scarlet-laced ice kuchang. As I headed to the cyber-room, I knew what the *pondok* reminded me of. Not Peter Pan. Switch of genre: the witches' ballet-school in *Suspiria*, the third scariest movie of all time. Fuck knows how terrifying the scariest and the runner-up must have been.

TO: VICE VERSA
SUBJECT: TORTURE AND MASS DESTRUCTION
DATE: 02/12/200-
FROM: LUDORUM
YOUR DRAFT HAS BEEN SAVED

I apologise for not having been in contact for some time. Now I have plenty of information for you. You are looking for a single head to what you call the Snake of Terrorism here in the South. I assume this is because you mean to end with one decisive intervention. But it is a hydra or many-headed snake. You are correct when you refuse to believe the Siamese government who claim the various attacks are simply the work of criminal gangs, smugglers, and drug-dealers, rather than secessionists and religious zealots. But the zealots and autonomists have no single leader. We all fight in the dark.

Think of us as football teams all competing in the same league but never visiting each others' home grounds. We have different captains, managers, playing fields, and act entirely without co-ordination but share the same goals and risk the same penalties. We never play each other but only the enemy's reserves. Of course, some teams have more talent and are better captained than others. Some may excel in attack and in offensive skills; others may be difficult to track down or capture and can be said to present a strong defensive line-up or to possess a resourceful goalie.

There is one particular team amongst us all that is so superior to the others it has become legendary. They are some 60 km distant from us, although I cannot be sure. These have scored so many successes and won so many victories against the Siamese that they are admired even by their fiercest rivals among the other *juwae*. Led by one Abdulrahman Eskander, known to his followers as the Great, they have achieved nearly all their goals. Like Philip, the father of the historical Alexander, this young man's father had lost the sight of his eye not in battle but in manufacturing a bomb in the early days of our little local *"intifada"*. Eskander's own skills in the manufacture of munitions far exceed those of his father. I have tried in vain to come up with a translation of his nickname among us and the best that I can find in my searchings is "Boffin" from the old movie *The Dambusters*. There are different descriptions of his physical appearance. All of these are at third-hand. No one seems to have personally met him but is acquainted with someone who knew someone who once heard a senior Mujahid say they were in his company. He is even said to give his orders from behind a screen and to write down his commands for someone else to read out in case his voice should ever be recognised. What is universally agreed is that this captain of *juwae* is extremely young and probably still only in his twenties. He is reputed to be fond of music. I can tell you that Eskander studied physics at Nanyang Technical University, Singapore, on a scholarship where he gained distinctions but he is also a very practical chap, as you would say. His knowledge and skills in mechanical engineering are the admiration of everyone. His projects include refitting an old freighter ship, filling it full of fertiliser and fuel-based explosives, to make a floating bomb of this type and size never envisioned before. You can imagine the devastation this would cause from the one truckful of similar type which brought about the destruction of the large federal building in Oklahoma City. This is low explosive as opposed to high explosive.

Boffin has plans to armour the bows, bridge and engine-room so that the ship would be invulnerable to small-arms fire as it proceeds from Singapore Roads by night into the river and business areas. He says only small-arms fire can be brought to bear on the *juwae* at that stage and it would be superfluous to provide them with more protection. "Over-specified" is a favourite expression of his. Having stopped the boat, there would then disembark a large number of Mujaheedin, heavily-armed, to attack the airport, embassies, schools, and TV stations.

Boffin always says that the theoretical principles for manufacturing an atomic bomb are very simple but that securing the raw materials and machinery for condensing or removing the contaminants from the fissile matter and concentrating it into weapons-grade is the difficulty. He says a devastating explosion equivalent to the TNT yield of a small nuclear device could be matched or exceeded by a ship crammed with low explosive. To emulate the contamination or lethal radiation of a nuclear weapon, he would simply add low quality non-weapon grade radioactive matter to the cargo to be scattered far and wide by the blast. This, as you know better than me, is colloquially known as a "dirty bomb".

Our Leader, the Milk Sheikh, says the best targets for this would either be Singapore at the time it hosts a large sporting event, say the SEA Games, or London, using the Thames river as a highway during a similar occasion. Our Leader is quite witty – unlike many of his kind, he does not lack a, somewhat wicked, sense of humour. He said, "Atrocity – the blockbuster coming soon to a venue near you."

An infantry attack could also be launched in conjunction with such a device or in isolation. Ten brave men with small-arms created havoc in Bombay. Can you imagine what 500 could do? It would be easy enough to train them over a two year period in Waziristan or Mindanao and no problem at all to bring small arms into a Western capital from the Czech Republic or Rumania.

Our Leader actually favours Singapore as a target, saying example is more important than actual casualties: a large metropolis like London or New York would not be completely destroyed by such a device but with Singapore an entire nation of Unbelievers could be obliterated at one stroke. Of course, this would necessarily mean the cancellation of the proposed attack with conventional explosives and commandos. Either project is expensive but we have already secured the promise of foreign funding. Arranging this through Islamic and Caribbean banks is Jaffray. Jaffray is the designated paymaster and quartermaster for this project. He believes it is achievable for much less than US$5 million – a trifling sum by the standards of Middle Eastern Terrorist groups. We might, however, need to pay Boffin a "transfer fee" to bring him over to our team and league.

To conclude, I have a personal problem jeopardising my security or threatening to "blow my cover". I have already been abominably tortured and can show the scars as evidence if ever we should meet (the last thing I am asking for is an appointment with your local agent, though I find his scepticism regarding my reports to be both offensive and hurtful). I repeat I am giving you fabulous intelligence such as no one else could possibly invent.

Under torture I was able, with a huge effort, to preserve my identity and be consistent in my answers under severe cross-examination. However, I am extremely concerned about the following personalities who could be instrumental in unmasking me. You may gauge my sincerity in that they are personal relatives of mine and of my friend here. My half-brother, Adi, sometimes visits the *pondok* and is a danger and embarrassment to me. When he is here, he openly mocks my lack of faith, my infatuation with American culture, my foreign friends, and states that my loyalties do not lie with my Brothers here. He threatens to out me for what I am. I need hardly tell you how perilous that would be. I would simply be killed and vanish. My friend's two brothers also speak of me in the same way. Can you solve this problem for me? I should be very sad if harm should befall Adi but could not reproach you for it. I attach a jpeg of Adi for your identification.

You have told me you will not act on the *pondoks* in the south until you have more information; however, you can act further North at Sukhothai without jeopardising me. A prominent Northern politician's son is involved in the arms trade, not just to secessionist groups in the south, but the fundamentalist rebels in Aceh at the Northern tip of Sumatra, and the Tamil Tigers in Sri Lanka. He meets representatives of these away from Bangkok in the South here in Krabi and Phuket (both of which have international airports). He also has ties with Libyans, with the Irish Republican Army through Libya, and with a major Ukrainian arms-dealer. Our Leader says if we ever get an old Soviet bomb it will be through the Ukrainian's military contacts and he values him highly. The name of the Thai is Mad Dog Chon. Your local contacts cannot touch him – his family is too powerful in national politics. His father, a former soldier, is regarded as too influential. Many national, as well as up-country, politicians are in debt to him for the speedy executive solution of their problems. It would take a foreign agency to accomplish Mad Dog's removal from the scene, perhaps when he travels overseas. He could be discovered with arms (or, indeed, as I well know, drugs) in his baggage or appear as the victim of a robbery turned violent. I believe that with this man prevention is the best cure. He should be removed from the picture. The Ukrainian does not affect me and could be allowed to operate freely while under surveillance.

I understand Boffin is arranging a meeting with him in the near future as he is using him as an intermediary or middleman in the purchase of canisters of Caesium-137 held for many years by a five-star general in the Thai Air Force who secured them in 1975 along with the atomic clock at Samae San base used to guide B-52 bombing runs in the Vietnam War (30 years being as the blink of an eye in the life of an isotope).

Finally, as a minor matter, some gun-battles took place on the East or Gulf Coast of the isthmus last week. Boffin's team fought a "turf-battle" against a notorious Chinese smuggling cartel with members on both sides of the Thai-Malay Border.

Large numbers of heavily armed men were involved in this encounter, amounting to perhaps 50 on each side. Casualties were correspondingly heavy. Much like the skirmishes between Viet Cong irregulars and US Marines the "body count" was deceptively low as both the smugglers and the Mujaheedin took great pains to recover their dead and especially the wounded in case they might be traced back to them. As the Americans like to say, no one gets left behind which is certainly not the case with third world economic development in the age of globalisation. In this battle the cadavers on the battle-field would amount to only the tip of the iceberg. Three corpses recovered by the Siamese military or police would represent a true toll of 20 or even 30 killed. Allowing for exaggeration, but not for the minimising of losses suffered by one's own side – the inclination would be to increase the number of martyrs so far as Boffin's team was concerned – and after lengthy calculation, I believe the score to be Boffin's Mujaheedin 28-Chinese Cartel 16. Some of the bodies were found headless.

Pardon my levity (a curse on both their houses, as Zeffirelli says), for I believe a series of bets on these numbers could be instituted in the way that gambling is based on English soccer scores in Malaysia. Perhaps these figures could be fixed by the Chinese businessmen in return for bribes to the players/combatants. As I say, pardon my silly sense of humour. From it you can see I am not offside but instead playing with your team.

Our Leader is planning a trip, which I think involves travel by boat, and I may well be included. No definite date as yet but before the end of the year. I would be appreciative if measures regarding my security could be undertaken before I leave.

I say again, I myself have been abominably tortured and will carry the scars for life. I will not put the details of the ordeal before you but the marks of my ill-treatment are still fresh on my back. I was under suspicion but did not betray myself during the ordeal. I cannot guarantee that I would be able to do so again.

TO: VICE VERSA
CC: BLANK FIELD
BCC: À VOUS
SUBJECT: CLONE PHONE
DATE: 03/12/200-
FROM: LK-FLOREAT-50/50
YOUR MESSAGE HAS BEEN SENT

Ask your man (?) or nancy boy to supply us with precise details as to the make, model and colour of the cellphones used by the pesantren leaders. They have to be absolutely exact as we will be supplying replicas. The information he is supplying is not just "fatally flawed", as you put it, but a load of baloney. Despite your strictures, I trust what the technical people at the Singaporean and US offices here could give us down the phones far more than your "human source". I remind you I was sceptical about all this right from the off.

TO: LUDORUM
CC: LK-FLOREAT-50/50
BCC: À VOUS
SUBJECT: STIGMATA
DATE: 04/12/200-
FROM: VICE VERSA
YOUR DRAFT HAS BEEN SAVED

As you so correctly surmise, I am at a loss to account for the very frivolous tone of the last part of your despatch to us. Are you in your right senses? If all you say is true, then every moment could be your last. I admit to being so mystified by the gay abandon of your tone that I had your whereabouts checked. You do, indeed, appear to be in the madrassah and not at home or in Bangkok. I have also checked and there does appear to have been a large, running gun-battle involving high-powered weapons in the very place you describe, plus some mutilated corpses. In view of this, my colleagues ask me if this "Boffin" received training in camps in Pakistan or if he fought against the Soviet army in the Afghan war of the 1980s.

So far as preserving your cover is concerned, it is my task to protect you insofar as it lies within my power. However, I would inform you that Western governments are constrained by the rule of law and cannot simply assassinate people at whim. In my experience from woollier days long gone by, these things also have a way of getting out of hand. What your local handler is permitted to do is quite another matter entirely and I will – with extreme reluctance – raise the matter with him.

I most eagerly await information from you as to your group's projected trip overseas. I appreciate you are not in charge of this but a preciser timetable than "this year" is necessary. May I point out that this would be in your own interests, in case you should need to be extricated if you encounter awkward or dangerous situations overseas in an environment that is unfamiliar. Include everything, no matter how irrelevant or unimportant it seems to you yourself. Thank you for the "jpeg" of your brother. Take more of others. It would be particularly useful to have some of the teachers. You may find it safest and most discreet to take group photographs in a very public way. Done like this, individuals do not feel threatened and focus upon you as an object of suspicion. Will you be going to Aceh? Ambon perhaps?

We also need you to perform another practical and useful action as well as provide information. This will be a demonstration of good faith and show us the benefit of your continued usefulness. What kind of mobile phones do the *pondok* teachers in question respectively own? We require details of brand, model, and colour. Do they leave them unattended at any point? Before prayers? Further instructions for you will follow.

TO: VICE VERSA
SUBJECT: THE REAL BAD GUYS
DATE: 05/12/200-
FROM: LUDORUM
YOUR DRAFT HAS BEEN SAVED

I have done better than that. Find attached photos of the phones. I think you are going to ask me to put in new SIMS or switch the originals themselves for identical new models. Sir, I REALLY, REALLY do not want to do this!!! It is SO RISKY!!! Think about it: what if I am caught? You lose all my valuable input and under mistreatment I am sure to divulge everything. You will not even have the information off the phones. If these are booby-trapped phones that explode and take off the user's head in the MOSSAD manner, then – with respect – I cannot do this at all. I may just dial your man in Bangkok and hold it to my own head.

Further to my last message, I enclose photos of myself with two recent recruits (not studying at the *pondok* – you must stop calling it a madrassah) who are being trained for something novel: a suicide attack on the British Embassy's Garden Fair in Wireless Road (I used to enjoy this, though I never saw the Queen). They are the brothers of "Abdullah K.", my childhood friend, whom you have asked me about so many times. I cannot give you a photograph of Jefri himself because he is uneducated enough to believe it is *haram.* You need to eliminate these two men as potential dangers and a threat to myself, whom they do not trust at all – and publicly say so. With respect, if you say Western intelligence agencies do not kill people, I do not believe you. This is not the result of seeing a surfeit of Hollywood spy movies. Please protect me.

As to the trip overseas, I cannot supply further information at present. The leaders keep details about place, time, transport etc to themselves for obvious reasons. I will "enlighten" you when the plans are firmed.

You inquired as to the mathematical classes the leader gives. These are more in the nature of a one-way seminar or solitary musings to which the rest of us are admitted solely as audience. So, for instance, he will speak about the Nash Equilibrium which he tells us is a perfect model for the state of affairs prevailing in the South here. This is a mathematically provable balance where no one side can, by altering its strategy or actions, improve its position so long as all other parties involved in the conflict persist in their old actions. An advantage can only ensue if another party agrees to change its actions at the same time. Although in the realm of calculations some alliance of convenience would occur, in the real world it is difficult to secure such co-operation among people who hate and distrust each other, for instance between the different groups of Freedom Fighters, the criminal gangs, the army, the police, the Malaysian authorities, and Mujahoodin overseas. It does occur to me that a simple word for this would be stalemate.

Our teacher also talks of the Shapely Rubik Power Index, the Captive's Dilemma, and Stag Hunt vs Hare Course. The Rubik PI measures a group's influence or authority among its allies not by, say, its numbers or its wealth but by how much its casting vote in any decision can swing a result. Thus a tiny group with few weapons could in fact be quite powerful in holding the balance between two stronger opposing groups. Again, this is seen many times in the small political parties in the Siamese coalition governments (we called the most flagrantly corrupt of these the "buffet cabinet") or with extremist Christian groups or the NRA during American elections.

The Captive's Dilemma, which our teacher diagrammatised on the board with numbers and squares, illustrates how loyalty can be more advantageous than betrayal, while silence might prove more in one's interests than treacherously "spilling the beans". This situation would be quite common in the real world when two suspects could be released scot-free if both kept silent. Alternatively, one of them could secure a reduced sentence if he incriminated the other who would then receive a harsh punishment. Logically the first course of action – or inaction – would be preferable but your knowledge of human nature – far profounder than my own – will teach you that the latter pessimistic course of action prevails. Perhaps this is because the criminal class suffers from low self-esteem, where Jihadists do not. Stag vs Hare is a similar conundrum to do with allying and accepting diminished reward in return for reduced possible loss. Once more, a friend who worked (briefly) in the finance industry told me this was a frequent gambit when "gearing" or "hedging" investment. I should immediately add this friend was female and the citizen of a Christian entity. I have also come up with my own game theory to do with the horrendous traffic jams in Bangkok. Such is the Siamese social culture that no driver is prepared to behave altruistically and yield right of way. To do so would merely lead to an interminable flow of cars blocking one's path. The result before long is gridlock for everyone. Yet, if everyone politely gave way (without, of course, causing mass collisions and a pile-up by taking hands off the steering-wheel to give a *wai)* we would all move much faster.

The question is: if one sacrifices oneself on a daily basis for long enough, will the example eventually set a trend, so that it is in both one's own selfish interest and that of the wider driving community to behave considerately?

I await your instructions and hope these insights into our leadership's way of thinking may be more profitable to you than my account of their teaching of *hadith*.

TO: LUDORUM
CC: LK-FLOREAT-50/50
BCC: À VOUS
SUBJECT: STIGMATA
DATE: 13/1/200-
FROM: VICE VERSA
YOUR DRAFT HAS BEEN SAVED

Thank you for the photographs. I have now raised for the second time with your local authority the subject of securing you. Whether he complies or declines, we shall not allude to this unpleasant topic again.

It is possible we have alternative means of finding detail of your travel plans, so refrain from inventing a spurious schedule to "take the heat off" yourself. I prefer no information at all to an unreliable source. Bear this in mind.

I conclude by expressing surprise that you cannot convey emphasis without recourse to the upper case and no less than three exclamation marks. Even a single one is otiose, *pace* Fowler. And yet you are still able to explicate fairly subtle philosophical discourses. I feel I am dealing with two people. I am only interested in preserving one of them. But thank you, seriously, for the insight into the way of thinking of the Leadership of the cell (for that is what it is). I don't actually find a contradiction between the calculations and formulae you tell me of and the other more archaic machinations. The fashionably contemporary spells and psychological mind-games of modern sociology are simply your earlier riddles, medieval adages, puzzles, quotations, and quaint tableaux brought up to date. *C'est plus de la même chose.*

I appreciate that people who live in glass houses should not throw stones and I apologise to you in advance for any errors I have made in my typing or should make in the future. For obvious reasons, I cannot entrust the transcription of my handwriting to my usual secretary and I must rely on my old and arthritic fingers. Those that I have left. I am told – I can hardly credit it – that there exist computer programmes that turn a human voice into the written word. Funnily enough, my eyes are not too bad but I have become colour-blind and I have an especial problem with the blue squiggles that suddenly appear on the computer screen. They are virtually invisible to me and operate on the unwary much like textual man-traps or the staked pits of the hunter-gatherers of an earlier human era. May I assure you, finally, that the preservation of your safety remains of paramount importance to me.

To: VICE VERSA
CC: BLANK FIELD
BCC: BLANK FIELD
SUBJECT: DEPARTMENT OF DECEPTIONS/OPERATION OTHELLO
DATE: 29/1/200-
FROM: LK-FLOREAT-50/50
YOUR MESSAGE HAS BEEN SENT

Not a problem at all. In fact, rather easier than swatting a mosquito. Consider it done. Thanks for the history lesson, by the way. I would have been happy to go to Sherbourne just for those. I had no idea you old-timers got up to tricks so dirty. Taking a leaf from that book, we will plant on one of the bodies documents incriminating TARGET T. which will serve as the codeword for the Head Teacher or Tok Guru's enforcer, the cove with the hook and eye-patch. Christ, where do they dig them up from? As with your fake D-Day plans all those years ago, it will be more convincing if the body appears the victim of accident. Drowning, as was the case in 1944, is not suitable. It leaves too much to chance. The body may not be retrieved from the river at all, or not by the people we want. I suggest a traffic accident involving a motorbike on the main highway. We have enough of those not to excite suspicion. Statistically, it's safer to go into orbit than ride a moped in the Kingdom of Thailand. Of course, our chums will be pre-tranquillised before we drive a truck over their heads. Don't want them coming to life like run-over kangaroos.

I don't believe a word of the stuff your Nancy Boy is sending you out of the pondok and I'm the native. Say the word, I'll be only too pleased to take him/her off your hands. Game Theory, Shame Theory, what does it matter if he loves his mother? What (s)he/it seems to be playing is the old Bait-and-switch ploy. Know that one? An ancient Cockney scam pulled outside Selfridge's in Oxford Street by blokes in cloth caps and also a hallowed gambit in the City of London practised by chaps in bowlers wearing my old school tie.

This brings me to the point. As you very well know, I haven't been to Blighty for several years and, if I did, certainly wouldn't bother you, but thanks for the kind thought. I wasn't impressed by Merde at all, by the way. He's not inaptly named – as big a bullshitter as Our Nancy Boy in Yala. I just know I'll be the poor sod picking up the pieces. I'll probably have to see Monsieur Merde at the Thinktank sometime next year – could you kindly disinvite him? – but it's a Moveable Feast. I haven't Blind Carbon Copied him in, as you can see.

2

Shaykh

In the Name of God, most Compassionate, most Merciful.

I was born of rock and ice but I find myself among a people of sand and mud. Where the path is crooked and treacherous, where it is soft and mired, I can lead them to the road of cleanliness. That path is hard and it is straight. I can point the way of submission to God.

That is the face I turn to my followers and it is the face I show myself for encouragement. The peaks and glaciers seem immovable but trickles of water — weak, formless water — over time will degrade them into slurry. And that is what the weakness of men can do to their belief.

Tariq has no such uncertainty. But his is the strength of stupidity. The simple have many uses. One is to sustain the wise in their time of infirmity. Doubt is a luxury. I may never show it.

Without God, men are nothing. In the end this is what I know.

They are thinking I am being a Saudi, maybe even a Saudi prince. I am not even a Yemeni. I am from Pakistan. I will tell you a dirty secret. If he can be thought something else, no Pakistani wants to be thought a Pakistani. I was born in North West Frontier. Later we went to what is now India, then to Punjab. My father served the British. He was havildar in their army. He was an upright man. I am not ashamed but I keep what he was to myself. He made a joke he should not have done, a Hindu joke. He called it the warrior *caste*. Nevertheless, from him I inherited straightforwardness and, I hope, his steadfastness. He never betrayed his salt. That was an expression from the old days which he still used. The British invented concentration camps, you know, for the Bores in South Africa. But he never betrayed his salt.

In my childhood I was having strong discipline. Sometimes I was beaten with his belt. This was only good for me. I was quite headstrong. Afterwards he would make me shake hands. Most of all, he despised those who had left the British and gone to fight for the Japanese. They betrayed their salt.

I studied the sciences. I was good at Physics and Mathematics, Applied Mathematics, not the more academic branch. There is a name for this most abstruse branch of Mathematics but I will not use it, for it is properly one of the attributes of God. Men cannot attain, only strive for, this condition. Applied Math is useful. I had a special aptitude for Fluid Mechanics. It was difficult but it was also realistic. It concerned velocity, tension, viscosity. It was not at the level of the atom. We want to harness the energy of this to be the equal of the Crusaders but it is not at the level real life takes place. I pondered for a week and I already understood such things as the Stokes-Navier equations, Goldstein's Paradox, and Porterfield's Conjecture. Unusually, only Goldstein was a Jew. Jews have dominated this field – so far. Game Theory I also found interesting. Many of its methods and lessons are applicable to the situation in which we find ourselves here in Siam. I sometimes speak of them not just to the cleverer students – who will understand the concepts – but to those whose ardour is unquestioned (that is to say, whose Faith in the Providence of God will not be undermined by those very concepts). That means just three or four of them. Fluid Mechanics were more practical, not like the Arts. The Arts people I found to be weak-faithed, weak in head and weak in heart. They talk too much. Their talk leads to doubt; they would call it scepticism. They say the scientists become atheists but it was always the arts people who were the scepticals. The Bible of the Christians states, "In the beginning was the Word." But God was not a talker, he was a Doer. The Worlds are not to be described in speech but understood in Mathematics. We Believers, my brothers in Jihad, those of them who had education, we were tending to being engineers, chemists. This is but natural. The great Scientists during the Christian Dark Time were all Muslims. Their beacon burned and it was an age of brilliant light in the Muslim world.

We invented chess, algebra, even universities, long before the Oxford and Cambridges. We protected the Jews of Spain from the torture of the Christian Inquisition. This is where the word torture comes from, from the name of the priest Torquemada who stretched people on the rack. At this time the British had not yet invented the concentration camps. The Moors, who were Muslims, saved the Jews then but we could not save them hundreds of years later from the Germans, a Christian nation, who took the invention of the British, the concentration camps, and used them on the Jews. This is what they call Christian civilisation and they try to call us uncivilised cowards. A civilised bomb drops from the air and kills hundreds or thousands of people and the true coward who dropped it flies away all the time in his comfortable seat. An uncivilised bomb kills only dozens and the brave martyr gives his life with the victims. That is their civilisation of cowards.

I was born in 1941, six years before Independence. And 1947 and the year subsequent were years of slaughter. Hindus slaughtered the Muslims where they could find them. In the North Muslims were the majority. But in what would later become India, where the Hindus were a majority, they went from house to house with their swords, sparing no one. Women they butchered with their children. They cut the babies from the wombs of pregnant women. On the trains carrying the fleeing Muslims they killed every single person. They stopped the trains and, as they had gone from house to house, they proceeded from carriage to carriage. The colour of the cars turned red. The vultures and buzzards gathered in the sky above. The bodies hung out of the windows and lay sprawled on the carriage-roofs and along the tracks where they had tried to flee.

They are talking about the Dachau and the Auschwitz but this is much worse. And it is Muslims, not Jews. My uncle took me to see such a train. It had reached sanctuary too late with its freight of corpses. Trains just keep running on their rails; they want to move. You cannot thwart the will of the steam even when you try to deny it and disengage the controls and apply the brakes. It will have its way. All that pressure, it is an unstable force. The engine can go without a driver and reach its destination; it is not like a truck. The rails guide it. It is like the heart guided by Holy Teachings. God wanted me to see this train.

The steam builds up; it hisses and puffs; the wheels turn, sliding at first on the slippery metal. All this time there is no one in the cab. The driver and fireman are dead. But finally the great steel wheels catch the rail in their grooves and slowly, slowly the train moves forward, until finally it is clattering side to side with speed. The bodies shake with the motion; they seem alive but it is an illusion. Finally, the dying steam takes the engine gently into the buffers of the station.

I have never forgotten that terrible sight. Ever since I have hated the sight of red and white together. I do not even like to see the flag of Indonesia.

My uncle held my head. He said, "Look and remember."

A stupid Arts teacher, British woman, said to me years later in Sheffield, "But you were looking at a train full of dead Hindus, murdered by the Mohammedans. You must have been, if where you were was to become Pakistan. Didn't you see the turbans and saris? The train must have been put into reverse. Only apply the mathematical logic you're forever wittering about."

I told her, "If they were wearing turbans, they were Sikhs attacking the train, whom the brave Muslim men were able to slay when they courageously defended their women. Muslims do not commit atrocities like this. It is expressly forbidden, so they cannot have committed them."

I can say this sight was the most forming memory and experience of my life. It has influenced me ever since. It was a train of events.

Now the Hindus have nuclear weapons, not just swords. They can slay all of us and lay waste our lands, not just butcher a train-load of women and children. This is why I wished to learn Physics, not the useless Arts. Now we have the Muslim bomb, now we have the Sword of God.

In one respect only was I ever stronger than my father. Our sister, his daughter, disgraced us. She was the youngest daughter of his third wife. She did the unimaginable. I will not even mention it. At the time she was 14. She still ornamented her body with bangles and jewellery, wore kohl, bright colours. All this should have stopped when she was younger, but he had indulged her; he had wished her childhood, that is to say her irresponsibility, to go on a little longer. This is what comes from breaking rules. All his life he had followed them. He had been upright. He relaxed his strictness once and this was the consequence.

My own mother was the one who found out about it. She said she was doing her duty. There was a family conference, of the men. My father, myself, my brother, my half-brothers, (my uncle, the one who took me to the railway station, had been shot in Kandahar in 1953 by an unknown hand). There were tears in my father's, that strong man's, eyes. His moustache drooped. He said, "But Ayesha . . ." He was not someone who usually quoted holy texts or precedents. (This was a wrong and blasphemous one). My own brother said, "She is not married and she is two years older than Ayesha was. She is old enough to know the difference between right and wrong. We do not need witnesses."

Her own brothers were angry but not as zealous as we were. They still knew what had to happen. She had been seen walking and holding hands and sitting.

"I will undertake it," I said.

My brothers looked gratefully at me. My father left the room. We decided on the method. There was a conventional way but there was also room for individual choice. Her brothers preferred strangulation, my own brother the knife, while my mother proposed burning to me later. And this was *haram*, it was Hindu in its cruelty. I looked her calmly in the eye. I said, "Woman, be gone with your wickedness. Be satisfied."

I told her brothers their choices of despatch were flawed: strangulation took time. We had not lost our humanity. Watching her choke out her life would distress her brothers. They might call a stop. Stabbing entailed the spilling of blood, to which I was personally averse. I told them I would hurl her from a height. Our roof-top was not high enough. Nor were any of the buildings in our town. There was a quarry with steep sides, several kilometres out. It also had the advantages of privacy. It could appear an accident. We did not want the whole world to know our shame.

We took her there in the back of my cousin's truck – his Uncle, that is to say my own father, had financed him in the haulage business to Afghanistan. These were brightly decorated vehicles but our task was sombre. My half-sister knew what was going on but she was in denial of it to herself. She spoke brightly, desperately to us. My brother answered her cheerfully. There was always guile in Murad. To me as his elder brother it was a source of regret that he did not take after our father more. One day Murad would betray his salt, but that is another story. My half-sister's own brothers did not have the heart to keep up the pretence but answered sorrowfully.

At the quarry she would not leave the truck. I picked her up while she screamed and beat at me with her fists. I was already much taller than everyone else. I took her to the edge and I threw her over. I had to break her grip on my arm and at this point I became angry with her, personally annoyed, by her awkwardness and lack of co-operation. It was her who had done wrong. She seemed to fall slowly, like a flower, her clothes ruffling around her like petals. It would have been beautiful if she had refrained from shrieking.

I recovered her body from the bottom. Picking one's way down the zig-zagging mule track was difficult but bearing the body back up was a penitence. Her full brothers were waiting for me. Murad did not help. He had wanted to leave her. I slapped his face for this. Of course, we had to bring the body back. We had to show we had honour. The deed was black but our hearts were clean.

Unlike the Indonesians and Arabians in our brotherhood, I have never regarded the Crusaders as our worst enemies. The Hindus were – are – far worse. They are slaughterers. The Americans, the Israelis, I do not think they would drop the atomic bomb on us without warning. The Malays (like Hassan and Umar) also hate the Chinese but the Chinese are a minority in Indonesia and Malaysia, just as Muslims were a minority amongst the Hindus. Of course in world terms, the Chinese are a majority. And just how powerful they are, we in Pakistan know. They defeated the Indian Army in Assam in 1962 and supplied us with all kinds of military equipment to fend off the Hindus. My father had the highest regard for them, for the precision and logistics of their artillery net. I cannot say it, but sometimes I feel sorry for the Chinese in Indonesia during the riots and attacks on them. In the Caliphate we will tolerate the Chinese. We will tolerate them for the same reason the Christians tolerated the Jews in their lands. They ran the businesses. I tell my woman this when I give her the housekeeping money and she covers her face and laughs.

Interestingly, the current rulers of China are not Arts. No, they are a hydraulic and an electrical engineer. That is why the country has prospered, even though they have persecuted the Uighurs. For the Malays and Indonesians to hate the Chinese is to localise the struggle as an intifada, whereas what we are wishing to consummating is the pan-national Jihad. And to be Chinese is not to prevent one from being a good Muslim. I have met Chinese Muslims. And they are speaking the beautiful Arabic.

There is insulting expression for Indian in the Malay language.

It is *Kling*. They call them black *Kling*. I like to use it. Fortunately, unlike Murad, I do not look like an Indian but an Arab. The Hindus, if they had the chance, would bomb Pakistan. Maybe not the leaders but the mob certainly would. But the mob only have swords and clubs. Jesus was a Prophet of Islam, the greatest after the Messenger of God himself, may peace be upon his head. The Hindus worship worthless, ridiculous idols. They worship . . . the cows. They follow painted, red-eyed lunatics whom they call teachers and holy men. They drink the filthy water of Ganges in which dead bodies float. Their religion is gross; it is an abomination. God cannot be touched, represented in a doll of wood or ivory or brass. God is a distillation and an abstraction. God is in algebraic equations. God is on the clean wind of the desert and the high mountain ranges. God is pristine. God is Great and Merciful, even if men are not.

The Christians are more like us. The Protestant Christians do not worship idols at all. Compare this with the Siamese – these people worship a fat, golden doll. In his chubby belly and navel they are seeking wisdoms. They will look for it for a long time. The man they call the Dalai Lama – the man is a clown. He is a licensed fool. I cannot hate the Christians, although I fear and fight them.

I fought the Communists in Afghanistan. But a funny thing – the Marxists are clean. They are godless atheists but they are unfouled.

I went to school in Rawalpindi first, then Karachi, then Lahore. Yes, my life of restless movement started already at a young age. My father worried for my safety in Karachi. It was a turbulent place as most ports are, except for Jeddah. When I think of my subsequent life, the thought of my father being concerned for my physical safety makes me smile. Maybe it would make that bemedalled man smile, too. He was to become a commissioned officer after Independence, not just a non-com.

In Lahore I was at school with rich boys and clever boys. My father had made some money, I don't know how. You just have to possess wealth – no one cares how you got it. Some of the fathers and grandfathers of the students were even "Sir" Something or Other. The Queen had tapped them on the shoulder with a sword when she should have cut their heads off. One of these rich boys went to Oxford University in England. I did not go there. His head was full of Communist ideas and, though he was rich, he was quite sincere. He was all for taking the land away from the rich land-owners like his own family. I liked him. My eyes had not been completely opened to Allah, although they were medically perfect then, as now they are not.

In England this boy made a name for himself as an orator and agitator. He went on marches, he was on the television. I cannot be on the television but my foolish Tariq has, standing on a wrecked Soviet helicopter. Then this young man, as he was now, visited Pakistan again. Of course, he was followed everywhere by the police. His mother, the Begum, a very gracious lady as I remember her, would send out cold drinks (in unopened cans) to the police and soldiers. The family would even tell the police where the chauffeur was going to take them in their car to make the task easier for the police. My father was one of those assigned to oversee this duty.

He told me, "At the end of his stay, when he was going to the airport, I went to shake his hand. I wanted to tell him how much I admired him, how much we all admired him. He was dumb-founded – he said, 'How can an old soldier like you admire a young pink-o like me?'"

(You have to imagine my father with his huge moustache in full military regalia and standing 6ft 5ins and then the Communist boy with his long curly hair and in his jeans and Hawaian shirt).

My father told him, "Sir, you are clean. You are moral. Of all the dissidents and exiles we have followed, you are the only one who did not go to the brothel."

Of course, it was being commendable but it was for all the wrong reasons. There was no religious reason. He had come back with his head full of all this Woman's Lib he had learned at university. He was one of those who did not study science.

I have to admit the Hindu Maoists, the Naxalites, that they were clean in their way, too. They were not corrupt. They stopped at nothing, but they were clean, too. Godless and clean. It is strange. They were cleaner than many of our Brothers. More honest than any of the Indonesians I ever met. I can say the Indonesian imams are the most guileful men I have ever known. It is not Islam. It is the being Indonesian. It is the Arts. It has been well said – there are those who are dirty but not dangerous and there are those who are dangerous but not dirty.

All the time I was applying myself to my Physics and Mathe-matics and Chemistry in Sheffield. I began to find the Arts not just a waste of time but sacrilegious. The Literature was the worst. God gave you the one life to lead – your own. You should not enter into the lives of other, imaginary people in stories and books or take their experiences to be your own. You must lead a real life in the service of God, not in entering another's man's fantasy. I find that disgusting. It is a masturbation. And the impressionable minds will lose focus, lose purpose; their own lives become diluted, sullied with the infirmity of another. Watered kerosene cannot catch fire. There is no such study in my *madrassah*, this *pondok*. Only the holy texts. They can find all the edification and instruction in the life of God's Messenger and all of the excitement and entertainment in the world in the stories of the *hadith*. They need no more.

My father loved the General Zia ul-Haq. He wept when he died in the air-crash. He was murdered, of course. There was a bomb. They covered it up. I did not love him like my father, his fellow-soldier, did but he was preferable to Bhutto. This was a dirty man. The stink of his crime and his corruption rose to the skies. He did not die well on the gallows, like Saddam died well. The Jihad has taken me from South Asia to South East Asia, to a small corner of the big world, but Bhutto's type is here and that of his family. They lie, they cheat, they steal, they kill the innocent.

Sukarno, the Indonesian. This man was a Communist and lover of the Chinese but, unlike the Naxalites, he was dirty. He was corrupt. Suharto, the General who threw him out, became even dirtier. The Generals who are in charge there now wear suits, not uniforms. They are not like Zia, they are not devout. They kill and arrest our brothers. Here in Siam, the politicians are even worse. I call them the Forty Thieves. If there is an honest man among them, his life is in danger already. Get in the way of their money-making, they will kill you. The soldiers murdered those sheltering in a mosque. They piled innocent boys into trucks, hundreds of them on top of each other to take them into an army camp. They suffocated and died. In Bangkok this man – I am sorry to say he was Chinese, with the square Chinese face – said, "Oh, the Muslims were already weak from fasting. It is Ramadan." His iniquity rises to the sky. Surely the warriors of God will punish him. Here Bhutto would have been safe. Here the generals do not hang their politicians. Instead everyone goes into exile and enjoys their dirty money.

They have their King. He is the real power in Siam, more so

than the generals and far more so than the politicians. Even here in the *pondok* they are frightened to speak ill of him. What do they think? A crowd of Buddhists will break in and beat them to death? They speak in whispers. It is enough to make me pull my beard. I do this a lot since I gave up tobacco and my water-pipe. I wish Umar would stop smoking those pungent clove cigarettes of his. You can't stop an Indonesian from doing that, like you cannot stop a Siamese praising his King. Ahmed is the best educated of them and in that respect the least subservient but he is also the worst example of what too much Arts can do to you. It can also make you a eunuch mentally. I know his head is full of books and films, the lives of others.

As an example of how God makes lives cross and intersect like the lines of geometry in the most unexpected ways, the Communist boy my father respected so much in Pakistan for his temperance and abstinence – as a man he was being seized in his hotel in Bangkok by the Siamese agents, pushed into a car without further ado, taken to the airport, and expelled from the country. This was some years ago. What had he done? He had criticised their King to a newspaper reporter. The Siamese agents laid their hands upon him. They, the dirty, judged the clean to be dirty. In Sheffield the leader of the Student Union once called the city police "The Filth". It was one of the rare times I could agree with their motions.

That eunuch of ours, that Ahmed. He always has a glib reply. I should have let him suffer longer with the removal of his tattoos with the sulphuric. I stopped it because I was worried we would deplete the battery and then the truck would not start when we needed it the next week. What if it wouldn't start when we had to drive it away with all the bags of fertiliser in the back? Trucks and trains. I have never liked them.

I was talking of Kings. The Saudis, of whom I am supposed to be one, have one as well. We shall bring him and his family to the dust. They flog the poor Pakistanis for distilling liquor but I have seen a prince – one of their dozens of such – drinking the malt whisky abroad. The Kingdom of Saudi Arabia, though, and the Kingdom of Siam – I mean Thailand – the two countries had a difference. The wife of a Saudi royalty had her jewellery collection stolen in Arabia by a Siamese servant. This servant fled with the gems to Siam. There was a famous blue diamond. He did not have the enjoyment of them long. The Siamese police got their hands on them. The jewels returned to the Saudis were fake, what they call paste. Three Saudi diplomats came after the original jewels to Thailand. The Siamese murdered them, too. They shot them in their car. Diplomats even! Then they kidnapped and killed a fourth Saudi. Even Tariq would pause before such a quantity! Well, the Saudis cut off diplomatic relations with the Kingdom of Thailand. They would have liked to cut off hands, I am sure, but it was only the diplomatic relations. To this day they have not been restored. A general of Siamese police was arrested. I would say he was just a scrapegoat except his career did not suffer. He was promoted! I sometimes think it is not just the Wahabbists but the kind of corrupt Saudi who lays up his reward on earth in shiny baubles, rather than with Allah, who smiles to see the punishment we inflict upon south Siam, how we make its tail thrash restlessly. Yes, we whip the thieves that no one else can punish.

Now is not yet the time to make our final effort, the big push, as my father the havildar used to call it. That moment will come when the old King is no more. When Siam is divided against itself. Then they shall see, the Infidels that they are, how the worst we have done up till now was but play. Even what I will have my young warriors do next will be as nothing compared to what lies in store for the *kafirs*. In the meantime our horizons are not restricted to Siam.

Of all the jewels we shall put into the crown of our Caliphate, Cambodia and the Philippines are the worst muddied with the corruption of the politicians. The Philippines have a woman President with a husband, just as Bhutto's daughter had a husband. The crimes and greed of the politicians there, both *kafir* and the Muslims in Mindanao, sully the land with their blood-shedding and filths. The Cambodian Prime Minister has a glass eye, like the Siamese King, like Tariq, too. From the Cambodian students in the *pondok* I hear tales of brigandage and blood-wit that could be from Afghanistan 200 years ago. We have much cleansing to do. I know this washing will be done in blood. I will purge them. I rely on God.

But the metallurgical skills of my Cambodian students are extraordinary! Better than the cottage gunsmiths of our mountain bazaars in Pakistan. They made souvenir samurai swords for the Japanese before but now I have them manufacture kris. We will use these in the creation of the Caliphate. The kris will be gifts like a calling-card or a box of sweetmeats or a bouquet of flowers. Khmer or Kamen Muslims from Cambodia are called Cham. This I did not know before, or that we had brothers like these.

The Siamese do not despise the Cambodians as much as they despise the Burmese, who are as low as the Hindu Untouchables in India, but still they look down on them. You can tell the Burmese apart. They like to stick a paste of flour and water on their faces. This makes them look not unlike the worst kind of wandering Hindu fakir. Even our Burmese-Muslim boys do it. They come from near East Pakistan, Bangladesh as they now call it. My Cambodian students worked as boat-boys before at Rayong, the Burmese at Ranong. The Siamese place-names sound so similar but can be at opposite ends of the country. I make our local students lower themselves before the Cambodians and the Burmese. They do not like to do this but they must obey. This is how we will make the seamless Caliphate with odds and ends and pieces and parts into a great whole. Then we will make what they call the ethic cleansing. Yes, the ethic cleansing they tried upon our Brothers in Bosnia. Except those who admit and accept Islam. They will not be subject to the ethic cleansing. That was the way of the Messenger of God (peace be upon his head).

Look at all the abuse and injustice of the world. To be happy and content in such a place is to be deaf and blind. We need first a religion of hate, not love. We need followers who will surrender themselves to a hate that is fuelled by love, who will surrender all personal pride and seek exaltation in the cause only of the Caliphate. I say to them when they serve and lower themselves before the Cambodians that personal modesty is a social virtue but humility is a weapon. It is a weapon of the holy. I cannot pretend to offer justice, not yet, but I can confer, like a mathematician, exactitude, equivalence. One day, but not rendered by me, there will be a Holy Reckoning.

I would like people intelligent and honest so they do not elect these rogues and rascals, these rascalpillions. But I cannot stop them from their foolishness; I can only correct their mistake once it has been made by eliminating the consequence. I will bring them cleansing by fire. I will bring fire to the world. Mercy is the prerogative of Allah. It would be presumptuous and impious of me to show it. Then we should have *sharia* in the Caliphate and there will be justice at last. I will bring fire to this verminous world.

The *koti* Ahmed asked me how we will support ourselves in the Caliphate. (I told Tariq to refrain from using the Urdu word for his like, as it has a good meaning in Arabic. Besides, *koti* sounds like their local word, *katoey*). I answered that we will be an agricultural society. The city is adulteration and pollution. But we will also be having centres of mathematical and scientific excellence. Technology does not necessarily mean the urbanisation or Westernisations. We can sell our expertise in such matters. You can also calculate in the countryside or the desert, just as you can in the town. Better, for the stillness and lack of distraction.

The Malays were on the verge of their own industrial revolution when the colonisers came and wrecked it. Not many people know that. I have read it in the book of Alatas. Alatas, not Atlas. The *koti* looked as doubtful as he dared (not very), before he asked me a very useful question. What language we will all be speaking in the Caliphate?

Mostly, I ignore Ahmed. He has nothing of consequence to impart. I am disgusted by him and his kind – to use the organ of defecation for the act of procreation. It is a filthy act and a usurpation of one's anatomy from God. But sometimes, just sometimes, I stop, reflect, and find he has contributed a useful point. Take this one, for instance. There are so many languages used now in what will be our Caliphate. When you include the dialects, there are hundreds of tongues.

You must ask yourself which is being the most widely spoken language, which one has the most mouths? Then the answer to this question is clear: Malay, whether it is Bahasa Indonesia or Bahasa Malaya. Haji Hassan tells me these are basically variants of the same tongue, like US English and UK English, like Hindi and Urdu. They say the Malay Malay sounds the more refined. Even the Indonesians readily admit this. Of the Indonesians there are 250 million and always increasing. They are not just the biggest nation of Islam here in this corner of the world. They are the world's most populous Muslim nation. They will supply nearly three-quarters of the peoples of the Caliphate. So clearly Malay must be assigned an importance. We are doing the Will of God. We are in the grip of an idea that transfigures our pettiness. But we are working through men who are not clean and transparent like is an idea or a theorem.

The Caliphate must meld all types and races into the *ummah* – but by political means as well as by belief and observances. That is where I am different from Hassan and Umar and even Tariq. I am practical, I am engaged in a form of engineering, human engineering, as well as devotion, when I strive to build the new Caliphate of God. Therefore, I must indulge the speakers of the majority language. This will be what they call our *lingua franca*. They will feel comfortable and reassured with this. But our master language must be Arabic, the language of the Prophet and the Holy Book. That will be our language of communication across the old imperialist borders, that is how Filipino will communicate with Acehnese, Javanese with Cham. Many of the intellectuals already know it. I have myself spoken with the Chinese Muslims of Sinkiang when I was in Lahore. They spoke and wrote it as well as an Arab might. Maybe better than the commonalty. Then, in time, Arabic would supplant Malay. It would be the language of prestige and achievement as well as the tongue of holiness. It would be as English is to the rule of the Crusaders, as English is to the Internet. And Islam would then be one.

But we have so far to go on this road yet. They say our aim of a Caliphate is a dream but it is a dream we can make precise. I can put it in exact numbers. Our Caliphate will extend from 22° 37' 43" N until 09° 04' 18" S and from 95° 16' 33" E to 132° 01' 03" E.

What we have to do first is take over the middle part of the equation and make it our battle-ground. We must destroy our own moderates. They, not the Crusaders, are the worst enemies to the Caliphate. God knows no such thing as a "moderate" Muslim. How can you be half-hearted in the service of God? We can defeat the Crusaders, overthrow all their puppet governments here, yet still not have the Caliphate unless we are energising the torpid middle. The majority of the Indonesians are luke-warm when we need them not just red-hot but white-hot. The anger of the just and holy is white-hot. It is clean. We must put a Bunsen burner to the Indonesian moderation, no, a blast-furnace, until, like the metal foundry we visited in Sheffield, all the slag and dross is forced out and their belief is like super-hardened steel.

The young people of Indonesia take drugs, they are going to

discotheques. The girls wear Western costume. They wear the jeans and the tight T-shirts. As many go bare-headed as cover with the veil. Between Malaya and Indonesia we have a paradox. Indonesia is the scene of action, the battle-ground of the Mujaheedin. There we have the bombings, there the Jihad against the Christian islands. Yet bulk of population are apathetic to our cause. Malaya is peaceful – no bombings, no guns. For the impious it is a holiday and a sanctuary. Yet it is the Malay intellectuals who are the most fervent in our cause, who supply the leadership, who shelter the exiled Indonesians. And it is in Malaya that Jihad was planned to strike the Crusaders in New York and their interests in Asia. Those who flew the airplanes into the Towers (may God be well-pleased with them) had meetings in Malaya.

There is a pamphlet of the bald Communist, Lenin. It says *What is to be done?* I like this. We can learn, too, from the methods of the godless Leninists and Naxalites. He also said Soviets + Electrification = Communism.

I can say about ourselves: Leadership + Followers + Weapons x Fervour = Force of Jihad[3].

On our greenboard I show to them my 8 *Steps to Zeal*, followed by my next stage of 4 *Steps to Militarisation*. Umar, I think, not Hassan, though neither of them would admit to it when they saw how angry I was, wrote *Opening of the Eyes* above the former and *Path of the Warrior* over the latter. I rubbed it out. It was Arts. With a firm hand I then wrote: 13th *Step: Martyrdom*. The first steps, you will notice, are even.

Of all the peoples of the Caliphate, the Filipino Muslims are the most persecuted and the most accustomed to arms. In the camps of Afghanistan and Pakistan, the Filipino Mujaheedin were renowned for their zeal and their courage. They had nothing to lose but their lives, which were already a gift to Allah.

We can think of the Muslim island of the Philippines called Mindanao, in the providence of Allah situated just North of Indonesian island of Sulawesi and ripe for integration into the Caliphate, as the fuse or detonator of a bomb.

It was the core of the old Sultanate of Sulu. Itself, it is not large enough to make the powerful blast but the explosive is high grade and reliable. It will always bang. It is the detonator and the initiator charge. Below it, Indonesia is damp, inert explosive material but huge in quantity. It will never explode by itself. Even there is a barrier between Mindanao and the rest of Indonesia, being the province of Manado, nearest the Philippines, which is Christian. This is Protestant Christian not Catholic Christian like most of the Filipinos, so it is not as bad as it might be. Still Indonesia can never explode by itself. But Mindanao and maybe our fighting in Ambon against the Christian can make it.

The invaders of the past ages made many obstacles for us – the Hindus in Bali, the Dutch missionaries. We will squeeze these pockets like you squeeze a boil. The flame which lights the fuse will be the Malays' hatred of the Chinese (I have to allow it for a while) and this is nearly as strong as the hate between Muslim and Hindus. Then we will replace this hate with the love of God. If Indonesia can be made to explode, the blast will shake the world.

I am being an outsider here. More so than the Chinese who were born here. How can I ever forget that? There are weaknesses to this position but also strengths. That is why they brought me here, appointed me to the *pondok*. My old comrades, even my former students, are more senior than me now, but they respect me. I can see clearly. With my wretched glaucoma, I can still see the future more clearly. I am not partisan, I am not biased. I see, I think, I calculate.

The big companies, the multi-national companies like the Chevron, the Microsoft, the Philips, the IBM, the KIO, the Dassault, the Samsung, the Boeing, the General Electric, the Toyota, they have executive directors who do the everyday administration. They also have the non-executive directors. These people give them the objective, neutral view, the outside calm, cold opinion. I heard a Arts use an expression once. The one who tried to contradict my memory about the train. She said, "Icy dispassion." They need this to avoid making mistakes. We are also a multi-national, the worldwide Jihad, and I am the non-executive on the board. Of course, I keep this comparison to myself. Our international committee is called *Rabitabul Mujahideen*. You can learn from the way the Naxalites organise themselves and also the multi-national companies. In-country we are Naxalite; that is, we are organised in cells whose members know little of each other. We call it by the Malay word *flah* (do I say that correctly?) which sounds in English like Flower. I like this and it is a good code. I think of it like a frangipani flower with the individuals as the petals which cannot survive by themselves. *Pondok* school itself is simply a large individual *flah* or Flower. I myself, I know only as much as I require to know in order to operate. I do not have the national picture.

Cell system is a good defensive form of organisation but less effective in offence. It means we cannot co-ordinate a big attack. It is good in our time of weakness; we can change later. If one cell is betrayed or destroyed, the damage stops there. It is like the rip-stop material sewn in squares on Tariq's back-pack. In defence, though, it does have one limitation – we cannot communicate very easily and warn the other of the tricks, or tactics, the enemy is using. It isolates us and, say, the Siamese found a way to hurt us stealthily we could not alert the other *pondok*. Usually there is safety in numbers, in a school of fish or the pod of dolphin I saw in Oman, but in this case we would be eliminated one by one, in silence. I do not think the Siamese have the subtlety or cunning for this. Praise God, we are not fighting the Indonesian imams! They would find the crafty way. Meanwhile, up to a point, we are secure against treachery and torture. Even Tariq would give way under the tortures they have, if he could not kill himself first. The ones you would least expect resist the torture best. It is not always the mighty, bearded warrior with cartridge belts glistening across his chest and a pair of daggers in his belt. It can be a woman. I have to say that *koti* of ours surprised me with his fortitude. The H_2SO_4 is terrible stuff.

Out-country, when it is coming to the international, then, as I said, we organise not like the Naxalites but like the Sony or the Shell. We are organised, like them, into regions comprising several countries, or as the Malays call it, *Mantiqi*, and from there downwards into branches and smaller and smaller units. Except we do not produce, or exploit, or sell, but we kill. Actually, I am, as usual, being too modest. The *pondok* is much, much more than a *flah*. More like an entire branch than a single bloom or fruit. Maybe it is a giant seed-pod.

You learn from the successful, not from failures. We can learn from the multi-national company. They have already come up with the solutions. Our own organising, our own financing, resembles theirs in many ways. I can regard ourselves as an overseas subsidiary of a great Middle Eastern enterprise. They give us so much autonomy that Hassan was imprudent enough to use the word "franchise" in front of me. I looked at him the once and he was abashed. He never saw blood spilled, not even in the anti-Chinese riots in Medan. We have planning department, we have research department, we have recruitment department, we have financial department. Hassan is our Quartermaster. This I am not so keen about, as they say. I could almost feel insulted by the lack of trust. They trust me to die but not to keep my hands off the money.

Hassan has half the password and half the account number of our funds. Other half I am knowing. The *hawala* is not adequate for this kind of amount, though Hassan uses it quite skilfully, I admit, for remitting smaller sums to Aceh or the Philippines. Most of the money is from the Saudis, of course, the richest among the warriors of God. It comes filtered, as water is filtered through strata of rock, and cleansed through several levels of charitable organisations. Some is the "hot" money; some, Siam being Siam and one of the world centres of the filthy trade in drugs, is very dirty money. This does not matter. It becomes clean when we use it for our holy purpose. Hassan once used the word "laundered". I refrained from saying the Chinese is the best laundry. Hassan and I turn our heads away while the other in-puts his code into the computer. As if we needed to, as if we were both not half-blind already. The serial numbers we have by ourselves will not work alone. We therefore need each other, our lives are mutually precious. This is good and it is bad. The good is that Hassan must preserve me and my knowledge from harm. I do not fully trust him. He has the Indonesian slyness, although not as badly as Umar. I was told he was the assistant manager of a bank in Medan many years ago but he expressly denied this. In fact, he swore it with some vehemence.

But Haji Hassan can say what he likes about the Americans and the British before them, for they have been successful. Now it is our turn. Now we will make our empire. We will take their methods and destroy them with their own technologies and organisation. They should not just fear us; they are their own worst enemies. The George Bush did as much for us against our own middle, our own "moderates", as our martyrs did.

So, when we have brought them down to the dust, what will we put in the place of the juntas of generals, the prime ministers and presidents shoving gold as quickly as they can into their back-pockets, the members of parliament, senators, and congress-men giving contracts and backhanders to their cronies, the police generals torturing the martyrs of God?

The closest existing example we have, like the examples at the top of the page in my childhood algebra textbook, is the governing of Iran, although they are followers of Ali and are not a federation of many races and languages as the Caliphate will be. They are called theocracy. Just as real power in Indonesia, in Siam before, in the Philippines, in Burma, is controlled by the army, so real power in Iran resides in the clergy. Iran can be regarded as our control experiment. This priestly control will be the same in the Caliphate. But I want young Imam. I do not say this to Umar. But I think he will be long dead. If God is willing, maybe I can see the Caliphate but I think it will be the grandsons of the boy Jefri. I want young Imam. You can learn from your enemies. Whose is the most successful army, the Syrians, the Iraqis? Of course, it is the army of the accursed Jews. Are their generals old men? To the contrary, not one of them is older than 45. You can learn from your enemies.

Naturally, we will need an older Head Imam, a stabilising force, a figurehead. He has to be Malay, most probably Indonesian. They are the ones with the great numbers of supporters at the moment. Something in me wishes that this was not so. The Caliphate is not yet at hand. God willing, it will be soon. God willing, not *too* soon. It will be better if Head Imam is a first among equals, not a para-mount figure as that *shia* Khomeini was and it will be better if he is a straightforward man, a man without guile. I cannot say this about the Indonesian Imams. There is something of the Pakistani about them. I mean of the Pakistani politician. They are impossible to pin down. They cannot give a straight, scientific answer. I never liked the lessons in logic and rhetoric I received in Lahore. It was a sly dialectic, a perversion of mathematics. Some of the Indonesian Imams excel at it. I have something of my father in me. In my life I have lied and deceived but I can say this – I never enjoyed doing it. I try to be upright and clean, I strive for the bright and unsullied in my life, but the circumstances will not always allow it. I will build a society which not only permits but is being conducive to it.

What society has been most conducive to this? Certainly not Iran under the Ayatollah Khomeini or his successors. Maybe Kalkalli would have cleaned it up. He was a Russian. He liquidated the unrighteous in a way never seen before or since. He purged like the most dogmatic communist. However, for every Muslim the answer to my question is clear. Medina after the *hijra*, Medina in the time of the Prophet (peace be upon his head). His was a time of war and uncertainty, yet he still achieved so much in what would now be called the secular sphere. It has been remarked (not just by the impious) that the Messenger of God (pbuh) could neither read nor write. That he dictated his words to a Follower. Were this the case, we should admire him all the more. But there is no definite proof on either side of this contention. I feel that though no blasphemy is entailed, it is not altogether a respectful discussion and the devout will chew it. Where there are no proofs, no evidence, no final QED obtainable, just vague speculations and muddy conclusions, only the Arts will venture. It is the idle chatter of the Arts. The Black Arts. Did anyone think the less of Khomeini for being unable to operate a computer?

As we are dealing mostly with Malays and speaking their language, I feel, most usefully in the early days of our Caliphate, we can adopt the political forms of their past. I say the forms – it will be names and titles but not the reality. No Sultans and Sultanates. These rulers, even now, with their Rolls Royces and their polo ponies and their women are a reproach to Islam. We would have a Supreme Spiritual Ruler who would be a respected Imam. He would also ultimately control the organs of state and finance but administer through delegation. Ahmed asked me, "Would we call him the Grand Mufti?" I replied, "No, it is the Caliphate. We would call him the Caliph." He looked as if I had hit him over the head with a piece of wood. There is an English expression I heard from a Arts but, for a change, it is a good one. The *koti* never sees the wood for the trees. The Malay name for Caliphate would be *Daulah Islamiyah* but even the Malays prefer the name Caliphate, so we would use it.

Under the Caliph would be the Grand Vizier. We would, however, not use the Malay title but the Arabic name. Under the Vizier we have the *Timengong*, which is a Malay word. The *Timengong* was in the old days the high official in charge of the defence of the state and the Caliph. Not a general, but a minister. He would also have what you would call now a spying function. He was in charge of anticipating as well as repressing plots and assassinations, both internal and external. (I called Tariq my *Timengong* – he did not laugh). Alas, rule by the righteous is not of itself a guarantee of peace. We know this from the early years of Islam. So many of the Caliphs died untimely deaths. The solution is for the Spiritual leader to be of such high prestige that no one dare conspire against him; it would be unthinkable. Instead of hierarchy among officials we would have a series of geometric steps and relationships, a perfect harmony and symmetry. They talk of the democracy – which is once more a word of the Greeks. One man, one vote, and then they count. The problem with this is that the stupid and the intelligent have the same voice. The venal will also sell their vote. Much better a Council of the Wise in which all sectors are represented but with the Holy having a larger vote.

I liked studying Euclid – the exactness, the pattern, the rigour, the clarity. There is nothing you can be touching but it is a masterplan of the solid world. I could also draw up a periodic table of desirable and undesirable human qualities in the Caliphate – how they would combine with each other, some neutralising, some catalytic, some reactive. For instance, I put the boy they call Jefri with Ahmed, the *koti*. This was not just because they both come from the same town. They are opposites as acid and alkali are opposites. They complement each other's strengths and weaknesses. Jefri is the calmest person under strain that I have ever seen, even more so than Tariq. He reminds me a little of my father, without my father's ire. Jefri's temperament is mild, his manner modest; in stature, he is short, even for a Malay who are a slight people. But appearances can be deceptive. He is a true soldier of Islam, a true follower of Jihad and was born to be one. The unlikely warrior is the superior warrior.

Ahmed, on the other hand, is the least reliable person I have ever taken into the cause. He flutters, that is what the *koti* does, he flutters like a bird in the fist, like one of the tiny caged birds the Buddhists here release from cages to accrue merit. Tariq says he was about to desert, to betray us in Hat Yai. But I believe Ahmed himself – he just froze, he went into a daze, a trance.

How can such a weak person be being an asset, a foil to someone as admirable as Jefri? Simple. The weak dependent makes a strong person stronger. Their weakness calls to the strength in the hero as air rushes in to fill a vacuum. Nature abhors a vacuum and Jihad abhors cowardice. Jefri himself is too brave, too self-sacrificing. He could waste himself. The *koti* is meaner, smaller-minded. He will balance this tendency in Jefri. He will add to Jefri's chances of survival until we need him. Like myself, Jefri is guileless; he has no cunning. Ahmed is slyness itself. Most of them are. If they are not so, I am afraid we make them so. To this native guile, our own Ahmed adds intelligence. He has that, I admit. He seems to know nothing at all but his wits are quick. This cause requires all kinds of instruments and, if God wills, there will arise a use for him. He can also be of use to me.

I admit the cunning of the Indonesians is too much for me. When Ahmed first came to the school, I confess I had strong reservations about him. He stood under the banyan with no expression at all on his face. I wondered if he was mentally retarded as well as a eunuch. I wondered if there was life in his brain, if there were any thoughts at all going through it, and if they were too brutish to be put into even the simplest words. Then he stood under the white flowers of the frangipani before recoiling from it as if he had seen an evil spirit. I have to say it is one of the most tranquil and beautiful spots in the whole grounds.

At first, I thought I would keep him a month or two then let him go, but he flourished in the special class in the map room. I was still unsure but he then exhibited such fortitude under the pain of the acid, I decided to make a permanent place for him. If he had screamed and made a fuss, I would have let him go. They say nothing compares with the pain of child-birth and it is, of course, the women who endure that. I will give the *koti* tasks where the requirement is not daring or strength but the capacity to endure pain, terrible pain, with passive fortitude. I knew he would welcome the honour of that, the honour of enduring for Jihad in a way all of his own. However, he is not proof against travel-sickness. After I told him of the destiny I had in mind for him when we were on the way to buy fertiliser for the vegetable garden, he vomited over the tailboard. Jefri handed him a white handkerchief, pristine as snows. The eunuch returned it fouled. That is the essence of Jefri for you. That is the nature of the *koti*, too. He has found his place with us.

In general, this is what we can offer those young men who come to us so lost and confused. A few come to us from the obscurity of their villages, the *kampong*; most come to us from their foreign studies or from a place, the modern city, which frightens and confuses them but from which there is no retreat. I, of all people, know the feeling. I was so lonely in Sheffield. These young men cannot return to the *kampong*; they have already lost their place there. I say to them, "You matter. You are of account. There may be no place for you in the new city and none where you were born. But I can give you a place. God can give you a place and a role. There is no more isolation, an end to bewilderment. Now there are only certainty and purpose and brotherhood. Come."

This was not how Tariq and I began Jihad. We had no doubts when we were in Peshawar. As I said at the start, the Malays are a softer people than us. Their past was not like ours. It was they who massacred the Chinese, not the other way around. They have a childish horror of blood, yet the next moment they are exulting as they wallow in it. They gave a word to the English language – *amok*. I need to take the amok's rage and focus it. I need his mind calm even as his heart boils. And to do this, I need to simplify. I need to make the world less complex to them, in the way that Euclid can be so simple. I can end their bewilderment by a solution that is diagrammatic, that requires only one moment of decisiveness to accomplish, even if it has been preceded by months and years of irresolution.

We were discussing the *intifada* against the Jews. Then one of the students, he is a Bruneian from quite a wealthy family, someone who was a Arts too long, said the problem was the Arabs should have thrown the Jews out or united and slaughtered them at the very beginning because now the descendants of these original interlopers had been born there and their children to a third and even fourth generation who felt the land was by birthright theirs.

Now here is how I made it simple. I answered, "If I stole your cellphone and gave it to my son and he gave it to my grandson would it make it any less yours? Would it stop you from repossessing it if he had made a lot of calls on it? Would it assuage your indignation?"

I do not seek the approbation of those I teach but I record that there was a burst of applause.

My wife here is considerably younger than myself and of child-bearing age. She is a Malaysian, a Chinese. Of course, she is a Muslim now. I feel no embarrassment about this. She lives in the town where

I visit her. It is not that I am embarrassed to have her at the *madrassah*. It is simpler like this. The great Tungku's mother was a Siamese and his wife a Chinese! Yes, Abdul Rahman himself! This did not come about through the weakness of an infatuation or a lust. It was the strength of his large-mindedness which permitted this union. I do not believe the stories of Jinnah, the father of Pakistan, eating pork but Hambali himself also had a Chinese wife. She was with him when he was caught in Siam. The great Hambali. He is an Indonesian. He was betrayed to the Americans in Ayuttayah, the old city on the same river as Bangkok to the North. The Siamese had nothing to do with it except kick in the door. The Americans and the Singaporeans did it all. They sent him to Jordan and tortured him terribly for two years. Some things he divulged. It would have been super-human not to, even for a Mujahid. What things he revealed, I can tell from who of the Brothers have been caught or eliminated by the Crusaders and their proxy sums.

Us he never betrayed. We are still here. Hambali is now in Cuba. I think the torturing stopped. I admire this man, I admire him. I could fill Ahmed full of false informations and have him be captured. He would not hold out as long as Hambali but long enough to convince his interrogators.

I believe my time here is limited. Not as limited as Ahmed's or Jefri's, but still finite. After a certain stage, they will be better led by one of their own. Then I may return to the bigger world, not to Pakistan, maybe to Egypt or Dubai. First, I will connect them to other links in the chain. We will go to Java, Jolo, Tawi Tawi, Maguindanao. Tariq and I know the former Mujaheedin there personally, the ones who fought in Afghanistan. We will cold forge the new personal links with our students and our old comrades.

Actually, it is not a question of link by link but much easier – joining up separate lengths of chain that are already quite long in themselves. The Caliphate is an idea, a vision, a dream, a crystal as yet unformed. But never forget – the shining diamond of the idea is made from the dirty carbon of life, from the entwining lives of men: their triumphs, their tragedies, their hopes, their disillusionments, their anger, their mistakes – and their virtuousness. God guides them, His Believers, always. They go astray but He brings them back to the path of correctness and cleanliness. I praise God, so be it.

3

Snooky

Snooky can't begin to tell you how much grief the Mac was starting to give her. For four years it had been rock-steady. The little white block had been reliability itself, immune to every virus and worm known to man. I had always thought of it as an extension of me, of my own mind, but purged of the flakier side of Snooky. I guess I thought of it as my super-ego. Now it was as skittish and erratic as Snooky on ketamine. It would stall, crash, throw up gibberish and symbols fit to adorn ancient tomb friezes; then behave properly again. Look, it didn't need a technician, it needed a shrink.

Life at the *pondok* was on the roil as well, on the cusp of changes one could feel but not articulate. We, the Maproom, got lots of spare time. This had been virtually unheard of. But it didn't make you feel relaxed; it got you tensed up. You thought of lulls before storms, darkness before dawn (assuming the breaking light facilitated something you didn't wanna do). Shaykh sent us on exploits which I couldn't – unlike everyone else – regard as minor victories. I thought of them as trial runs – insofar as the Emperor gave kamikaze trial runs; insofar as one's whole preceding life had not been the trial run.

Our fellows were not to know the less than glamorous or flat tering details of our little raid – its fumblings, redundancies, its huge tracts of boredom and momentary flashes of terror. They saw three bold and efficient killers. Jefri's bashful *my pen wry*, "It was nothing," served only to reinforce the aura of calm heroism that had been his in waiting for some time. Iskander's finger-snapping bravado was the perfect contrast. Haji Tariq even persuaded Shaykh to let him keep his iPod, to Imam Umar's utter fury.

As for me, initially, very initially, I did my best to shuck off this undesired mantle. I did not wish to wear SuperMuslim's cape. Shit, no. Then something inside me kicked in. Snooky adored the limelight. It was what every *katoey* strutting her stuff on Saturday night wanted. Look at me, look at me, willya. Never mind that it wasn't exactly the catwalk of Miss Gay Universe or Miss Queen Tiffany's. Never mind I was in a skullcap and not a tiara and wearing a quite different kind of gown (definitely no sequins). Oh, all her life Snooky wanted to belong, just to be accepted, to be loved for what she was. I could only love a straight man. The straights who went with me, drunk or sober pretending to be drunk, would reject me in horror afterwards, as if that single act had turned them into queers. But I never thought of them as fags; they had been with a woman. A woman of the second category – me, Snooky. I so much wanted to merge into the unremarkable crowd and be unexceptionable. And yet . . . that accursed desire for the limelight that was every shemale's tragic flaw, the urge to camp it up to the gallery for all I was worth, undermined all my resolutions.

Then it came to Snooky like a blow to the head – in her new *pondok* role she had it both ways: she was one of the crowd and she was a stand-out, too. I was a *waria* and I was a warrior.

WHAT LOOKED TO everyone else like a series of haphazard events, quite random and entirely unconnected, unfolded to Snooky like a logical strategy. It resembled math. It was like solving text-book exercises, example by example, in ascending grade of difficulty.

Let me begin in order.

Highway police boxes in Siam are generally designed as gigantic motor-cycle helmets, complete with brim and badge. Two men in the small-sized outpost and four, or even six, under the larger brims, could shelter beneath from sun and rain. Of course, the open sides of the North had been replaced by a curved wall of sand-bags which, neatly piled and serrated, with observation slots and loop-holes like so many eyes, mouths, and nostrils, resembled the human face beneath the helmet. It looked like the head of the Scarecrow in the movie of that name.

All Southerners hated the sight of the things. Even my metro-politan self. In the North of Siam it might have been a visual pleasantry which merely ceased to be amusing with time. In the South it was like holding up the dirty finger to us and thinking we'd like it. A Buddha idol would have been less provocative and, of course, a lot easier to vandalise. A drive-by strafing of the police boxes was a relatively common event but the collective wisdom of the Maproom was that hurling several Molotov cocktails made better practice. This was cheaper, left no ballistic fingerprint, was potentially more destructive of property and infrastructure, and the flames and smoke covered your already rapid passage, where even a hail of bullets would provide only momentary distraction to the frantic retaliation of the frightened fuzz.

We made a stack of bombs: *haram* whisky bottles – the Black Cat brand broke more easily than Mekong – filled with gasoline and sugar. Behind these, sacks of non-dairy-creamer which ignited, believe me, with a simply enormous flame. Sometimes Snooky missed the obvious: it took Imam Umar to point out it was what you would normally put in a cup of tea or glass of coffee. "Let them savour that," he chuckled.

Despite dozens of practice runs – when we had spent hours lobbing water-filled bottles from moving bikes against plank targets on the *pondok* meadow – the actual day of our attack, our first few Molotovs missed the police loopholes. The cops were able to get a few pistol shots off against us before Jefri, never the best *takraw* player in the world but typically finding the mark when he really had to, sent a bottle spinning in like a fat five baht coin into a slot. *Whoomf!* out flared the flames. Even with sugar, it wasn't an explosion but a soft incandescence. Actually, it reminded me of the time we'd lit Do-Ann's fart. It had gone straight up her back vertically and not horizontally outwards at us, the audience. Even the sugar sparks of the Molotov were reminiscent of her pubes and stubbly ass-hairs carbonising and borne upwards, ever upwards, on the burning methane.

Nevertheless, soft or hard, explosion or no explosion, out rushed the stamping, rolling, swearing cops. Every shot I fired at them from the pillion missed (and my dodgy wrist ached for days from the recoil) but, baby, baby, did Haji Tariq's secret weapon ever prove the clincher. I hadn't been in on this; I think only Jefri had an inkling and, to judge by the surprise which replaced the triumph on his face, not a complete one.

In the deep ditch behind the police kiosk where excavation works were going on – ironically to lay the big concrete pipe-sections that would deny our likes the opportunity to set culvert-mines – came a series of bangs. As sound-track, they were rather more impressive than the Molotovs. Signal puffs, then gouts of thick black smoke, rose into the smutty air before, with a great roaring, the serrated maw of an iron beast extended itself to view.

Its appearance had the effect of the Sherman or Tiger tanks in *Patton* or *Battle of the Bulge*. Caterpillar tracks rose vertically, then dropped like toppling ladders. Sitting in the cab of what I later learned was called a back-hoe (a good name for any one of The Gang) were Shaykh and Haji Tariq. We all knew straightaway it had, just had, to be them but they were outlandishly accoutred – for our part of the world – in the traditional robes of Meccan sheikhs, including gold-banded head-dresses. Shaykh retained his reflective shades but Haji T. was wearing a latex mask, commonly vended on the sidewalks of Phuket and Samui at Halloween. Accurate down to the hairs of the moustache, it was recognisable at once as the rubberised countenance of that hammer of the Shias, Saddam.

I have to record that Shaykh possessed many qualities but among them were not numbered a sense of humour. Actually, he had totally zero sense of humour, though Haji Tariq did possess a grim semblance. But now Shaykh was laughing! Cackling, in fact. Sitting side by side, our redoubtable pair of teachers and exemplars resembled kids on a fairground ride.

Down went the mechanical arm as Haji T. pulled the lever. Up went the entire police post in the scoop: chairs, plastic water-bottles, a transistor radio still blaring Isarn pop, two walkie-talkies, and a shotgun and an armalite, spilling over the edges of the shovel.

"Get the guns," Jefri ordered Iskander over the rumbling rackety-clack. Poor Iskander scavenged the long firearms but just missed being brained by the rest of the kiosk which, with an expert jerk of his gears, Haji Tariq unceremoniously dropped over the reeling and crawling cops. I could lip-read what Shaykh was shouting. It was, "In the Name of God!"

One of the cops, the fat sergeant-major with the potbelly straining at the tunic, was slower than the others. He could still run faster than the back-hoe, of course, but Snooky was gonna be startled by the monster's manoeuvrability. Haji T. expertly stopped one of the caterpillar tracks by engaging the lever with his metal hook and swinging the roaring beast within its own length as if he had reins. He then turned immediately again in the other direction, employing his – as it were – good hand to heave on the opposite lever, blocking the policemen's getaway.

Down came the shovel. Into it went the portly cop. All heads craned upwards. I felt we were on *Amazing Police Videos*. The cop regained his feet – not so easy if you happened to be wearing patent-leather boots with metal half-moon clackers on the inside of the heels.

Drawing his service pistol, he took aim with Earp-like deliberation at Shaykh, rather than Haji Tariq. The former did not move a muscle. Just before the policeman fired, Haji T. dropped the shovel and sent him sprawling. The bullet shattered the exhaust funnel, sending thick black smoke everywhere as a volley of shots from the pillion-riders of our motor-bikes knocked sparks and rust off the bucket. The Haji was bringing the bucket up again when Shaykh shook his head and signalled to him to dismount. Haji T. did not fully stop the vehicle, but slowed it to a crawl, enabling himself and Shaykh to jump off as it bore the sergeant away at snail's pace. He was standing, looking bemusedly back at us, when I turned precariously with Iskander doing the ton down the road.

If my relation was a movie, I would have invoked artistic licence and left this preceding scene until last because everything that followed it was anti-climactic. Our next exploits would be the comparatively mundane ones of knocking off a police Colonel and a village headman. The former was absolutely more than a little step-up from hoisting a Sergeant-Major in the air and certainly never to be found under the shelter of a highway patrol helmet. For their part, sensible headmen would ensure they were always accompanied by an escort of thugs armed with 12-gauge shotguns. I didn't figure that even 20 years of prayer would save you from a blast from one of those. But the thing was, we planned to catch them unawares and alone. Milky-eyed Imam Umar, unworldly but malicious, cynical but saintly, had a way. "These men," he croaked, "are safe while they follow their course. It is when they leave that path that they become vulnerable."

Haji Tariq looked askance at him – not disrespectfully. He respected Umar as a buffalo might a rattlesnake. "Gambling," said Imam Umar. "Women. Money. These are what lure men to their destruction. Surprise them on their way to those." He nodded grimly as it appeared that he had won Shaykh's approbation, for the latter said, "Imam Umar is, as he so often is, with the Will of God, correct. The resorting to prostitutes is as strong an addiction as that to drink or hashish or gambling."

"I was thinking more of mistresses, minor wives," the Imam swiftly interjected, looking round furtively with his less vitreous eye.

"As it may be," Shaykh said. "The details differ but the results are the same." His already lean face was quite taut. I would have said with fury, except there was no reason for that.

It turned out that the police Colonel was the one with the mistress, while the headman was not a gambler himself but part-owner of an illegal "casino" on the outskirts of town. Haji Tariq had them assassinated expeditiously, bullets in the head from behind: the Colonel as he was parking his Lexus at a discreet distance from his minor wife's apartment, the headman while he was at a coffee-shop counting the take reposing in his money-belt. Neither of them can have known their fate.

Alerted by the shot, the Colonel's mistress had come running. "She didn't seem sorry at all," said Iskander. "Not a single tear. I saw her taking the Rolex off his wrist."

"Fake that one?" inquired Haji Hassan.

"She didn't cry at all, Haji," Iskander repeated patiently.

"No, I mean the watch."

Shaykh looked coldly at Hassan. "There will be no looting of corpses," he said, "not under my leadership. Not while there is breath in my body."

Hassan protested mutely with his hands and shoulders. I did notice he wasn't wearing a watch himself.

WE WEREN'T THAT BIG on acronyms at the *pondok*. It was more of an Indonesian thing. TNI, GOLKAR etc. The Malaysians used them much less, though speaking the same language. And we, Malays at one remove, employed them even more seldom and not just because they were in the Roman, as opposed to Arabic, alphabet. However, one acronym doing the rounds with us was IED. It was on everybody's lips. Haji Tariq started it. It might as well have been H-bomb. We couldn't make one.

It was quite beyond our capabilities. You didn't just, you know, manufacture one as easily as you packed your bag. Shaykh and Haji T. were in the laboratory hours on end, the Haji, to my surprise, deferring to Shaykh in all aspects of this enterprise. So far as I could gather, there were two problems: making it go reliably off from a distance and focussing the blast so it was effective. The pillion-bomb was a sling-shot compared to the moon-shot of this.

Shaykh covered his greenboard with line after line, row after row of his calculations. Three times we went off to a distant meadow to test his theories: all in vain. We had a diffused, ineffective blast. No way would it topple a Siamese armoured car, which was what Shaykh wanted to do; it wouldn't even knock over the galvanised iron sheet we had laid against a post. The object in mind was as symbolic as Shaykh's algebra: to show nothing of the Northern state was invulnerable. All we did was send a few goats scampering.

As we left the field, I heard Haji Tariq say to Shaykh: "No focus. It's got to be a single jet. It must be concentrated. Your copper's too hard or the flame's too soft. We learned that with the T-72 and the BTR's. The only ones that worked were the ones Zia's armourers made for us."

Shaykh was already pretty pissed off. No one else, not even Imam Umar, maybe even especially Imam Umar, or Haji Hassan, could have criticised him with impunity. As it was Haji T., Shaykh merely contented himself with a baleful look, muttering, "That's the problem with the whole Jihad here. No focus."

Haji T. replied, "God willing, you can change it," to which Shaykh, of course, found it impossible to retort.

Shortly before we accepted second-best and settled for planting a culvert-bomb, I was charged by Haji Hassan with the task of purchasing a lithium coin battery for his calculator and three new gel pens which we all found more reliable in our climate than ball-points. "Get green – that is what is used for accounts – and a blue and a red."

"Yes, Haji," I said, delighted to have the chore and some variety in my life. Oh! how the mighty are fallen. Then, in town, I caught a glimpse of a tall, familiar figure in unfamiliar costume: Shaykh in a short-sleeved shirt and loose but well cut trousers alighting from a motorcycle taxi. It must have been an uncomfortable ride; his knees would have been touching his ears. I hesitated, then followed at a discreet distance, telling myself I was protecting him. Or, rather, providing myself with a line if I was observed. He stopped at quite a nice house with a well-tended garden.

Two kids rushed out and embraced his knees. The smell of the pilaff I knew he was fond of emanated from the kitchen. A veiled woman emerged with a cry of delight. They all went in. I found I was smiling, too; the same ashamed smile that shmaltz in a crappy movie could extort from me in the darkness of the preview theatre: a tribute, y'know, to the inherent power of the medium. I used to check out the other faces in the gloom to see how many other sophisticates in their soft chairs were as vulnerable to corn as I was and it was this reflex that saved me from discovery now in a completely different situation. Rounding the corner behind me, clearly as Shaykh's rearguard against surveillance and entrapment, was one of our very youngest juniors of about 13. Only the fact that he had his juvenile nose and fingers in a bag of entirely non-*halal* salted, deep-fried scorpions and silkworms saved Snooky.

I retired backwards round the corner, then legged it. Even while doing so, I racked my brains for an explanation of what I had seen. Then I had it. I figured this was the family of a martyred Mujahid whom Shaykh was consoling. Not just that – supporting through brotherly alms as well as his inspiring presence. I thought how much I admired him, as well as feared him; I thought how he exemplified the noblest attributes of sternness and mercy, usually unattainable by a mortal. With a moist eye I remembered how he had extended his compassion to me during my ordeal when I was being put to the proof.

Back at the *pondok*, Haji Hassan brought me down to earth with a querulous scolding. In my stupor, I had bought an LR32 coin battery and a black pen with a green cap on it.

He was still irritable when we went on our next, or third, exercise. Which was to say, the culvert-bombing. Ah, the culvert-bombing. We would all rather draw a veil over that. Mixing the diesel and fertiliser for this with dairy-creamer and birdshit was child's play by comparison with manufacturing an AP shaped-charge. Making mayo and getting the proportions of yolk and oil correct actually required a steadier hand and nicer judgment if the mix was not to be spoiled.

The only problems lay in concealment and surprise. And for this task Shaykh chose Haji Hassan and myself. It was a little baffling to Snooky until she reflected he had selected what he would think of as the slyest, if least practical, members of the tribe. That offered food for thought.

Haji Hassan had no intention of defiling his hands with manual labour, excavating spoil and putting the device in the culvert. If Shaykh thought good Muslims abhorred cities, Haji H. wished to put as much distance between himself and his bumpkin *bumiputra* students as he could. He assuredly did not think of himself as a bucolic son of the soil and the two-inch long nails on his pinkie fingers were as the horns of the most recalcitrant bull.

I was supervising the kids at their digging after the prayer break – the Haji still telling his beads in extra devotion on his mat, a posture I was sure he intended to sustain for at least a further half hour – when I became aware we were under observation.

Two kids, only slightly older than our own earliest intake, were regarding me from the boughs of an acacia tree which I had mentally earmarked as a dummy observation-post. Let the remnants of the army patrol waste their ammunition on that.

I beckoned to the boys. Although they were Malays and we were all united in our detestation of our oppressors, I still felt it advisable to come up with the ready-made alibi that we were drain-repairers. Looking, just looking, at Haji H. this was not a fiction Snooky was gonna invest with more than a quorum of conviction. Haji Hassan could have been many things: scholar, executioner, judge, sage. Hole-digger was not one of them.

The two boys appeared extremely reluctant to come over. Perhaps they were frightened of being sodomised. Snooky couldn't blame them. I waved in a friendly way before sauntering over. I was encouraged they remained.

One of the reasons we had chosen this particular spot was that the culvert was just round a bend where vehicles had to slow down. The boys were on this corner and as I rounded it I realised why they had not fled my approach. Behind them were a dozen bearded and heavily armed men, far more mature and formidable than my own youthful detachment. I had only a moment's panic before I realised they must be *juwae* like ourselves. Or not like ourselves. Then I panicked more.

"Who are you and what are you doing?" asked the biggest, darkest, and most hirsute in no very friendly tone. I noted they were the kind of group where supremacy was based on physical presence rather than intelligence or moral authority.

"God Willing," I replied, "we are about the same business as you." I had quickly noted they were all provided with pick-axes and spades as well as a reel of electrical wire and some rusty barrels which probably contained similar proportions of ammonium nitrate and diesel as ours did, assuming they'd been using the same excellent Crusader search engine.

"Then in the name of God, go and find your own spot," he answered truculently. "With the women." Snickers from his band. Even with facial hair and in the costume of the convinced, I could be outed. Annoyance made me territorial. "No! You go and find your own spot. We got here first."

Weapons were already being raised when six Maproom stalwarts came round the corner, too. Expressions of astonishment on normally phlegmatic countenances, followed by frantic fumbling for handguns under robes (we were not as well-off for small arms as the competition clearly was).

"Stop! Stop!" I shouted in unison with the leader of the other group who was clearly nowhere near as trigger-happy as he would like strangers to assume. Just then Haji Hassan appeared, his age, bearing, costume, and entirely assumed severity of countenance inspiring the respect among our fellow Mujaheedin that guns could not.

"In the name of God, identify yourselves at once!" he snapped, as if he were dealing with so many jungle, not desert, djinn.

"We're, we're *Barisan Islam Pattani*, Haji," stammered one of the youths whom I'd initially spotted in the boughs of the acacia. Haji Hassan scowled at them short-sightedly through his pince-nez.

"Don't you recognise us, Haji?" asked one of the acacia boys piteously. "We're from the King Faisal school in Aceh." Haji Hassan's face remained irate. "Haji, you used to lecture us on Islamic Finance on Tuesdays. We still remember. Muslims cannot receive interest from a bank but they are permitted by the Prophet, peace be upon his head, to accumulate capital gains."

"Oh-oh!" said Hassan now, with all the false joviality of the slant-eyed Santa Claus at my favourite Bangkok mall. "You must be . . ."

"The Abdullah twins, Haji."

"So you are, so you are."

The leader of the troupe was clearly impressed, despite himself, but his nervousness also made him impatient and, together with his desire to be respectful to a dangerous Imam, inclined him to cut the ludicrous figure of a man desperate to relieve himself with propriety but discovering himself without a lamp-post or a tree. "Haji, we only have a few hours to set a bomb under the soldiers . . ."

"Well, we were first here," replied Haji Hassan with deceptive mildness, "which, God willing, is nine-tenths of the law."

"I think you mean possession, Haji," ventured one of his former pupils, greatly daring. Haji Hassan chose to let this go, but the big, hairy fellow – regaining his natural obstinacy – now insisted, "We have our orders from our leaders and we must obey them."

Haji Hassan reflected, then brightened. "By all means, you may dig the hole," he said. "We for our part will keep lookout for you, er, protect your, er, flank."

"Thank you, thank you, Haji, thank you so much."

"Think nothing of it. Er. *My pen wry.*"

Haji H. went to sit under a tree with a Kuala Lumpur newspaper and a clove cigarette while Jefri and Iskander set out sentries. I dared not only to sit by the Haji but to say, "Haji Hassan, are we not profiting from the efforts of others while we sit idle and enjoy the fruit of their labours? That is surely the spirit, if not the letter, of the Prophet's injunction against usury?"

To which Haji Hassan's startling reply was to go, "Hee, hee, hee!"

It was not unpleasant, I have to record, watching the big brother Mujaheedin dig a deep hole. Certainly they accomplished it much faster than we could have done. At the end of two hours, I turned to speak to the Haji but found him fast asleep, rasping lightly, with the newspaper over his mouth and nose against the flies and his pince-nez precarious as ever but still on the bridge of his impressive nose.

"Ha-er. Show the client in," he burbled in his somnolence as I lightly shook his shoulder. "What? What?" he stammered.

"They are filling in the hole, Haji. They will be finished soon. What are your instructions?"

"These are for the depositor, er, for the client to give upon maturity of fixture."

"Haji, no. We are here on the hillside overlooking our ambush-point. What are your orders? Will we let the other Mujaheedin detonate the bomb?"

"Ah, ah. Let me think."

This was bad. Usually the ancient Haji was glibness itself in class but on the rare occasions he came out with this, it meant either a protracted interval or no reply forthcoming at all. However, on this occasion self-preservation was a powerful concentrator of his thoughts, for he said, "If God is Willing, let them have the distinction of springing the trap on the Infidel Northerners but let Ibroheng and Maruding mingle with their number in the aftermath and participate."

"But Ibroheng and Maruding are the least reliable among us. Maruding was a drug-addict before and in jail for thieving and Ibroheng even peddled *dada*."

"Then you may join them if you wish, Ahmed, and, God Willing, inspire them. For then," said Haji Hassan, with eyes sparkling behind their little aids, "there would be three of you."

"God is Great, Haji Hassan. With His Aid just the pair of them can suffice."

To cut a long story short, Maruding panicked and fired his pistol early. The mine the other group set also failed to go off (whereas one of Iskander's or Inginir's would not have) and everyone had to run as fast as they could from the furious Siamese soldiers. As Haji and the rest of us were at some distance, we were not in any danger of being caught but Jefri waited for our pair on his moped. Ibroheng had been hit in the leg but hopped along with encouraging agility. It was all the more surprising he bled to death on the way home.

Jefri smiled a happy smile at the *pondok* next morning. "He has joined the martyrs in Paradise." I was a bit disappointed in Jefri. Iskander said to me, "If he had been wounded too badly to bring back, Jefri would have had to shoot him. The torture is bad. Maybe only you could withstand it, Ahmed. That's why Jefri is happy."

Shaykh actually looked no more sombre than usual. I had been expecting him to bawl us out over the royal fuck-up. Maybe it was because Haji Hassan had been with us. He said to him gravely, "Your life is precious, Hassan. Remember that. Do not jeopardise it, or we are all high and dry."

"God willing, I only wanted to contribute outside the classroom. I thought there was little peril."

Shaykh went so far as to lay hands on Haji Hassan. He actually tapped him on the temple. "Your contribution is in here, Haji. It has been entrusted to you. Never forget that. We will never be parted again. We are like the two hemispheres of the plutonium – one is useless without the other."

HAJI HASSAN was, of course, highly respected within the *pondok* as scholar and teacher, as *kyai*. The Maproom set, however, whilst never explicitly formulating an adverse opinion of Hassan, were less sold on him. It was perfectly possible to be both saintly and incompetent while practical qualities were, as you can imagine, coming to be more esteemed with us. I was, therefore, not the only one to be implicitly rebuked by Shaykh's words to him.

I explained to Iskander and Inginir: "You have men of action and men of thought, like our two Hajis, Tuan Tariq and Tuan Hassan. But men like Shaykh are such an inspiration to their followers because they partake of the qualities of both. You have to be both a scholar and a warrior and you have to be both a Believer and a scientist. That's what Shaykh was saying."

To which commentary of mine Inginir replied, "God Willing, I try, I shall always try."

What was becoming clear to me was that our activity occupied a tiny space, both of actual physical territory and of the world's attention: we were a niche insurgency, a boutique Jihad. Our petty struggle was highly parochial. In one sense that might induce a strategist to think our victory was all the more achievable. We did not compete for strategic territory; we did not have a Suez Canal, a Straits of Hormuz, or even (like Haji Hassan's homeland, Aceh) stand at the top of the Straits of Malacca.

We had rubber, some tin, and the only oil we possessed was palm oil. Not the raw materials of the future. The problem was we were so insignificant as to be highly undesirable. We wanted to join our Malayan brothers but the Malaysian government wanted no truck with us – all trouble and no contribution. Then while our insurrection appeared as multi-headed as the Hydra (and therefore unkillable) another way of looking at it was that the different groups of Mujaheedin were rival predators competing on the same hunting grounds. If you believed the laws of nature, some of us had to go extinct. Shaykh first mooted, then quietly dropped, a notion of us joining with other groups of God's warriors to raid the government's southern arsenal.

Someone had been very smart to bring Shaykh and Haji Tariq

to our part of the world. They plugged us in to the wider picture. We needed outside help if our freedom, that overused word *merdeka*, was to be achievable. It could only be meaningful within the Caliphate. And my own small part in it could be summed up in terms not totally dissimilar to Shaykh's: from global entertainment to global Jihad.

About three weeks later we read, just like everyone else, just like the ordinary citizens of Bangkok, that the government arsenal in the Deep South (e.g. where we carried on our existences, which seemed central enough) had been raided by over 100 armed insurgents. Hundreds of rifles and thousands of rounds of ammunition had been purloined. The embarrassed looking Colonel in charge of the depot muttered to the camera something about serial numbers. To Snooky it seemed about as useful as knowing the DNA of an escaped dog.

Shaykh had more original ideas for us than this glorified piece of shoplifting. Our brothers in Jihad, our rivals, too, had cut down a banyan tree; we would fell a frangipani. "Phuket!" squeaked Imam Umar with a glee that would have been wicked, except he was a priest, and turning his milky eyes skywards. Cataracts not of milk but foaming blood!

Like all the brightest ideas, Shaykh's notion left you wondering why nobody had thought of it before since it seemed so obvious in retrospect. We all knew of the Bali disco bombings carried out by our brothers in Jemaah Islamiyah. Indonesia had a small tourism industry. We had one of the largest on earth. Why had we never targeted Westerners before?

What foreigners did in Siam was considerably more abominable than what they did in Bali. If we wanted to hurt the Siamese politicians, and we did, we did, the place to hurt them was in the pocket. It was as if the Brothers had been fighting a giant in a physically uneven combat and neglected to kick him between the legs.

"Ever been to Tin Town?" Haji Tariq asked me brusquely. I knew he meant Phuket with its Chinese mining past. I knew Shaykh didn't hate Chinese or Christians as much as our Indonesian imams did. "No," I replied. "Only Hua Hin. A lot, actually, Haji."

Haji looked at Shaykh, who shook his head. "Too far," he said almost wistfully. "We can't get the requisites past all the checkpoints."

"Boat?" ventured the Haji.

With a rare, a very rare, flash of sarcasm, Shaykh said, "You go 200 miles across the Gulf of Thailand in an open boat, if you want to."

Haji T. looked surprised; actually quite difficult with one eye and a huge beard. "Is it that far?"

We all smiled. Everyone, absolutely everyone, in the Maproom had the Lat and Long of the Gulf clocked. It would be our village pond in the Caliphate. Shaykh sighed.

Haji Tariq said innocently, "Train?"

Shaykh blanched. I thought his reaction disproportionate. Thai railways ran ancient American rolling-stock (which made you feel you were in a romantic old b&w movie). It clanked, lurched, and banged but the railway offered the most punctual and accident-free transport in the Kingdom. An old guy with a hand-crank came round before Chumphon on the Bangkok-Hat Yai run to turn your seat and the luggage rack above into comfy, daintily curtained bunk beds with integral ladders. Total privacy, complete discretion. More than once I'd caught someone's glance and taken advantage of the secret space, but that's another story.

"Very safe, Shaykh," I contributed blithely, aglow with tender memories. "No one gets left behind." For answer he stood up and cracked me across the cheek. It was open-handed and it didn't really hurt so much as shock. Nevertheless, I burst into tears. Shaykh stalked out the room, followed at a prudent interval and distance by Haji Tariq. Snooky still doesn't understand what she said so wrong but it didn't get her dropped from the trip.

Haji Tariq did get his way in one thing. A group with the explosives went the short distance up the West Coast to Phuket by fishing-boat. This was a week in advance. If caught, they were to say they were going blast-fishing and accept the prison sentence without a murmur. All our teachers knew they could depend on us to do that. Wow, that was the very least of the expectation. Greater sacrifice would not, Haji T. told us, necessarily be required but, of course, we should all be prepared for martyrdom so that the "great opportunity should not find us surprised." It would not be a "one-way mission" (the surprising euphemism of Shaykh) because the Siamese authorities and the foreigners would be unsuspecting, there never having been a precedent.

Well, you could certainly have knocked Snooky down with a

feather when Imam Umar let the cat out of the bag with a cackle and told me I was to lead the charge.

"But, but . . . I've never been to Phuket," I said.

"And when you get to Paradise, that will be the first time, too, *koti*," Tariq rejoined to the Imam's frowning disapproval.

Don't say I didn't take my responsibilities seriously. I might be an objector but I was still conscientious. A day before the boat set off, I made a reconnoitring expedition of the resort with Iskander. A rehearsal of some kind would have been standard procedure but I decided to forego it as too risky.

Actually, you could say there were several resorts on the one island: there was the old town in the centre, more or less *farang*-free; there was the biggest public tourist beach with its strip of bars, dance-halls, and restaurants now stretching back to the enclosing hills; then, along the coast, two quieter beaches with smaller tourist development. In fact, it was all at extremes. The first beach was a neon hell, throbbing the whole 24 hours and probably living up to our Hajis' and Imams' worst expectations, while the third had no tourist development at all beyond a forlorn and antiseptic five star which was quieter than a Bangkok mosque outside prayer time.

Iskander and I wore Southern costume and stayed outside the discos. They were very empty. I saw a group of ladyboys outside The Shark – provincials compared to Do-Ann and the Gang but with much better rhinoplasties and boob-jobs than us, thanks to the local hospital.

The next morning we checked out the little port at the very southern tip of the island, the one with the enormous mile-long pier as disproportionately elongated as a new septum in a flat Isarn nose. The boat had arrived and we would carry this news back as Shaykh was adamant that there should be no traceable cellphone calls linking us to the event.

At the *pondok*, Iskander told Haji T. a blast of ball-bearings down one of the larger side-streets would cause more havoc than a bomb in an empty disco. Haji looked disappointed and started talking about walls focussing an explosion. Snooky figured he was disappointed we wouldn't match Bali. Shaykh waved him down with weary flaps of his long hands, like some cynical stork. "This is the very reason we sent Iskander and Ahmed. He knows," he said, smiling at me. Earlier, he had personally opened a durian for me with his own little silver fruit-knife.

But fortune was to favour the Haji. I was surfing Phuket sites when something that would have also attracted my attention in the old days caught my eye. A famous English entertainment conglomerate was opening the biggest disco floor in Asia near the edge of town. I'd actually seen it and assumed it a hangar. In fact, the big foreign firm had swallowed the local company which owned the Cha-Am disco where Do-Ann had got hit by the stray shot. The opening night would see the disco packed. We could bomb the inside and get a stupendous result. I went running for the Haji and the rest was history.

As always, we travelled separately and on different buses. This time we were not in our white gowns and skullcaps. I was wearing duds purchased by Iskander: a black T-shirt emblazoned with a huge red tongue and a pair of those baggy dun-coloured, knee-length shorts with cargo-pockets, zips, poppers, and tassels. "I thought you'd like them," said Iskander, trying to look hurt. "Yes, suits you, Ahmed," said Jefri, who was sitting this one out at the *pondok*. We had but one mirror at the school (good thing, I sometimes thought, as I'd be the only one with a reflection) but I replied, "You guys have no taste. The bigger the bling, the lamer the thing."

When I went to the john at the bus station half-way to Phuket I did see myself in the mirror: tall and kinda manly in a vicious way. Those macho shorts didn't usually suit Siamese boys but they went with my dizzy legs. Dizzy was what I went. Then I fainted. When I came to, Inginir was splashing water on my face. He looked so worried I knew it couldn't relate to myself.

"It's OK, Inginir," I said, speaking in English. He and Iskander were the hippest of the brothers and had the most English. "I'm cool, I'm cool," I said, using the Tarantino line. "It's got nothing to do with nerves about the mission. It's a, er, personal issue. OK?"

"Oh, *my pen wry*," said Inginir at once, reassured straightaway and extending me *kreng jai* – heartfelt consideration.

"*Insh' Allah*," I concluded as Haji Tariq, disguised, despite his protests, as a Sikh, came in for a leak in his nattily creased slacks and short-sleeved shirt and tie. We were all supposed to act like we were strangers but Haji's glare was downright personal. Purely as a subterfuge for the assortment of leather sandals and rubber flipflops visible under the doors of the squat-pits, I remarked to the Haji, "Dig the duds, dude!"

He was still smouldering, figuratively, when we alighted in Phuket Old Town. It was funny. The entire Maproom would have martyred themselves for Shaykh. But a little stiffness and tiredness after a five hour coach run, a smidgeon of tedium, and all discipline was gone.

We all piled on to the same microlet to take us to our lodgings instead of waiting for different conveyances and it was all I could do by scowls and significant nods to stop everyone from engaging in general conversation.

"Where do you come from, Big Bro'?" I asked the Haji – for the pleasure of demoting him – and was aghast when he replied, "Waziristan." Not that our driver could have had the faintest understanding where it was.

At the lodging-house was therapeutic Siamese massage. That I ordered for all of us in a communal room, clad neck to wrist to toe for decency in baggy cotton suits, our joints cracking and popping in fusillade as the blind attendants made Chinese script of our bodies.

Next day I took Tariq to the port where, at the end of our ten mile ride, he became embroiled in an altercation with the microlet driver over the exorbitant fare which ended with him half-pulling the driver out the window of his tiny cab. "Haji! Haji!" I implored him, "please, people are looking!"

As we started for the infinite length of the pier/causeway, he struck me on the shoulder and hissed, "Mr Singh, you eunuch! Call me Mister!" Rubbing my arm, I had to admit the justice of the reproach, but came back with, "Er, Mr Singh, tomorrow how about taking off the eye-patch?"

During the pedal-trike ride, the half-mile down the pier to the boat, we did not exchange another word. We spent a few hours preparing the explosives, interspersed by two prayer-breaks, then returned to the boarding house in the Old Town. I checked the net again on my temperamental Mac – the grand opening was the next day.

Our plan was simple but effective. Getting explosives inside the hall would be risky and difficult. Driving a van up or even leaving one parked was very easy but would cause less casualties than detonating a bomb inside – unless there were people milling in the street. Therefore, we needed to get everyone inside to leave – and the quickest way to do this was with a bomb scare or a fire.

"Make it both," said Haji Tariq shortly. Sometimes, Snooky thought, the simple mind is the best mind.

From our point of view there was one good thing: inside a Thai discotheque there exists no shortage of combustible materials. Come to think of it, I could say the same about the cavernous venues in which I had enjoyed my Manila cavorts. If you wanted to burn a bunch of people to death, no better place existed. It might have been purpose-designed for it: enough ceiling height and volume to feed a blaze but insufficient ventilation thereafter for breathing to be possible or smoke to escape; loads of couches and cushions stuffed full of foam; shiny balls and streamers; sufficient dangling cable to climb Everest. The clincher to this death trap was a problem for us, however. Insufficient fire-exits, chained bar-levers on those that existed. Narrow passageways. All this was great for trapping people, not so good if you wanted to channel them into an outside killing-zone.

"We need a small blaze that looks under control," mused Inginir, "so that people don't all stampede at once but still leave."

"Let off a flare," suggested our boat captain, a Maproom boy from a fishing *kampong* south of Trang. "That's intense but very confined."

"Gas," said Haji Tariq, making all heads turn. "That's what gets you out of a confined space. Cave or house, all the same."

We were all silent, thinking of how the Haji had come by this piece of knowledge. In the end we plumped for an eye-irritant, nothing as formal as tear-gas or CS, cooked up by Inginir from an obnoxious cocktail of LPG, paint-thinner, and (to be kept dry and separate until the last moment), swirling red chilli flakes.

The great day, or rather evening, came. I requested Haji Tariq to stay on the boat but he refused. I looked him over in despair. You could have decked him out in medallions and leather trousers; he was still no one's idea of a raver.

At the disco the whole scene had changed. The street was jam-packed. It would be empty again tomorrow. The business enterprise would probably be a failure but for a few hours it was the place to be. I recognised fashionable faces: starlets, *look khreung* singers, a famous comedian. And . . . there was some security. Not a lot, pretty vestigial, but an upgrade from non-existent. I decided to ditch the idea of LPG and paint-thinner. "Get two more big packets of the hottest flakes," I told a junior. "Will we be able to eat it all, Big Brother Ahmed?" he asked. "Just get it," I replied. Off he went. On the whole I had been getting implicit obedience. Maybe it was our system – submission's name itself, y'know – maybe it was a question of the uniform, not the man, the skullcap not the tranny, or maybe it was the testosterone pills.

I had not lost my old touch, not with facial hair and a voice octaves lower. No one had circumvented disco security better than our Gang.

"And where are you going, Big Bro'?" a bouncer asked me. For the first time it struck me that the studs and leather wristlets on these would-be heavies were absurd as intimidation. "Gonna smoke these, aren't I?" I replied, flourishing the chilli bags. "I'm with Noi on the sounds, OK?" There were more Nois in Bangkok – of all three genders – than Johns in New York.

Two of the bouncers laughed. The third wasn't more conscientious, just meaner-spirited and to his cavils I countered, "Ask the *farang* guy, then." Well, he wasn't gonna do that, not in a million years, and I was in and free like some spiky virus in search of a receptor. It was quick work locating the main ventilator intake and aircon-grille – the safest place for us to light up a joint in a disco. When I looked at the party streamers and bunting overhead, I knew all I had to do was stand on tiptoe and wave a 10 baht lighter with the flame switched to jet. The place started to fill at a relatively unsophisticated hour – they had to make the print deadlines in Bangkok. In the gloom I recognised a few familiar faces, including the *farang* who'd given me my first job on his give-away ad-sheet, 1066. I found I wasn't too troubled about what might happen to him. Next moment I had what would be the second biggest surprise of the night (nothing compared to what was gonna be the biggest). I was in denial even as I saw it – the swarthy, bearded, eye-patched face of Haji Tariq at my elbow.

"Haji!"

"Get on with it."

"What are you doing here. How did you get past the security?"

Haji's teeth glowed in the ultra-violet as he drew his finger across his throat.

"Jesus Christ!"

"What? What? What did you say, you accursed *koti*?"

"Nothing, nothing, Haji."

He took me by the throat. His grip was superhumanly strong, like a mechanical device. "I've never trusted you, you eunuch. The Boss is easily taken in. He's too good for this world. But me, I know dirt when I see it. You don't fool me."

"No, Haji. You're wrong, you're wrong."

"Set the blaze, the tear-gas. Do whatever you have to do. I am telling Inginir to set the van off in five minutes."

"Fifteen, Haji."

"Ten." And he was gone.

After he had shoved his burly way through the dancers, people turning angrily round and then thinking better, much better, of it, I wondered why I'd tried to delay the moment of truth. Now I wanted to get away as quickly as I could, before they discovered the bodies of the security guards, before Haji told Inginir to let everything off.

I had torn open the cellophane on the chilli flakes when I got the night's biggest shock. There was a short-haired, female, *farang* face in front of me.

Avril.

I felt fainter than I had in the bathroom of the coach station.

"Hey, likewise, gorgeous. Did the earth move for thee, Siamese?" She patted the couch beside her. "Siddown."

She was drunk as a skunk. I recognised all the classic Avril signs. She didn't go completely red in the face the way I and many Asians did but the flush was confined to the bridge of her nose and the lower forehead. The nose I had so often envied. "That's a 20,000 baht nose you got for free, girl," I would say and she'd reply, "Yeah, with other things you don't have."

Now Avril, the real flesh and blood Avril, not the idealised friend of my memories, patted the space beside her more insistently. There was very little time to waste; the clock was moving against us all the time. I sat. My body was still but my mind was speeding, speeding. As a preparatory gesture, I took Avril's hand. I ran my lines quickly through my head but I had to compose them myself: this scene could not be plagiarised, my uniquely crazy situation had never been imagined by Southern, Schrader, or Sorkin.

I saw my words as black characters on my screenwriting software: Avril had to trust me for old time's sake. Completely trust me. I knew something she didn't. I was risking my life for her. In turn she would have to promise not to betray me. Leave with me now and keep everything completely secret, never tell a living soul about it.

All this took about three seconds to go through my mind. Believe me? Just as Snooky was thinking, "Hell, Avril keep a secret? She couldn't keep the smallest one for five minutes. I might as well place a three column ad in the *Bangkok Post*." Yah, just as I was thinking I couldn't leave her to die, be ripped into pieces and charred (could I?), she squeezed my hand back.

"Hey, you're fast," she said flirtatiously, then put her warm hand on the thin fabric encasing my thigh (the long, slim thighs she so envied).

It dawned on me. Avril didn't know who the fuck I was!

"I don't know why I like you so much," she said dreamily, "but I do. Call it love at first sight." She held her face up at me from below, angling for a kiss.

"Oh, you slut, you," she'd tell me in the old days when I would recount to her – in copious, technicolor detail – my beachfront adventures at Hua Hin or Jomtien before she would tell me about her own totally (by comparison) innocent weekend, marked by insipid moments of hetero affection rather than the chemically-fuelled and anonymous lusts of mine.

So now I knew she was hoping for me to brush my lips against her neck which, gritting my teeth, I did. *Shalimar*, at *eau de parfum* concentration. The copycat. It had been Snooky's signature fragrance when she couldn't afford the Chanel *No 19*. I remembered telling Avril that the Chanel *No 5* she favoured was for old ladies. "Catherine Deneuve uses it," she would counter and I would say, "Auntie Catherine Who?"

"Let me freshen your drink," I said gallantly, disentangling myself from her.

I found myself the nearest ladyboy. "Big Sista," I said. "I need Knockout Drops. And quick with it. I'll pay you what you want."

"Why the fuck are you asking me?" she snarled indignantly.

"Because you'd look just great in a pharmie's white coat with your stilettos throwing your ass up and no knickers on. C'mon. Gimme a break. I'm desperate. Three thousand, no questions."

"OK, good-looking, one deck of Rohypnol coming up."

"Nix, Mary. Not date rape pills. Animal tranquies. Kayo drops. The kind you starch your Johns with. And fast. Make sure it's the real stuff. It's 4,000 if you're back in two minutes."

"Two seconds is OK? Here." She pulled the phial from her bag. "Come back later. If your girlfriend's out of it, she won't be able to put your dick in her mouth and I can do it better than her conscious anyhow. I do the best BJs in the world."

"So do I."

"Get you, *tea ruck*."

Thirty seconds later I was handing Avril the spiked drink.

"Have we met before? You're kinda familiar, your voice and all."

I deepened it. "Maybe in my dreams."

"Hey, you've got cute lines. Are you Thai? You're kinda tall for a local guy."

"Drink up, Avril. You've got a lot of catching up to do."

"I'd say I had a head-start on you with the drinks." She put her glass down without touching it. "Hey, how d' you know my name?"

There was nothing for it. I turned away and put the rest of the phial on my tongue. Then I thrust it into her mouth. Ugh! I didn't want to leave my tongue too long in her mouth both for reasons of disinclination and, more cogently, because I didn't wanna pass out. In my enthusiasm I'd probably given her enough to fell a bull-elephant.

"Hey, don't tease," Avril remonstrated. Then she frowned. I do believe she was remembering. Voice, height, (dare I say it?) wit. We clicked. We had always clicked and we were a couple who were clicking now.

I caught her glass as it was dropping from her fingers and laid her on the couch. I was in such a hurry to tear open the cellophane wrapping of the chilli flakes, I got some up my nose and in the eyes. Ouch! I was already sneezing helplessly as I poured it into the air-intake but none of the bulk would irritate my mucous linings further: it was sucked in as if by Do-Ann's magic mouth.

I had to get Avril outta the disco. Already prone, she'd be trampled in the rush to escape. But I also had to lay her down well away from the van-bomb. I put Avril over my shoulder in the same fireman's hoist as I'd carried Crab and Do-Ann when they'd OD'd on smack. "Gangway! Gangway!" I called, "*Farang* chick's passed out!" This had the desired effect of creating a pathway and also having the curious (e.g. everyone) craning to look at my cargo rather than me, specifically finding Avril's panties – which I took pains to display – more interesting than my skirt-shrouded face.

Out in the street, I found the pondoks verily hopping in agitation. Haji T. had ordered them to set the timer and scamper. Inginir, bless him, in the back of the van and inaccessible to the Haji's wrathful fists and feet, had refused. Now he started the clock, slid the doors shut, and still had the presence of mind to saunter away.

"What, in the name of God," asked the Haji in a very tight and dangerous voice, "have you got over your shoulder?"

I was going to say it was a trophy, like a fox stole, then thought better of it. "Just some drunken floozie, Haji. To cover my face as I left. There was CCTV at the exit we hadn't noticed."

"Why didn't you cut her throat in the van?"

"I didn't carry a blade, Haji," I said reasonably, "the security frisk you at the door," but I quietly lowered Avril and propped her against a lamp-post. "We need to get to the boat, Haji, as quickly as we can."

Inginir had not set up an initiation by cellphone but by clock as we did not want to be traced to the port.

The Haji fiddled in his pocket. "My knife, my Peshawar blade. Where is it when I need it?" I was already appalled but my blood froze when he unwrapped his turban and said, "Strangle her with that."

I had brought Avril from the frying-pan of potential harm to the fire of certain death.

I shoved Tariq as hard as I could – thanks for the testosterone, Haji. "The cops, Haji! The Tourist Police! Move!" I think he was quite prepared to make his stand then and there except that Inginir came back and helped me pull him away. At that moment Avril slid off the post and bumped her head on the kerb. I went back, picked her up, and took her at a run 800 metres down the road before making her safe in a shielded alleyway with an illegally-parked car protecting the entrance. She mumbled a few indistinct swear-words (she liked to do it in French), then, "Get your cotton-picking hands off me, you goons. I'm Press, I'm the film critic of the *New Sentinel*."

"Should've left you in the disco, honey," I thought as I caught

Inginir up, "you stole my job." But I was smiling. Better Avril than one of the illiterate *farangs*.

I could already hear the beginnings of commotion behind us. Clearly the chilli had worked. For once both Siamese and *farang* were suffering equally from the prick of *prik*. Inginir whispered to me, "I gave us 15 minutes longer than we were told." For answer, I squeezed his hand.

We were over the hill and in the valley when it went off. What a result for Inginir! It was of a completely different order from our under-the-seat moped bombs. It was like the end of the world. The ground shook beneath us. Then a huge red glow appeared over the top of the mountain. What can I say? It was more like a volcano erupting than just a car bomb.

"What the f-. Uh. What did you put in it this time, Inginir?"

"Just the usual, Tuan Ahmed. Diesel, fertiliser, peroxide, quite a lot of non-dairy creamer in cloth sacks, ball-bearings. OK, there was a lot of it. The van was sitting right down on its suspension I had so much in there."

The Haji rolled over from the front passenger seat to shake Inginir's hand. "You have done a great thing, my son!" he exclaimed. After this, the thunderclap of the blast, taking till now to reach us, was like the endorsement of God.

We embarked at the port without further incident. It was dead quiet, no one around. We might have been in a different country, not just ten miles away. The boat's exhaust already burbled attentively in the water. Haji threw off and we were away on our magic carpet.

By dawn we had Satun town off the port bow and were ready to say our prayers with more than ordinary fervour. We might as well have been off the rings of Saturn for all the chance of retribution finding us amidst the spray and sunbeams. The pondoks surrendered themselves to joy. They basked in the sun and, even more warming, the beam of approbation on the Haji's face. What did I feel? In the unpolluted, fresh, and salty air, my clothes damp with abrasive spray, I felt scrubbed and alive, clean and exultant. To possess life was justification in itself. Yah, Snooky felt clean: alive and clean.

Umar

In the Name of God, the Lenient, the Merciful!

I can no longer tell you where I come from. I am jesting, of course. But in the old days I used to hop backwards and forwards over the frontier so many times, I felt like a hare or a kangaroo. Not to mention the frog's leap over the Straits to Aceh when the need really arose. In the old days the crossing from Siam to Malaya was as easily done as said. It was simplicity itself. It was like a child's game on a chalked-out grid, where one quick step to a certain square gave you sanctuary from the touches of others (meaning the Siamese authorities). In those times there was thick jungle. Even 20 years ago it was thick as the locks still on my head then. We have thinned together, the hills and my scalp. They talk about conservation and saving the forests for the orang-utan. They call it the rain-forest now. What happened to the jungle? You could have cut down as much of that as you wanted, as far as your servant was concerned. It was impenetrable. It was not convenient. You could stand on a mountain-top, watching the boys carrying the heavy things and glad you were not doing it, but still wet with sweat, and see miles and miles of jungle rolling before you with the sea nowhere in sight. They say Malaya is narrow – narrower than the minds of the Chinese – but you might as well be in the middle of Borneo or the Amazon. You could not see the sea! Ha, ha! My English is as good as that of the Indians, those cheating *Kling*.

When the heat got too much for us in Siam, we looked for shade in Malaya, in Kelantan. Why not? We were among our brethren: we spoke the same language, wore the same clothes, looked exactly the same. We believed in the only God. They sympathised in our persecutions at the hands of the Siamese. At that time, even the Malaysian government did. Our lands and people longed to be joined. We should have been as conjoined as the famous Siamese twins.

Whether Malaysians, Indonesians like Hassan, or – as I am – of Patani Darussalam under the oppression of the Siamese, we are all Malays. This is more than I can say for Tariq or His Lordship. I cannot bring myself to say his name, the foolish name they call him. I would whip them for that, if I could. Alright, I will say it. I will say it but once to show I am above these petty issues of nomenclature. I am not jealous of the one they call our Shaykh. It would be ridiculous to say that. This Caliphate of his – it will only make trouble. I would be happy if Narathiwat, Jala, Singgora, and Pattani were conjoined to Kelantan in the manner of the old Sultanate and we left it at that.

Why did our Arabian benefactors make him the head of us here? Over my head, I mean. I had served many years. I am Malay, too. I know what our people need and want because I am one of them. Of course, I am all too well aware we are merely an outpost, a reflection of the great Arab world. It is the Arabs who are the real Muslims, with nothing else mixed in. It was them from the earliest times. But I know this interloper, lording it over us, is no Saudi prince. He is not even a Saudi, still less of the royal family. It may have 300 princes but he is not one of them. He is just a wretched *Kling*, he and his pirate thug with the eyepatch. Lost his hand fighting the Russians? They cut it off for stealing from the gold shops in Riyadh. He drove a bulldozer. He was a labourer. He was a manual worker. He was the lowest of the low and now he is swaggering around the *pondok* looking down on me who has never laboured a day with his hands. I have never had to engage in manual toil. My father was a teacher, too, you know. That is a vile story about him washing dishes in a Chinese restaurant. He could not have engaged in such polluting work, such a defilement. The Chinese eat pork, you know. They love it. And me being his son by his unmarried female cousin. I would cut off the ears and tongues of those who spread it or even give credence to this wicked rumour. I admit I achieved everything through scholarships, through the munificence of the Sultan and the Tungku but my family could also have afforded it. It is unfortunate, I admit, that my complexion is not a little paler. Anyway, I am now a scholar. I am an intellectual. I am an intellectual who punishes. I am learned and I am stern. It would be ridiculous to suggest I could harbour feelings of envy or resentment. I just see the pair of them for what they are. They have no sense of respect because respect is rooted in tradition and they have none.

When I teach the *hadith* to my pupils I tell them that they are at the end of a mighty anchor-line which secures them to the Messenger of God, peace be upon his head. The line itself is indestructible but each individual link in the chain is composed of a fragile human life, culminating in your own teacher, who happens to be a frail old man. So the story will have been narrated by a relative or close follower of the Prophet to a descendant or subordinate and sub-narrated in turn to another and yet another, fitting together like boxes inside each other but, however many boxes there are and however differently decorated, the gift inside them – the example of the Prophet's Life – is always the same and unchanging.

But the scenery around has, indeed, changed. Now we are in Singapore, after the rail journey the length of the peninsula. Quite a comfortable journey, even for the pampered sons of the rich whose buttocks have been used to soft cushions all their lives. My father could have afforded first-class for us when we travelled but he preferred we should know the hardness of the wooden seats in third class the better to appreciate luxury. Those born into it rarely appreciate it. In any case the Communists in Malaya, as it was then, always set off their bombs under the first-class compartments. I should have liked to have seen that. I can imagine my 10-year-old self wagging his finger at them amidst the tatters and splinters and saying, "See? See, what comes of your lives of ease and privilege? I am glad to look at you as you lie there groaning with your limbs blown off and your intestines on the dusty floor and I stand unhurt."

His Lordship – there was a good expression the Malaysian politician Anwar Hossain always used, His Nibs, which makes it sound like a scholar who is getting above himself – His Nibs cannot be faulted for lack of nerve. He had a lot of nerve coming here in the first place. Usually, he is much calmer than me (not saying much) when physical danger threatens. I close my eyes (what is left of them) and put my trust in God. But at Hat Yai, getting on the train, I never saw a man in such a cold sweat. I use the expression advisedly. I saw one of the Sultan of Brunei's polo-horses in just such a lather: wild-eyed and clammy. His Nibs' eyes rolled back in his head; if he had possessed hind legs he would have reared back and pawed the air with his front hooves. The one-eyed thug had to pull him back with an arm round his chest. I cannot explain it, I simply cannot explain it. It was so out of character. The man has many faults (apparent, it seems, only to the superior discernment) but lack of courage is not one of them. The train carriages were unusually crowded, people standing on the couplings between the cars, thronging the corridor, sitting on the roof, sticking their heads out of the windows.

The boy Jefri was already on the roof, so he couldn't see. I only wish he had; it might temper his hero-worship and it would get back to the others. But he scaled the carriage like a monkey and came down even quicker. You'd think he'd done it 1,000 times. I had just sent Ahmed the Waria to buy me an ice kuchang – that sweet tooth of mine will be my downfall! – and the fool dropped it on the platform floor. I had a mind to make him lick up the scarlet slush as it melted and got trodden on. Then some oaf spat betel juice on to the one-eyed thug's gown. He looked like the flag of Indonesia. Hoo! Hoo! Hoo! I could barely forebear to rub my hands in glee at his predicament. But his master, His Nibs, turned grey and that was when he had to grab him. He looked like some child in the grip of a nightmare, not the great Mujahid the students think he is. I can only assume he lost his nerve for a moment at the thought of the perils ahead of us. I decided to wait upon myself and proceeded to the ice-stall, hearing some small disturbance behind me but ignoring it. There was a peal of childish laughter. Perhaps they were laughing at what a fool the Cyclops looked. I was long in choosing the ice-condiments – then there was the fumbling for the coins and remembering the phone-number – and I had to run to catch the train. His Nibs gave every evidence of a full recovery of his faculties but the students were still tittering over the missing Cyclops' mishap.

This was no doubt as amusing to them as to me but we have still left a hornet's nest behind us which is anything but laughable. The other holy warriors and even the young hot-headed *juwae* are not pleased with us. In fact, they are furious.

We have single-handedly taken it upon us to disrupt the whole pattern and strategy of our war of freedom. There is little co-ordination between the *juwae* here but we are Brothers and many things did not need to be said. We kept our struggle, our own *intifada*, local. We purposely did not connect our own struggle in our backyard to the worldwide Jihad. This was not because we were not devout Muslims. It was because we knew we would have more success if we did not, as they say now, globalise our fight against the Siamese. The Brothers refrained from attacking foreigners and tourists in Siam. They never dreamed of it; we never dreamed of it; I never dreamed of it. It would only bring the attention and the resources of the Americans and Australians upon us. Well did the Shia dub that nation the Great Satan. It was not that we lacked foreign infidels to attack. We had more here than the Indonesian Brothers and martyrs – may Allah be well pleased with them – bombed in Bali. I watched the video of the discotheque – those are indeed Halls of Shaitane – and rubbed my hands. Even the blaze on the video warmed them. It was not that attacking *farang* would cause less damage here. Their money is more important to the Siamese government than it is to the generals in Indonesia. The Indonesians have oil-wells, after all; the Siamese have none. It is just that it would swell the number of nations against us and increase the aid to the Siamese. Maybe we can beat the Siamese in three decades, God Willing. God Willing, it would take three centuries to defeat the Americans.

There must be some good reason that they overlooked me, some good cause to appoint His Nibs and the Cyclops over my head. Many Arabs, even wealthy ones such as our sponsors, are Wahabbis. Maybe they are sacrificing us to what they see as a bigger matter. Maybe that is why His Nibs insisted that I accompany them. I think that it is a matter of time – sooner, I fear, rather than later – that they will track them to our *pondok*. In fact, I would not like to be there at that time. We may regret not taking up that interesting offer from the Chinamen.

I only went to our brothers in Jihad to serve our cause the better. I am no traitor as Judas was to Prophet Jesus, as Ali was to the memory of his Uncle, God's Messenger, may peace always be upon his head. I went to our so-called rivals to preserve the *pondok*, not to destroy it, the *pondok* that was there before they came and will be there long after they are forgotten, the Cyclops and His Nibs. I know many of our brothers in our struggle to be free of the Siamese yoke. I studied with many of them. They are not gangsters as His Nibs calls them. How could anyone I know be a criminal? They told me, kindly and respectfully, that I was not responsible, that they held me immune from responsibility for His Nibs' reckless actions, crimes really. He is the real criminal. Only they asked me to tell them in good time when I would leave Pattani on our folly of a journey and whether we would be going to Medan first or Singapore. This would be so that no punishment should be visited on the *pondok* while I was there and by accident should be involved in it. I should find that most undignified as well as dangerous. I am the one who gives punishment, not receives it. Of course, should the Crusaders or the Chinks seize His Nibs and the Cyclops if we are in Malaysia or Singapore, well, this would not be of my direct doing. Not my doing at all. But I should not object witnessing it. I was, indeed, able to supply the information from the railway station when I went to replace the iced sweet that Ahmed dropped. God's Providence was in his clumsiness. I thought I would have to wait till Singapore to tip them off – I mean, to provide the information. It took a coin to do so. One thing about the Siamese, the public phones are good. Much better than Indonesia. It was remembering the numbers which was the problem. Unlike Hassan, I do not possess an inkling for them. Still, I am a scholar and before you are a judge, you have to possess the attainments of a scholar.

Bearing all this in mind, I would not like to be thought the ignorant son of the soil, with his eyes to the ground where he will cut the next rice-stalk. I was in Cairo, I was in Riyadh. I am familiar with the world. I remember watching the whippings for drunkenness. I would have liked to have seen the Cyclops' hand when it was cut off. I felt as I did when I was in my room as a child, dry and comfortable, watching the people scurry in the rain.

We could do with rain here. The haze hangs over Singapore. The airport is closed. The pilots cannot see even 100 metres. I am glad we came by the train, even if His Nibs did not like it. I wish a plane, an American plane or the Kwantas plane, or, in fact, any plane, would crash in the haze. We could go and look at the corpses like Khalkhali did those of the American helicopter pilots. He was a *shia* but he was just. I would poke them with my toe. It is on the spot, this airport, where the Japanese imprisoned the infidels in Singapore. I can remember my father pointing and laughing at them behind the barbed wire at Kanchanaburi in Siam. They were very thin and very young, though, then, they looked old to me.

Many died building the railway to Parma for the Japanese. They call it the Death Railway. Yes, it is good we came by the train. Our airplane would maybe have crashed and the Chinks would have poked my charred body with their toes. The haze bites my throat. I feel nothing in my ruined old eyes but the young pupils rub theirs and sneeze. I say, do not rub; it will only make it worse, but this useful advice seems not to be appreciated. No one can see anything in Singapore. It is, of course, the fires set in Sumatra. It happens every year and the rich Chinks in Singapore can do nothing about it! Ha! Ha! Ha! The *bumi* in Indonesia set the blaze to clear the forest for planting – bad for orang-utan, bad for Chinese.

Shortly before we left for Hat Yai and Singapore something irritating to the sight also took place on the edge of our own forest. There was a motorbike accident on the highway. Quite how this occurred it is difficult to imagine as there is precious little traffic in the small hours, though I admit the young people all drive at reckless speed. This is the judgment of Allah as many of them are inebriated. I think a big truck must have struck this one as the machine was hopelessly crumpled and beyond even our talented machinists' ability to repair for our own use or re-sale. I arrived later than everyone else to find Hassan already inventorying the effects of the three deceased, while His Nibs was reading a blood-stained piece of paper with a frown of disgust more intense than its admittedly revolting appearance warranted. The bodies were sprawled in the careless and meaningless postures of all untimely deaths (except for the significant end of martyrdom). Someone whispered that they were the brothers of Jefri and Ahmed. I looked closer and did indeed recognise them. Although the machine and helmets were badly damaged, their faces, by the providence of God, were not. They must have slid on their backs. Weeks ago I had brought the Cyclops to shoo them off our grounds, not trusting in their ability to render the respect due to character, venerability and learning, rather than brute force. (The Cyclops has the latter quality in abundance). I was congratulating myself on standing looking down on disaster once more and not being – thanks to God – involved in it when I saw His Nibs suddenly look up from his perusal of the gory scrap and stare hard at the Cyclops. It was not the way he usually looked at his henchman. On the contrary, it was the kind of look I sometimes caught him giving me.

Then he kissed the Cyclops on the cheek, encountering, I should think, entirely beard and no skin. The monster responded like a dog shown affection by its master. If he had possessed a tail, he would have wagged it.

"I count on you, Tariq," said His Nibs. "I do it without even thinking about it."

"Of course, Boss," replied the Cyclops. The monster is incapable of thought, still less feeling, but it was the closest I have ever seen to a look of puzzlement on what is visible of his face.

This talk of dogs: last night we ate at a public housing estate. Each estate in Singapore has its own food-hall. You know what an Indian wrote about the Singaporeans – he was a Singaporean, too – he said they were dogs, content in the way a hound might be satisfied. They were comfortably kennelled in the public housing and their stomachs were kept full so that their heads might remain empty. Ha-ha! This man's name was Go-Pal and he was a surgeon as well as a writer. He was admittedly a *kafir*, not to mention a *kling*, but he was a perceptive one. I am a Believer, I am a thinker, and I am also a surgeon – not of bodies but of societies. This food-hall we ate in was enormous, as big as a covered football stadium – it had more than 100 stalls, each serving a different variety: Chinese, sea-foods, satay, soup, noodles, even *halal*, desserts both iced and fried. It was far better than the expensive restaurants we passed in the city area and, of course, cheap. It was delicious and even cheaper than at home. Hassan was heading for the Chinese noodles when I stopped him and re-directed him to the *halal* stall.

"Ah, Imam," he said, "for once your eyes are better than mine!"

"Your nose, Haji," I replied, "you were following your nose!"

The cheapness of the viands pleased Hassan who, as at the *pondok*, is our paymaster. I like to call him our House Jew and we chuckle over this. He is certainly shrewd as we saw when there was that interesting proposal to purchase the *pondok*. Its land, I mean, as really quite extensive and being one of the few holdings in the area not prone to deep flooding. It is not the physical build-ings but the spiritual reconstruction which goes on within that makes a religious school unique, I told Hassan. We should not be sentimental about land or buildings. He was actually not in need of much encouragement. Of course, the property is owned by the charitable foundation but these things are always flexible. Then the young Chinese fellow came round (representing the old Chinaman, his father, no doubt). "We'll pave Paradise and put up a mega-mall," he said. Hassan and I ignored this. Unlike the Cyclops and his master, we know when self-control is best. Anyway, this was all just before the time of His Nibs. Hassan made an appointment for the young Chinese fellow to see His Nibs in his study that used to be mine. The next thing you know, the Chinaman is running for his life to his car which the chauffeur, a good Muslim boy, too, had moving even while he was opening the rear-door. Out comes His Nibs, shouting, "Over my dead body!" with the Cyclops close behind roaring, "Over his, you mean, boss!"

And that was the beginning of the reign of His Nibs.

Hassan actually makes no secret to me about his early career as a bank manager in Medan, even though he is reticent with the students. I would like to think we have no secrets from the other but, sadly, this is not the case. Of course, I would not insult him by calling him our House Chinaman. When I look at Hassan, I do see something *peranakan* about his eyes. However, we were the old teachers at the *pondok*. We have something in common. Sometimes we catch each other's eye during a specimen of vulgarity or barbarism from the Cyclops. I say to Hassan, "The Gentleman Jihad, Haji, we two are the Gentleman Jihad!" We are unspoken allies against the arrogance of the interlopers. Hassan is scared of His Nibs and the Cyclops; I am not intimidated. Not intimidated at all. Hassan clearly is more privy to their schemes than I am. There is something he does at the computer and on the mobile phone with His Nibs. Hassan turns away and punches numbers into the keypad of the little white computer or the screen of the Nokia. It is an expensive one. I know the one with the cut-out of the apple on it is called Nokia. It is from Sweden, not such a bad country as the Great Shaitane. Why do they need that? Whenever I speak to Hassan about this he becomes evasive. I mean, even more difficult to pin down than usual. He gives me the same glib, crafty responses he gives so often to the others and in which I abet him. He treats me at these times in the same way as, united, we jointly cope with our own awkward colleagues. Only this time, I am the awkward colleague being coped with. I don't think it could be about a sale of the land. I would dearly like to get to the bottom of this. Maybe, God Willing, one day I shall.

*　*　*

OH, DISASTER! OH, WOE! Allah is Mighty but his servant Umar is weak. Something terrible has happened. I was on my way to the mosque. His Nibs prohibited us from attending any public prayers while we were in Singapore. Usually, I keep my mouth shut when I disagree with him. I know if I question him, humiliation and indignity are waiting for me just round the corner. I do not excel in such situations, to say the least. Theological exposition, academic debate, exercises in logic and disputation, explication of the chain of narratives in the holy accounts relating to the life of the Messenger of God – peace be upon his head – even legal argumentation, are more my style. To be frank, my notion of an ideal situation would be for me to explain a decision or announce a punishment from a physically higher place – of course, while comfortably seated – to someone who is forbidden to reply and, if very obdurate, gagged. When there are no rules or framework, I tend to hesitate. When I wish to speak in a polite, but nevertheless firm and confident, way to His Nibs, it comes out as an old man's quaver. I do detest hearing a recording of my own voice. A silent film would be pleasanter and more dignified and do justice to my bearing, except that is *haram*.

Bearing all these things in mind, I went myself to a well-known place of worship, not troubling to recruit any companions or disciples. In fact, my pupils pray by themselves with an ardour that cannot be matched in any *pondok* elsewhere and in a group their zeal, as they rock in bliss, can be truly inspirational. I have been their teacher. The youngest even volunteered to accompany me but I had to disappoint him. I wished to be alone or, to be more accurate, in the company of my coevals rather than my juniors. You may not know that word – but it means equals. Now you know it. Nevertheless, I confess to feelings of slight disappointment that the youngest alone requested permission to accompany, though I would only have had to refuse the others too. No, I wished to attend prayers at the mosque for the pleasure of it. I am an ascetic. I have few physical pleasures other than clove cigarettes and sweetmeats. My pleasures are of the mind, not the senses. I like to go to the mosque to be in the company of the like-minded, to hear news, maybe to impart it as well, mostly reports of people. It is most definitely not idle chatter and certainly not gossip. It makes me feel part of the world, not an old man surrounded by *bumibumi* in the boondocks. That means up-country amongst bumpkins. I was surprised Ahmed the Waria also knew the expression, to judge by his smile when I used it in class. Yes, I want to stand there among the older imams and teachers and be known for what I am and respected. Praise be to God! The prestige is pleasant.

All the greater my discomfiture, then, when a taxi slowed down by me and when I refused a free ride – even though the driver was dressed as a Muslim – my elbow was roughly taken from behind and a rude voice hissed, "Get in, you old fart."

The door swung open. The next thing I knew, I was toppling in. It was most undignified. My gown flew up; my sandal came off. This was not so much thrown in after me as used to administer a stinging blow to my posterior. "Take that, Sir," said the same voice. The door closed with a solid sound, much more expensive-sounding than our own taxis, followed by an unreassuring click. The windows were also tinted which made it nearly pitch-dark for my poor eyes. Usually, I can see the meter glowing in the taxi but not read the numbers, trusting only in the driver's respect for his religion and my position. Quite often, you know, I ride for free. "Kindly turn on your meter," I said, and my voice shook as it does when I have to contradict His Nibs. "Oh, the clock'll be running the whole time, Older Brother," said the voice in Bangkok Siamese. It was a young Siamese voice but he gave the respectful address *Pee* a horrible, disrespectful twist. My heart started to pound. Of course, I already had an inkling of the hands into which I had fallen. "God is Great," I found myself saying and to my joy my voice rang firmly in my own ears.

"He most certainly is," replied my unwanted companion.

I bit my lip. He was obviously an infidel. And so was the driver to judge by the grin on his face. A *kafir* in Believer's costume. Tuan Anthony taught us the excellent expression wolf in sheep's clothing when I was young during that single year in Malaya. I would be deceiving myself if I said I had not been feeling increasingly uneasy during what had started as a carefree saunter but I had half-sensed with my cloudy eyes someone following me on completely the other side of the road from where the actual assault and eventual abduction took place. I suppose the explanation is that either my sight has degenerated to a condition even more impaired than I feared or that my enemies were numerous as flies on blown sweetmeats. Both explanations are equally plausible and perhaps operating at the same time.

I preserved a dignified silence until we arrived at a nondescript building I knew not where. They talk about Singapore being a small place but, like the Malayan jungle, it seems big enough when once you are in it. God is Great but I was very scared. There was no one I had to show an example or put a brave face on for. Even the martyrs to the cause – may God be well-pleased with them – have someone to watch them at the end, in case their resolve falters (as is only human). Of course, so far in our *intifada* we have no martyrs in that most exalted sense. There have been deaths among our own *juwae* but no one has sought death in order to take the life of the infidel. I do not like the term suicide bomber at all. That is the term of the Crusaders. But as I entered this place I wondered what lay in store for me. They made me wait alone in a locked room and that was terrible. I was my own worst enemy. At length I was taken into another room. I could sit but see nothing and no one. A bright light was shining in my face. Of course, this did not inconvenience or incapacitate my poor eyes as much as it would a young man gifted with perfect sight. I could not forebear smiling quietly to myself. When someone asked me politely in Southern language and then Jawi what was so funny and I remained silent, I was seized by the hands of what felt like invisible djinns but which were, of course, all too human. I was turned and twisted in the air. I knew it was less than my own inconsiderable height above the ground but it might as well have been 20,000 feet up in the sky as I took the precaution of closing my nearly useless eyes.

I felt as I did as a child when the fair came up-country to our town and I rode the helter-skelter with my father, his hands still smelling of suds. Everyone thought I was so daring but my eyes had been shut all the time! My father's female cousin kissed me when we alighted and said, "My brave boy!" Now I began to drown. Again, this might as well have been in the ocean's profoundest abyss but was not even a fraction of an inch deep. Everyone knows the technique now. It is sufficiently notorious that I need not dwell upon it. I do not know how long it lasted. Then a voice said, "That's enough. We don't want to give the old codger a heart attack." They all started laughing. This was a mistake. Humour is always a mistake. It is the error and solace of the weak. Those who are sure of themselves do not need it. You see, I was able to realise I had not more than three tormentors. This did not immediately help me – knowledge is seldom of immediate practical use other than the knowledge God vouchsafes us – but it aided my morale in that I was able to look down on my tormentors for their stupidity. So far, it was all wrong, topsy-turvy. I was in completely the wrong place. It was always me in control, watching others wriggle under just and condign punishment. The voice of the one who had disrespected me so much in the taxi said, "The venomous bead wouldn't like it anyway."

Someone else said something indistinct and the first speaker said, "No, he's first and foremost a don, not an Apache, never been on a warparty. Well, not at least for 60 years."

It had been plain to me for some time that I had been kidnapped by the intelligence services of the Shaitane and their allies. Now I knew those Mafias were in on it, also. I know that word Don. I know the Shaitane all too well. Who does not? Their filth – I cannot call it culture – pervades and pollutes the world. Well, we will take fire to it. Fire beats water. I know the history of the earth. As His Nibs always likes to say, Islam and Science can go together. Naturally, I know God made Man (and maybe Woman, too!) We did not develop from monkeys or orang-utans – or maybe only the Chinks did, ha-ha. But I am wandering. Actually, I don't want to remember but I will force myself.

Suddenly the room was quiet. The whole atmosphere had changed. A new voice said, "Would you like me to turn the light off, Imam?" It was an old man's voice. Now there are some compensations for the failing of a faculty. Others develop in its place. I did not need to see this man. All his qualities were evident in his voice. He was a *farang*, not an Asian. However, he also was not an American. He was English, educated English. His voice was not unlike that of Tuan Anthony who taught us in Malaya, as it was known then. We call it the BBC English, or the Queen's English, or the Oxford accent. Not the way the squaddie soldiers spoke among each other, going up on the railway to fight the Chinks in the jungle. This voice now said, "I apologise for the treatment you have received. This was not the way to treat a scholar, still less a great teacher such as yourself."

I inclined my head in polite acknowledgment. Of course, I knew he was merely speaking with a sweet mouth.

"I am afraid," the voice continued, "the world does not value us according to the store we set upon our own heads but by its own debased standards. Nevertheless, among ourselves in educated circles, we can pay respect where respect is due. Even if the scholarship belongs to different traditions. A scholar is a scholar and can recognise another."

Now I did not know whether I heard the voice of a Shaitane or an Angel.

"What is your name?" I asked.

"You can call me the Voice of Ages. No, that's conceited of me. Call me . . . Winner. No, how utterly thrasonical. That's boastful, in other words, for you. Call me . . . Vice Versa."

"Well, Tuan Verser, if you respect learning, please let me go on my way. I am indeed a scholar and a teacher but not the man you think I am. There has been some mistake."

"As to that, my dear Imam, I believe I must be the better judge. You are both right and wrong. You are incorrect in that, of course, there has been no mistake made, but I very much hope you are correct in saying that you are not the man people fear you are."

"I do not understand."

"That honest admission is a first step. It could be a step towards common ground. You and I are indeed more similar than you would think. I, too, made my progress by dint of my wits. My family was wealthy but I was — how can I put it – not an official son of my father. Islam is, I am happy to say, somewhat more tolerant in this regard of the weakness of men. I think the situation is far from unknown amongst the Chinese here. Money was often in short supply where my mother was concerned during my childhood. So we can say we have both risen from difficult origins to knowledge and our present positions."

Tuan Verser spoke in soft tones he obviously thought were soothing but he succeeded only in lowering himself in my estimation and offending me also. Offending me deeply.

"I cannot imagine why you should think I come from lowly origins," I said coldly, taking care to show him the two-inch nail on my left little finger. "I have never had to engage in manual labour at any time in my life. I am a scholar. I have held books, not a hoe. As to being the offspring of a mistress, I do not say my family were poor, but if they were, at least I could hold my head high as a legitimate son."

"I did not mean to disparage your antecedents. Far from it. If I was wrong, forgive me. I only meant to find some common ground. It is surely more commendable to travel far and thus ascend a greater distance to your own exalted position than to start out with unearned advantages of birth nearer the top?"

"I cannot think where you have got these notions from," I sniffed.

"In that case our information is clearly incorrect. Perhaps you would care to supply us with some that is nearer the mark?"

"I can do no such thing. Martyr me now." Even as I spoke I could not believe it was me saying these words. And I meant them. My voice did not shake as it would when confronting the Cyclops and His Nibs. I can only assume God was in me at that moment, filling me with strength.

"My dear Imam, I really could not contemplate such a thing. Please. Accept my assurances. We are talking teacher to teacher, scholar to scholar. And I might add, your colleagues do not appear to respect your intellectual attainments as they should. Am I correct in this supposition?"

"A little perhaps. Not really."

"Those with integrity and of high intellectual attainments are frequently passed over in favour of the more wily and worldly. It has happened to me many a time and I daresay to you too. The one who has served the cause the longest and the most faithfully is passed over in favour of the new and the meretricious, the interloper in fact. I think there can be few chagrins greater than that, surely worse than seeing one's juniors and pupils promoted over one's head, for at least one can take pride in being the architect of their attainment. In these brazen times, the simplest brute is preferred, it seems, over the subtlest scholar. I see from your rueful smile you have seen this happen to your unfortunate colleagues. But I am forgetting myself. A cigarette? One of your own clove-flavoured?"

I bent my head with alacrity while he lit it. Then I remembered that unfortunate and humiliating incident with the Dutchman years ago in Java when I was riding the train from Bandung to Bogor. "But you will find the odour too strong," I said politely.

"Not at all, it's an extremely pleasant fragrance, as if you were smoking a slice of cake."

There was a long silence after this. It was not uncomfortable at all but still I did not want to be the one who weakened and broke it. I cannot be sure how long it was before Tuan Verser spoke again. "I shall take steps to discipline those who treated you so brutally. It will, believe me, not amount to a simple reprimand and these are not mere blandishments I am offering you. I could almost wish you were there to sit and hear me mete out censure to them."

"I should like that very much," I found myself saying eagerly, the words jumping out before I knew it. "They should receive double, no, triple what they did to me."

Tuan Verser replied – and his voice was no longer stern as when he spoke of punishing his subordinates but soft as one wooing a bride. "I have to say we all admired your fortitude under duress. It does you every credit. Lesser men would have broken."

"No, no," I replied, fluttering my hand.

"What I am saying, my dear Imam, is that if you were to help us now, it would not be a question of want of courage on your part or lack of appetite for martyrdom. No, not at all. You have proved your courage as a Son of Islam. We are not asking you to betray your beliefs or your friends. You would simply be hastening a process, the process whereby men like yourself would be in a position once more to influence the making of decisions. We would only, in a sense, be smoothing your progress and removing obstacles to it."

"Why you do this?"

"Oh, call it a residual sense of fairness, don't you know. I take it you want to be the head of the *madrassah*, do you?"

"We call it *pondok* or *pesantren*."

"You could be the head of the biggest *pondok* in Malaya, if you so desired. Sorry, Malaysia. I'm a dinosaur, I know it. Or do you fancy Brunei? After that maybe Celebes, or should I say Sulawesi? It's all up to you. Tell us. We wouldn't ask much in return and it would always be to your benefit. I know wealth doesn't interest a scholar but there's always money available for whatever schemes interest you. The thing about it, one doesn't want it for oneself – who wants to drive round in a Rolls all day? – but it gives you power over those who would want to. And that means most of the world. No need to submit accounts. We don't have much time, I'm afraid. I'm going to have to force some kind of an understanding from you. Purely makeshift and temporary for now, always change-able later. Maybe a signature on something. A photograph of us together. I'm afraid if you don't, I have to leave soon and it may be the thumbscrews again from our young friend. While the cat is away, you know . . ."

Despite Tuan Verser's remarks about there being little time, it seems to me that I spent several more hours closeted with him. I had been abducted on my way to morning prayer and it was nearly dark when they dropped me off for what they thought the final prayer. I must have spent nearly 12 hours altogether. I did, as he predicted, sign something. I have no idea what it was. That and the fact that I did so under hardships make it invalid, not to mention I was not foolish enough to use my correct signature. Perhaps he anticipated that. The photograph of us while I signed was un-welcome. It made me look like the Japanese signing the surrender while the American general looked on with a stern face. The expensive phone with the design of the apple on it was entirely undesired by me but apparently they wish me to exchange it with Hassan's and the Cyclops and they will want nothing more, maybe for years. More fool them if they think I believe that. Yes, I must have spent more than half the day there. Much of it I cannot now remember. Oh, yes, the numbers and letters he gave me. He was talking of pins, or was it needles or, indeed, pins and needles which I had in my foot. Something to do with banking but not to do with banking or money. He made me write down sequences of numbers and letters. Maybe I will ask Hassan. On second thoughts, I will definitely not ask the Haji. I did have the presence of mind to write the key in an antique form of Jawi that few at the *pondok* can read, certainly not His Nibs. Some of the day not only can I not remember, I also do not wish to remember, at least not too clearly. For the most part I am confused. I am very confused. I have for the first time in my life the feeling that I am standing outside myself, watching myself as a stranger but privy to all my history and most secret thoughts because, of course, it is me.

4b

Snooky

We would travel in three batches: under Shaykh, under Haji Tariq, and under Jefri. To have gone in a single big band would clearly have attracted attention; however, the whole *pondok* went together in public buses to Hat Yai under the pretext of hearing a famous Imam from Jogjakarta speak. After that most returned, under orders to draw attention to themselves with a zealous but still seemly exuberance. Some 30 of us remained. At the railway station Jefri and Tariq saw off Shaykh's company (in which I found myself with Imam Umar and an increasingly querelous Haji Hassan).

Snooky had made herself useful. It was she who had secured a stack of fake Indonesian and Philippine passports through a syndicate Air Fun knew in Bangkok. "It's better than the real thing!" Iskander had exclaimed, admiring the handsome embossing and, most of all, the photo of his even more handsome self.

"That's what they always said about me," I sighed.

We were going to Singapore, then onwards to Kalimantan and the Philippines by a relatively direct route. Jefri would cross into Sumatra, proceed south-east to Java, then north through Sulawesi, Manado, and the Sangihe islands to Mindanao. How Haji Tariq would get there was anybody's guess: ferry, magic carpet, train, plane, telekinesis, levitation, hijacked oil tanker. Despite your headstart, you just knew you'd find him already there, glowering, mono-orbed and baleful, demanding to know what had taken you so long and not excluding his revered Shaykh from his grumblings.

Jefri accompanied us a few miles over the Malay border since he knew all the dodges from his cigarette-smuggling days – which palms to grease, which stations and check-points to avoid. Since his teen heyday things had got considerably worse, or better, depending which way you looked at it: much higher-ranking officers on both sides of the border were now involved in the heroin and amphetamine business. Duty-free gasoline was also pouring through. Smuggling a few cartons of cigarettes seemed innocent. Jefri took his old station on the roof with a grin.

Although I was a senior Maproom member by now and a battle-hardened *juwae* to boot, Imam Umar despatched me to bring him a plate of beans and scarlet ice-shavings with jackfruit or durian. Unlike Jefri, I was not happy with my temporary reversion to junior status. I am sorry to say, I did actually spit in the frosty splinters and the gore from my now constantly bleeding gums only made my copious expectoration the less conspicuous. Fuck him, I thought. I would never have done this to Haji Tariq, seeing us off at the railway station, not just through fear but respect as well. I was doubly content with my piece of spite. I was kinda sick of being the macho Mujahid. This was Snooky paying tribute to the holy bitch that still lurked inside her. Fortunately, or unfortunately, I couldn't push through with it.

I was wending my way through the platform stage-army of water-bearers, green mango 'n chilli dip vendors, newspaper boys, pickpockets, peanut-roasters, maize-broilers, single-stick cigarette and chewing-gum sellers, satay-grillers, lotus-wristlet plyers, and the prayer-saying devout, with my paper platter significantly heavy with the Imam's frozen delights, thinking I'd ask him half-way through if he was enjoying it when, with his back still to me, the Imam removed his skull-cap. He'd doffed it to scratch his pate and, in doing so, incidentally revealed his bald patch. I didn't see the testy, pompous dotard who liked to make our lives more difficult than they already were on a daily basis, who'd tried to get me flogged harder for having a tattoo. No, I saw my vulnerable, trusting teacher who was absolutely small-minded and vindictive but not so much that he could ever suspect treachery from a pupil.

I called his name, "Imam Umar! They had only durian!"

Then as he turned his milky, delighted eye upon me, I pretended to trip.

Unfortunately, choosing this moment to say his *ultimo adios* to Shaykh, Haji T. crossed my path, fielded a gob of betel juice from a squatting crone selling fragrant garlands, and got a 40 baht serving of ice *kuchang* from me over his pristine white gown, to boot. Imam Umar's expression of greedy joy turned within a second to one of appalled shock, then virulent rage. I was sorry I hadn't just given

him the fouled ice. Next moment he saw the dreadful, sticky predicament of Haji Tariq (of whom it may, or may not, surprise you
he was none too fond) and his expression turned again to the
habitual one of vicious glee. His veined, milky orbs resembled
the most prized of the marbles Jefri and his chums would roll as
kids at school.

Haji T. didn't cuff or even sneer at me. He had to grab Shaykh
who, taller than everyone else on the platform, was swaying like
a Dubai tower in a gale of wind. I didn't know if it was something
as insignificant as delayed travel-sickness from the bus or if he was
about to get dengue or malaria at the worst time. You see, that
would have put Imam Umar in charge of us, not Haji Tariq or
Hassan. Haji T. was speaking quietly to Shaykh, while supporting
him, in a language that was neither Arabic, English, nor Malay.
Then he said, "A train is a train, nothing more."

Shaykh said, "It's a time machine. Change your gown."

Haji T. then said something to Shaykh in the foreign language
again. I had never heard the sounds before but I knew exactly what
they were from the look in his eyes and the tone of his voice. It
was an exhortation he often addressed to us in Malay or, rarely,
English in our flakier moments. *"Get a grip on yourselves."* I imagined
he'd used it not just on us but on the Mujaheedin in extremer
moments in the past in Afghanistan. From anyone else to Shaykh,
including Imam Umar, it would have been an impertinent piece of
insubordination but so obvious was Tariq's attachment to his master
that it could be construed as simple brotherliness. It worked.

Shaykh's colour returned to his face. He said, "What God Wills,"
and patted the Haji's supporting hand.

Imam Umar had the strangest look on his mug, quite uncatego-
risable. What was on it? Bafflement and contempt would be too
strong. They would be the black and red to the grey and pink of
perplexity and disdain. Mixed in with it were disappointment, yet
also awe. There is the Siamese expression "to look cheap on
someone." This was what Umar was doing to Shaykh but he was
also incredulous at the same time and just a little behind it was fear.
At that moment I realised he hated Shaykh, had always hated him,
and whatever joy he took in our petty misfortunes would be
as firecrackers to the atomic explosion of rejoicing in anything
calamitous that might befall Shaykh.

It was at this point, too, that the roaring station hullabaloo around me became fainter and fainter, dizziness assailed me, my eyes became as dim as Imam Umar's, and the ground came up to me faster and faster. It was a good thing we climbed up the fixed steps of our American train-car from ground level and did not enter from a raised platform in the European style or I would have fallen through the gap and injured myself.

I then proceeded to vomit up my *halal* coffee-shop breakfast of roti and mutton. I figure it was ten per cent shock which was the trigger but 90 per cent was genuine preceding unwellness and fatigue. I couldn't sleep any more, what with the profuse night sweats and my throat so sore I could hardly breathe. It was Shaykh himself who grabbed me. I saw myself in his polarised lenses. I didn't look too hot. The glands on my neck were prominent as Skullcandy earphones at rest on the collarbone.

"Ahmed," he said with great gentleness. "Ahmed. This makes two of us. Are you alright?"

"God willing, Shaykh, I am fine."

"God willing," he replied and mounted the steps as if they were a scaffold. My peers crowded round me, taking their lead from our master. To their unspoken query, I replied, "No, it isn't morning sickness," and that's how we left Siam, in a cascade of giggles turning to laughter when Imam Umar came into view, having to ditch his self-purchased *cendol*, pick up his skirts and run for a slowly creeping train.

The hand Shaykh extended him was strength and reliability itself.

I was watching with more than usual interest. Haji T. had made an unusual pick, you see, before he left with his crew of budding desperadoes. The Haji's one good eye darted here, there, and everywhere, like a wounded bird of prey. What with scarlet syrup and betel all over him, he looked like he had been shot in the chest. Finally, his gaze settled on . . . Ahmed. I could see it coming but I was still bowled over.

He beckoned to me. "Mind the Boss," he said. Not "Shaykh" but "Boss". His prosthesis (today flesh-coloured plastic, rather than the hook, not that it made him look any more innocuous) jabbed me so hard in the chest I checked myself for crimson seepage afterwards. "Take care of him," he said. The unspoken corollary was, "or else."

"Of course, Haji," I answered. "God is Great. If He is willing, we shall arrive in Singapore in one piece."

"If not, God Willing, I will cut you into more pieces." And he was off.

I was more flattered than menaced to be chosen as Shaykh's carer but I did keep a careful eye on him. I'd already worked out what to do. I would misdiagnose whatever his attacks were as travel-sickness and pop him a Ketamine and a GHB under the guise of Dramamine or Stugeron. Shit, Ketamine was a racehorse tranquilliser and ought to work even on a superhuman like Shaykh. Yah, OK, I'd scored them at the same time as the kayo drops I used on Avril in the Phuket disco and stashed them safely ever since. Well, does Snooky have to own up to everything?

As luck would have it, Shaykh, so far from having epileptic seizures and frothing at the mouth, sat tranquilly but untranquillised all the way down the isthmus, cracking salty black watermelon seeds between his teeth like an old Chinaman and sucking up cup noodles with lashings of chilli. I wondered where he'd picked up the habit. We sailed through the border formalities, making me wish we'd taken the risk and all travelled together. Long past KL, well on the way to Johor, Shaykh bought a copy of *The Straits Times,* then removed his shades. I was shocked by how bulgy his eyeballs were. He produced a monocle from the depths of his robes and screwed it in.

Then he started doing the crossword puzzle. He looked up at me, with a smile, in response to my open curiosity. You could see he wasn't yet back to normal. Normally, he'd have ignored Ahmed the Abnormal. Just for the duration of our time in the carriage there was a bond. "My father's," he said, tapping the eyeglass with his pencap.

Beside him Haji Hassan scowled through his pince-nez. "You are setting a bad example, Tuan," he rebuked the leader. "Better to read our holy books. The students have prayer-beads."

"Here," said Shaykh, dividing up his newspaper. "Have the financial pages."

"Oh, thank you," replied Hassan, forgetting himself and speaking to Shaykh in Siamese. Quick as a flash, Shaykh replied, *"My pen wry."*

In Singapore Imam Umar's clove-cigarette smoking started

to go through the roof. He was fuming away like Krakatoa or Pinatubo. This got worse after the day he vanished during the hours of light. Shaykh had taken a group to the Riau islands that morning, so I think Shaykh never knew about it and those of us who remained would never have presumed to inform on the Imam, though privacy, as you well know, was a concern alien to our hearts.

I kind of figured he might have gone to the brothel, probably the cheap Indian ones in the Geylang district, little sub-divided brick terraces like concentration camp gas-ovens, packed with Hindu crones with six folds of belly showing through the sari. He was grave, he was dignified – was Umar – but there existed flight-iness in his nature only semi-trammelled by the half-blindness. It took me to see it. It took the TV, the TG, the ladyboy to see it.

The other half of us got taken over to Riau a couple of days later. It was Indonesia, one of the oldest sultanates, fount and origin of the best Malay dialect, the accents in which my half-brother Adi spoke but (much like Adi) gone to seed and become variously an illegal casino, a whorehouse, and an industrial park of Singapore.

A filthy, smoky haze lay over the city-state during the equatorial dry season. It came from thousands of fires set by loggers in Indonesia, which the tidy and law-abiding Singaporeans had to endure. It made the eyes sting and the throat rasp. Normally, you couldn't see these islands from Singapore (some larger than the island republic itself) but you could see the looming skyscrapers of Singapore from most of the islands. This was a paradigm. Singaporeans never thought of the archipelago – except as a weekend retreat – but the islanders were always thinking of Singapore in the way in which the ancient Central Asians might have thought of Golden Samarkand.

When we went there we couldn't see a thing through the smog, not even the ferry pier from 50 metres. But at night it was different. Then you could see the twinkle of Singapore and mistake it for the constellations in the heaven.

The islands had totally different characters. Our first group had gone to the most developed: huge shopping malls, three lane highways but with the earth on the most recently scalped hills still raw and red, surmounted by plank and palm-thatch huts that were the same as the most backward *kampong*. Or you could say they were the skullcap which surmounted my head of advanced thoughts.

We prayed at a tiny mosque with a huge sound-system and I thought this is how Shaykh wants our struggle to appear on the stage of the world: noisy beyond its stature. Not 200 yards from the mosque were the pink lights of a karaoke. One of Jefri's cohorts whispered to me, "This is where the Malacca pirates come to celebrate their heists when they take a tanker," and Snooky thought, yah, could be be the stage-set for a modern Muslim *Pirates of the Caribbean*.

We didn't stay long in civilisation, such as it was. Shaykh got us on a smaller, more ramshackle ferry to a minor island: no lifejackets at all and this time no airport X-ray machine to scan our bags for bombs and guns. Snooky thought it was lucky the Singaporeans had not yet invented something that could scan your head for subversive ideas, though no doubt they would have employed it on their own population first.

There was one stop, where no one got on or off – the now deserted island where the Vietnamese boatpeople had been imprisoned for years and years. The lucky fucks were now gangsters or billionaires, or both, in California or Norway, you name it. After two hours of *putt-putt* as the island came into view we all gave a sigh of recognition. You could have put our *pondok* down here. It was Shaykh's perfect idea of the bucolic idyll, pastoral innocence.

And you could see the flimsy, narrow, but over-engined fast ferry, fitted with second-hand airliner seats, was a time-machine just like Shaykh had said mysteriously of the train. This was what Singapore had been not so long ago: mangroves and hardwood giants. And, of course, pirates, real ones, not intellectual counterfeiters.

Here, for the first time on the trip, we were met. Even when they were just wraiths in the smog I knew it was us they were waiting for. We stood and pulled down our striped zip-bags from the crudely nailed overhead shelf. Indonesians and Malaysians both spoke the same language – Malay, surprise, surprise – so most of us were instantly at home. In fact, though Haji Hassan was Acehnese, his accent was similar to theirs. It was the Caliphate, honey, manifesting itself in tongues.

Our reception committee carried our bags for us after some polite demurral on our part. Not for the first time, I thought that even the most macho Thai lads could exhibit the coyest behaviour sometimes. I then noticed that each of us had a welcomer of our own, no more, no less than our own number. They knew exactly how many of us were coming.

We stayed in a dark, dank tenement full of cell-like rooms. What would have been the top four floors of this and similar buildings were blank-walled, save for slots the size of loop-holes. Indeed, my first thought was we had a fortified pill-box or bunker above us. Then, as I saw the swallows swooping in and out, the truth dawned on me: they were artificial caves for nesting, for harvesting bird's nest soup. Chinese commercial enterprise on top of solid Muslim foundations. I wondered if the boats were culling shark's fins as well as smuggling cigarettes to Singapore.

Town was about 150 metres by 150 metres or the size of the huge French supermarket where Do-Ann and the Gang would go shop-lifting in Bangkok. There was the whole island with its undeveloped interior – larger than Singapore – but we were being crammed into our concrete coffins.

We washed our feet, prayed, all without Shaykh. That night I dreamed I was in a giant honeycomb. Avril, lower thorax black-and-yellow striped, was the Queen Bee. "But, darling, you could have flown away," she said. "Off with her head – I'm doing you a favour, Snooks, just like you did me. It's not the transgender thing that sets you apart, honey, it's your brains that make you different. You're lonely because you're smart."

Breakfast was standard Indon buffet, heaped on cheap tin trays: fried rice or noodle, crispy deep-fried fish-fry (you fry, I cry), all washed down with scalding black coffee or luke-warm red tea. Yah, Snooky the luke-warm contented herself with tea. I usually sustained myself with healthy papaya and rice porridge at the *pondok*. *Joke* was the Siamese word for this rice congee. A *katoey* won't choke on your joke, I used to say to Do-Ann. We're used to swallowing. Fruit, as you will see, I was to taste later.

Our host took us out to his orchards. These were an hour away, through jungle even thicker than our own. He specialised in unusual fruit: the least unique of these was the pink Vietnamese dragon fruit I'd peeled and sliced once for the *Sentinel*'s geriatric restaurant critic: I now saw it growing on the plant up concrete posts, as opposed to reposing on the supermarket shelf, and realised it was nothing more than a cactus pear (mystery solved). Exotic fruit from foreign locales which now flourished in this soil included a black globe I'd never seen before which made delicious juice the colour of ink and came from Central America; sapadilla; golden egg-fruit; apple-mango; brown chico; June plum; noni; maney.

Shaykh was already there. He was standing in front of an unknown tree with Hassan and Umar. He had his shades on again.

"Yes, very unusual," said Haji H. as I was approaching. He was, I have not told you, the Keeper of our Groves. "I have no idea what it is."

A branch of the tree lay on the ground, gnarled as the main, living trunk but no more so. "See," said Shaykh, "it has been down a long time. You can see the mushrooms, er, fungi on the ground all around it and it has already dented a hollow of its own but no mushrooms have grown upon it."

"Praise be to God, I can see nothing," remarked Imam Umar and they all laughed. It was strange watching men whom I knew disliked each other sharing a self-deprecating joke. We couldn't have done it. I suppose that was why they were elders and we were juniors. Imam Umar prodded it with his toe in the spirit of a man testing if a recumbent enemy was still quick. "I cannot move it," he said in surprise.

Shaykh said, "God willing, I shall give you a lever and you can stand on the moon and move the earth." He saw me. "Ahmed, pick it up."

I complied. "It's heavy as iron, Shaykh," I said. "Like metal, not wood. It would sink, not float. You could not make a raft from it." It was true. It was like hefting a girder. "The wood is quite black, Shaykh."

Shaykh touched it. "God is Great! I know what it is," he cried. "It is the wood the Chinese make furnitures from. I have some in my house."

"Ah, yes," said Hassan. "So it is. Well-spotted. That's clever of you. I would never have realised it myself, in its unpolished state. God willing, you would have to own some to know it. But, wait. You don't have any of this in your rooms. We wouldn't have Chink stuff in the *pondok*, even good quality Chink stuff. I had to auction back to them all the heirlooms the bank distrained in Medan after the riots."

"Yes," said Imam Umar, his head to the side and almost gloating. "I rely on God, I have never seen it."

Shaykh's face was expressionless, as perfectly expressionless as, well, a Chinese poker-player's. I swiftly interjected, "Of course you have never seen it, Imam. Not with your martyr's eyes."

His expression changed instantly. I have learned jests do not get a reception on their intrinsic merits, so much as on the status of the quipper. I knew I had made a dangerous enemy. Was it my imagination or did Shaykh pat me softly on the shoulder that was away from Haji Hassan?

Shaykh reached up. "Look, the fruit of the tree." Only he could have managed it with his great height and long arms. Not even Snooky, the lissom *katoey*, always taller than real men, could do that.

"But it's white," I exclaimed. "The tree is black and the fruit is spotless white, like, like . . . a snowball."

"Or the Shaykh's gown laundered by a Chinese laundry," said Imam Umar and if his milky eyes could have flashed they would have done, like lightning in storm clouds.

"Like a Clean Draft or the unblemished pages of a Valid Will," contributed Haji Hassan.

Shaykh reclined his lean length along the branch to retrieve the fruit. In his bug-eyed lenses he looked like the monster in *Anaconda V* or had the franchise only reached IV? With a final stretch he grasped and plucked the white globe. "Here." He handed it down to me. Fuzzy, firm on the surface but yielding to sustained finger pressure, it resembled nothing so much as an albino peach.

"God willing, let the Imam have the honour of first sampling it," Shaykh said.

"Oh, no, no," declined Imam Umar, tittering.

"Your hands were clean, Ahmed? Praise be to God, mine were and, God willing, so were those elegant fingers of Ahmed. Do not fear, Umar, it has not fallen to the ground yet. Rats have not urinated upon it. I assure you it is quite *halal*."

We all allowed ourselves a laugh. "Come, you cannot hide your sweet tooth from us of all people. Come, in the interests of science."

"God willing, in the interests of knowing His Creation." Umar sank his yellow incisors into the luscious flesh. He shuddered. "Praise be to God, it is absolutely delicious."

"Praise be to God." Shaykh removed the fruit from Umar before he could desecrate its virgin skin a second time. "Ahmed."

I pointed to myself in incredulity.

"Yes, you, God Willing."

I felt in myself a great reluctance but the hypnotic lenses were on me and I was as a rabbit. I saw myself polarised in them: furtive, curious, sheepish, afraid. My toes were turned in like a ten-year-old girl and I had my hands over my balls like a gay footballer facing a free kick. I closed my eyes and bit, making sure it was the other side from Imam Umar. I didn't want what . . . gingivitis, piety, rabies? I thought of the Turkish aubergine dish, The Imam Swoons. The fruit of the ebony tree was tart and sweet in the same mouthful, soft but crunchy, succulent-fleshed but delicate-fibred. If marzipan dormice grew on trees from their tails, they would taste like this.

I opened my eyes and looked at Umar and saw in his face what that blind seer saw in mine. "It's wonderful, Shaykh," I mumbled. "God is great, it is wonderful," and I felt the earth unstable beneath me, except it was not the firm and reliable ground but my treacherous legs trembling. "Praise be to God, I never thought I would eat the seed from which a chair springs."

"Now you know, Ahmed," murmured Shaykh. "Praise be to God, now you know, Umar. Now you know and now I know what you know, too. I seek the forgiveness of God. What it is to know. What power knowledge confers on the knower. God is Great. I know. I seek the forgiveness of God, as you should."

"But Shaykh," stammered one of the Maproom, "you have not sampled the peach."

For answer, Shaykh tossed it aside.

Imam Umar was older and frailer than me but he had recovered. "According to the Chinks," he said, "the peach is the longevity fruit."

"You shall see," Shaykh said. "I rely on God."

At his counting-house, the orchard and lodging-house owner, a good Muslim successful in business among the cut-throat Chinese, as unlikely as a Tokyo sumo champion from Peru, had a selection of his other produce for us. I think we weren't meant to have chomped his rarest growth.

There was salt to sprinkle on the fruit. "Salt?" said one of the juniors, wrinkling his nose. I wasn't surprised after my studies in Manila. "We mix sugar and chilli powder to put on fruit," I said. "People like the Filipinos put salt on it."

Shaykh said something I didn't quite catch about a tray of their salt.

"What's that, Tuan?"

"The Pashtun, the Pathan."

"I thought no fruit grew, Shaykh. It looks so arid on *Geographic Channel*."

"Keep to your salt, Ahmed. God is Great. God willing, it is never too late."

"Shaykh?"

After our fruit repast (it occurred to me that you could feed a troupe of monkeys or a band of gorillas quite successfully on the same viands) we were taken to the orchard's prize exhibit.

We all gaped, not politely but genuinely. It was a six metre or 20 foot python skin. That meant the live animal had been even longer. It had been caught and killed, we were told, three years ago but not before it had crushed and killed a six-year-old Chinese boy.

"In this very orchard," said the (Chinese-looking) manager. There was a collective intake of breath from the *pondok*.

You mustn't forget, we had limited TV and no movies, as these were, in Haji Hassan's and Imam Umar's view, sinful and corrupting: not even Thai ghost films (the very nadir, will you believe me, of the horror genre). Even Iskander's iPod had been confiscated for weeks before being restored for valour – i.e. our elders needed him bad. So this was fantastic to our poor imaginations, with the added kick of being real.

The frayed web shivered in the slight breeze. Apparently, the mother and father had gone ahead only a few steps with the boy's even younger sister. The snake must have stalked the boy. Then quickly wrapped itself around him and suffocated him before swallowing him whole and slithering away, all with the parents within its own length.

Now we were taken to the grove of rubber trees where the attack had taken place. What was striking was the sparse cover, the trees widely spaced, just an ankle-deep covering of leaves on the hard grey earth. It made you respect the cunning and silence of the python and appreciate the beauty of its camouflage.

Our guide pointed to the hollow of the big tree where the snake had been found with its distended coils. "As soon as we saw it, we all suspected the worst, of course."

"Of course," echoed Imam Umar in a whisper.

The father was personally allowed to kill the python with an axe-blow to the pinioned head, the size of a small dog's, but could not bring himself to slit the belly. The boy was entirely intact – the snake's digestive juices had not had enough time to work – but crushed to a jelly, his limbs plastered to his torso, like pressed chicken in a delicatessen bottle.

God forgive her, Snooky thought:

(1) Now we have blood-wit with a snake and

(2) Why don't they bottle the boy as well?

In order mainly to suppress her traitorous giggling, Snooky said solemnly, "It shows how effective constriction is for a predator. You'd think fangs or claws, or even poison, would be more effective. But if you're hunting not a solitary animal but one that lives in a group, a co-operative group, you're safer as a predator like this: the prey dies in silence, it cannot cry for help. You can go right into the middle of the herd or group and make your kill and get away."

Shaykh regarded Snooky a long time. "Yes, even better than poison," he said finally.

Back in our lodgings that surprising man had yet another surprise for us: an unexpected change to our travel plans. We were not going back to Singapore. The first group – now returned to the city state and waiting there – would have to make the ferry trip back to Riau a second time in order to join us. The most junior *juwae* over there (he was by far the youngest among us) was to return home to the *pondok* by himself as too tender in years for the potential hardships we faced. Shaykh hadn't even brought him to Riau but left him in Singapore all the time. I was quite surprised as it was precisely him whom Shaykh always trusted to run not his riskiest but his most delicate errands where discretion and loyalty were of the utmost essence. For instance, taking petty cash to town once a week back home to support the family of the dead Mujahid he accorded *sadaqah* out of the goodness of his heart. OK, call me snoopy, not Snooky.

Haji Hassan, however, was to be neither silent nor accepting. "We have return tickets," he remonstrated. "We have paid good money for these. Why did you not buy single fares? This is wasteful. The planning was poor. It is, forgive me, Tuan, *spendthrift*."

"God willing, Hassan, you are pardoned," said Shaykh. "The one-way fare was Singapore $21 but, Praise be to God, return was S$25.50 cents. It was prudent to pay the extra. Had we decided to return but only purchased the one-way fare it would have been $42, leaving us to pay extra . . . er . . ."

"Praise be to God, $16.50 cents each," said Hassan.

"I commend your accuracy and precision, Haji, or rather that of your calculator, but what the device in your palm cannot tell you is that there is balance of risk and reward. Only a trained mathematician could know this. Your little circuit-board could not tell you this. God willing, risk was very small, in fact $4.50, while reward was greater. Thank you, Ahmed, I see you remember the Game Theory. In any case, among the Faithful though by appearance we are obviously numbered, they may not have let us in without return tickets. Those of us unlucky enough not to be in your shoes and possess an Indonesian passport, of course, Hassan."

Snooky had glimpsed Shaykh's own travel document at the Tanjung Batu ferry terminal where they had been not only (of course) slower and less efficient than at the Woodlands crossing in Singapore but had paused to heft it significantly by way of hint. It had been a Pakistani passport – obviously less attention-grabbing than the Saudi or Yemeni article Shaykh was entitled to – and he had got hit for the US$20 visa fee non-ASEANS got charged. Poor Haji Hassan paid as if he was watching himself donate life-blood.

Actually on hearing of the alteration to our itinerary, it was Imam Umar who was affected by the most dismay. Whether by accident or design, he heard it alone from Shaykh's lips. He'd been out of the room smoking or relieving himself (the fruit had been a heaven-sent loosener of all our travel-bound bowels) or perhaps both simultaneously when Shaykh told us. The old man's face had dropped a mile. He looked – I choose a nice word and do not exaggerate – flabbergasted. "My books," he gabbled. "The rakoum and pistachios. Everyone will think I have run and deserted them. What are you thinking of, man?"

"*Bapak*," said Shaykh in a steely voice I had never heard before, "*what* did you just call me?"

Umar's expostulations ceased. Had Haji Tariq been there the Imam would have been in jeopardy of having violent hands laid upon his dignified person. "Do not," said Shaykh, "forget yourself again."

"God willing," quickly interposed Haji Hassan, "he will not. Shaykh, we are both prepared to travel third-class to the destination of your choice. Singly or jointly. Accompanied or unaccompanied by baggage. Receipts will be submitted in proper form after due interval." Poor Hassan. Like many Indons, he detested unpleasantness more than he feared bloodshed.

I also couldn't stand it any longer and went to see to my stripey bags. I was in charge of several of these. They contained 3,793 bootleg DVDs. Many people seem to think that China is the worst IP rights violator. In fact, it is not. Malaysia is. Of course, this is a footling academic distinction. Malaysian *Chinese* dominate this particular black market. You didn't seriously think it would be any other ethnic group, did you?

It was gonna be our alibi. We were posing as smugglers of these harmless objects. If Chinese made the disks, it was Muslims who smuggled them into the Philippines by the southern backdoor. That was Plan A. If that failed to convince, Plan B was to admit we were *dada* or drug runners and then pay a bigger bribe to whomsoever.

Snooky had done her best. I mean, to uphold certain cultural standards. It is interesting how degradation occurs across a gradated spectrum. Mostly, the DVD counterfeiters did purvey mass market crap, with the odd great director by accident. You could say quality protected you from victimisation. I was able, however, to get a dozen disks of *Seven Samurai*, two of *Rashomon*, and one each of *Dersu Uzala*, and *Sanjuro* and *Yojimbo*, plus a couple of *The World of Apu*, and *Shadows of a Hot Summer* by the Czech director František Vláčil and one of a superior Taiwanese love story entitled *One Day at the Beach*. I like dramatised documentary, which may surprise you, y'know, factions as they call them. Shortly before I left Bangkok I had discovered the British director Nicholas Broomfield – or is it Bromhead? My memory, so sharp and retentive once, is becoming dulled, not, I think, through repetitive worship and study so much as physical indisposition. Anyway, this Bromhead was a helluva handsome guy, if that was really him on the bootleg cover.

I also got Nick Roeg's *Performance*. They should have had someone from the Factory do Jagger's role – I mean get a real TV for the movie. Trouble was, once you'd relaxed your standards infinitesimally you'd do it again and there'd be a multiplier effect. From *Mr Hulot's Holiday* you'd go to Mr Bean – which I liked a lot – but then pretty soon you'd be wallowing in the trough amongst American Fraternity House comedies. I'd start with *Battleship Potemkin*, allow *Tora! Tora! Tora!* then wind up with *McHale's Navy*. Drop your standards, like your knickers, once and you'll do it again and again. Each of the film's neighbours was respectable but, as the road got longer, it soon got sleazy and in the end people would leap out of demolished houses and mug you – the cultural zombies. It was a lesson for life. Finally Snooky just crammed what she could into the bags with some honest hard-core porn in the middle, like a bag of sanitising mothballs in a urinal.

To cut a long story short, our first group came over from Singapore, unchaperoned, with the bags of movies. It worked so neatly I figured Shaykh must have been planning it during the long hours on the train. The first group knew the ropes, such as they were, of getting over the meek stretch of water and Shaykh would not be around if there was hassle with the contraband. (The borders we'd go through later were far more primitive and porous). Perfect. For Shaykh.

In the dilute dawnlight we prayed united among the mangroves of a small islet. Imam Umar led us. Shaykh was prostrate behind him. The new arrivals acceding knew nothing of the strain between them, such as it had been. I did not see a flawed old man before me but a zealot of the true and the clean, his physical frailty transmuted into the strength of ages by his own conviction and that of the generations who had gone before him, imbued in their belief in God and their Brothers. I felt one of them. For the first time I felt one of them. One of us. In short, I had a starring part as the stoolie in *Infernal Affairs*.

Of course, I was a long way from the arm of retribution and revelation. The Crusaders could reach out to get me in the *pondok*. But not here. And not there – where we were going. We were going into the unknown, the violent and contingent unknown, but the paradox was it acted as a sanctuary for Snooky.

Before we boarded the small boat that would take us through the shallows to the larger, waiting craft, Shaykh spoke. It was obvious he had been working on this one for a long time. It was far from extemporaneous but one appreciated it more rather than less for that. Who wants to be sacrificed on a moment's whim?

He said, "My Sons, my Younger Brothers in Jihad, you are the unsullied, the brave, the righteous and virtuous warriors of God. Given the prevalence of weakness and malice in this world, the victory of strength and goodness is far from assured. In the next world God will provide His reckoning.

"The Mujaheedin and the martyrs will assuredly enter Paradise and the Unrighteous will know agony equivalent to the joy of those Blessed to enter Paradise. But in this world it is for us the Mujaheedin, you the *juwae*, to do God's Work for him in the interim, to castigate and to chastise the Infidel. So far we have erred on the side of moderation. In fact, far too much. Moderation in personal dealings within the Ummah is usually a good thing but not in the Jihad. Jihad is extreme and severe.

"From now things will change. From now you will change. God willing, we are journeying to a part of the Caliphate, as it will be, where the Holy War is already extreme and the Infidel enemy cruel and brutal. At home at the *pondok*, our Jihad is lukewarm; it does not yet simmer. Where we go, it is hot enough to scald the hands of the Crusaders and their minions. And, of course, in Afghanistan the waters of Jihad passed boiling point long, long ago . . ." He permitted himself a sardonic smile and we all laughed.

"You will learn where we are going, you will train and, God willing, you will participate. You will return home and you will begin a new and stronger Jihad at home. God is Great! Now let us board."

We all let out a cheer, even Snooky. Yah, I was full of the essence of the *arabica* bean and as the contents of the black glass had also moved my bowels I did not fear a long boat journey. I was about to splash through the shallows to the prow with the rest when Imam Umar irritably gestured to me. He turned my face to the horizon, mounted my back, and told me to carry him. If I was Snow White and Shaykh was the Prince, he was Grumpy.

GIRL, *tea ruck*, it was a good thing we didn't know what awaited us. Mindanao was a pocket Afghanistan in the making and Jolo even worse. How can I put it? We'd been playing. Cutting heads off, blowing people up – we'd done that, been there, got the T-shirt, but we'd still been in kindergarten. This was for real. This was for keeps.

It started well. Haji Tariq and Jefri were waiting for us. If it had been the gates of Hell they'd have been waiting for us with indomitable grins on their faces. Haji Tariq simply stepped into the water and did willingly what I had done under compulsion with Imam Umar. He carried Shaykh ashore. This doubled as the embrace of welcome. Haji Hassan was last off the outrigger, frowning and telling off the milling boys on the sand with his forefinger in a vain attempt to count their number.

"God Willing, we're all accounted for, Haji," yelled Iskander, seeing what he was doing. "No one has been lost!" Iskander had his player on. Tinny Arabic pop meshed with the rasping of the cicadas' legs in the acacias and talisay trees.

"God is Great," muttered Imam Umar, sounding almost disappointed.

As the pondoks led us to our quarters, Snooky thought, "Shaykh is a showman. We weren't dawdling, he wasn't inefficient. He wanted to arrive last. He wanted our arrival to be the centrepiece and finale for the others." And he had kept Umar and Hassan with him – the tetchiest of travel companions whom the Messenger of God himself (peace be upon His head) might not have tolerated in his caravan – so that they could not create mischief in his absence.

For others, like the Imam and the Haji, the few weeks of the journey in the evenings of their existence were as a few hours to us in the morning of our lives. But for us it was an aeon: startling transformations could take place in that time.

Jefri had changed.

You could see that straightaway. It wasn't physical. He was still a runt who was never gonna gain even half an inch more in height. I would always tower over him. His whiskers remained sparse as the goat-nibbled grass on this dirty beach. Quiet and restrained he still was; respectful to his elders, considerate to his juniors, he had always been. But the schoolboy magnetism had turned into a subtler charisma. In the old days you'd be drawn into Jefri's orbit and the circle of his friends and then be faintly disappointed that there was nothing more. I mean no programme, no agenda. Now he had purpose and will, assertion and belief. And an edge. He was equable, he was kind, and that made his ruthlessness all the less resistible.

"Ah, Jefri," said Imam Umar as I dropped him off my back next to my old school-friend, not at his request. "The children have found their way home unaccompanied, I see."

"God willing, Imam," said Jefri, "the grave will be my home and yours." Umar was visibly disconcerted. "With your blind eyes, Imam," Jefri continued, "I shall be your guide. God is Great. He may yet open them. Be one of them, Tuan."

"*Insh'Allah,*" stammered the elderly cleric and, as I led Jefri to Shaykh and Haji Tariq, I saw the fury on Umar's face.

"So," said Shaykh quite jovially, "the boy has become a man."

"The boy has become a man," said Tariq. Shaykh's words were a question, Tariq's the answer. Shaykh kissed Jefri on both cheeks, a salutation he had never employed on anyone before. The page – in those bathetic Hollywood jousts and tournaments – kneels, is tapped on the shoulder, and rises a knight. This was the *pondok* equivalent, with Jefri as poor Heath Ledger.

I looked round. The trip had been beautiful. Island after island, atoll after atoll, thrown down like glowing amber beads in a backing of Navajo turquoise. This scrappy beach had also looked ravishing from a distance. I wasn't sure which country we were in. No good asking Haji Tariq. "In the Caliphate," would be the gruff and unhelpful answer. Most of the pondoks had no idea where we were, still less curiosity. Yah, Snooky didn't like it at all. If she didn't know who or what (or which) she was, it was essential to know where. I began to feel giddy. I smelled the same smell of aluminium in my nostrils as I had at Hat Yai railway station. I figured at least if I keeled over and no one caught me, sand was softer than a concrete platform.

"Here," said Jefri. "Have a tissue." He used our lovely transliterative word *cheechoo*. "Your nose is bleeding."

"Thanks, *kha*."

"It's nothing."

"Where are we, Jefri?"

"Couldn't you work it out?"

"Don't be a smart-alec."

"What's that?"

"A wise-ass."

"I'm not. It's easy."

"How?"

"Where was the sun most of your trip? It has to be the same as ours." (Jefri, it turned out, had gone to Manado in North Celebes by ship, then onwards by smaller boat here).

"I didn't notice."

"That's a shame. Think about it. The sun sets in the West and rises in the East. It was always at our 11 o' clock on the high left at our second prayer. That means we were heading North-West . . ."

"Of course, he could also have just taken the teeniest peek at the prayer compass Haji Tariq gave him," interposed Iskander, punching Jefri on the shoulder.

"It dropped overboard from my hands when I was feeling seasick," expostulated Jefri. "I had to get the direction of Mecca from the sun."

"Yah, yah, yah," I said, joining in the sport, Jefri-baiting. I really think we were different from the older generation. We could admire Jefri and still poke fun at him.

"So," continued Jefri, undaunted, "we could be in Indonesian Kalimantan, Sarawak or Sabah, or the Philippines. It depends how far you travelled as well as the direction. And you'd have to work it out from the speed of your conveyance and the hours travelled. You travelled too far to be in Borneo still, so it's the Philippines or no-man's land like the Turtle Islands. If we're in the Philippines we're clearly on a small island, so it's not Palawan or Mindanao. Which leaves Tawi-Tawi or Jolo."

"Which is all part of the old Sultanate of Sulu anyway," said Iskander. "Remember the lessons?"

As it was all sinking in, something occurred to me. "Hey, black heart. You led your group. You knew the destination all along."

"God willing," said Jefri, "always look for the simple explanation."

Iskander and I chased the nimbler Jefri up the beach. Behind us, Shaykh, Tariq, and Hassan followed more sedately but engaged in animated discussion, while Imam Umar brought up the sulky rear.

WE WERE IN Tawi-Tawi, actually. Tawi was the string of islands right at the end of the Philippines. You could think of them, like I said, as a necklace of amber beads, getting smaller towards the end. They were mostly reef and atoll, very low-lying. Looming a little to the North-east under a fleecy skullcap and more substantial was Jolo island, with its mountains and jungles, like a re-sectioned slice of our own joint in Pattani.

Even for us, as opposed to the likes of the vacationing Avril, the seascape was stunningly beautiful, a word I tended to reserve for the winner of Miss Gay World, Tiffany's Theatre, rather than a mere vista. Turquoise, white, blue and green, were the prevailing colours and I resolved to remember this particular combo for mix 'n match in my attire on future and happier occasions.

Every now and then the scaffolding of fish traps and occasionally whole stilt villages whizzed by us in the thunder of our outboards and the slap of the spray. The Venice of the East. Well, yah, if the metropolis of the Doges (I can spell it but not pronounce it) had been ramshackle and filthy instead of grand and imposing. The refuelling stop at a sea-gypsy village had been the same anti-climax as the scruffy strand on which we had greeted Jefri with such joy. From a distance, it was glorious; once there, you stood on the municipal land-fill. Did I share these thoughts? Snooky did not. Reflections are not welcome at the Vampire Ball.

Darkness came like an invisible wizard had waved his wand. It conferred even more romance than distance did. I am not talking about girl-boy or even boy-boy, silly; I am still rhapsodising about that darn beach. Suddenly it became Camelot, Manhattan, Hollywood Boulevard. In the distance the dusk was adorned by the soft dots of multiple cooking-fires. I knew it was only the sandiest rice and the coarsest of little fish – more needle-bones than flesh – but each spark of flame held the allure and promise of the unknown. Closer at hand, the impending darkness softened and glamorised daylight's banalities. What was ugly was beautified, what nondescript made special. A black sand hillock became a couch fit for the Grand Mufti. My companions' homely faces became as profound and striking as the countenances of the sages and warriors of legend and our teachers were as the lower angels. Shaykh himself seemed . . . but in my enthusiasm I have strayed close to the frontier of blasphemy. Honey, honey, *tea ruck*, our mean circumstances, transformed by the alchemy of evening, became the frame for a *sura* rendered by Cecil B. DeMille.

Above us, the star-field seemed the reflection of the cooking-fires in an ocean now dark and inverted. In my heart I knew it was all illusion, that this was the still centre of the typhoon passing over and next time it might tear my life apart but I pushed reality away with all my might. I wished I could do a tab of E or even some ketamine.

This benison of evening was naturally nothing novel to me. The same happened nightly in all the beer gardens, BBQ stalls, and brothels of the Kingdom, not to mention the Christian Republic in whose insurgent nether regions and rebellious rump we now found ourselves. Yet my mood was not impervious to its magic.

As good Muslims we had neither spirits (other than our own high ones) nor (if Imam Umar had anything to do with it) music, nor was our feast of welcome more than the materials of Prophet Jesus' Sermon on the Mount.

It had been a long journey; we were all tired, not just the old men. At first the wine of joy exhilarated, then it exhausted. Inebriate it never did. Stereophonic buzzing and rasping told me many of my companions had found oblivion. We had got on to a time machine again. No electricity, just the twinkle in the heavens and the grey and orange ash of the driftwood. We could have been a seventh century Arab raiding party recuperating in the sands of time.

Beside me both Jefri and Iskander had closed their eyes. I sighed and stretched my long length luxuriantly. My mind, even without speed, was always too active for sleep to come quickly even when I was physically finished. Not so my companions. Sleep came easily to them, the clean, the simple.

Snooky had her arms out, again to cite Prophet Jesus, in the position of crucifixion when many hours later Jefri rolled sideways and wound up with his head on her shoulder. I hardly dared move. If it had been my arm I would have got cramp or pins and needles. Like this, I could tolerate the burden indefinitely. A quiet joy built up in me and never diminished in the long hours. Snooky has never been so contented before or since. How I long to have that moment again. I do believe it was the still point, the centre, the eye of my life – not in the chronological sense (this epiphany would have had to occur for me at the age of 13) but in the symbolic sense which conferred meaning on my entire existence. It was a moment of fulfilment, chaste and decent. There was nothing dirty about it, nothing of the lewdness I had been no stranger to. I knew I loved Jefri and I loved him as a sister might. While it was still dark, Jefri opened his eyes and realised where he was and who he was with. He smiled.

"Snooky," he said, looking up at me. Not Ahmed. Snooky.

"Go back to sleep," I said. "Go back to sleep, my brother."

FROM Tawi-Tawi to Jolo was the hop, Jolo to Basilan the skip, and Basilan to Zamboanga the jump. Straight from the frying-pan into the fire. But at first it was playful. It was like hopping across a ford from a small stepping-stone to increasingly larger ones, Snooky not omitting to shriek, of course. Our guides became more ruffianly, our reception-committees more daunting with every crossing. After the customary Arabic salutations uttered by Shaykh or Tariq, our own burbling pleasantries of conversation became ever more perfunctory and stilted until finally, in Zamboanga del Sur, they withered and died on our lips.

Our escorts had always been armed but the weapons got heavier and more modern every time and their accoutrements and costume less ragged until on the mainland they no longer cut the piratical figure of Malay myth but were indistinguishable from the regular soldiers who were our mortal foe. The strong-faced robots who met us in broad daylight carried the latest American carbines and wore camouflage battle-dress and boots. Only the black handkerchiefs they wound round their heads distinguished them from our enemies (as I thought, until I discovered that the Philippine soldiers and their US advisers wore them, too).

Haji Hassan actually ducked below the gunwales of our motorised skiff when he saw them, then pretended all he'd done was lose his prayer-beads rather than his dignity in subservience to his fright.

Haji Tariq missed this demeaning piece of uncoolness but Iskander and I didn't. Our faces remained those of dutiful disciples but we read each other's thoughts. Here, one Haji T. was gonna be worth 20 Haji H's. Trade with you, cutie, I thought, Iskander having offered to swap me the pod 'n phones for the red heart-shaped shades I'd brought along for the sea-rides. I'd hidden them, as items of high contraband, at the *pondok* with my chemical stash but on the boats Haji Hassan, for one, had not been too conservative to borrow them. In fact, I'd had to re-possess them from his cloth bag on the sly. They were patterned, the sunglasses, after the ones worn by Sue Lyon in the opening credits of *Lolita* but did not really make the Haji look nymph-like. More like the Christian take on Satan.

FROM THE coast of the huge island of Mindanao our steps led us ineluctably to the mountains. The inclines grew steeper, the vegetation changed, the temperature dropped, the earlobes of the inhabitants lengthened. Jefri saw his first conifer. "Oh, haven't you seen evergreens before?" I asked carelessly. I had seen them once before in my life during a class trip to Baguio, the Zermatt of Luzon. With every step upwards Shaykh and Tariq seemed to draw strength and Haji Hassan and Imam Umar to become visibly disheartened and physically (if possible) weaker. Shaykh would pause during our ascent, not to recuperate but to suck the peppermint-scented air into his lungs for sheer pleasure. "Home," said Shaykh to Tariq, "the scent of home. It's the same. Clean." And Tariq would soften for a moment.

IT TOOK US four days to get to Camp Baku Babu. Hard even for the young, harder still for the elderly scholars. We had to carry them in the end in the same slings as the Moros would carry their wounded. I don't know if Shaykh knew it but it made Umar and Hassan very unpopular after the second day. It was kind of a physical emblem of their total uselessness in this context. Once, it rained hard for three hours. Imam Umar cursed the rain and cursed the students carrying him. Shaykh looked on with strange satisfaction. As the drops slapped my cheeks, I thought, "I'll trust in God and keep my powder dry. My face-powder." I must have laughed out loud for, "That's good, *koti*," Haji Tariq startled me. "Keep your sense of humour." Coming from him, that was rich.

Camp B.B. stunned not so much with its fortifications which were both prodigious and medieval – as with its brazenness. I mean, it was huge, honey. It was a flagrant provocation to the Christians and their seat of government 1,000 miles away. It shouted, loud enough to be heard at that remove, "Here we are and we will not be moved." No attempt was made at concealment. Like, everyone knew where it was. It comprised, though of irregular shape, many square miles – maybe more than Jomtien – and was a honeycomb of bunkers, tunnels, and shelters as well as a thriving surface township of schools, dwellings, and – of course – places of worship. For the local Air Force the Moros held less regard than they did for the dengue-carrying mosquitoes. They were inhabiting a little piece of Tora Bora transplanted to Asia. They did not so much defend a sanctuary as assert an immunity. For them the most immediate danger was not the soldiers supposedly hunting them but their family enemies. These historic feuds and antique vendettas, known as *rido*, usually with an origin in sisters seduced or irrigation interfered with, could reach out and claim their lives at any time.

We'd been guided by relays of escorts. The last of these melted into the scrubby hillside without a word of farewell – this would have been asymmetrical, as there had not been a word of greeting. Jefri snubbed my rueful glance which I had been planning to follow up by slitting my throat with a finger. (I'd been growing my nails on the sly, ready with the excuse I was following the Imam's example. Good Muslim boys weren't really supposed to do this).

From a well-concealed outpost, now identifiable as a machine-gun nest situated to fire down the entire length of our path, stepped Haji Tariq at the head of a retinue of bandolier-swathed cut-throats. Even by the Haji's standards this was startling as he had been behind me, well to the rear, addressing unwanted words of exhortation to Imam Umar and Haji Hassan. Somehow he had covered 20 metres of distance in the time it took to blink, um, one eye. This was the thing, though; his eye had healed and was no longer pirate-patched. Looking closer, he had also transferred his hook to his uninjured hand and the missing one had regenerated itself. Otherwise, the Haji remained himself: ferocious beard, baleful countenance, dwarf legs, hook-nose, burly chest straining through the confines of his gown and waistcoat.

"Tariq, my brother!" he called. "Be one of them!"

From our rear, next to Imam Umar, who was doing a flabbergasted double-take as if Tariq might be the veritable Shaitane of his suspicions, Tariq himself bellowed, "Imran, my brother!"

Of course, it only took a moment for the penny to drop with even the slowest of us. The Haji had a twin. But it was like pain – you felt it immediately but it was a while before you appreciated it. Through our tiredness we smiled glazed, idiot smiles. The two substantial figures advanced towards each other like colliding trucks. They embraced. The hooks patted each other's back. Now they were mating crabs, identically shelled except our Haji had a knapsack while Brother Imran bore on his broad shoulders not one, not two, but three rockets. These turned out to be as much a fixture of his daily appearance as his boots; so that one imagined him able to blast off to safety in the next valley should the security forces ever get their act together and overrun us.

He and Shaykh knew each other, apparently well. Imran treated Shaykh with as much respect and deference as did Tariq, while Shaykh was easy with his underling's obeisance.

"How is the old soldier?" Imran asked Shaykh at our dinner of roast goat. "God Willing, well?"

"I am sorry to tell you he died these many years," Shaykh replied. "God is Great, unlike his two brothers, my uncles, he died peacefully in his bed, safe from the spite of his enemies."

"May God be well-pleased with him," said Imran.

"I rely on God," said Shaykh. "In many respects he was blind and misguided, but even in his obstinacy he was always the companion of valour and honour. And, this is something, he was being loyal to the last."

"Yes," said Imran. "He was of the old school. And, God Willing, so shall we be faithful in our constancy."

"God is Great. Certainly you and Tariq, but not everyone. I have things to impart."

This conversation took place round our own fireside but if I have to describe the camp canteen or mess, it resembled nothing so much as the inter-galactic bar in *Star Wars I*. All kinds and descriptions of insurgents from every corner of the world would come to train here, now that Afghanistan and Libya were closed to them. Many of the Philippine Mujaheedin commanders turned out to have been graduates of the Waziristan camps of the 80s during the war against the USSR. These camps were no more to the warriors of God, but from being the most zealous students the Filipinos had in their turn become Professors of Jihad. And as Brother Imran put it, "From the number of the warriors of God, they were always the most valiant and zealous," meaning had killed and mutilated the most Russians. Now everyone came here to learn the unholy techniques of Holy War.

We had firing-ranges, explosives labs, demolition sites, building mock-ups, on site jungle-training (joke, honey), first-aid lessons including non-*sharia* amputation, a rusty airliner hull (very small, as Cartoon liked to reassure her prospective customers), a rappelling cliff, a two-span suspension bridge as often re-built as demolished, and, as you will see, a plethora of sacrificial victims.

Where we relaxed from these endeavours and ate, every language as well as the most virgin Arabic could be heard. Just like the variegated rasps, clicks, buzzes, squawks, and squeals of the droids, tentacled aliens, little green men, and furry space yetis of the Lucas movie, we heard the tongues of impassive Mongolian giants, Somalian stickmen, grinning Egyptian dwarves, sombre Chechens, volatile Iraqis, dour Saudis, chatty Palestininans, even Chinese Uighurs who spoke Arabic of a perfection to match the Yemenis. Then also Uzbeks, Tajiks, Dagestanis, and Syrians. Only one representative from the Star Wars saloon was absent – the bounty hunter with the ray gun. He'd never have made it within ten feet of the gate guards without being raygun-incinerated. The likes of Imran preyed on predators.

We had brought gifts with us to propitiate our stern hosts. It was a Filipino custom, the *pasalubong*. Ours were *kris* from the *pondok's* own workshop; that is to say, the Malay sword or dagger with a blade wavy as a mermaid's tresses. Snooky figured if you got stabbed with one, the wound path would be as circuitous as the disputational logic we learned in the Imam's rhetoric class. Every knife had its own character or spirit. Antique ones would be possessed by the ghosts of those whose lives it had taken. The white-hot blades were quenched in a special cradle under running water during the full moon; their history was visible only to a baby, or the blind, and I watched Umar's face closely as he handled one. Nope. He sure wasn't seeing ghosts as he chuckled over the fine workmanship.

"Tch, Tch," clucked Haji Hassan. "There was no need for ivory and pearl for the inlay on the scabbard. Wasteful."

Tariq was showing Imran how the kris handle was completely different from all the other knives in the world, Arab as well as Crusader. You didn't grip it in your palm. It was a T-shaped grip. You made a fist and the blade protruded between the serration of your fore and index fingers. The horizontal of the T lay in your palm like the grip of Do-Ann's knuckleduster. You didn't stab, you punched with your full weight and a straight arm, imparting a force that could puncture a coin.

"Mmm, mmm," said Imran. You could see he was longing, just longing, to try it out; hopefully, on a dog or goat.

If this talk of spirits and visions vouchsafed the blind and the unknowing sounds un-Islamic, yah, it is, but then so is stabbing people. In the last resort, even the Haji and the Imam, even Jefri, were Malays and a certain permissible cloudiness went with the territory. Anyhow, the kris were well received, though not with the rapturous delirium Shaykh might have been hoping for. The traditional Moro versions, with plain *narra* or Philippine mahogany handles, were kinda more barbaric but also more business-like than ours. They didn't look so outta place, stuck into a sash or belt, next to a smoke grenade or a pistol; they looked as neat and appropriate as an old tiled mosque next to some glassy Dubai skyscraper.

Snooky can say the training offered in tertiary terrorism was way in advance of the *pondok*, though we did have to pray every time we re-filled the armalite magazines on the range and every circuit we made of the obstacle-course. We were filmed doing this, in black hoods, by an Egyptian Haji Hassan either knew already or became close to on the basis of his youthful years in Cairo. Why I personally had to wear the hood, I don't know. I mean, *tea ruck*, I was unrecognisable. No one from my Bangkok days would possibly have realised it was Snooky. We were told to look at the lens and shout "God is Great!" in the spirit in which the cute American boys on CNN would shout "Airborne!" or "We own the night!"

By the way, our pirate DVDs made more welcome gifts than our knives. Not the Japanese classics, of course, but the Taiwanese and Hong Kong kung fu flicks. I recognised my own subtitles on some of them. I had an unpleasant moment with the Twin Brothers, whom I had privately named the Left Hook and the Right Hook. It was something to do with Shaykh. I still don't understand it. I'd put a Satyajit Ray classic, set in 1947, into the Chinese DVD player that was so universal it could have played an egg sandwich, if that's what you'd laid on the tray, and was over-cautiously waiting for any glitches with the remote in my hand when Tariq shoved me roughly aside. He didn't know how to operate it, just pulled the plug out.

"Idiot!" he bellowed. "You want to set him off again?"

"What, Haji? Ahmed doesn't understand."

"There is plenty you don't understand but, God willing, you shall! Understand this!" And he drew his fist back.

It was Jefri who grabbed it. "Haji!" he remonstrated. Jefri was not a complicated person but he could achieve subtle things thoughtlessly that other people couldn't if they pondered it for a million years. Like now, he could do firmness and deference all in the same line. Tariq went off to join Imran, muttering imprecations in the language I couldn't understand.

"Hair-do," said Iskander, "that's *bahasa* hair-do. Some of the Afghans know the language, too. Put on another war film. How about the Korean one?"

We'd sneaked a look at this by ourselves already. Movies were a grey area. Banned at the *pondok* along with pop music, films appeared to be allowed in Camp BB. Like, our hosts were incomparably more bloodthirsty than the Malayan clerics but, by way of compensation, cut themselves more slack when they hit the pause button on Jihad. Of course, there was no liquor to be seen and absolutely not a pig in sight. The Moros were the absolute opposite of Snooky – grave where she was skittish, brave where she was cowardly. If nobility meant a marmoreal head as well as a heart of flint, they were noble.

Unfortunately the DVD sleeve contained the wrong disc – I think Iskander had been slyly viewing either the porn or *High School Musical* – and I no longer held the remote. God is Great, it wasn't Japanese schoolgirls in sailor-suits going down on each other, but it was a Spielberg combat movie. Snooky's heart sank. The remote lay propped in Imran's hook while he fast-forwarded with one of the four fingers of his "good" hand. It was too late to do anything. Brother Imran pressed PLAY just as Shaykh arrived with Haji Hassan and the Imam. Umar saw what was on and flounced away with Hassan in tow. Shaykh seated himself next to the Twins.

Five minutes later, I dared look. Shaykh was rapt, the same expression as he had when talking about the Caliphate. It did not leave him for five episodes of the miniseries before we had a crap break. (The *lack* of spicy food was depriving our bowels of a bacterial bodyguard). "Sorry, Shaykh," Snooky mumbled. "God Willing, you can forgive Ahmed. I did not mean to show you Crusader propaganda."

Shaykh looked at me in surprise. "On the contrary, Ahmed. I rely on God, we can learn from this."

"What?"

Shaykh patted me on my shoulder. "They were indeed brothers. They were loyal to each other, they sacrificed for each other, they gave their lives. They never betrayed each other. They never betrayed their salt."

"C-rations," contributed Iskander cheerfully. "Those guns, they call them Garand. The older Moros have some here. They must be 50 years old. I mean, the rifles."

"The best," said Imran. "God Willing, the most powerful still."

"Better Lee Enfield," Tariq contradicted his Twin. "They are 100 years old and still carry further than the AKs."

"If it was up to you two, we would still be carrying jezails," said Shaykh, laughing. He saw Hassan and Umar conferring on a log and frowned. "Some of us will not see the age of 100," he said. "Come, God Willing, we shall see more."

More turned out to be even more surprising. Our Shaykh was transfixed by a movie about a schizophrenic American mathematician, played by an Australian actor who normally did action. (As great a change as Tariq writing a tome on philosophy). I had to repossess the remote from his elegant hand while he was talking to Imran as, like all our senior members, Shaykh was absent-minded enough to misplace the device and forget where he'd left it.

ALTHOUGH ALL foreigners at the camp ate together, we divided into sub-camps otherwise and we were placed with Indonesians and Cambodians, there being some overlap with the likes of Haji Hassan and our own Cham knifemakers from Pailin. So this meant we were spared the attentions of the severer Saudi and Yemeni Wahabbists. These guys had been more in evidence at the first camp, Camp Abubakhar (Camp AB), which had been captured a couple of years ago by the Philippine army under the Presidency of the B-Movie actor, Joseph Estrada, who can be described as Ronald Reagan gone Latino. All this put fancy notions in my gay little head. After pistol practice, where Imam Umar scored a bull's eye – in Jefri's target – I broke the idea to Shaykh. He just smiled quizzically. Quizzical Shaykh could do. It was beyond the rest of them. I mean, they had never known a moment's doubt, still less a lifetime's scepticism.

What did Snooky venture to suggest?

We were gonna make a Mujahideen Movie, something that could have been entitled Band of Zealots.

Imam Umar was vehement in his opposition. "The Talibs interpreted the Will of God correctly," he pronounced. "In the Caliphate there will be no music, no images, no pictures. And this is a picture. They call films pictures. Am I correct, Hassan?"

"Correct, Imam. You are always correct. God Willing, will continue to be."

"Think of those films of the Mujahideen in Iraq which you so much enjoyed, Imam," Snooky persisted. "The ones Jefri 2 showed to you on Youtube. The one with the Humvee blown 20 feet in the air? The sniper shooting the American marine through the helmet? And the replaying it in slo-mo ten times, him falling and resurrected again? And Haji Hassan told Iskander he liked the score, he remembered it from the cafés in Cairo?"

"The music was amusing, Ahmed," said Haji Hassan primly, "because it was what they call incongruous. It was cheerful and did not go with the shooting. That is the only reason I laughed. I rely on God to acquit me."

"It is called a counter-point, Haji," Snooky said.

"God created Eye and Ear to work together, Ahmed, not against each other," Imam Umar said. "This is the work of Shaitane."

"God is Great," Haji Hassan said. "His Balance was never in Trial."

"For every action," Shaykh said, "there is a reaction. For every transgression there is punishment. God is Great. For every betrayal there is a retribution. Ahmed, there is being no problem here. If it helps the cause of the Caliphate, God will bless it. The end justifies the mean."

"It will be the propaganda of our cause, Shaykh," Snooky said.

The conversation went on for some time after this. What Hassan, Umar, and especially Shaykh agreed on, though, was this: that the events should be real, based on something that had actually happened. "The Brotherly Bond – they were real people," he said. "You see them as old men first talking about the things they did when they were young. This was why I did not stop viewing immediately."

"It's called talking heads, Shaykh," Snooky said.

Now Tariq interrupted, "Heads cannot talk. God is Great. That is the whole point of it. Their mouths are silenced for ever. Shaykh?"

"God Willing, I think the word Ahmed is looking for is interview," Shaykh said, patting me on the shoulder. "Talking head is being the very simple expression of the uneducated. It is like calling a gun a shooter or a cup a drinker, if you do not know the word. You are forgetting your English, Ahmed. Maybe that is for the good."

I bit my lip, my moustached lip.

Haji Hassan said, "He cannot forget it. We can burn the tattoos and bury them beneath a scar but we cannot do it to words. You can burn the books but not the thoughts in them. They are an indelible record."

Shaykh said, "God Willing, numbers, too, Hassan," and to my shock they both giggled like girls.

The AV equipment in the camp was top quality, both expensive and modern. It was a poor country and we were in the most impoverished part but the movement itself was awash with cash. *Zikat* or charity flowed in from the *ummah*, supplemented with local windfalls such as ransoms, free passages, immunities, and blatant loot. The cameras and recorders were as good as their guns but while the latter had been employed expertly, the former had been amateurishly used. They could set great ambushes – so Iskander and Jefri related to me with awe – but the standard propaganda shoot was a line of hooded Mujaheedin, festooned with rifle grenades, coming out the forest in single file.

They lopped heads as readily as we plucked fruit but had never put the deeds on what Shaykh called their "spidersite" (I did not repay his earlier words to me by correcting him). As for the genre of the martyrdom video, the suicide attack was as unknown here as it was in Pattani. There was also as big a gap between their rank and file and their leaders as there was with us. To the man, the Moro and Abu chieftains were pious Afghanistan veterans whose physical presence rivalled that of Tariq and Imran. But they led hillbillies. They were the directors at the head of a mob of milling extras who had to be positioned, used, paid, fed and watered.

The way to circumvent our elders' prohibition on anything made-up or fictional was to offer them something historical. I offered them an epic from the past. I had a ready-made subject.

Our hosts in Jolo had told us fireside tales of the infamous massacre American troops had carried out on their island in 1906. This was The Massacre of the Moro Crater where 600 Muslims, just a few hundred of them warriors, the rest women and children, had been shot like fish in a barrel by US soldiers standing on the lip of the dormant volcano. It was modern weapons against sharpened poles and knives. My Lai had nothing on it.

The corpses had been piled up like fat pork in an adobo stew. Even Americans had been shocked when they saw the photos of the atrocity in their newspapers. The massacre in the crater had finished the Hassan Uprising (yah, we all laughed at that, the Haji the loudest). It had begun when the local hero had krised an American officer (stabbed, OK, not smooched) but the fate of the rebels had been sealed when Moros in the service of the Americans had refused to surrender their guns to their fellow Muslims. That was hilarious when you looked at what the modern Moro freely bought from rogue sergeants in the Philippine army. Shaykh, oddly enough, had nodded almost in approval when hearing of the native soldiers' misplaced fidelity. Our own Hassan, his usual mildness gone, snapped, "The same as those Dutch dogs, the Ambonese. They fought against *merdeka*."

"They did not betray their salt," Tariq said stolidly. (If not 'Kander, Snooky at last had worked out what Tariq and Shaykh were saying).

"God Willing, they will go to hell," Imam Umar said, himself backing his ally, Haji Hassan.

"Then, in the name of God the Merciful, they will march into hell with honour," said Tariq. "And this is more than can be said of traitors who call themselves good Muslims. God Willing, for them the flames will burn brighter, the pigs' cunts."

One glance from Shaykh was enough to abash Tariq. Shaykh hated, abominated vulgar words and dirty language. His decent words of rebuke chilled the recipient in the way the hottest oaths would not.

I had assumed I would recreate *The Massacre of the Moro Crater* within the precincts of Camp BB. Believe Snooky, the place was full of large holes and depressions: disused bunkers, drained reservoirs, some shell-holes, and a bomb crater from an aerial attack when Camp AB no longer took the brunt.

But Shaykh was adamant. "Oh, Shaykh, please!" I wailed. "Ahmed has to go back? All that way back? The jungle and the boat-crossing?"

"God Willing, it must be accomplished in the very place where it happened," Shaykh said. "We cannot have make-believes. God is Great! We live in the world He made, not in the invention of our imaginations. The traps of Shaitanes are laid there. It is the refuge of the weak. It is an opium, a hashish."

Snooky kind of didn't like the last words. But it was her own bright idea. She had to stick with it. "Can Jefri go with me?" I asked "Maybe Iskander? And also . . ." I named the toughest, most capable boys; those who could protect Snooky best from the lethal American "advisers" lurking round Zambo and Jolo. "We don't want to lose the Moros' expensive cameras. They would certainly make us pay for it, brothers in Jihad or not. Maybe more than they paid, if I know Filipinos."

"God Willing, we would not want to do that," Haji Hassan said quickly. "Or at least I would insist they write down depreciation of asset due to, er, what is it . . . ?"

"Wear and tear," Snooky supplied.

"Thank you, Ahmed. Yes, Shaykh, God Willing, 40% write-down for tear and wear. I rely on God."

I got 'Kander but not Jefri. On the way Snooky had time and opportunity to reflect on the wisdom and merit of zipping her big *katoey* mouth. Werner Herzog had to trek through the Amazon to make *Aguirre, Wrath of God* and *Fitzcarraldo*, so I was not the only director in the history of cinema to have to go through the jungle and across the water to make a movie but none of them had to complete the journey, 200 miles there and back, through hostile territory under threat of ambush and aerial surveillance, not to mention attack. I suppose it contributed to Shaykh's notion of *cinema verité*. Nor was I the first critic to make the leap to director, nearly as big a leap as Poo's op, as there were always the examples of Bogdanovich and Talese, though neither of these had to direct protected by an armed retinue.

Where *Band of Believers (Kris vs Krag)* resembled *Paper Moon* and *The Last Picture Show* was the technical circumstance that it got shot in retro B & W. Snooky had no choice. The Sony Steadicam got dropped down a waterfall, landing – God is Great – on a flat rock, and lost the colour spectrum. So, yah, what Snooky ended up shooting was a homage to *Seven Samurai*, right down to spears and swords taking on firearms. Remember that shot of the master swordsman, Kyozo, fighting in the mud? A musket shot rings out – the bandit chieftain has treacherously shot him in the back from the safety of a hut – he staggers, then flings away his sword in his dying gesture. Kurosawa follows the flashing blade as it twirls in the air and then sticks upright in the filthy mud, the flower of bushido in the shit.

Apparently, that shot was sheer fluke. They got it the first time and could not have reproduced it if they had done it 100 times. Snooky knows because she did the take 489 times before she got it right. Thanks be for digital. It would have been a mile and a half of celluloid. We used the longest kris we could find, with a conventional sword hilt, about half the length of Kurosawa's *katana*, so figure on 489 x 2 = 978 takes.

To pursue the figures, which both Hassan and the Shaykh jointly enjoyed doing on my return, some 600 Moros died in the American encirclement of 1906 as opposed to the US casualty list of 15 troops killed and a few more wounded. No Moro wounded survived. Mountain pack artillery, Krag carbines, and Maxim guns poured their fire down on the Moros in the dormant volcano. Time and again, the Moro men with pole and kris charged, while behind them their families huddled. Even had the warriors been given quarter, they would not have taken it for themselves. Yah, their courage was sublime. They say the .45 calibre Colt pistol round was adopted by the US Army after that day on the strength of the Moros' ability to take revolver bullets and keep running forwards.

Charlton Heston starred in *100 Days at Peking*. Did the Yanks ever make a film of the Jolo Massacre? They did not. But Mark Twain wrote a denunciation of it which did him credit. The yellow tatters of the article were framed in the local vegetable market. Snooky will have to find a different path to immortality, beyond the grave.

Unfortunately for Shaykh's stipulation that the movie should correspond with real life in all details, the local headman would not allow his people to be cast as their murdered ancestors, so we had to recruit from areas miles and miles away on different islands. Not a problem. In these parts, even more impoverished than Pattani, a dollar a day attracted film extras to the set like a magnet might iron filings.

Snooky began her movie with shots of villagers tilling fields (Kurosawa's last scene in *Seven Samurai*) and then Tausug fishermen bringing in their silver catch, in baskets first, then neatly arranged in the market side by side on ice. It looked just great in black and white and made you see the field furrows picking up the rows of fish, like thematically. It was also a premonition of the bodies heaped in the volcano. But you'd have to be a film buff, or Japanese, to see my link to Kurosawa's other shot.

I used his initial framing take in *Rashomon* of narrators sheltering in a ruined temple (it was also his concluding book-end shot as well) for my own fade-out: the six survivors from the massacre (that was Kurosawa's original number of samurai), beginning their tales in the shelter of a burned-out mosque. To focus the general story, I fixed on two individuals in the massacre: one who survived, one who didn't; one an old warrior, one a farmer with a young family whom he watched gunned down by laughing Americans.

We were not allowed to have females in the film. Instead Snooky cast young boys, garbed them in long sarongs, hid their toes in latticed sandals, concealed their bristly haircuts under scarves, and a puff of talc here, and a dab of cream there, completed the transformation. Oh, Snooky knew how. Snooky hadn't lost her touch. I showed the boys how to run round screaming piteously, waving their palms, wringing their fingers.

"Uy!" exclaimed the most intelligent of the extras, playing the historical village chief nearly as well as Kurosawa's professional actor had done. "You're so clever. I could really believe you were a girl!" My friends grinned but did not betray me.

As always, you needed conflict; strife was the motor of drama. No scenes work without it. I don't mean in the sense of bang-bang, dukka-dukka. We had that built into the story. I mean between people and then also interiorised within them. I did the struggle in the native troops' minds, the fight as to where their allegiances lay and whether they should give their arms to their fellow Muslims. I took liberties with the facts (Shaykh never knew) and had one of the Moro troopers, fighting on the American side, run into the crater unarmed to save a child but get caught in the crossfire, still protecting the child with his body.

Sarid, the one who started the revolt by krising the American officer, was probably an amok, an automaton with a blade, but I cast him as a gentle, clerical soul, tormented by his belief in his religion and his natural kindliness. I made the American he stabbed to death his friend. (If I had dared, I would have made them lovers).

The one big casting problem Snooky thought she was gonna have was portraying the Americans. I could have the taller Moros pull the floppy hats I had the local tailor make for them over their faces but the officers needed humanising, even the US Commander, General Wood, if only to show the cruelty on their faces. As much as a hero, a villain needs an individual face.

I consulted the extra who was playing my village chief. (Unable to separate acting from real life, the cast had started to accord him the respect he commanded from them in the film). "Uy! Plenty of *Amerikanos* here," he said. As to this, I remained slightly wary. I remembered it was a common figure of Filipino speech. In fact, most commonly and confidently used when what you were talking about didn't exist at all, e.g. the prevalent local saying, "There are many vampires in England." Or, inquiring after that mythological creature the *sigpin*, half-badger, half-wolf, reputed to live in the mountains of the southern Philippines: "We have *plenty* of *sigpin* in our town."

I said, "A *mestizo*," (their word for a *look khreung*) "would do. Or even a Filipino with a long nose who is not completely black."

"No, no. Plenty of *Amerikano*. Just wait first."

Well, time was just what Snooky didn't have much of. Usually, a director only has the accountants chasing him if he is over-schedule, not Scout Rangers and SEALS. Usually the director simply eliminates scenes there is no time to shoot; mostly, it has to be said, these terminations are greeted without tears by either director or cast. Only the poor screenwriter tears his hair out as his brain-children fail to see the light of day. Only the poor caption-writer smudges her mascara at the thought of the lines the audience will never read. Only poor Snooky ever grieved.

But under the circumstances in which *Kris vs Krag* was shot, delays meant attack and capture. Snooky bought as much time as she could by shooting the scenes without Americans first: the end, followed by the beginning. This naturally created even more confusion in the simple minds of the cast. In fact, I am sure they believed in the intervention of Allah as everyone was brought back to life.

Finally, the head extra came to my bower or lean-to – the set was kind of our dormitory – to say he had my actors. At that stage I was ready to use the village's single albino deaf-mute or paint coconut cream on the faces of the orange-haired Badjao sea-gypsies and take care the lens never caught them in profile, or do it myself. (The lack of iron in their diet gave the Badjaos the rusty hair colour, just as surely as lack of iodine gave them guava-sized goitres).

I came into the sun to see seven walking skeletons whose parchment-skins had more infected sores and ulcers than healthy area. They stunk and were clad in rags. It took longer than it should have done to register. I was used to seeing rich, comfortable, healthy Caucasians. In fact, I only recognised what I was seeing because I'd been to Kanchanaburi on an office outing where we'd toured the Death Railway Museum before embarking on the floating River Kwai barge disco. These people were more emaciated, sicker, more miserable than the ancient photos of the Dutch and British POWs the Japanese had used to build the railway to Burma. I only made the connection when I identified the filthy scrap of cloth one guy was wearing as a floral shirt.

"*Mga Amerikano,*" my head extra said with the same proprietorial pride that the 14th century Chinese eunuch admiral Cheng Ho might have exhibited his African menagerie of giraffes and zebras to the Emperor in Peking. The *Amerikanos*, as the headman described them, were actually two Danish missionaries, an Italian Roman Catholic priest, and four French divers, taken hostage at different times in different places but collated by central casting just for Snooky's uses.

Tariq and Imran would shake their heads over this later, the putting of all the eggs, or hostages, in one basket – something the Iranians had taught everyone to avoid; it was deep in the Shia soul, they implied – but I looked on the positive side: everyone criticised the Moros for being just like their enemy, the Christian Filipinos. That is to say, factional, disputative, unable to work together. Willing to cut off their short noses to spite their own flat faces. Now here were all sides, groups, splinter groups, splinters of splinter groups, working together practically and logistically, as well as in modifying their personal behaviour, to make a *movie*.

If the Northern Filipinos had spent 400 years in a Spanish convent, followed by 40 in Hollywood, the Southerners had spent 600 years in a tiled Grenadan mosque and the rest in Loony Toons. Snooky gave the Caucasian captives water. When we were by ourselves I gave them each a *puso*, a plaited coconut frond purse of rice about the size of one desperate mouthful or three polite bites. They were desperate.

One of them was a woman, dressed in Muslim garb, including a headscarf. It was a way to end the sexual assaults. Garbed like that, even a *bayot* or *katoey* like myself would avoid a kicking from the devout. Snooky told her to sit down. Snooky couldn't use her in the film. At the turn of the 19th century the American army hadn't had female soldiers, just nurses, and, yah, she looked more like patient than nurse.

The elderly Italian priest didn't look like one of Roosevelt's Rough Riders, either, but the French divers fit the bill perfectly. We didn't let them hold a razor but shaved their beards ourselves. Their captors weren't worried about them attacking us; they were concerned they would kill themselves and the ransom would be lost. I admit they looked kinda morose. After a few days the re-growing stubble, dirty cavalry scarves I gave them (just the ubiquitous Filipino bandana moved from head to throat) and floppy Smokey the Bear sombreros had them looking more like the originals than the originals had themselves. (To judge by the sepia photograph in the market).

I just took care to make sure the frame never strayed below the waist to their bare feet. The local banditry dug up, literally, some antique bolt-action Springfield rifles (if they were realistic enough for Peckinpah's opening roof-top ambush, they were good enough for Snooky's crater-lip climax) and the illusion was complete. The way I'd done the shooting during the massacre scenes beforehand had just been smoke and muzzle flashes and Moro bodies going down. Now I would cut in the projected shots of my Frenchmen aiming, making them march from place to place on the lip of the crater, so that with all angles combined they could appear a veritable stage army, delivering a single fusillade.

I had already decided it would be 1. demoralising to the *ummah* and 2. disappointing to my prospective audience, just as audience, if they failed to see Americans being slain by the valiant Faithful in any quantity. So I beckoned three of the Frenchmen deeper into the crater and told them to spare no pains dying spectacularly prolonged deaths, giving them a flamboyant rendition of my own, not so much the dying swan as the expiring ladyboy.

I clambered over the lip to check what was in the camera monitors when I saw 30 extras, men, women, children, young, old, rushing my actors with poles and kris. I waved my clapper-board, improvised by Iskander out of the thwart of a broken pump-boat, and shouted, "Not yet! *Not yet, Kato!* Wait!" But, not to discourage them, added, "That's good. I like it!" It was no more than the truth. It really did look like Kurosawa, a pell-mell mob of civilians, finding their confidence and identity and going after the bandits. It was only the first take, too. For amateurs, the acting was great. Far better than the earlier scenes. I could see why the great directors sometimes coaxed miracles out of a non-professional cast. Method – that was the secret.

As no one had taken any notice of my shouts, I could also see why the early directors carried voice-trumpets. The boots and jodhpurs Snooky could do without. I had already decided I would cut the sound-track and use white on black intertitle cards to introduce each scene change and carry on the plot-line. Yah, a tribute to my own pedigree as well as the history of cinema.

The Moro villagers showed no sign of slackening. The French hostages were also acting with far greater animation and conviction. A pair of Moro men reached the first Frenchman. The leading Moro stabbed him with a bamboo spear and the Moro behind grabbed the end of the green pole and added his impetus to his friend's. The point came two feet out the Frenchman's back. He grabbed the shaft. His mouth fluttered. He took a half-step rearwards, sat down abruptly, then fell on his back, the spear sticking skywards. Two boys and a young woman caught up the leaders. Swiping with agricultural bolos, not the antique war kris, they missed the Frenchman's head as he fell back. They were used to cutting cane, which hardly moves even in a gale.

"No!" I screamed. "Stop!" The mass of Moros arrived, trampling over the dying Frenchman's body to get to the others before they could clamber out the crater. But the three Europeans were malnourished, stiff from being kept in chains, and paralysed by shock. The Moro wave broke over them like the tsunami.

"Action! Action! Cameras roll!" screamed Iskander, forgetting to invoke the Merciful and the Compassionate first, as stipulated by

Imam Umar, and I added my punier shriek to his. There could be only one take, though for reasons entirely different from Kurosawa's experience of non-professional extras.

Three young Moro warriors grabbed a Frenchman, while a fourth buried his kris in his heart. Meanwhile, the last Frenchman slipped on the lip and slithered inexorably down, down, down. I thought of the railway car full of huddling Belgian civilians, running uncontrollably downhill to where the Simbas, waving spears and machetes, would rape and butcher them in MGM's *The Mercenaries*, starring Jim Brown and Rod Taylor in Technicolor, soundtrack by Todd-Ao. I figured this would be on Haji Tariq's censored list for Shaykh.

Reversing the gender situation in the Congo film, a gaggle of Moro women wound their scarves round the first Frenchman's neck and began throttling him. Just then my headman arrived with the light, innocuous striped rattan cane that was not so much a weapon as a symbol of a *tanod* or watchman's authority. He began laying about the women with it, at one point simultaneously striking one across the shoulders, while kicking another up the butt.

"Did you get that, did you get that?" Iskander called up to the guy with the Steadicam.

"I rely on God, we did," called back a young *pondok* student, trying to reassure his elders, but of course as much in the dark as we were.

Finally, unwinding two scarves from the black-faced, frog-eyed Frenchman, the headman escorted him to safety out the crater.

"God is Great and Merciful! That village chief has behaved like every good Muslim should," groaned Iskander, "but he has ruined the continuity. How can we explain the deviation in the narrative? And if we cut it, how can we explain why there are only three corpses?"

"May God be well pleased with him, Iskander," Snooky replied. "It is called a plot twist. And the headman, may God commend him, only wanted to save the women from throwing away $100,000 of ransom on the wind. But don't worry. God Willing, I know how to splice the incident in."

I saw the white on black intertitle on the card already: *At great risk to his own life the saintly old Moro rescues the American who saved his grandson from hanging.*

Following that, I'd have a Christian Filipino treacherously shoot the headman in the back as he retreated down the crater to share the fate of his people. I would synchronise the audience's roar of rage with the film's final image: the extinct volcano exploding into life, the lava streams cracking and spitting as they poured down the mountain like gore down a water-buffalo's black back, super-imposed on a montage of the Faithful wheeling clockwise in white around the Kaaba. I'd get both these images from stock on the net. The volcano would turn out to be Etna, wherever the fuck that is, but so what.

Back to Camp BB we traipsed. You can tell Snooky's relation is real. Fictional narratives are neat. Hollywood never tolerated divagations or loose ends. They're expensive, they're an extra cost. And however fantastical the tales of Borges or Robert K. Dick (yah, I know) they were always ordered with satisfying economy. But real life, actuality, is ragged, messy, haphazard, inconclusive, with sums never added to a final balance. It repeats, retraces, winds us all in its sneaky coils. Of course, the ordinary cannot slip life's web. Only the very brave, and also the very weak, may. They make a starry choice: courage and cowardice are but separate paths to the one terminus of doing away with oneself.

Our return journey passed without event. I showed *Kris vs Krag* not just in our section of Camp but in the Indonesian, the Acehnese, the Saudi, the Chechen, the Albanian. I became an instant celebrity. I said modestly, "Of course, it's only the rough cut, Brothers."

After dinner, I heard Haji Tariq say in the tone of an expert to a Libyan trainer, an explosives instructor with the specialty of the shaped conical charge: "Of course, it was only a raw slice. Ahmed's final version will be something to behold."

Shaykh button-holed me a little later on my way to a poison class, demonstrated on a dog by a former Associate Professor of Toxicology from Odessa. He (Shaykh, not Toxicologist) asked: "What is the meaning of this thing *Reality Show* that Iskander talks about? I am liking the sound of it, Ahmed."

"God Willing, Shaykh, Ahmed hopes you would hate it."

I explained. I told him that, as with Kurosawa's great films being influenced by, and in turn influencing, the genre of the Western, the Japanese had refined their game shows to the point where they were the model for contests in both the States and Europe, not to mention India and ourselves. I did mention *American Idol*. Oh, honey, was that a mistake on Ahmed's part. By themselves, could there be worse single words, greater affronts to the chaste and fastidious souls of ruthless Mujaheedin and severe Imams than those? *Idol*. *American*. I ask you. Unite them and it was like assembling and then shoving together the two plutonium hemispheres of the nuclear football Shaykh was always using as an analogy.

He exploded in wrath. The firestorm broke over Snooky's head. Haji Tariq saw and came with his heavy leather sandal in his heavier fist. Ahmed had been upsetting Shaykh yet again. Keeping a wary eye – one on one, as it were – on Tariq, I suggested to Shaykh: "But we can take the form of it, the empty shell of it, and use it on them. The format itself is neutral. It is a means, not an end. Don't we use radios, rifles, jeeps?"

"A good Muslim invented radio," roared Haji Tariq, swiping at me with his footwear. "I rely on God."

And that was how it was born. From homage to Kurosawa to *Big Brotherhood House*, *Mad versus Mild*, *The Amazing Chase*, and *Deadliest Batch*. Snooky also thought of a raid show, in the footsteps of a TV dating or matchmaking series of some years back, which she would entitle *Blind Hate* but this one failed not the reality but the propriety check. Nevertheless, based on the British version of *Celebrity Squares*, she did stage *Have I Got Jews for You*, only slightly marred by the inadequacy of Iskander's lens which could not create a chessboard of multi-mug shots but only a simple square of four pixelised talking heads. Yah, once again from global entertainment to global jihad. Snooky personally put the fun into fundamentalism.

For obvious reasons we couldn't have in-clear close-ups of contestants' and judges' faces, where the real joy of such programmes is to watch the evocation of emotions, the naked feelings playing on the faces of the participants as they stand there with the spotlight on them after their performances, vulnerable as actors in the dressing-room, as the judges render their withering criticisms or heap unstinted praise.

We couldn't do that, not unless we wanted to find our contestants jailed or killed. We tried darkness, we tried black hoods in the manner of Badawi's videos. It didn't work at all. Then Haji Hassan had the bright idea: *wayang* puppets, or indeed any kind of puppets, as avatars of the real Mujaheedin, with the actual person supplying the voice. All on-line, of course. In his childhood the Haji had been enthralled by the Indonesian Rama puppet saga. The poor kids of then had no other outlet of entertainment, just sat for hours in front of the tiny stage and watched the shadows behind the illuminated screen. Shaykh's ascetic soul was appalled by the prospect of using such a Hindu genre but Hassan dared to point out to him that millions of good Muslims, in the most populous Islamic nation in the world, had appropriated it as their own over centuries. As I had said, in the right hands it was neutral as Semtex or C-4.

The only human faces you saw on our show were the *kafirs*, the Unbelievers. It wasn't so much like that genre of movie – which has never really prospered, has it? – where Toons interact with a human cast, so much as *Planet of the Apes* where the highly evolved simians appear more human than the humans.

Paralysed by crippling fear, stiffened by dour resentment, or stymied facially by complete lack of mental activity, our *kafirs*, white or brown, had less vitality and individuality than the faces of our puppets whose carved features were made motile by Iskander's cunning use of shadow and lamp-light.

We had moved on from silhouette cut-outs to solid puppetry. For these latex is usually employed, whether in satirical shows about politicians and celebrities or in horror movies, but wood worked best for us.

The kind of nose Shaykh, Tariq and Imran had in common also worked better in unyielding wood than in flexible rubber but the ears were fashioned three times as quickly in latex. In practical terms, this didn't matter much as there was no danger of running out of the commodities in the part of the world in which we found ourselves. Wood and rubber, I mean, not ears.

With my own hands I made a tiny, felt eye-patch for Haji Tariq's puppet. I wondered whether to use a fish-hook for his piratical prosthesis then, deciding it was too dangerous as I might well skewer my finger-tip, hit upon the screw hook from which mugs hang on kitchen cabinets (these mugs in Camp BB were enamel rather than clay). Apart from anything else, this kind of hook was designed to screw into wood. Tariq's skullcap was simplicity itself to fashion from a cake doily. Our panel or jury of three was completed by a puppet Jefri, accurate down to the three bristles from a broom which I glued on his chin. Jefri's was to be the voice of reason and moderation, Tariq's – of course – the one of the nasty critic, the one of belligerent truth with its own private jet. You know the programme.

In the background, a final jury of seven black burkha-clad harpies – absolutely the easiest of the puppets to fashion, they were no more than a cross of bamboo inside – handed out verdicts of life or death in a silence that was more eloquent than the most gilded sermon. Then they sashayed up to the victim to hand over, with a wild cackle, either a golden key or a miniature black crepe coffin. Snooky spiced things up (as if they needed to be) at this entirely *halal* buffet of the audio-visual senses with the participation of a rival puppet gang, our evil twins: Southern Thai smugglers and contract killers, masquerading as leering Mujaheedin. They formed a dissenting chorus of jeerers and hecklers (with the sound track speeded up so that they sounded like the Chipmunks) which only added probity and gravity to the real tribunal, the one with the vote.

I thought gang, I thought rivals. I thought movies, I thought musicals. I thought (God shall acquit me) of Audrey Hepburn – whom I am told on a good day I can resemble – of Julie Andrews, of *West Side Story* and the Sharks and the Jets, and of Natalie Wood starring therein as Maria. I picked up the puppet of Imran and in a quavering approximate to a baritone sang, "I'm in love with a code called *Sharia, Shari-aaa!*"

Iskander snickered. I don't think he knew at what. Jefri's expression did not change as, say, Tariq's or Umar's would have done. He said levelly, "Do that again Ahmed, my dear friend, and, God Willing, I will find the strength."

I knew then the transformation was complete. I loved Jefri as a brother, he loved me as a sister. And he had the resolve to kill me. Jefri was no longer human. He was an angel of vengeance. Being Jefri, he was more the former than the latter but still the incarnation of an absolute; unalloyed, uncompromising. There was a simple word for what he was, but I could not find it in all my sophisticated lexicon. I felt a mixture of awe and love. I had never admired anyone so much.

At that very moment my raw gums began not to ooze but to pour profuse quantities of blood. I had been getting worse for weeks, sweating heavily in bed, almost fainting during the long marches. Nausea was as much a part of my day as blinking or respiration. Like I said at Hat Yai station, it was just a shame the sickness was not in the mornings, yah? I had that moment of syncope again, my recurrent, reverse epiphany. When I came to, Iskander was dripping water on to my forehead.

"Where's Jefri?" I asked, surprised I wasn't looking into his concerned eyes.

"He went to prayers with Tuan Imran," said Iskander.

"No, I saw him drinking *Milo*," said a junior *juwae*.

"After his prayers," said Iskander firmly.

WE NEEDED to take the penultimate show, *Maguindanao's Next Top Mujahid*, on the road. All game shows are cut from a common template but the devil lives in the local details, the little twists that give the appeal to the national audience. Jackpot prizes work everywhere but it's the means to the golden and universal end which differs. So: the American Reality Shows stress self-reliance, inventiveness, rugged individualism. The British emphasise fortitude, resilience; the stiff upper lip, in short. The Japanese game shows reveal the path to fulfilment lying through humiliation at the hands of sadistic hosts.

What had we in the dismal place we discovered ourselves? Well, to start with, love of song and dance and well-established local traditions of brigandage and piracy. Or, equally true, love of brigandage and piracy and well-established local traditions of song and dance. We had two strands to the show. The first involved our competitors aspiring to the title of Top Jihadist. The second, minor, skein involved their victims. We didn't just knock them off. It was Imam Umar, backed immediately by Haji Hassan, who pointed out that this was wasteful in the extreme. Not so much that it was a shame to throw away the lives of *kafirs* like rice chaff but that it deprived the show of additional suspense and drama. Me, Snooky, I've always felt that these two things are overrated, for the uncouth and stupid only, but, yah, I realised we weren't making *Citizen Kane* or *The Godfather II* (Snooky's favourite of the trilogy). It was a game show, girl, a Jihadist game show. So we made the victims compete for their lives as well as our Mujaheedin for the victor's crown.

Snooky isn't sure she really wants to divulge the details; you might not like her for it. For instance, the part where contestants had to compete to see who could extract information the quickest from hostages without using flame or drawing blood. If the *kafirs* could hold out for 15 minutes they could go free. None of them, Snooky can relate, ever did. Imam Umar, ever merciful or merely wanting to heap added humiliation upon their suffering, gave the Infidels a final chance to jive and sing for their wretched Christian hides. The most mellifluous, the most fetching, and – by definition – the most plangent, but at the same time least depressing, of the renditions, would secure the prize of continued existence for the performer. The merry twist was that the losing hostages would go to Shaitane singing and dancing, as if being Christian wasn't already a ticket to hell.

Our contestants for most accomplished Jihadist would originally have numbered a Chechen, an Ossetian, two Filipino Moros for the local appeal, a pair of Indonesians, a Bangladeshi, and one of our own number who was, of course, technically a Thai, and . . . Haji Imran. However, Shaykh intervened. There was to be no cult of the individual and, especially, no nationalism.

"Shaykh is right," said Haji Hassan with satisfaction. "What is this? Not the Olympic Games. I rely on God. We will not be playing the national anthems of the winners."

I took it upon myself to explain to Jefri and Iskander. "There will be no countries in the Caliphate. That was a Crusader thing. They divided us into nations the better to rule us in the old days." At this point Haji Hassan passed us and whispered, "Rely on God. The Dutch were better in Aceh and Ambon than the Javanese after *merdeka*, but I did not tell you that," and was off with that charismatic nod of his that was both sly and sage.

So it was teams, of course still with team captains, in the final and most hackneyed (and therefore successful) show *The Apprentice Fanatic* (that wasn't its title, it was how Snooky thought of it). Competition events involved bridge-blowing, message-relaying, field-stripping and re-assembling small-arms blindfolded, floating ampicillin and dried *danggit* fish across a swollen river on a make-shift raft, ransom-bargaining, collecting kidnap collateral from the families of Chinese traders who did not know their sons, fathers, and brothers had been killed within the first hours of their abduction, plus singing of the heroic Moro ballads glorifying the hundred year old war against the Americans, and Qur'anic Quiz and Classical

Calligraphy competition. Oh, yah, and, of course, the ambushes that took place in the final episode. The winning one was both ingenious and effective. Quite often, we would smuggle weapons and explosives through Crusader-territory in coffins, Christian coffins. The government soldiers would lever open the lids of the roughly-planed boxes with predictably tasteless remarks. This time, instead of crates of grenades and cases of carbines, the winning group of Mujaheedin contestants lay in the caskets, arms folded, clutching pistols in ashen hands, barrels nestling in the armpit. As the soldiers threw off the lids and stepped back hurriedly from the green faces, the undead Mujaheedin reared up in the box with yells of *"Allah Akhbar!"* and blazed away, sending the bullet-riddled soldiers sprawling into the jungle-side ditch. It was kinda the reverse of a Dracula movie where usually it's the coffin-occupant in recumbency who cops it through the heart and those in the vertical plane who go on to tell the tale. Imam Umar rebuked the winners for their poor sense of *halal* and propriety but Tariq commended their ingenuity and cast his deciding vote for them.

Our panel of hooded judges comprised Shaykh's puppet avatar as the emblem of sternness and fairness both, Tariq reprising his role of the harsh and outspoken critic whose brutal verdicts are what the audience really tunes in for, while Hassan's wooden and rubber image represented rationality and mercy personified (always overruled by the others but still an extant and moderating presence and general figleaf for native intransigence in our Mountain Eden).

And who were our hostages? I can say the slots were not vied for and there were no auditions. Perhaps our star was the Christian, naturally – or to be totally precise, Roman Catholic – nurse Edlynn Rodriguez, whom the Moro raiders/talent scouts had abducted from her clinic in Maguindanao. Oh, yah, she had the voice of an angel, that one and the face to match. Pity about the legs, as I used to tease Avril.

They talked, in an antique B & W swords and sandals vehicle, starring the long-dead English ham Charles Laughton, of Nero fiddling while Rome burnt. Edlynn sang *Come on, baby, light my pyre* while, as a brilliant counterpoint to the velvet backdrop of the night, the cottage hospital flared to the heavens in a moment of beauty as transient and fleeting as Edlynn's own song.

Said Shaykh, "No one with a voice like that should die. It would be to trample on the gift of Allah."

The flickering shadows lent his already ascetic face an extra dimension of unworldliness. Credit where credit is due. It was not Snooky who saw the opportunity but her ever-improving acolyte and trainee cinematographer, Iskander. Without removing his one uninfected eye (the season was one of universal conjunctivitis throughout the archipelago) from the rubberised viewfinder of the Steadicam, he called, "Shaykh, Shaykh, your shades quickly, quickly, put them on." Well, film had cast its universal licence and benison upon us. Without demur, Shaykh obeyed the exhortation of his Follower and donned the dark glasses that were his closest companions by day. Iskander zeroed in for the close-up.

For us all to see in the next day's rushes were – reflected in the reptilian mini-theatre of Shaykh's lenses – burning buildings and Edlynn's face and elastic lips transported in the ecstasy of song.

"We will release her by the nearest town," pronounced Shaykh. "Not a hair on her head shall be harmed."

Tariq nodded. His one good eye also wept pus and water. "And the others?"

He and Hassan were seated next to Shaykh behind the trestle table with which we formalised proceedings. (Without a table there was nothing judicial about it; they might as well have been Prophets inflicting ancient carnage).

"Kill them all," said Shaykh. "Kill them all, everyone." Behind him a diminutive pupil of Haji Hassan held up a card saying 6.3; Edlynn's had been 9.9 since perfection or 10 was Allah's alone. Art was flawed, or it could not be.

Shaykh himself was reliable in this: he was perfect unpredictability. Snooky was not alone in being unable to forecast the path he would choose. It had, for instance, nothing to do with the mood he was in. With lesser souls, Umar or Tariq for instance, if they were having a bad day, they would take out their exasperation on anyone handy, particularly a Christian hostage. Shaykh could be in his coldest rage when he showed his warmest clemency.

One day we ambushed a pair of buses. It was a conventional hinterland ambush. Jefri, Iskander, and Co. had laid a blockade of felled trees and bushes, worthy of the most industrious beavers, just round a blind corner on a jungled hillside. As the two buses skidded to an unsuccessful halt, snagging themselves into the vegetative maze, Haji Tariq roared out of a purpose-cut lay-by in a ten ton logging truck to block the rear bus in from the back. The cries of dismay and fright as we and our Moro friends emerged from the trees were as familiar to us as the cawing of shooed crows to a farmer. Higher on the hillside, Imran directed a rusted but still formidable American .30 calibre machine-gun, dating from the Japanese War. We had no intention of wasting the bullets on a bus full of civilians. This was Tariq's insurance policy in the unlikely event of the military showing up. Of the police being so injudicious as to expose themselves, there was no chance whatsoever.

"The high ground, Brother," Tariq had told his twin. "Take the high ground."

Imran had merely looked at him, as if to say, "I ain't stoopid." By now it had become apparent – through social osmosis rather than tittle-tattle – that Imran had spent most of his youth on the proverbial high ground, spraying gunfire on young Russian conscripts. Our bus-load were not even inexperienced young soldiers but a bunch of old women, grand-children, village defectives, chickens, and infants.

Getting closer to the vehicles, it became apparent that the rear-most had broken down and was under tow by a rusty chain. The fact it wasn't frayed rope inclined Snooky to think that it was the routine rather than the exception. Passengers hung out the windows, squatted thick-packed on the roof among cloth bundles. They didn't even have the striped or checked zip rectangles we'd used on our journey – the bales of the modern Sinbad. This land was poorer, more fucked-up than ours. They looked like maggots on a bamboo barbecue-skewer. Snooky must have spoken out loud; she was no longer completely in control of her nausea, her grip on reality. "No," said Tariq. "It is like a train in India."

The Moros were lining up the passengers on the road. It was a predominantly Christian area. At Camp BB we were homeboys, sober, devout homeboys. Here we were flamboyant raiders. Five Muslims had been riding on the bus. Of course, we let them go. Hassan gave them a gentle chiding for omitting to say prayers of thanks before departing.

Haji Hassan and Imam Umar still looked like the scholars they were but the rest of us were so many uniformed bandits in dire need of a good salon. Half the Christians were now on the road but, so crowded had the buses been, people were still hanging on the roofs and clambering out the windows. The leader of the Moro detachment approached Shaykh. He was a tiny, bandanaed killer about 18 inches shorter than our own Leader. He drew his kris across his throat with the cheerful grin that marked him as a Filipino, Mujahid or not.

"No," said Shaykh. The tiny Moro clutched his Garand more closely. It was actually longer than he was. His grin became more fixed – he thought it was a silly idea to waste bullets and alert the world with the noise.

"Take them for ransom," said Shaykh. "The ones with soft hands. Let the others go."

The smile left the Moro's face and he turned on his heel.

"Don't show your back to him like that!" roared Tariq. "You come back here. Now!"

Said Imam Umar to Haji Hassan, "These are sons of the soil. What do you expect? They show no respect to the learned."

"God willing, Umar, you may change them," replied Hassan.

"God is Great," retorted Umar, "but not in a million lifetimes."

The short Moro was muttering with his friends. Tobacco smoke hovered above them in the still air. The group split, like hawks coming out of a cloud. (Snooky wonders if that is original; she hopes so).

Tariq was still hopping mad but his anger never lasted long.

Inside the bus came two explosions, one shortly after the other. Then a few seconds later flames. The Moros opened fire on the line of Christians who were outside the bus. Imam Umar and Haji Hassan grabbed each other in a mortal embrace, pulling each other this way and that. After a while, I realised they were wrestling, each trying to use the other as a shield.

Shaykh looked at the line of people toppling over under the hail of rifle fire; he looked the other way at the pair of linked buses, with the corpses hanging outta the windows and passengers, whole families, clambering over them, trying to get out. The branches snagging the vehicles had caught fire, too. He ran towards the blazing buses.

"Stop, boss, stop!" Tariq shouted, always close behind. The Moros were using their parangs and bayonets to poke would-be escapers back into the fire.

Shaykh tossed his shades away as he reached the bus. His great height meant he could easily grasp the window-frame. He already had it in his hands when Tariq tackled him. Snooky found herself close behind. Snooky is nothing if not curious. Snooky didn't want to be left out, did she. Snooky is not brave.

"Have you gone mad?" Tariq shouted at his master. "Cease this insanity!" Tariq's beard had caught fire. He looked like the Archangel Jibreel. Sparks flew off his hair as profusely as they did off the burning bushes. Snooky patted at it with her snowy hankie. Tariq slapped it away but I had succeeded in preventing serious injury to his face. Tears poured down Shaykh's gaunt cheeks from his swollen eyes. "As a boy I was powerless to stop it, then, and as a man now I am impotent, too," he cried in a cracked voice that was not his.

"God is Great!" shouted Tariq. "And he could not stop it either! Pull yourself together. It is men doing this."

"They are devils."

"Men!"

"Then the devil acting in men. There is nothing of the Jihad in this." Shaykh had recovered himself. The stench of charred flesh filled the air. Snooky found herself retching. It did not take much to turn her stomach these days.

The Moros reloaded. They had executed able-bodied men first, the ones who could run away or resist.

"God is Great," said Shaykh, now speaking as slowly as he had been gabbling before. His moment of weakness, if it had been such, was over. "I could not save them in the carriages but I may preserve those without. I am not so debased that I can watch children burn. Give me your radio."

"Reflect on what you do," said Tariq but passing over the hand-held set at once. "God Willing, the past shall not warp your judgment of the present."

Shaykh began passing instructions to Imran in the language I did not know.

"Cease fire," called Tariq to the Moros. Unlike their leader, they carried M16s. For answer they pulled back the cocking bolts with the incongruously dainty pinch of thumb and forefinger employed

266

on that American weapon. I called that gun the Black Lady but it was also the way Mare had held my hated weenie to aim my stream of urine.

"Repeat – cease fire! Stop that!" bellowed Tariq.

Imam Umar's bafflement was matched only by his bitter disappointment. "You are wasting our chance," he remonstrated with Shaykh. "We can shoot all these *kafirs* and they will never know. I mean, God Willing, that I, er, we did it. They will not know I paid them in this coin, hoo-hoo. God is Great, I can watch but I will not be blamed."

Shaykh raised his long arm. From above Imran fired a short burst that drove up dust and pebbles within feet of the Moros. They vanished in the storm of dust. When it cleared, their hair and uniforms were white. Shaykh sauntered up to them. He contrived to swagger and be dignified at the same time. "Let these poor people go," he said.

The small Moro said, "They are *kafirs*." He wasn't smiling now.

Shaykh said, "God is Great. Let the Christians walk."

The Moro considered and said, "No."

Shaykh said, "God willing, you will find the way within yourself or be at one with your brave forebears."

The Moro said, "Your machine-gun cannot shoot at us without hitting you."

"Praise be to God," said Shaykh and for the first time in many days joy suffused his face. "I shall have the opportunity to swell the ranks of the martyrs, may God be well-pleased with them."

"They will not fire on you."

"Imam Umar," called Shaykh. "Take the radio from Tariq and order Imran to fire upon us. I ask for the forgiveness of God."

Umar's face lit up, like Shaykh's but for different reasons. If he had not taken possession of the hand-held, he would have been rubbing his palms together in unholy glee. The Moro picked up on Umar's total readiness to give the order, rather than Shaykh's willingness to die. The shamelessness of the weak is a thousand times more convincing than the composure of the strong.

"OK, OK, boss," said the Moro.

"God is Great," said Imam Umar abjectly.

Jefri beamed at an ancient, wrinkled Christian woman, who was probably 40. Her gums had been rotted by betel. "Just go, Auntie," Snooky advised. "Not too quick, not too slow."

The line of Christians moved off. They didn't look particularly grateful, just stunned, overwhelmed. One of them, a middle aged Chinese mestizo gay with a shaven head, from some crappy up-country town, offered a quiet prayer of thanks on the move. His hand stole to his pocket.

"That one! That one!" roared Haji Tariq. "What are you doing?"

Ten Moro rifles were trained upon the guy in an instant. Tariq levelled his huge revolver at him. The man produced a string of wooden beads. He had been telling the rosary. Tariq looked at Shaykh. His master did not disappoint him this time. The bald Chinese guy looked exactly like a Buddhist monk off-duty in Siam, say, on his way to check his bank account and his mistress after some charbroiled, definitely non-veg, ribs at Tony Roma's.

"Kill him," said Shaykh.

"What?" said the Moro. It was as if he was a child who'd had a sweet taken away from him for bad behaviour but then had it restored when he'd been even naughtier.

"You heard," said Tariq. "Or shall I do it myself?"

"God is Great," Shaykh said. "Let Ahmed be the one." Shaykh took the revolver and went behind the Christian.

Tariq pushed the man to his knees. "Here you go, *koti*," he said. Snooky smiled. She knew she was equal to expectation. She put the barrel to the victim's head and she . . . pulled the trigger. Click. The man fainted. So did Snooky. When she came to, people were wrinkling their noses. Ordure. Snooky feared it was hers. God is Great. It was not. It was Christian shit. The man had fouled himself, as well he might. Tariq slapped me on the back, knocking all the breath from my labouring lungs. Snooky was a shadow of what she had been. All my infirmity, I swear, was now physical, not spiritual.

"Good, eunuch, good," he said. "I was having my doubts about you, but the boss never did."

Shaykh smiled. It had been a test. He gestured to the Moro. "Decapitate the *kafir*," he commanded.

"Hah?"

"Cut his head off," Tariq translated tersely.

During these nerve-wracking exchanges – at least for Snooky

and the Christian – Shaykh's face had been unreadable. To all except Snooky, I mean. Usually Shaykh was impermeable to me. This time it wasn't a moment of understanding, more of telepathy. Me, firing the empty gun which he'd unloaded behind Tariq's broad back and which Iskander was now reloading – that had been the merest of afterthoughts. The execution of the Christian was the main thing. The Moros, simple souls, just couldn't figure it out: why would someone willing to die to defend the Unbeliever a few seconds ago now be willing to throw the *kafir's* life away? Whim it was not. Snooky looked at Shaykh. He looked at Snooky. He knew I knew. He knew that I knew he knew I knew. How can I put it? Sometimes the Master has to throw a bone to the dogs, if he is to preserve the rump of his own authority.

Ineffectual screams came and then, horrible, horrible gurglings told their own story. Baldie was dying the *halal* way. With a clean chop from behind the likes of the Iraqi dictator – or Imran or Tariq

could muster the courage to die with dignity and composure. But not with a slow sawing from the front. Give it to Snooky from behind any day.

OUR TIME in Camp BB was growing shorter by the day. I couldn't say we were outstaying our welcome and getting black looks in the way of a b & w Shakespeare vehicle for the late Laurence Olivier – not quite there, but nearly. Shaykh had spooked the bumpkins with absolutely Arab attributes of ruthlessness and forebearance, the two so much more compelling together, my dears. It was time for us to ride off into the sunset, providentially the compass direction in which both Mecca and our own *pondok* lay.

Some business was definitely going on in the background, which needed completing. Haji Hassan and Shaykh seemed to be waiting on something, Shakyh with coolness and Hassan fretfully. I always wonder if what happened next might have been averted, had we gone earlier.

We did not inhabit, literally or figuratively, temperate climes. We had too much or too little, never the right amount: of rainfall passing from flood to drought with no happy in-between, of nights of nipping mountain cold with days of gluey heat. Nights had now turned humid. Our seniors took all the mosquito nets outside and slept under them in the open. Imran and Tariq shared one, Hassan and Umar another, while Shaykh had one to himself. It was not just Snooky who felt a sense of relief. It was quite impossible to have a hand-job when Shaykh's recumbent form, within 12 feet of you, stood in for the long, rebuking finger of God. In fact, there had been the hideous, yah, mortifying occasion when a Junior's shrill cry of, "Haji, Haji, Ahmed is polluting himself!" had rent what had been the comforting darkness. Snooky hotly denied the accusation, saying she had been pulling the ejector rod of her hand-gun so that it should not discharge negligently. "I rely on God," Snooky vowed.

"He was doing it. I also rely on God," said the Junior indignantly.

When Tariq's snores announced he was unconscious again, Jefri and Iskander put a pillow over the informer's face and belaboured his stomach mercilessly, depriving him of the wind to shout for help.

Well, this particular night we were all dog-tired. We'd gotten up before dawn, on Tariq's command and to Imam Umar's delight (he was exempted) to trek 25 miles over the hills to preach in a remote village. We didn't even get to eat when we returned at dusk. Just passed out on the ground. Not even the mosquitoes could keep us conscious. Imam Umar had been there, rubbing his hands over our exhaustion, to make sure we did some completely unnecessary chores before collapsing supper-less, and ostentatiously enjoying the steaming *binignit* or sweet tuber and coconut stew Shaykh had ordered for him. He had a Malay tooth – even Thai Muslims, like myself, would have spiked it with a little sophisticating salt.

A hoarse cry woke us shortly before first light. Haji Hassan, under his net, sheet wound round his stringy calves, as ashen as the corpse he was not, pointed in horror at Umar beside him.

The Imam resembled the Indonesian devil puppet Naja Gengong. Stiff as wood, eyes bulging out his head, face quite black, yellow fangs exposed in an uncharacteristic snarl, with a tongue protruding in a cheeky raspberry, he was as dead as the Caliphs of yore. Hassan, for his part, though quite speechless and in a state of frozen immobility, was clearly still with us from the uncontrollable trembling of his shoulders.

"Ah-ah-ah," he now managed in a chain of traumatised gasps.

"Here, Haji," said Jefri, draping a military load-vest over Hassan's frail shoulders, "Iskander, hold his other hand while I clasp this one." He began rubbing the Haji's fingers. "So cold, Haji, so cold," he comforted him.

Imran was still shaking the world with his snores but Tariq was with us now and alert as an owl. He did not so much take in the scene at a glance as seem fully apprised by Allah. He said in tones of sombre exultation, "The Imam has given his life for the Jihad. May God have mercy upon him." I couldn't forebear looking sharply at him. He had sounded less sombre than exalted. Tariq was a crappy actor. In the man there was no dissimulation. What you saw was what you got. Snooky, she kind of respected him for it.

Jefri said, "He must have had a heart-attack." His tone was quite flat.

A Junior approached the corpse and exclaimed, "There are marks around Imam's neck!"

Now with us, Imran kicked him. "Mind your own business and keep your opinions to yourself!"

"But, Tuan Imran, I am just trying to help. I rely on God!"

"And, God Willing, you may continue to do so. Diligent boy," said a quiet voice, the calm voice that could be heard at the height of a storm, or penetrate the deepest dream. Sometimes Shaykh stirred up a whirlwind among his followers, sometimes he was as oil upon furious waters. What we got now was emollient Shaykh. "It wasn't a heart-attack after all, Boss?" Imran inquired. The poor guy seemed hopelessly bamboozled.

Shaykh knelt by the Imam's body. "God," he said, "is Great. He has gifted this boy to see what wise men could not. There are indeed marks around the Imam's neck. Look. Everyone may look. Look closer."

For his part Imran looked at Shaykh as if he was crazy. He gave the red weal around Imam Umar's neck the most cursory of glances. So did Tariq. We others crowded in.

"Someone has murdered Imam?" asked the Junior who had incriminated me in my happy proclivity.

Shaykh laughed, actually guffawed. We followed his lead and, though we had not found anything mirthful, discovered ourselves hysterical.

"Who would do such a thing?" said Shaykh, clapping Tariq and Imran both on the back. "Did Crusaders creep into the camp? The

Navy Seals? The Delta Forces? The SAS's? The Bond of Brothers? All the while Imran and Tariq were here? No, no."

"Imam hanged himself, Shaykh?" asked the Junior.

"That," said Shaykh, "is less unlikely, but where is the rope? Where the branch? I rely on God. He is flat on his back."

"Then what, Shaykh?"

Shaykh reflected. Light broke in on him. "God is Great! The Imam was suffocated in the coils of a snake! Within the labyrinthine folds of a mighty serpent! He was crushed by the twisting loops of the Tempter that tempted First Prophet Adam and, like the child in the grove with his parents in Riau, he had not the breath to cry to us for aid!"

A ripple of horrified satisfaction passed through the juniors. Man, this was as good as a Siamese horror movie.

We buried the Imam with expedition. It was like 24. We had a day to do it in but Tariq and Imran got him in the ground well before midday was upon us.

WHETHER UMAR'S FUNERAL was expedited because of our imminent departure or our departure was expedited because of the Imam's funeral, Snooky cannot be quite sure. She knows frantic haste, bordering on the unseemly, was the order of the day. Only Shaykh gave the impression of taking his own sweet time but then he didn't do his own packing, did he? A cursory farewell of the Chechens whom Tariq and Shaykh both esteemed the most – I would not like to say it was because the Chechens looked Caucasian but at the same time were as bloodthirsty as the Filipino Abus – then we were decamping without exchanging so much as the most perfunctory embrace with our hosts of the past several months.

Our return route would be the very opposite of our original ingress. We travelled . . . by bus! That is to say, we had our very own vehicle, one of the largest kinds of the class known in the Philippines as a jeepney and at home as a Twin Row. On the side Iskander painted in his best Roman capitals: MAGRAB PRAYER TOUR TO BRUNEI DARUSSALAM BY KINDEST PATRONAGE OF HIS MAJESTY SULTAN AND YANG-DI PERTUAN NEGARA HASSANAL BOLKIAH MU'IZZADIN WADDAULAH. Haji Hassan stood behind, correcting Iskander's over-enthusiastic spelling (he liked to double-up the letters, thinking it made it more important, e.g. KKINDEST PPATRONAGE). Shaykh with Hassan and Imran joined him.

"It's good, Shaykh, it's good," cackled Hassan, rubbing his hands together. He had made a rapid recovery from his catatonic state of two days before. In the mountains he had taken to wearing fingerless gloves, similar to those worn by Ebenezer Scrooge in all five versions of Charles Disney's *Christmas Carol* I had dozed through during my career as film critic. (If Snooky had her way, she'd have done something dire to Tiny Tim with his fricking crutch). "God Willing, no one will suspect," continued Hassan.

"Yes," mused Shaykh. "Sometimes shelter lies in openness and concealment not in secrecy but in boldness. The brazenness is not being suspected at all."

"God is Great!" said Tariq. "It is better than a coat of camouflage paint!"

"Winter or desert pattern," contributed Imran.

"Then there is no one, God Willing," said Tariq, "who will lift their hands against those sponsored by the richest man in the world."

"In Asia," said Hassan. "God Willing, in Asia. Yes, money talks. The Filipino soldiers will not cause us let. They will not know the Sultan has less knowledge of us than he has of destitution. The Americans . . . it is a different matter but we shall not encounter them, if we avoid Zamboanga."

As the greybeards left, Iskander asked, "The Sultan really helping us, Older Brother?"

"No, stupid," Jefri retorted. "It's a white lie. Get it? God Willing, a white lie. The Sultan and his sons and brothers are among those we shall sweep away in the Caliphate. Just as Brother Osama shall sweep away the Saudi despots."

"In the name of the Merciful, the Compassionate," said Iskander doubtfully, concluding his final painted word with an inappropriate, Arabesque flourish.

Our spirits lifted with every mile put between us and Camp BB. Home! We were going home! Back to our dear *pondok*! Away from these terrible mountains where it seemed every atrocity was permitted save cannibalism, as being un-*halal*. What were our little peccadilloes in the oil palms compared to the blood that had soaked into this parched and evil soil until it had become a raging flash flood of gore? Poor Imam Umar! He had been – as we knew him in his old age – a crotchety dotard but maybe he had been as us once. He certainly hadn't deserved his fate – to be broken in the vice-like grip not just of a wild animal but a reptile, too. Better the Inquisition's rack.

I did wonder why the python hadn't consumed him when it had gone to the length of asphyxiating him but perhaps his lean bones were hardly worth the effort of dislocating its jaws. At least it was only him we were leaving behind in this raw soil and at least it was the one of us who had the least years left.

We put up for the night in a school that had been built with Saudi oil money. I noted Jefri was happy enough to rest his weary head there, despite his earlier strictures on royal families.

A booming metallic voice shattered our slumbers at 3 a.m.

"You are surrounded! Resistance is useless! Give yourselves up."

I was fully conscious in an instant. Cameras, lights, action, Snooky thought. Then: why are they speaking in English? Answer: because the idiot Filipino officer thinks he is in an American film. Or does he know who we are? A blinding light filled the room. We were all out of our cots on the floor now.

"Thunderflash next," said Imran. "That would be standard spetsnaz procedure. Close your eyes, open your mouths. Fire instantly at anything standing. I rely on God."

"Needless to say, do not stand yourselves," added Tariq.

"Turn your light out," called a voice I recognised as Shaykh's. To my surprise I then heard Haji Hassan's voice call with the pedantry of a checker bringing an unliquidated advance to account: "Are you Marines? Army?"

"Neither," shouted back the Filipino voice straightaway. "Amphibian Regional Assets Anti-Insurgencies Forces."

Hassan caught Shaykh's eye meaningfully. "Then this can be fixed."

Shaykh shouted, "Out your light. We wish to parley."

"You are in no position to negotiate," came the reply. "Surrender without conditions."

"That is not a path the warriors of Allah can take with honour."

"You dogs are not warriors. You have no honour."

"God is Great and we are his warriors in Jihad!" bellowed Imran.

"Let us discuss this confidentially under flag of truce," interceded Haji Hassan. "God Willing, all parties may reach a mutually satisfactory resolution and accord."

A long silence followed. To my great surprise, the Filipino voice called without a loudhailer, "One of you. No weapons. No monkey play or you will feel our shots whizzing you by."

To my even greater surprise, Shaykh said quietly, "Ahmed, Jefri, go with Haji Hassan." Then loudly, "Three will go. You send as many as you want." To Jefri and me he added in an even quieter voice, "Do not let the Haji out of your sight. Not for one moment."

As Haji Hassan joined us, briefcase in hand, Shaykh said within his hearing, "Rely on God, Jefri and Ahmed have orders to kill first you and then themselves if there is any danger of being taken. If the Haji is made to accompany them, if he shows you his back, shoot the Haji without qualms. This is the path of your duty."

"God is Great," Haji Hassan said calmly. "There will be no need to seek security in extremities. I am a true and faithful trustee."

Tariq grabbed him by his free arm, the one not holding the case. "OK, Hassan," Tariq said. "This is your thing. Get us out of this fix."

Hassan shook his hairy paw off, saying haughtily, "It is in the hands of God, not yours. God Willing, in mine, too. Delicate hands!"

"You," said Tariq, "sound just like Umar, with whom we trust God is well pleased."

Hassan said mildly, "God knows I shall pay all my outstanding debts and Umar's," but Snooky knew that was as close as he could come to cursing Tariq for four generations.

"Come, Haji," said Jefri brightly, "God Willing, we shall be back in five minutes." And Snooky is in a position to say that is exactly what happened, with or without God's Intervention.

Haji Hassan's case contained exactly what we had always suspected: bricks of tightly packed dollar bills. He conferred at a distance with the Filipino officer and his second in command, a handsome boy only a few years out of training school, Snooky would say, and as fresh-faced and wholesome-looking as his superior was seedy and unprepossessing.

Jefri and I were too polite to keep the Haji under direct surveillance and squatted, facing the rising sun, at 90 degrees to the increasingly heated bargaining going on. The weight of the two snub-nosed, or short-dicked, revolvers we had punctiliously informed the soldiers we were carrying, while refusing to be frisked, dragged our pants down reassuringly, like the full load of money the Filipino officer was getting. Haji Hassan's voice rose shrilly, like the squeal of an Isarn fife. "I am not accustomed to broken agreements . . ." while the deeper, insistent officer's voice was a menacing drum-roll.

Finally, Hassan rejoined us, wiping sweat beads off his tenuous hairline. "God is Great. Down payment of 30 per cent now. Five succeeding instalments of 10 per cent before journey's end and finally 20 per cent into escrow box, location of which to be divulged by line of SMS text at one mile stage of withdrawal, God Willing."

I noticed that the Haji no longer had the case. "Not to be nosey, Haji, and with respect, Ahmed wonders if you left the other cases with Tuan Imran for safekeeping?"

Haji smirked, then turned cautiously. We all waved instinctively and smiled for all we were worth – good Thais that Jefri and Snooky were – at the camouflaged Filipino thugs. "We rely on God, Ahmed. That is the only case we had."

"God will have mercy on you, Haji," Jefri said. "You had to tell a white lie?"

"No, no," Haji said irritably. "What kind of financier would I be then? I have always been a man of my word. As the *kafirs* say, my word is my bond. God Willing, I fully intend to pay the Colonel. I just omitted to inform him that I did not immediately possess the wherewithal at hand. Praise be to God: we shall not omit to leave him a promissory note in the drop-box."

With the whole of my back already flinching from the impact of imaginary rifle bullets, I still did not dare catch Jefri's eye for fear of laughing, as I knew my old friend still would.

"What's so funny, *koti?*" growled Tariq as we got back.

"Ahmed knows not fear," whispered a Junior. "God Willing, nor shall we in the cause," replied another awe-stricken youth.

"Where's the money, Hassan?" asked Shaykh without ado.

"God is Great!" wailed Haji. "The *kafirs* took it all!"

"Cretin!" shouted Imran. "Reading all those books and not an ounce of commonsense in you?"

"Speak to the Haji with respect, Imran," Shaykh said. "The

scholar's ink is worth more than the blood of the martyr. Haji, they took it by force?"

"God Willing, I would not just yield it," Hassan said reproachfully. "We only got away because your servant intimated there was more."

"God is Great! There is!" said Iskander. "I took the liberty of removing the bottom layer, while Haji was praying for Allah to preserve them."

"That," said Haji Hassan, "is a very great liberty," but, brightening suddenly, "I rely on God to forgive you the deception."

"We will need to keep throwing out chaff to satisfy them," Tariq said. "That is the only reason they haven't attacked us. Did you threaten to burn it all if they made a move, like Shaykh told you?"

"I rely on God. It was the very first thing I told them," said Haji Hassan.

"Very well," said Shaykh. "The glittering treasures of the Caliphate will make a box of dirty notes seem as wipings. Let us move before they change their minds."

Snooky needed no encouragement but Tariq was there barring the way, cuffing us with his doughty leather slipper. "Fools! Carrion! Never show a pack of dogs your fear! It only incites them."

We passed under the levelled guns of the Filipinos and I marvelled at the Fonze-like coolness of my Brothers. Iskander even waved a sheaf of notes under the soldiers' noses and stuck his tongue out at them. Their commander laughed and pretended to cut his own throat with a fingernail as long as Umar's had been. Once out of sight, we scampered – Imran and Tariq included – as fast as mice fleeing the cat.

"These," said Hassan that evening in our lean-to under three big boulders – not so much a cave as a granitic wigwam – "rely on God, are men of blood, men of the moment. They have no conception of contract or a principal maturing and then rolled and renewed. They would take less in the here and now rather than incomparable riches in the future."

"God is Great! The very opposite of martyrdom!" Snooky exclaimed.

Shaykh looked hard at her. Tariq said, "God Willing, Ahmed, that might be the near future. You would not have need of patience."

Jefri changed the topic. "Tuan Imran, we need to stay ahead of them. Slow them down by making the money difficult to find but still texting them as to its location."

"Then my teachings," said Haji Hassan, picking the yellow hulls off a maize cob with satisfaction, "have not been in vain. I rely on God."

It was a terrible night, such of it as we spent on our backs resting. At one point Haji Hassan pulled his old bones up with a curse, snapped open the locks on his briefcase, and began punching his calculator. At midday – no rocks around at all on a spongy ground, the spite of the sun untrammelled by a single cloud – we knew why. We needed to make our pursuers, our debtors, stop seven times on our escape to the coast but we had sufficient cash for only three instalments. This was why Hassan had been racking his wits in vain on his calculator.

Imran said, "Miss one payment. The dogs will still pursue us. Tell them there will be double at the next stop."

Hassan said, "God Willing, let us leave half of what is owed at one point, the rest of the instalment at the next and none at the last."

Jefri said, "Let us leave double at the second waypoint, none at the third, half of the correct instalment at the fourth and then no more but with promise of full reimbursement at the last stop."

Shaykh laughed. "My son," he said, "your arithmetic is as unerring as your psychology is being acute. We will make you a Bachelor of Science yet, God Willing."

You know, Snooky had a feeling she was in one of the folksier *hadith* but, like Shaykh, she had to hand it to Jefri. I kinda thought more of Jefri and less of Jefri for it. It was like peeling the layers of an onion, finding Jefri, straight Jefri, upstanding Jefri, sneakier, more devious than I thought. It didn't exactly make the tears flow but it made Snooky sad. Certainly sadder than the other thing which occurred.

We made the first few money-drops OK. The abuse and threats in the subsequent SMS texts to Iskander's mobile were only to be expected. In fact, we all chortled over Imran's fruity replies. Even Shaykh, before whom any salaciousness merited instant chastisement, permitted himself a wry smile. As we were making good progress and the soldiers were nowhere to be found in Imran's Cyrillic-branded binoculars, the Juniors could afford to snicker.

We'd just left Hassan's courtly credit-note in the bole of a gnarled acacia when Imran's head morphed into a pomegranate as luscious as any to be found by a good Muslim in the gardens of Paradise. Juicy red globules, bone-white seeds, skin-taut sacs flew into the air, as a scarlet fountain gushed from where his neck used to be. His skull had disintegrated.

One of the attributes of the twins had been their rock-steadiness, their balance, their firm foundation in all perplexities. Now Imran stayed upright for a small eternity.

Crazily, Snooky thought, it didn't take much in the way of a brain to control Imran. But, in the end, as we all knew it must, little by little, the Column that had been Imran faltered, lost its balance, inclined to one side, then over-compensated to the other, shoulders drooped, knees flexed, and in a crash of dust and earth the Colossus was over. It was like watching one of the tripods go over in *War of the Worlds*. The boom of the Barrett rifle, for such it had been, reached us.

Fear replaced frustration. Snooky dived behind the acacia. She might be the next one turned into . . . what? . . . a bolo-bevelled coconut, pineapple chunks? Actually, it was Haji Hassan who copped it. Prudent, sagacious old Hassan, who should have been the first behind the acacia trunk, rooted to the spot with terror, who took the .50 cal projectile straight through his skinny chest.

Jefri and Tariq had gone to Imran. Now they turned. Shaykh had not shown a flicker of emotion – grief or fear – as Imran was downed. Behind the reflective lenses you had not a clue what was going on. Snooky wanted to say, "Get down, Shaykh, you are so tall. You are the easiest and also the most important target they have." (Snooky also thought she would not stand too close to Shaykh, in the way you might not want to shelter under the mightiest oak during a thunderstorm).

Now Shaykh hurled off his shades. He ran towards Hassan. Instantly, bullets scored the soft loam around him. Tariq cried, "The *kafirs* have outflanked us!" The big bore rifle fired again and a Junior's entire arm came off at the shoulder before the thump of the cartridge in the breech reached us. Shaykh dashed through the bullet storm as if it were the merest rain-shower. He grabbed Hassan round his shoulders, less substantial than a wire coat-hanger's, cradling the dying old man's head with his own long forearm. Hassan's lips moved feebly. "Yes, yes, in the Name of God!" Shaykh shouted exultantly. "May God be well-pleased with you, Hassan, this is your last duty to the Jihad!" Blood bubbled from the Haji's mouth. The words could not be enunciated. Shaykh seized the Haji's forefinger and dabbed it on the failing scholar's own lips. "Write it down, Hassan," he urged. "Write the numbers on my robe!"

With a glare of concentration such as I had never seen before on the Haji's mild features, he raised himself and upon Shaykh's snowy skirts inscribed first a wavy upright line, then a diamond-head upon it.

"Yes," shouted Shaykh, "One."

Hassan shook his head with a ghastly rictus, then drew a nought. "Zero," shouted Shaykh but with more doubt in his voice than I had ever heard. "Go on, Haji, go on."

I think he had difficulty from his perspective deciphering what was written on him but Tariq saw it at once. "You traitorous old fool," he roared. "Will you spite God himself?"

Hassan's arm dropped, his eyes glazed – Snooky saw for the first time the film of death upon them – but the sardonic grin remained on his face long after his quiet soul had fled.

Shaykh

In the name of God, most Compassionate, most Merciful. Mindanao was a glorious trial and exercise of our youthful Mujaheedin and – eventually – a triumphant vindication of my methods. God chose for His Battlefield a veritable Eden. Even just being in the mountains made them clearer and freer, even the air was being cooler and more limpider. Being in high places you are mathematically closer to God. God Willing, it may even be susceptible to measurement, just as is an experiment in chemistry. In praise of God our experiment was to take our homegrown provincial *juwae* and enrol them in the greater Jihad. By this, they became truly swords of Allah.

Also, but not so important, it was expedient to go for a while. Our so-called brothers in Jihad were resentful about our exploits in Hat Yai and, especially, Phuket.

I, and those from whom I take my bidding, have no interest in the secessionist solution. Why would we want to integrate the three southern provinces of Siam into Malaya? (I keep calling it Malaya, just as Ceylon will always be Ceylon to me and not – what do they call it? – Sri Lanka). No, our ambitions are bigger, being loftier and nobler. It is a paradox that I would rather Pattani, Yala, and Narathiwat remained the property of Siam than were integrated into Malaya. The cause of Jihad and the Caliphate would be lost once this had happened. The toys of peace and affluence keep the people in childhood. The flame of belief burns the brighter in the hovel. Despite all the show, Malaya is a secular state. Many of its citizens are *kafirs*. Many of its politicians are as dirty and greedy as those of Pakistan, if cleverer at hiding it behind a seemly front. They are not even having the military to periodically purge them of their greed. Their cruelty to their holiest clerics surpassed that of the Siamese. That is why Umar, who always chose the softest seats, preferred Siam after all.

No, my orders – God always Willing – were to lift the struggle to a more exalted plane. I said the local *juwae* were the dough and I was the yeast, they were the fertiliser and I was the detonator. Jihad needed a new theatre. God's Warriors needed to find both a sanctuary and a proving-ground. Too often the Crusaders have chosen the site of battle – always a place of strategic importance for them. We planned to make them bleed on a ground where they stood to gain nothing. God Willing, that way our quick victory would be assured. That is to say, as opposed to our eventual and inevitable but long-to-be-awaited victory. To accomplish this, we had slowly to infiltrate the local territory, to make the native inhabitants' struggle our own struggle. But we were not an addition to the local forces, we were much more than a reinforcement. We were a multiplier. So, for example, Tariq, myself, and Imran – may God have Mercy upon him – were not just Three. I example you: if there were 300 *juwae* or local warriors in Yala, we did not make it 303 warriors. No, we made it 3 x 300 = the force of 900 Mujaheedin. In the process, we the foreign warriors in Afghanistan, Iraq, or Kashmir, would bring down the wrath of the Crusaders upon the locals' own heads.

Thus, as even poor, limited Tariq, saw, understood, and told me, the Afghans themselves would readily have compromised with the invaders but the Chechens and the Arabs among them – not to mention us from over the mountains – would not allow this. And in attempting to extirpate the Outsiders, the Crusaders and the Russians before them killed so many of the native peoples that they, too, became the Crusaders' implacable foes. Jihad thus became self-perpetuating and limitless: it was like the number *pi* or π. The Crusaders tried to divide this – like the clever of them tried to separate the integer into its separate parts, to terminate it and have a conclusion and a balance but, God is Great, they could not with the transcendental number (just as they could not do with the transcendental Jihad) and the infinite numbers which reeled off π every time they freshly assaulted the number were as endless sparks struck off eternal flint which flew to all corners and began conflagrations there. (I have often thought that algebra, which was the invention – I praise God – of the Arabs, always balanced its terms but geometry – as the delinquent child of the Greeks who were the fathers of the Crusader civilisation – gave them the devil's imp, π, which could not be stopped or balanced but lurched on for ever).

They talk of the collateral damage but their geometry was wrong. The collateral damage they wrought upon the locals was the central damage. God is Great – the more powerful the bomb they dropped, the more damage they did to themselves. Their chastisement was proportionate. Umar joked to me about this once. He said, "They have their *pi* in the sky." Umar thought – as he did with many other things – that I was unaware: in this case of this expression. It is called Proverb, like the chapter in their Bible.

Of course, proverb – a riddle for a Arts – is neither equation nor example. I often wonder how many Crusaders we shall have to kill before we prevail. For Jews the answer is simple – you would need to kill them all in order to make victory secure. As for Americans, by which I mean the Aryan race, it is problematic. There is a secure and exact answer but it needs to be approached from both ends. One million is clearly excessive to requirement, one hundred is too little. To kill 3,000 is merely an incitement. I should say ten times that figure would also be nothing more nor less than a provocation. Civilian casualties would also simply invite retaliation; it needs to be their soldiers in a place that is not valuable to them. In my mind 50,000, all at the same time, is a sensible interim quantity that would give us the result we desire. Far more died in their wars of conquest in the last 100 years.

Malays like Umar seem to think the British colonised only them. When I think about it, they colonised everybody, brown, black, yellow, white. They colonised even the Americans! The Americans invented the bunker defence to beat the English. They put them upon the hill. In those days the Americans did not have the strategic air power which was to prove so terrible later. The Wright twins invented this at Kitty Hawk. This is the kind of thing I know and which Umar did not. You have to use the weapons of the enemy against him. Once, the Americans fought the redcoat British. They could not fight them on the open battlefield or they would have been destroyed. They fought in the forests and mountains. And they won. Now the terms are reversed. We cannot fight the Americans in open battle or we will suffer the fate of the Taliban. We will fight as guerrillas, like the Americans did themselves three centuries ago, in the forests and mountains. And we will win. Tariq, who is as brave as he is devoid of imagination, is not ashamed to admit he soiled himself under the attack of the Russian MIGs and, especially, their Hind helicopter which was simply a tank with wings.

Aerodynamics are strange and fascinating, if more predictable than the ways of men. Once for a demonstration our physics teacher, whose hobby was model aeroplanes, attached a propeller and a tiny glow-plug engine to, of all things, a dog kennel and – God is Great – made it not only fly before our astonished young eyes but also loop the loop. He called it the Turn of Immelman which sounded Turkish – religious almost – but was just German. The Turks were once allies of the Germans and thrashed the English and the Austrians at Galapagos. This was where Darwin was struck with the devil's tale of evolution. God punished them on this ground through the Turks. Now the accursed military in Turkey persecute the Godly, harass the Imams, and prevent the women from dressing modestly. This is worst on the university camps where the veil was forcibly rent from the daughters of Islam. As for the Turks in Germany, they went in search of jobs – much like the Pakistanis in England – but, unlike the Pakistanis, Holy Jihad fell on fallow and sterile ground. The ambition of the German Turks and Kurds is not to drive a Talib Tank but a Benz. They have bought them off, bought them off with toys.

I know someone else who was seduced but by their clever words and flattery, not so much by the glitter of worldly possessions, though that was also in him, and him adjudged a scholar. I can say I have always despised material possessions and the corruption which the coveting of them brings. I, too, have been a scholar and a teacher and I will write the book of God's Will in the blood of my pupils and, if God Wills, with my own. I will correct the Calculations of the Crusaders and show them the Design and Reckoning of Allah.

Umar was one of those clever men who think not only that no one else is as clever as they are but that no one else is clever at all. He was wily (which is something we all know I hate) but also astute enough that nobody could practise wiles upon him (which unfortunately is not the case with your servant). Unluckily for Umar, he did not realise that he himself – caught, God Willing, against the light, as it were – might be as transparent to others as others were to him. I rely on God, this was his downfall.

We had always suspected, Tariq and I, that there was a traitor among us. I can truthfully say before God I never completely trusted Umar. Hassan was another matter. It is, of course, always possible with the help of God to redeem oneself. So many of God's warriors had pasts that were not as mine. They sullied their lips with alcohol and took and sold hashish and heroin and consorted with low women. They robbed and stole. I let the *pondok* students think Tariq lost his hand in Afghanistan against the Russians. Imran certainly did. No, the gold jewellery exposed in the lane of Riyadh jewellers was too much for Tariq when he was young and driving his bulldozer. I almost do not blame him. He came from direness of poverty and was an orphan. The poor country boys do not usually steal, that I can say. It is in the cities that they learn dishonesty and depravity. The Saudis removed the hand that had offended, surgically, of course, but Tariq hates the Wahabbis with an intensity. He does not love our principal paymasters – and, God forgive me – I wondered once for three seconds if he was not the spy among us. But, God is Great, redemption is possible and he is a changed man.

Too many things had gone wrong. Too many for them to be accidental or a series of coincidences. There is the law of averages and the actuarial logic. You must follow, be guided, and obey, overcoming personal prejudice. Numbers used like this offer the counsel of a compass in the white-out of a blizzard or the stinging grains of a sandstorm. The snow is cleaner but deadlier. The high altitudes and the cold can snuff out a life long before heat and thirst would ever take their toll.

I had him watched. I watched as the falcon might the rabbit before it starts its stoop. I had Ahmed watched, too. Tariq, my dear friend, my loyal follower, I had you watched. I am ashamed. For a moment I was deceived by the lies in the incriminating writings on the body of Ahmed's brother, the one who was killed on his motor-bike. For a moment I wavered. I took Hassan into my confidence, not Umar but Hassan. Hassan seemed to think that just because something was in writing in printed words, it deserved more credence. That is the thinking of a Arts. "Only numbers are trustworthy, Haji," I replied. I knew Tariq and his limitations too well to suspect him for long. The man I have known for 30 years was not the man named in the document as an apostate and traitor. It is not that he is too good, it is that he is too simple; he lacks the subtlety. Only Jefri I did not trouble to keep under surveillance. As for you, Umar, I trapped and snared you in your own toils of perfidy.

Too many times the police and soldiers, and even the criminals, were waiting for our young Mujaheedin. It was clear that, at the very least, there was a loose tongue in our midst. I say again, I did not believe for long the lies in the writings found on the brothers of Jefri and the brother of Ahmed. Bad as these men were, it was still a pitiful sight to see Muslims crushed like cockroaches. Their helmets had come off. They had been riding the one motorbike. I remember us riding as four with my own brothers as a boy, which is all very well unless you have an accident. Then all the family's eggs are in the one basket.

It was clear Ahmed's brother had been driving. His legs were entangled in the crushed carburettor and wet with fuel from the tank. He still retained his helmet but those of Jefri's brothers, sprawled at the side of the highway with their bodies twisted into the shape of the number 4 and the number 2, had come off. One helmet remained in the middle of the road, near the bike, while that of the other had rolled down the camber. Blood had also flowed in copious quantity down the incline. I was surprised to find I did not feel at all queasy. This was as the handiwork or illusion of the devil. It had, of course, really happened but it was like watching, well, Ahmed's film. It was as if it was beautifully staged but it was not the work of men, the evil men who carried out the massacres of my childhood and set off the train of events which would become my life.

Jefri was also composed, even though the corpses he looked upon were his own family. I still said to him I was sorry he had lost his brothers. There is the time for sternness and the time for softness. The eunuch I expected to be dancing and wailing. But Ahmed was as calm as Jefri. "What God wills, Shaykh," he said.

I admit I was very impressed for it being all the more unexpected from his quarter. Sometimes, as with his – I would say stoicism but that is of the God-less Greeks, great mathematicians though they were – his martyr's fortitude under the acid – I am simply amazed by his qualities. I would have left him behind at the *pondok* and not brought him to Mindanao but for this most recent proof of his constancy and his endurance. He loved his brother, as I loved even Murad, but Ahmed was strong enough to refrain from shedding public tears for them.

The letter incriminating my faithful follower was stained with blood but its lies were still legible. I believe the brothers were hastening to show it me when they overspeeded and were struck. I think it emanates from the *Mourners of Haji Sulong* or the *Group 453*, more likely the latter, who are common assassins and smugglers. It was a piece of blackest navelry but my straightforwardness, my simplicity, and yes, my sense of honour enabled me to see through the trick. Had it been true I would not have hesitated to condemn Tariq to a speedy death.

But Umar I had followed, just as I think he had me followed months ago to the house of my wife, my wife the good Muslim. I remember it was pilaff day which I always look forward to. I could feel the hairs prickling on the back of my neck as when the Russians had us under observation from the hillsides during the holy war in Afghanistan. My little *juwae*, the youngest of my followers, the one who flies above me like a sparrow and watches, also told me he glimpsed the hem of a gown and a pair of leather sandals (not the rubber ones he wears) rounding the corner in a great hurry. At that time Umar's turpitude and treacheries were not yet of the blackest dye. He was only liaising with our rivals at that time. Even though most of them were just criminals and bandits thinking of money – they were more Siamese than they would like to think – this was not yet apostasy. Umar, too, was against our inflaming actions that widened the secessionist struggle to Jihad. He was frightened the Crusaders would come against us in strength when that was exactly the result I desired. I left him to his own devices in Singapore by design and he condemned himself. I do not know exactly when he turned, when he changed, where was the tipping-point. But by Singapore he was an apostate to the Crusaders. He got into the taxi with the half-caste Siamese following him. I know because I sent the little *juwae* to observe him. Only this time he was a sparrow-hawk. The young are the reliable, not the old. The young are the clean and the candid; they have not yet been contaminated. Afterwards, I still took the precaution of sending the boy home and not bringing him to Mindanao with the others. In his innocence he might have been vulnerable to the wiles of Umar or at least have spoken too ingenuously. This word sounds the same as ingenious but has quite the opposite meaning. The boy said it looked as if Umar was pushed into the taxi and struck a blow with his own slipper. What I would say is that it would have been typical of Umar to compound his failings with hypocrisy as well as treachery. His pretended remonstrances were as those of a woman of easy virtue or an adulteress to their seducer. And we know how their sin is punished.

I took no pleasure in it, I rely on God. It was only the *kafir* story, the *Bond of Brothers*, which influenced me. And, while it was going on, every moment I had to fight my desire to call an end to his frantic strugglings, to spare him. The students slept like the dead Umar would soon join. That had been Tariq's idea, sending them on an exhausting route march. God Willing, sometimes the un-educated can be more cunning than the highly learned. God forgive me, it was like being the only spectator at a puppet-show. In the moonlight they were as the shadows of the *wayang* upon the screen; or like the marionettes of the *kafir* jerked this way and that on their cords. At last, all was still. Within the hour, long before the roosters crowed, poor Umar was stiff as wood. He had succumbed to temptation, God have mercy on his soul. I did not succumb to the temptation of mercy, just as I had succeeded in preserving our family's honour when I was still a boy.

Imran and Tariq were not boys. They did their work with the silence and efficiency of the Hindu *thugi* sending their slumbering victims to Kali.

I want to be surrounded by the efficient, by engineers, by chemists, not by the foolish Arts. China is now a successful rival to America. That is because their President and Premier are engineers. I want to be surrounded by the holy and the efficient. Then there will be no contradiction. As Ibn Rashd combined and made the synthesis of Aristotle and Aquinas, so shall we, the humble servants of knowledge and God, continue the Sciences and the Arts in the Caliphate. Except, God Willing, Science shall surely prevail and be accounted the senior partner and the Arts be as handmaidens. When Hassan raised the alarm, the crime had been committed – God is Great! – I mean the punishment had been administered – barely an hour before. I was still shaken by it. How did I manage, so against my nature, to dissemble so glibly? Simplicity itself! It came upon me in the instant as I strode towards the scene as if it was the first time. I should simply pretend I was Umar himself. He who so revelled in the misfortune of others. I should tell the quick and ready lies he was so expert in. This was the sweetest of revenges. Then I thought – I had committed what I had long ago identified as the fundamental crime and fallacy of a Arts, to abdicate the certainty of self for the relativism of the other. Then I thought yet again – how sweet to use the weapons of the Shaitane against himself.

It is done.

From the inception in Mindanao my faithful students all knew we had arrived in a special place and they resolved to improve and uplift themselves accordingly.

Even Ahmed – whom I have forged from the basest and softest of metals into a Sword of God – even Ahmed who personifies all that is worst of the City, of the New York and Gomorrah – raised his arms as he saw extending before him the virgin, unspoiled forest of Mindanao and the solid, unyielding rock on which he would rest his head. Even Ahmed, I say – God is Great! – lifted his hands to Allah in thanks and gave vent to an inarticulate howl. Of joy and thankfulness! I saw the tears upon his face.

At first I was filled with horror at the notion of making an entertainment of Jihad. It was, oddly enough, Tariq who changed my mind. He said, "To use the enemy's weapons against him is not to become the enemy. Did we fail to pick up the Kalashnikovs the Russians dropped? If, God Willing, one day we get an atom bomb, will we fail to detonate it over Singapore or London because a Jew invented it?"

I hid my surprise, saying with a laugh, "London, God Willing. We will let the Chinese off the hook this time."

For answer, Tariq waved his own hook and his intelligent moment was over. Perhaps it was God speaking through him, God speaking through the mouths of babes and huge, hairy idiots.

I watched *Bond of Brothers*. To my surprise I greatly enjoyed it. There was indeed a bond between these young *kafirs*. Of course, they were about the devil's work, stopping the Germans from eliminating every Jew in the world, subtracting them from the sum of the world and arriving at the correct balance. I must point out it was not a frivolous fairy tale nor "creative" invention of the Arts. It actually happened. Actors portrayed real people, except the actors were young and the actual people they pretended to be were already old. Ancient, I should say. Old as my father the havildar, may God be well-pleased with the honourable old soldier. He was misguided but admirable. I admit this is a paradox but it is also an equation. You saw the real people talking first about what had actually happened in the war 60 years ago – they were wrinkled, grey-haired. Then, as if they had drunk the devil's elixir, you saw them miraculously young again. Suddenly their leader's grey hair became red as the carrot. To do this, they chose actors who resembled the real people. I knew a red-haired boy at school – he was from Kandahar. Naturally so, I mean. Not dyed with henna. Ahmed called them "Talking Heads". Tariq said, "Heads don't talk, ho-ho." Maybe all this was *haram*. Maybe it was not right to reverse time and make the old young again. This is the prerogative of Allah, this is the condition of Paradise. Still, I was glad I had listened to Tariq, as I had listened – God forgive me – to his offer to remove Umar from the sum of things. I acceded after I had watched the fifth – or was it seventh? – episode of *Bond of Brothers*. I was angry. I compared – God have mercy upon his servant – the loyalty the young *kafir* commander enjoyed from his loyal lieutenant with the treachery of my own dotard.

I can certainly say Ahmed's film is not the work of the devil. To look at, it is not so pleasing as the saga of the young *kafir* Brothers. For a start, it is not in colours. I was very surprised. The camera he used – from Singapore, of course – was very expensive, unless Hassan was put up to tricks with the receipt by Umar. It was surely within its capabilities – or features, as Iskander called them – to have colours but Ahmed launched into a long arty explanation as to why it would look better in black and white. I was about to cut him short when Tariq muttered, "In colour less *haram*, boss," and I was pleased to leave it at that. It is of an outrage that actually occurred in the past and will serve the cause of the present Jihad.

The competition which Ahmed and Jefri staged – this was even better. Reality show. That is an excellent expression. Yes, the Mujaheedin have a dream and they will show the *kafirs* it is a reality, God Willing. I was concerned when the point of the competition had been clearly explained to me by, of all people, young Iskander (they compete to see who is the most zealous warrior of God) that it should lead to excessive zeal on their part. I cannot condone or allow this. Atrocity in the name of God is still atrocity. To accomplish any objective a precisely calculated quantity of force should be used. This is the solution of the engineer or the architect or even the physician when administering a medicine. We, the Mujaheedin, administer a *dose* of violence. It may be a single dose or it may be regular over a prolonged period, like a course of the anti-biotic. Let us be clear, it is a planned schedule of anti-biotic violence. (I can tell you anti-biotic means "against life"). It is not some random and unplanned orgy of revenge-taking. That would be wretched. That would be *haram*. It is not to be enjoyed. It is necessary – regrettable, but necessary. Most important – I rely on God – it is not banditry.

Our brothers here fell into this error – this trap – long ago. Also our brothers in South Siam. The other *pondoks* – justice compels me to say – are mostly free – God is Great! – of criminal influence. I cannot say the same of those fighting for secession. In their number are included drug-smugglers, hired killers, kidnappers for ransom, and extortionists who with menaces demand insurances for immunity from the hard-working and devout who otherwise would see their businesses burned down around their ears. These are precisely the criminals my father detested the most. My mother said, after he was gone, that he had been part of the bands of soldiers and police in plainclothes who had dealt summary justice to these criminals at night, but I never believed her. The misdeeds of the common criminals in Pattani taint our great and holy cause and delay the accomplishment of the Caliphate.

For a while, I could tolerate and even encourage it. We needed, as I said, to lift the temperature of the flames beneath the pot of water that was Pattani. Civil disorder, the breakdown of the rule of law – if anything other than *sharia* can be considered a law – were necessary as the first condition of the coming of the Caliphate. God is Great! It will be a precisely gradated series of steps. This is why I was able to condone communication and cooperation, but never the friendship and respect that exists among real Mujaheedin, between us and the Pattani fighters who were no better than gangsters.

That night-time affray where shots were exchanged between our students and the smugglers in Pattani remains clouded in mystery to me but I am confident – God Willing – that I will eventually have the truth. We were supplied with false informations. If someone had wished to start a conflict between ourselves and these people it could not have been better designed.

It is my belief that the Crusaders do not know who destroyed the den of iniquities called the discotheque in Phuket. No one suspects us, except for the local Mujaheedin. They do not suspect, they *know*.

There is no contradiction between my earlier calculations and the Jihad we took to Phuket. We needed to kill hundreds, as did the glorious martyrs – may God be well-pleased with them – in Bali. We needed to attack the foreign target, the tourists, that our brothers – our often criminal relatives in Pattani – refrained from attacking for so long. They were frightened to widen their national struggle for secession and connect it to that of the greater Jihad. As I said, they feared the wrath of the Crusaders upon their heads. They thought it would impede, not hasten, their struggle for independence.

In this calculation they were not mistaken! It could and did! God is Great!

I killed, burned, and maimed 203 *kafirs* in the Phuket attack. I care not. I rely on God. I looked on those photographs with a heart that was calm and indifferent. I saw the arms, the legs, the torn and charred flesh. Mighty Allah was with me.

Mercy and ruthlessness, compassion and cruelty, are but opposite sides of the same equation. God Willing, you must have them both to balance. They will work better together. Their effect is a synergy.

From the strong, forebearance is more appreciated. From the weak it merely appears as weakness. From the compassionate, in turn, sternness is seen as justifiable. The Messenger of God himself (peace be upon his head) was as severe in his punishments as he was generous in his forgiveness.

A Leader has to be feared, by his followers as well as his foes. When he becomes predictable, when his wraths are foreseen, he becomes controllable. We fear nature just because she is not controllable, except by Allah. I do not say a Leader should be capricious but he should surprise, even shock. Then, God Willing, later they will see he was right.

292

And sometimes, God have forgiveness, a Leader has to give them what they want after first refusing it, so they appreciate it more.

These are not wiles, as were the false and crafty habits of Umar and the politicians of Pakistan. These are the lineaments of Man. And without God we are nothing, we are less than the dust between our toes.

The middle part of the sum must be taken out. By this I mean not just those Muslims who are lazy and shirk Jihad but also the good Siamese. They are redundant, the "moderates", the word is otiose. Just as ⅝ is re-fractionalised to ¼, so they must be reduced. Of the good Siamese, there are few enough and, God Willing, we shall make them fewer still. It is regrettable but necessary. It is a calculation. As to our own apostates, a fiery end awaits them and we shall not be slow to despatch them there. The "moderates" we can change – the Crusaders, rather, will transform them for us, God Willing. Moderate is a word for lazy, for coward. We shall fill these empty vessels with the rage the unwitting Crusader shall provide in torrents. The Crusaders shall provide the fuel for the Jihad that will destroy them. As a Follower, I would rather have the awakened "moderate". They make the better recruit to Jihad. God is Great! They can be even more zealous in the cause of God than the hardened and calloused criminal with blood upon his hands! They are more dependable. They are, at the end, the fiercer fighter, too. Look at Jefri and Iskander, even Ahmed who led a life of sin in the city. There are many more like them in Pattani, so many heaps of black and dusty charcoal bricks and dirty newspaper, waiting for the clean flame to ignite them. I, God's servant, focus the jet of burning gases upon them. I am Allah's Bunsen burner.

Imran was a grievous loss, not just to his other half, Tariq, but to all of us. If possible, Imran was even more stupid than his brother but more manageable for that. He would have been as useful in Pattani as he was in the camp. God Willing, we will still turn Pattani into another Mindanao and Mindanao into a second Afghanistan. But Tariq says nothing. I suppose he was without his twin for many years and can face the prospect of many more. I already cautioned him against seeking a swifter reunion. He replied, "I look so crazy, boss?" He spends hours at a time sharpening his kris. I have also warned him against exacting sudden and arbitrary revenges upon the unsuspecting and unoffending.

Had I participated in Ahmed's project – I would never do so, of course: as the exemplar at the head of the exercise, at the top of the page, as it were, I could not permit myself to come within 10,000 miles of anything contaminating – but had I been younger, with less responsibilities, God Willing, I would have liked to have been filmed cutting the heads off ten Americans, then rushing into the burning fort to save the son of the American Commander I had just decapitated. That child would be brought up within *sharia*'s strictest precepts to be an adornment to his religion and – God is Great! – his name would have been Muslim. He would have been as a janissary. I shared this thought with Hassan at the time. He had been smoking the water-pipe while we watched. This was more tolerable to his neighbours than Umar's clove cigarettes. Maybe the heady clouds of his exhalation had given me a euphoria, for it is a rule with me – confirmed by experience – that it is better for a Leader to keep the innermost workings of his mind to himself. I speedily corrected myself. "This is a fantasy, Hassan," I rebuked myself, "our concern is for the actual."

Hassan removed the tube from his mouth, then blew wreaths of apple-flavoured smoke away from me. The Haji's were the courtesies of a bygone age, formulaic but practical. He changed the mouthpiece so that it was hygienic for the next user – he knew it would not be for me. I thought he felt my comments did not merit a reply – they assuredly did not – when after a long interval he said, "Our aim to bring about the Caliphate is also a dream. God is Great but men are at their most noble in their dreams; it is then they are redeemed."

I was about to reply when Hassan added with a cackle, "The redemption date of a bond is also a distant dream for the lender, the *kafir* creditor." That was the trouble with Hassan. He was what you would call a pedant but he was also a clown. There was no spite or vanity in him, unlike Umar. I rely on God – at the end, I do not believe he was trying to thwart us. I disagree with Tariq.

I find myself brooding over the recent events. I shall put them behind me. It is another life and you should lead the present one, the one you have and which God gave you in all its immediacy.

Our resources are depleted. But Allah was merciful to his warriors. It is our financial resources rather than our human which have been lost. At least, God Willing, money is more easily replaced than people. Umar was no loss at all. I still have Jefri. Iskander is a good boy and will be a better man.

We have to take stock, solidify our position in Pattani. But not for too long. We cannot let the other groups – Mujaheedin, criminal, whatever they are – have an inkling of our true situation. One of the late havildar's precepts was that offence is the best defence. We need to conduct a great exploit – different in kind from what has gone before, even the Phuket attack. I shall use the resources I have sparingly and to greatest effect but I shall use them to their utmost. In the Name of God I shall get the utmost from them and not spare them. I may have to sacrifice some of those for whom I feel the greatest affection. That is the anguishment only a leader can know. God will give me strength. It is beyond personal likes and dislikes now. That I disliked Umar and liked Hassan and that I cherish Jefri and not Ahmed is of no relevance. I know right and I know wrong. I am not soft like the Arts, full of doubts and uncertainty. I have studied. I can recite the sura in my dreams. I know Set Theory. I know the clear theorems, their unwavering posits. God is Great.

5

Snooky

Snooky can't stop herself. She follows the example of the late, hard-faced Polish Papa and throws herself upon the red earth of Pattani. She kisses this and finds it . . . unpalatable but friable. Reeling with fatigue, her brothers are about to imitate her before Shaykh shoots a furious glance at them and she gets Tariq's rocket-propelled sandal wedged up the butt. Fortunately for Snooky, Shaykh doesn't get the true origin of what he thinks is Ahmed's impromptu homage.

He hisses, "A martyr's house is everywhere he lays his head. His love is for the Caliphate, not this . . . this . . ." Words fail him, until he passes Snooky by and a good five seconds later spits, "Snake-pit."

Snooky's balls, and she never likes being reminded of them, throb for the rest of the day as much as her fundament but she doesn't care, not even for the rebuke of Shaykh. Yah, it's home and Snooky knows it at last.

Jefri and Iskander take an arm apiece and lift her up. They do it as if she is light as a wisp of aromatic smoke from the clove cigarettes they will never see nor smell Imam Umar wheezing on again. They speak into her ear at the same time.

"Brother, do better," Jefri exhorts.

Breathes Iskander, whose fraternal words are innocuous of even the mildest reproof, "It's nothing. I feel the same."

And Snooky replies aloud to both of them in Iskander's very words: *"My pen wry."* Oh, it's nothing. Poor Snooky – the depths of her inconsequentiality, the virile face she has to show her brothers.

Later, it becomes clear another of her tribulations is gonna be anonymity – what her kind hate most: *Curse of the Katoey*, not Karloff's *Curse of the Mummy*. Snooky just isn't the strong but silent type. Relegated to the shadows, outta the limelight, in her sarcophagus in the blackest reaches of the mausoleum, it's just hell. She won't be getting the teeny-weeniest bit of a credit, not so much as unreadable white letters travelling rapidly up the screen at two feet per second. The *auteur* of that historical epic *Krag vs Kris: The Moro Greater* will forever remain as anonymous as . . . Snooky doesn't know: the author of the anthrax letters, Jonbenet's killer? Whatever. The movie would be a cult success, not just on the Mujaheedin circuit but to a wider audience on DVD and the net. Snooky sees it for sale on the barrows at the local market where it has been rapidly pirated, no doubt by Chinese hands. *Sheikh of Islam productions proudly present*, it says on the garish cover. Someone has been dictating because *Moro Crater* has become *Moro Greater*. Snooky hadn't exactly hoped she would walk the red carpet sparklingly begowned on Tom Selleck's arm at Venice or Cannes but still . . . she sulks as much as she dares. Not Jefri or Iskander but Tariq is the chosen message bearer. He says, "Your moment in the sun will come. God Willing, the boss promises you. You will be world famous."

"Fifteen minutes of fame," says Snooky bitterly.

"God is Great! Instant and Forever!" insists Tariq, with a terrible joviality harder to endure than his rages.

Snooky needed encouragement. Home again, happy in spirit, she had declined physically. Maybe because she didn't have to make the effort to stay well every day – or die. Snooky was frail, *tea ruck*, frailer and more fragile by the day. There'd been no full-length mirrors in Mindanao, just cracked shards of glass and circles of stainless steel to shave by. In the *pondok*, too, something like a tailor's reclining mirror was also unknown as a hog. It is in town (where Shaykh spent his first week back) that Snooky catches a glimpse of herself as she really is when she passes by the window of a Chinese roast meats deli. There, mingling with the red-lacquered duck carcasses and ghostly pale chickens, she sees herself as others do: skinny as a latex tree, gaunt as Mount Kinabalu. If you wanted the human opposite of golden, fat Buddha then Snooky conformed. She had lost 15 kilos, maybe more. Both hands fly to her face. Now she does look like a dead gander, with wings folded.

Dr Cheuan's words from all those months ago, her cautious prognosis, come home to roost. "Are you sitting down?" she had asked me on the phone before she had taken the ground of my Bangkok room from underneath me. "Of course," she had encouraged me, "there will be remissions – maybe for years at a time. Maybe something else will carry you off. But it will always be there, lurking under the surface, waiting to pounce." I laughed hollowly, no manically, as I thought of her final exhortation. "Make the most of life, Khun Snooky. Do the things you want to do while you're still strong enough. Don't put off anything you can enjoy today until tomorrow. Stay well-nourished. Get plenty of sleep. Take care of yourself. Try not to worry too much about anything. Avoid stress at all costs."

A year in the *pondok,* learning Holy Koran by heart, Snooky bored out of her tiny little mind when she wasn't crapping herself at the computer with her heart in her mouth. Six months in Mindanao alternately massacring and being massacred, sleeping five hours a day in the company of Khun Dengue and Khun Diarrhoea. Drinking from puddles. Being chased by the Armed Forces of the Philippines. Oh, yah, great, it had been a vitamin-laden, worry-free ideal existence. Just what the doctor ordered. Even at betrayal she was mediocre. Snooky's whole life was a failure and a sham. Snooky wanted to be something she could never be.

What did Snooky do? She took her love to town. No, of course, no one desired her scabby, emaciated body anymore. She took the only physical consolation she could.

She sneaks out the *pondok* – all the Mindanao veterans are permitted liberties even *ulama* or haji are not – and scores some junk, some oxycontin, some ketamine, and some ice from a gang of Trannies, in a larger township four stops down the train-line, who never guessed she was one of their own. Then she does something she has never, never resorted to before: she mixes them all up into a milkshake speedball and shoots up in the train's bathroom. The rickety engine takes off and impales itself in the moon, the moon. Snooky alights, alit, a stop down the line further than she should have done (a metaphor for her wretched life), entering the *pondok* path long after curfew, under the light of the crescent moon.

Her Brothers cover for her. They trust her with their lives, the poor fools. She loves them for this, she despises them for this.

Next day she feels worse than ever. Euphoria is longer-lived than its more active cousin, elation, but not by much. For every action, Shaykh liked to say, there is a reaction.

Snooky's old friends, Su and Ana, come to visit with her. Actually, Ana didn't come. Only Su. You had to have some self-regard left, if you were to entertain Ana. Khun Su whispers in her ear. No one can see her seductive presence, only Snooky hears her beguiling suggestions. Cord, O-D, poison, slit veins, on the train track under the Surat Thani express, electrocution, drowning, or that huge macho gesture, the shot in the head? (Oh, anything, anything but that).

Snooky thinks: her means of departure can be a means of cleansing, too. Of atonement, restitution, a chastisement masochistically desired.

She feels her forehead. Hot as Do-Ann's ceramic curling tongs. She heads for Shaykh's study. The rooms of Umar and Hassan are as yet unfilled. The rumour-mill has it that Jefri will get Hassan's and a new *alim* is coming from Yemen to fill Umar's slippers. A friend of Umar's had hopes of being Tok Guru but was gonna have his pious ambition thwarted.

It's like vomiting. It builds up in you a long time. One is nausea, the other guilt. At the moment the bile rises in the gorge, at the moment you decide to admit your terrible guilt, you actually feel a sense of relief. I confessed to Shaykh, haltingly at first, then the words of shame spewed out.

In his lenses I saw myself auditioning. For infliction, retribution, the punishment that might restore as it destroyed. My gestures became theatrical, my voice throbbed with weakness and self-pity. I imagined how Shaykh might see me, the impression of falsity I might produce. I pretended I was Shaykh. I had no idea what was going on behind the shades but I imagined a combination of Cannes jury and firing squad. At last I stopped.

Silence ensued. Snooky, babulous Snooky, felt no desire to break it.

After a long time, Shaykh said, "I know."

"What?"

"Praise be to God."

"You always knew?"

"God is Great. He gave me the penetration to add all informations together and be supplied with the correct answer."

"Yes, Shaykh."

"I have been waiting for you to tell me. This is good you have told me. Tell me more."

"More, Shaykh?"

"Yes. For instance, about Hassan. Did he tell them the numbers? Did he mention them to you? Do you remember them?"

"Er, Shaykh, Haji Hassan had no part in any of this. I can show you all the old emails and any that come through after today."

"Good, Ahmed. God is truly Great. I was merely checking, cross-checking, your veracity and I am glad, truly glad, to find that you have not lied. I am sorry I had to set you a trap. I hate slynesses of all kinds myself."

"I would not lie to you, Shaykh. My heart is sick of lies and deception. I want to be true, true to myself and true, too, to our Cause. I want to be nothing other than I am. If you decide I should die, I will go with a joyful heart. This is nothing other than the truth itself. You may find it hard to believe but that is the simple truth. I deserve to die as an example to my Brothers. Shaykh, I ask you as a final kindness, let it be quick. I ask for the Mercy of God, I ask for the mercy of my leader. Let me feel no pain. I do not ask for leniency, just a merciful departure. God Willing, Tuan."

"Go. Go with God, always."

Shaykh's words were enigmatic. Snooky had not been forgiven but nor had she been condemned. In fact, there was a slight presumption, no, in favour of forgiveness? You could go with God to your doom but, in normal usage, it was used to address those you hoped to encounter again.

Snooky would be a liar if she said she slept well that night. She kept imagining a great, coiling snake with obsidian eyes approaching her in the darkness. It wore dark glasses and it hissed, "Your days are numbered!"

In all this turmoil, there was one thing Snooky could be glad of. Thanks be, Imam Umar was no longer there to rub his dry hands as he devised some intricate and classical, but barbarous, penalty for me.

I waited in vain for my unveiling as traitor to the Caliphate. At the least, I had expected a public confession, some tearful auto-criticism supplied by myself, maybe a vote from the senior Brothers on my fate. I hoped for a meticulously placed shot in the back of the head, from a loving friend like Iskander or Jefri, in the palm-grove. But nothing happened.

For sure I knew Tariq knew. As I passed him on my way to the Maproom the next day, he drew his fist back and growled, "If it was up to me, *koti*, I'd cut your balls off."

What made Snooky reply, "Promises, promises, Haji," and then run to her Brothers for sanctuary? The funny thing was: we should all have been scared of Tariq but after Mindanao we treated him as a pussy-cat. It was Shaykh, ascetic, reserved, and controlled, who petrified every single one of us.

None of us could really put a finger on it. We respected him, no, we adored him, but he spooked us.

Behind the kingly exterior – for us he was the Caliph-in-waiting – we felt there was no pity in him and that clemency was not forebearance but a gambit. We spoke of Haji Hassan in whispers only and of Umar not at all.

In the seventh week of our return, three after my confession, Shaykh summoned me, Jefri, and Iskander to his presence. He said, "God has a prize, a great work for you."

TO: LUDORUM
CC: LK-FLOREAT-50/50
BCC: À VOUS
SUBJECT: A ROLLING STONE DOES NOT GATHER MOSS
DATE: 25/11/200-
FROM: VICE VERSA
YOUR DRAFT HAS BEEN SAVED

Thank you for your report on your journey. As you say, not much happened during this time but it is good to make contact once more and it is incumbent upon you not to allow such a long silence to occur again. You might let me know exactly where in Nusa Tenggara the two old Imams decided to retire. It will be an easy matter for us to check should they ever decide to return to the school, in, say, a matter of a few months. This quieter interlude gives me the occasion to reflect upon your position and how you came to arrive in it. I am well aware that you have been impressed into our service willy-nilly, if not by physical means and short of actual maltreatment – which one abhors – then by moral and minatory suasions which could be said to have verged upon blackmail. Nevertheless, some of the greatest naval heroes in history arrived on the quarter-deck via the press-gang, senseless with drink or rendered so by a knock over the head. I would like to offer you thanks – compensation in an entirely immaterial sense – and appreciation for such assistance as you have rendered us. I believe you have acted not dishonourably and you have no reason to feel ashamed of yourself. You may hold your head high and should refrain from proceeding to extreme courses of self-reproach.

In your last report you note the flagging of Eskander alias "Boffin's" Yala cell and Eskander's own waning star and the rumours of his impending retirement. (You have referred to them as a "team" as if they were playing soccer and mentioned "own goals" and "relegation"). This may simply be following an analogy as the simplest course when writing quickly under pressure and fear of discovery – I understand this – or it could lie deeper and indicate the development of a more communal or committee-run form of organisation and a less charisma- or individual-dependent style of leadership. The deaths and wounding of their most daring operatives in battle may simply be seen as occupational hazards – footballers always seem to be getting themselves injured – but one can almost feel regretful about the secession of Eskander's former lieutenants under the blandishments of the criminal gangs. When you continue the analogy and speak about "transfers", do you actually mean to imply that financial inducements were proffered in the way that sportsmen might be offered fees? The treachery and, in due course, execution of the religious leader as opposed to the tactical commander is almost disappointing. Photographs of these personalities, though deceased, would still be useful and go a long way to allaying the doubts felt about you by your local handler.

Your remark that old terrorists do not die but simply fade away brought a smile to care-worn features. You could say the same about spies, if that cheers you up.

Your local control informs me there has been no activity either from this group but he remains extremely sceptical of them and of you. I repeat – you are in a delicate situation and very much dependent on our good-will. I can be a good friend to you in the way that your local handler cannot and, perhaps, will not. Evince all sincerity and you may expect liberty in due course. We may, before then, require you to meet the local contact. He says Ayuttayah would be most convenient for his purposes. A convincing cover or pretext will be manufactured. There was a Roman word for the formal freeing of a slave or indentured person, usually, like your good self, a person of education . . .

TO: LUDORUM
CC: LK-FLOREAT-50/50
BCC: À VOUS
SUBJECT: ABSOLUTELY YOUR LAST WARNING
DATE: 12/12/200-
FROM: VICE VERSA
YOUR DRAFT HAS BEEN SAVED

I really think you need the Riot Act read to you, preferably through a loud-hailer at the *pondok* gate and in the stentorian tones I can no longer muster, if I ever possessed them. We are given to understand through independent and highly reliable channels that one of the elderly *pondok* scholars you assured us was relatively sentient is, in fact, recently deceased. I think I can safely tell you without prejudicing those sources – who are youthful, legion, and heavily-armed – that they are American. The departed in question would be the gentleman who had made the pilgrimage to Mecca while studying in Egypt and had once been a bank manager in Northern Sumatra. We are told he was given his quietus by an American-trained sniper, embedded, or perhaps enmired would be the more appropriate choice of word, with the Armed Forces of the Philippines. Or do you still persist in saying his obituary is premature? I am appalled, frankly appalled, by your deceitfulness and insulted as to your estimate of the degree of our gullibility.

So, when I ask of you: How fares the Imam? perhaps for once I can expect a straight answer.

We are virtually certain that Tariq, the spectacularly intimidating-looking enforcer, has also gone the way of all flesh. Your half-brother and the two siblings of your friend "Jefri" were able to describe this character and the Imam himself to your local control before they were tranquillised. (If you are concerned, I can assure you they never felt a twinge during the "accident"). The enforcer's facial features were completely destroyed in the ambush in Mindanao but habitment, girth, prosthesis, and DNA analysis all give the lie to your asservation that he is still quick. We have two reports as to the circumstances in which he met his fate: that he was shot by the same sniper who killed the Haji or that he was executed as a traitor by the "Milk Sheikh". By the by, this latter's physical description appears not to tally with the one you have given of a short, nondescript man as we have the report of a tall and distinguished-looking gentleman imposing himself in the ambush party's gunsights.

We are also informed the enforcer became an object of suspicion to the leader some months before his end, at the time your brothers met with their unfortunate mishap.

I need to know how exactly the enforcer met his end. In the unlikely event you maintain he is still alive, I do need what I am told is called a date-stamped digital "Jay Peg" image as proof of life. And, again, if you are actually able to supply this evidence as to his existence perhaps you can inform us whether or not he has been able to re-insinuate himself into the good graces of the leader. Kindly also reveal if anyone else can be said to be in bad odour at this moment in time, how they arrived at this perilous predicament, and what means they could take to extricate themselves from this impasse. Do not give me your own name!

Give us accurate and executable intelligence and I can guarantee you an end to your bondage by the middle of the year and perhaps even a small gratuity to help re-establish yourself in a new life. We might even be able to secure you a minor journalistic position in Brunei or Goa. The younger part of my acquaintance tell me the latter is a perfect den of iniquity and drug-taking. Sounds right up your street.

I had hoped to meet you personally but, alas, have shelved plans to visit the Kingdom for the foreseeable future. That is, unless you care to defer your de-activation ten years or so just for that pleasure? I am, of course, indulging in pleasantries. Do not trifle with us and we shall not mock you, the afflicted.

PART THREE

Trapdoor

Many men would take the death-sentence without a whimper to escape the life-sentence which fate carries in her other hand.
- T.E. Lawrence, *The Mint*

Girl! nimble with thy feet, not with thy hands!
Curled minion, dancer, coiner of sweet words!
Fight; let me hear thy hateful voice no more!
- Matthew Arnold, *Sohrab and Rustum*

Pesons le gain et la perte en prenant le parti de croire que Dieu est. Si vous gagnez, vous gagnez tout ; si vous perdez, vous ne perdez rien. Pariez donc qu'il est sans hésiter. Oui il faut gager.
- Pascal, *Pensée #318*

Secrecy is not a dirty word.
- John Sawers

Notwithstanding the modern emphasis on sport techniques, whose proper province is the competitive mat, the age-old street deciders of the kick to the groin, the eye-gouge, and the head-butt, remain the staples of any system of self-defence worthy of the name. With these techniques the weak may realistically hope to overcome the strong. In general, most systems of unarmed combat actually follow the principles of an asymmetrical military strategy: as in guerilla warfare, the weak, the elderly, the diminutive, or the outnumbered, may select a target and, through applying all their force to a sequestered part of the opponent's anatomy, by instrumentality of the heel-hook, the arm-bar, small-joint manipulation, or the triangle choke, actually prove themselves stronger than the foe – at that moment in time and at that *point d'appui*.
- J.M.M. Trelawney, *On Restraint*, HMSO 1958

We should seek the greatest value for our action.
- Stephen Hawking

The golden evening brightens in the west;
Soon, soon to faithful warriors cometh rest;
Sweet is the calm of paradise the blessed:
Alleluia! Alleluia!
- William W. How, 1823-1897

Victor

I mounted my chariot of fire and ascended into the empyrean – rather grey over the Home Counties – without excessive trepidation. They say when Chamberlain flew to see Herr Hitler (as the BBC still liked to call him then) it was his first time in an aeroplane and that the "Peace in our Time" agreement was as much the product of his funk aloft as a sense of weakness at the negotiating table. Others might say the cunning old fellow was simply buying time for us to construct more Spitfires and Hurricanes. If the Few had fought the Battle of Britain in 1939 they would assuredly have been far too few. I arrived in Siam, or Thailand as I must now learn to call it, comparatively refreshed on my jumbo. (Which makes me think of pachyderms and not the product of Messrs Boeing).

I flew Nob Class to Singapore little over a year ago, but it was Steerage this time. Still, it was as nothing compared to the old Dakotas they'd cart us around in for most of 1943-44. Those were less comfortable and slower than the jets of today but probably sturdier. I was always suspicious of the circumstances in which Orde Wingate died. They talk about Churchill or, more likely, Philby, having Sikorski's plane sabotaged but I am among those who strongly suspect Woodburn Kirby, but of course not Slim, of having a hand in the death of the detested Chindit. How can I put it? I'm not sure they did do him in but I'm not sure, either, that they didn't. Woodburn Kirby, if I'm right, did Wingate in twice, the last time with a character assassination in the *Official History*. As always, there's the public narrative and there's the real story.

Anyway, I'm on *terra firma* again physically, if not as regards the flights of fancy, the De Lisle safely in Jerry's golf-bag. We had more difficulty checking it in at Heathrow than with the gun's check-off in Bangkok. Jerry insisted I bring it, can't think why. He might want to swap it for some marbles. He's an old codger now but there remains something terribly Bevis-like about him. He turned up, all 5ft 6ins of him, with his raincoat primly buttoned right up the collar.

Why am I here? Having been wrong-footed and slow off the mark so many times before – Falklands, Kuwait, London bombings etc – SIS now wants to be, or be seen as, more likely pro-active and not reactive, prescient and not dilatory.

As I'm always saying, since 1975 SE Asia has been not just a quiet corner of the world but also something of a sanctuary – a holiday-camp as well as a conference-room – for the most extreme kind of zealot, like Fountains Abbey or Sherwood were for the types in Lincoln green. All kinds of mischief can safely be planned here. No drones overhead. National sovereignty and all that rot. As the exchange student from the Sorbonne said to me when the bulldogs nabbed him coming in over the low kitchen-garden wall of Brecon, *"C'était la ligne de moindre résistance."* The situation in Southern Thailand is clearly out of the control of the government and, in fact, tipping over from the stage of low intensity conflict to an unstoppable insurrection. The Bangkok authorities and the army are incapable of remedying the situation, yet national pride precludes them from calling in overt foreign assistance. As yet it remains, in Lawrence's words about the Arab Revolt, a "sideshow of a sideshow". So a discreet hand has to be played in the shape of a superannuated, and apparently masterless, old retainer and fogey like myself. Despite the oleaginous flatteries proffered me, I am aware my role is purely symbolic and merely represents an acknowledgment on both sides that a channel of communication has been opened. Of course, in these straitened times they sent someone on their last legs – Veridian – and by economy class, too, the skinflints.

What really lit a fire under everyone was the forestalled sabotage of the nuclear plant (no, it wasn't Calder Hall), involving *inter alios* a pair of Thais and a Malaysian, as well as a quorum of our very own home-grown Cabbagestanis. The vetters had no inkling that radical Islam existed in Thailand! Somehow everyone managed to keep this narrow squeak under their hats and out of the news. I would like to think on the basis of not putting ideas into other impressionable little heads, rather than "not alarming and panicking the public", which we all know means "not embarrassing and inconveniencing the government". It was felt that while, as far as the UK was concerned, most of the dangerous plots came out of Pakistan, from now on we'd better field a couple of long stops in SE Asia to supplement the plethora of silly mid-ons in South Asia.

The real thing is, our Cousins want a finger in the pie here but cannot justify a too direct involvement. Nor would they want to burn that finger after their previous experience in this part of the world. Who better a proxy than us, the old imperial power who owned two of Siam's neighbours, Burma and Malaya, boast of a successful counter-insurgency history in the latter, and historic on-going personal connections with the Siamese elite? It is a bizarre irony. I was the Americans' rival here in 1945. Now I'm their glorified errand-boy.

As an Englishman, I can say what we did in our imperial phase here did not, for a refreshing change, by its greed or its ruthlessness contribute to the present dismal state of affairs in Southern Siam. What happened was, we were far too abstemious and moderate. We didn't cut ourselves a big enough slice of the territorial pie when we were the ones holding the knife. It relates to the breaking up and re-apportionment of the old independent Sultanate of Patani by Britain and Siam. Not totally unlike the dismantling of Poland by Hitler and Stalin, really. We, meaning Perfidious Albion, by the Anglo-Siam Treaty of '09, or was it '08, grabbed the Southernmost rump of Patani and annexed it into Malaya, whereupon it became the Northernmost state of our protectorate. We conceded the Northern (from our point of view) portion of the Sultanate to the Siamese which promptly became the Southernmost tail of Siam. i.e.what happened was that we carved a fairly sparing chunk from South of Siam's nether regions and slapped it on to Malaya as Kelantan, Terengganu, and I forget the names of the other pair of successor states. Had we annexed more territory, it would have constituted, to mix the metaphor further, an entirely benign piece of historic heroic surgery. Today the agitated, rebellious Islamic provinces of modern Thailand would be dozing the peaceful nap of their Malaysian neighbours in a unitary Malay state (forgetting the Chinese and Indians). The cancer would have been excised from modern Thailand at an early stage before metastasis and enlargement. Alack and alas, Carruthers of the FO for once was too restrained. We could have done with Napier's precipitate *peccavi*.

There is the local canard – put to me at Teddy's by one of his Malaysian pupils – that Kelantan was secured from the Siamese – the wheels of the transfer greased – with funds derived from our Chinese opium monopoly, or indeed the raw commodity itself, but I dismiss this as precisely that, a canard.

Just looking at the map, or even driving, you can see the balance of the modern nation-states is all wrong. Thailand is far too long – from Chiang Mai to Yala is a prodigious distance – nearly Calais to Gibraltar – while Malaya is too short: close your eyes driving and you'll be hitting the brakes at the Causeway to Singapore before you know it. Incidentally, relative levels of Anglophilia may be gauged by the fact that the Malaysians drive on the right and the Thais, like us, on the left.

Siam was renamed Thailand just before World War II, the word Thai often erroneously said to mean "Free." Certainly Siam was the only SE Asian nation never to have been colonised. Annam, Cambodia and Laos owned by the French, Java and Sumatra by the Dutch, Malaya and Burma by our good selves. But here's the inglorious truth: Siam only stayed independent because it formed a convenient buffer between the French and ourselves. Whoever got Siam would have upset the balance of power. The French would certainly have had no problem overrunning Siam militarily at that particular time. Poor King Chulalongkorn (the present King and Queen's grandfather) had to run for his life from his island holiday palace on the Gulf of Siam in 1893 when the French navy first shelled it, then landed, and burned it down. The French were the real wolves, although the Burmese have always been seen as the invaders and natural enemies of the Siamese. It was the Burmese who burned the old Siamese capital of Ayuttayah and forced the move to Bangkok 250 years ago.

We, the Anglos, by contrast went for what would now be called the exercise of soft power, through the education of the Siamese elite, as we did with the Egyptian King Farouk and the Maharajahs. King Rama VI was at Sandhurst and Oxford (Christ Church) and then commissioned into the Durham Light Infantry for his sins! His brother Rama VII, the last of the absolute monarchs, was put to school at Eton and then, after the "Shop", or the RA's Woolwich Academy, placed in the Royal Horse Artillery.

The Siamese, correctly, trusted Britain as a counter-weight against

French ambitions to expand their sphere of influence from Cambodia, while the modern military education which the likes of Basil Liddell Hart imparted to the Siamese monarchs clearly bore fruit when the country squared off against the French 47 years later with superiority both in the air and in heavy armour on the ground.

An army coup in 1932 had ended the old absolutist monarchy and replaced it with a constitutional monarchy which was simply a cloak for military dictatorship. Field Marshal Phibun played the nationalist card cleverly. As I say, well-equipped with the latest kit of the day and acting in cahoots with the Japs (notably the pilots who, it was persistently but, one must suppose, incorrectly, rumoured, flew his Mitsubishi dive-bombers for him), he defeated the French Vichy regime in Indo-China in 1940, thus exacting revenge for the humiliation of 1893. After the defeat of the Japanese in 1945 Siam escaped punishment by the Allies, the only Axis affiliate to do so. Phibun himself was put on trial at the instigation of the Allies but acquitted in a great wave of xenophobic fervour. One could say the Thais were not so much the free as the scot-free.

Phibun, a slim, trim cavalryman of Chinese extraction, was overthrown by his corpulent, womanising deputy, Sarit, in – off the top of my head – 1957. I might be confusing *anno domini* with the number of mistresses Sarit was reputed to have maintained. Sarit promptly promoted himself to Field Marshal but also presciently began the public relations promotion of the monarchy, too. He it was who started the throne's rise from an all-time low, after the mysterious shooting death of the new young King in his Palace bedroom in 1946, to the zenith of its power and influence today under that dead boy King's younger brother. Sarit was not to see the full fruition of his scheme, dying of cirrhosis in his mid-50s.

My own small part in all this seems to have taken place so long ago it might as well be in the B.C. era and yet sometimes it seems to have happened yesterday. I spent a very pleasant few months in a blacked-out London (when I wasn't touring stately homes with Howard Colvin) whispering into the ear of the Siamese Prince Chula, mostly at the Café Royal, during what turned out to be a working convalescence for me. Chula, I can say, was a patriot and an absolute gentleman. Devastatingly handsome and a pre-war fixture racing his Bugatti at Byfleet, he actually had a Russian mother. I flanked him two laps round a desolate wartime Brooklands to celebrate the day I secured his reluctant agreement to work for SOE. His Bugatti was far more powerful than my motorbike but I was a bit more agile round the hair-pins, so dead heat, more or less. SOE stumped up the fuel requisition note and thought it funds well spent. Only 12 years ago I passed by Brooklands on my way by Southern Rail to Aldershot on a doomed mission to put additional grey matter into the heads of subalterns. It was a ghost town (Brooklands, not Aldershot), made more, rather than less so, by the banshee howl of a jet engine in its test bed. I admit a tear came into my eye as I thought of my old friend, by then long dead. The last time I'd made the journey was in a baby-blue Rolls Royce, driven by the chauffeur of Prince Bira, Chula's cousin, who despite being a bona fide Formula One driver managed to live 20 years longer than he did. He sold the Rolls to an absolute cad from Newcastle by the name of Clifford Hall. *Tempora mutantur et nos mutamur in illis.*

It all started when I'd been one of the home-tutors for the teen-aged Princess Bejaratana, the exiled daughter of Rama VI, in Brighton. (Not that the concept of the "teenager" had yet been invented). I had been helping the chaplain out at Roedean, some way up the road from the Marine Pavilion and the piers, in the Long Vac before the War, so it was all quite fortuitous. Bejaratana was a talented gel but musical rather than intellectual. Our appointments were very erratic but she had an uncanny ability to correct my timetabling in an instant when the date I'd set by its number in the month turned out to fall on a weekend. Pleasant though the experience was, I have to say Chula was more my cup of tea. I was very tenuously assigned to him solely because of the slight pre-war connection with the princess. And, one suspects, in turn to this current case because of my ancient friendship with Chula. Thus are cast our destinies.

Chula had been educated in Britain, was happy there, and the last thing he wanted to do was parachute into a Japanese-controlled Siam on our behalf. Inveigling him was considered a great feather in my cap right at the start of my career with SOE. Officially, Chula had a position in Dad's Army in the Home Counties. On the side, I had him donning the cloak and the dagger. He undertook several (dinghy-borne) missions for us to the Andaman coast of Siam, though in the end we never had to activate Operation Roger, the invasion of the then obscure island of Phuket. I found his funeral in England in 1964 – as I recall – a very sad affair. He died, only aged 50 or so, of cancer. King Rama VII himself died in a war-time England in '41 though, with his Etonian and Gunner chums, he wasn't as lonely as one might think. After the War poor Chula wasn't desired in the new Thailand by the military dictators and was a forgotten figure both in Britain and there, thanks in no small measure to the policies of the Americans. He was, on not one but two occasions, in the succession stakes to the vacant Throne of Siam and could have been King. I suspect the admixture of foreign blood counted against him.

The seeds of our long, complicated, and ambivalent relationship with Cousin Jonathan, or at least those of our mutual security services, were already sown before the Americans hastily bombed Japan (to keep Joe Stalin out of Manchuria as much as to save the lives of the doughboys). We Brits in Special Operations Executive (SOE) Force 136 were at loggerheads with the Yanks in OSS (Detachment 404). To be frank, I disliked their methods and policies and detested those operatives I met personally. I was not alone in SOE in having those feelings. In fact, they were fairly widespread. Funnily enough, at that time the Americans were quite left-wing and very distrustful of us Brits and French trying to regain our Empires.

What all of us, Americans and British, were capable of, however, once the Japanese were beaten, was dumping loyal friends from the War for dubious new allies who had actually fought on the other side from us. After my Burmese days with Wingate I had the pleasure and privilege of working with half a dozen Free Thai lads in our Force 136 (they wore a British Army Tommy's uniform with their own shoulder-flash). The Siamese generals had, as I say, been enthusiastic Axis sympathisers who never paid a penny in reparations or spent a day in the glasshouse. After the war they used the police to murder any able person of overtly democratic inclination, including most of the chaps who'd worn our uniform. We supported these monsters to the hilt as a reliable buffer against Communism.

As for the Islamists in the south who had taken up the cudgels for us against the Japs (like the Siamese, perceived as invading Sinic Buddhists) we dropped them like hot cakes, too. The Patani Sultanate Freedom Fighters who'd blown up telegraph poles, mined roads, and sniped the odd laggard Japanese were abandoned to the tender mercies of the Siamese Field Marshals. Poor Haji Sulong (so long to him) who'd performed valiantly against the Japs was abducted by the Siamese police in 1954 – presumably tortured and summarily executed – and never seen again. All that without so much as a cheep from us or the Cousins. This was to be a dismal pattern, played out with the Montagnards and Nang in Vietnam and Laos and even as late as the Kurds and Marsh Arabs, incited to rise in the first Iraq War, only to be abandoned by Bush to the even tenderer mercies of Saddam's secret police.

I arrived in Burma first, not Siam. Towards the end of '42, after my wounds and the months recovering in London breathing down Chula's neck, I was posted as a youthful intelligence major, complete then with Clark Gable moustache, first to Calcutta, then very briefly to Chungking, and Imphal, liaising with the American General Stilwell (aptly nicknamed Vinegar Joe) and then our own two-star general, Orde Wingate, and later the American Brigadier Merrill and his Marauders.

Orde Wingate was absolutely the most remarkable human being I have ever met. "The most remarkable sub-human being," Teddy would snort. He loathed him. Had actually met him in Palestine in the '30s. Orde passed into popular legend for his creation of the Chindit force in Burma but his more lasting legacy, military and personal, lay in the Near East. What is today half-forgotten, despite the memorial in Israel, is his enormous contribution to the birth of the Jewish homeland.

To put it euphemistically, a highly practical one. As a captain attached to the British Forces in Palestine, he actively sympathised with the Jewish settlers over what he called "dirty Arabs" and went so far as to create the Special Night Squads, composed of British squaddies and Enfield-armed Jews from the Haganah who pretty well behaved like the Black and Tans of a decade earlier in Ireland. There were no hay-ricks for them to burn on the arid soil of the Holy Land but plenty of hapless Palestinians to pull from their beds, interrogate, maltreat and – if necessary – kill.

Wingate, I am sorry to say, not only condoned but participated in what he called "severe" methods which, of course, were nothing less than brutality. His customary retort was that war and weapons were a dirty business.

Among his recruits and students was Moshe Dayan, later to lose an eye but gain a black patch for his own empty socket and thousands of square miles of territory for Israel in the 1967 war against Egypt and Jordan. Dayan, all his life, not only spoke of Wingate with warm admiration but cited him as one of the founders of the aggressive, pro-active tactical doctrines of the IDF under its youthful generals (mandatory retirement *aetatis* 45). Also, Dayan did not add, of torture and the ruthless execution of rioters.

Among other things, Orde's Jewish thugs also protected the pipeline of the foreign-controlled Iraqi Petroleum Company from Arab sabotage. Beloved by future Israeli "hawks" Orde might have been but not by his superiors who, just as they or their peers had blackballed Dyer in India, shipped Wingate off to Ethiopia with a prohibition from returning to Palestine stamped into his passport. This was merely dumping a born trouble-maker on to other hands – Wingate promptly raised Cain in Ethiopia with his Gideon Force.

Orde's death in Burma did spare him the kind of anguish T.E.Lawrence had known when he had to betray his friends for his country. Perhaps Wingate would have betrayed his country for his Jewish friends. Interestingly, he was a remote cousin of T.E.'s, Lawrence who had so loved the clean life of the desert Arabs. These distant relatives were to re-write the book on what is now known as "asymmetrical warfare", though having not only completely different objectives (Pan-Arabism vs Zionism) but methods – in Lawrence's case the use behind enemy lines of hordes of untrained, irregular partisans to cut vital lines of Turkish railway communication across the open desert and, in Wingate's, the use against the Japanese empire, also behind lines but in the confines of the jungle, of small groups of highly trained forces dependent for their survival on communication and supply from the air.

I met Orde twice in '43 and can vouch for the truth of the stories which had already accrued around him. He did, indeed, hold briefings, much like a potentate's morning audience, from behind a canvas screen as he showered, occasionally emerging with a loofah (not a rubber or wire brush as related elsewhere), thoughtfully dabbing at unsavoury parts of his anatomy and working up to a zealous scrub as he became quite animated on abstruse issues of strategy.

He was, in my opinion, and that of others who would have

followed him at the quick march through the gates of hell, absolutely crackers and he had the unswerving love and admiration of those he commanded (at the time John Masters included, though Jack carped in print later) and, most importantly, of Churchill.

He was only 41 when he died, a major-general, in the air crash at Imphal. Wingate himself believed in the sixth sense that gave junior officers in the field a better chance of survival – so did Dennis Anstruther, actually – the prickling on the back of the neck that might forewarn of a Japanese ambush on the far bank of the river. And after his time in the Holy Land (can there ever have been a name less lived-up to?) Orde was no stranger to plots and treachery. One asks oneself why he boarded the plane, but perhaps it was in despite of his own better judgment. Better judgment is often a euphemism for weakness. The large-souled might feel hate and fear, both, but timid they are not. He took the leap into the dark: to trust in the good nature and honour of your fellow man is not folly but the sublimest courage. I hope I could live up to that challenge but doubt it. I will always help, if I can. Anyhow, bad weather and unreliable machinery – and perhaps the spite of others, meaning sabotage – secured his premature demise. Perhaps Zia ul-Haq had the same feelings as he boarded his Hercules for the last time. Not even gargantuan wills like theirs could cheat death. Still, Orde during his short life had proved himself the master of the cheeky ruse, the gambit that could pull the chestnut out of the fire at the last moment and give you an eleventh hour or even Pyrrhic victory. I could wish I possessed the same nerve, quickness, and general gumption. Might have changed the direction of a few Synods.

Montgomery, on a visit to Israel 20 years later, had this mean judgment to pass: that the best thing the madman Wingate ever did was to get himself killed in an aircrash. As this comment was made to Wingate's worshipper, Dayan, doubts can be cast on Monty's own mental health. By all accounts, Dayan nearly hit the old man.

With Field Marshals in general, Orde had precarious relationships. Wavell, who commanded him in the Near and later Far East, tempered personal admiration with formal reservations, while Slim, who succeeded Wavell, praised him faintly while he was alive but swung later to the Woodburn Kirby camp. You have to remember that Wingate's patron, Churchill, the arch-Tory, did not think particularly highly of Bill Slim. It was the Labour PM, Attlee, who promoted Slim to Field Marshal, so make of it what you want.

Orde, by the way, was far from being the muscular public school Christian without the higher ratiocinative faculties. He had a fine command of language, succinct and bracing. You saw everything in the faces: his was open, simple, ingenuous, noble in its frankness. His mortal enemy, Stanley Woodburn Kirby, never rose above the stilted and constipated lines of the *Official History* and his visage was a masterwork of malevolence, bile, and cunning.

Most of Orde's eccentricity can be attributed to his strict religious upbringing with the Plymouth Brethren – certainly his admiration for God's chosen people of the Old Testament.

I am going to give a lecture devoted to him at the round-table as well as the more contemporary stuff. You cannot understand the present without knowing the past. In some copious detail, prefer-ably, I might add. Wingate's career will demonstrate to the younger generation I address how, in the single person of a servant of the British Empire, an area of major contention, the Near East, has been historically linked to what might be regarded as the SE Asian periphery. I could say the same about David Smiley's exploits in Siam and Indo-China and, later, Yemen but most of what he did is still classified. Smiley was Lawrence without the neuroses.

On my flight I suffered no such fate as Orde Wingate but, gracious heavens, it would have been tedious without the reading material George's nephew, the Next Major Dramatist, was so good as to press upon me. We weren't too emotional about the send-off as I'll be seeing him shortly. Off my own bat, I took Carlyle's *On Heroes and Hero-Worship*, plus some Thomas Love Peacock, but he brought me Alec's latest, both bestseller and masterpiece, which I'd already picked up at Heywood Hill, so now I have two copies. The shop was always convenient for Curzon Street. During the war one carried a book in preference to extra rations. It was easier to cope with the gurglings of an empty stomach than the grum-blings of an empty mind. Alec's stuff isn't exactly Proust or Joyce and he endures the contumely of the genre writer – in silence, with dignity – but if I'm going to stifle the pangs of boredom, why, I want my corn well done. And no one does it better than him. I think Auden must have been thinking of Isherwood (wasn't he always) when he wrote of the Novelist having to grow out of his boyish talent but it could also be Alec being good among the Good, (or was it just among the Just?) and among the Filthy, well, filthy, too. Alec will be read long after the likes of Virginia Woolf languish for the last time.

He proved much better value than my official brief. I'm jiggered if I didn't detect the hand of Merde Mahler himself. *Storm-clouds gathering over the uncertain bark of the Siamese state*, indeed. Why Green even began considering Mahler's wretched ditty all those years ago, I don't know. Vivian was usually the shrewdest of the shrewd. Whoever the author of my synopsis was, he possessed little original knowledge. A gallimaufry of information gleaned from the newspapers, leavened with barber-shop speculation. And zero knowledge of the national history which might provide a centre-board to the dinghy of state. If the nation's future course is going to be set by the Grand Guignol of dowagers, prodigals, and revanchists of the dossier, then it is in dire straits.

In the bookshops of Bangkok was scant provender. I went to a particular establishment to re-stock, picked up some luridly jacketed volumes on the "Local Interest" shelf – much like the reef fish in an aquarium, though that's a disservice to even that twit Harold Acton – and was promptly stunned into open-mouthed silence. Dear God, the crassness, the vulgarity, the solecisms, the amateurishness. Never was the term "vanity publishing" better applied. In vain did they strive to reach the level of Macaulay's schoolboy. "Thrillers" that failed to thrill, other than raise the hair with a grammatical howler every two paragraphs, anecdotes of the sexual life as gratuitously detailed as they were forlorn, travel (I wouldn't have allowed them past the platform for the boat-train), and dictionaries for the bazaar and chatting up the local female (similar vocabulary, one suspects). As I departed (given a subservient but thorough frisking at the door) I was accosted by a trio of pubescent trollops on the corner who hailed me, "Hello, Sexy Man!" I would dearly have liked to station a pair outside the Hertford SCR just to have boosted Felix's morale while he was still sentient. (He was actually viewed as more promising than Teddy in their day – so much for the accuracy of contemporary judgment).

One has to admit the browsing (something cows and the

intelligentsia do) was strangely compulsive. Of course, I could also say I was generally sniffing around and being led a dog's life but then I've always felt the dog's life isn't half a bad one: free board, bags of exercise, a protein-rich diet, unlimited access to the female of the species, and the legal guarantee of a merciful end. Once again, deserting poor Carlyle, the spoor led me ineluctably before dinner to the bookshop's Local Interest shelf (fine oxymoron, that) where I was to enjoy a second jolly good laugh, much in the spirit of the bored 18th century bourgeois taking spouse and progeny to watch the lunatics cavorting in Bedlam for some harmless family fun of a wet Sunday.

Only a few years back the Malaysian terrorist Bin Armin was arrested while hurriedly vacating a Bangkok bookshop. Only now does one understand the indecent haste which was to inculpate him. He must have had literary standards.

Picking at a cold supper back in my digs (if you can call a suite that: my handler had obviously shrewdly calculated that it was more effective to scrimp on the airfare and splurge on the billet) my talk had clarified. I would pitch it much more strongly than I had originally adumbrated in London. Thus, stripped of polite circumlocution, the gist would be (and it bears repetition) that we had been in this part of the world longer than anyone else and our methods had been proven in the hard school of knocks and sordid experience to be by far the best. We hadn't just educated the Siamese elite. The senior Malay and Singaporean politicians had all come through Raffles School and, behind the "anti-colonial masters" posturing, were far better disposed towards us than the Indians, Pakistanis, or Wingate's Jews (who had gone so far as to assassinate a British Cabinet Minister in 1944, namely Lord Moyne). In Malaya the methods of Templer and Thompson (a Chindit veteran and admirer of Wingate, though his methods of quelling rebellion were as subtle as Wingate's had been ferocious in Palestine) are still to be learned from today. Nowhere else in the world has a counter-insurgency campaign proved so successful as it did in the Malayan Emergency.

Of course, what worked on up-country Chinese Marxists in the thick of the jungle might not be so efficacious today on ethnic Malay zealots in the cleared lands and petty townships but there would be certain general principles that would still be relevant.

323

Wingate was a shrewd social psychologist as well as bonkers (*sine qua non* to qualify as psychiatrist). He was adamant mere dislike would not turn anyone into an insurgent. It took a "burning hatred". This qualitative jump was usually caused by the perceived brutality of the occupier in combination with the catalytic agents of nationalism, ideology, or religion: or all three, God help us.

Robert Thompson always saw military enforcement as subordinate to social pacification, whereas Wingate, I am afraid, was in the shoot first and ask questions later category.

Thompson had read his Mao Tse Tung where the guerillas are seen as the fish and the sympathetic population as the sea. What Thompson did was relocate inhabitants of whole villages, denying terrorists access to food and sanctuary – in other words, he drained Hereward's marsh.

When seconded to the Americans in the Vietnam war, he enthusiastically hailed the strategic hamlets programme and always considered the war to have been still "winnable" at that stage. The contention of the US military was that they always had the gloves on and, had they been permitted to use unrestricted force, they would have won, too. The defeat was not a military debacle in the classic sense but a failure of civilian will.

I consider there to be truth in both viewpoints but that British finesse and experience could have secured a better result for the Americans – had they only listened to us. Of course, Wilson – or, if you believe Wright, the Russians through him – did us a favour by keeping us militarily uninvolved. This is not a dusty academic issue from half a century ago but a practical problem for the present. They would have done well to heed our advice for the aftermath of victory over Saddam. We have now learned religion is a far more potent motivator than ideology or nationalism and that our present enemies have the stomach for personal casualties that democratic electorates will not endure even by proxy within a professional military. It was proved long ago, in the days of the British Empire, that the most effective therapy for dissent was a multi-mode one: ferocious repression followed by extensive, almost philanthropic, welfare. There is nothing new in this system of Imperial Policing. It goes further back than 1934. As the Victorian General Charles Napier said, the lower races have first to be cowed, then melted with kindness. Remove the dated and objectionable expression "lower races" and it would still be a useful motto. Human nature, i.e. the old Adam, doesn't change. One could say the old Eve, too. Napier didn't explicitly say so but he would not have objected if "women" were added to "lower races". Of that I have no direct experience but I can say that I have always found romantic love between men and women to be an illusion invented and fostered by third-rate scribblers. To be fair, Catullus and Donne (to mention just two) were first-rate but, for the great unwashed, the words of love will be the maudlin lyrics of popular music, the very nadir of poetic composition.

Jesú, that fearsome cleft. It might as well have teeth. The relations between men and women, and indeed life itself, are founded on a gross physical act. We begin in revolting, hot slime. If there is no God, then human life has no worth. Honour, morality, affection are so much make-up on the ugly face of existence. Without God there is only self-interest; at the best, reciprocity. How noble is tit-for-tat? Without Him life would not just be cheap but valueless. To deprive someone of the worthless is not a crime. The body is just the integument sealing a sack of offal and excrement. We can only save ourselves through loving our dirty fellow man, undeserving though he is. If there is no God, we still have to pretend that he exists. In that case, Godhead can be created by Man himself as his own redemption. I am sure this heresy has a name! It is certainly the opposite of Eliot's diabolical proposal that it is better to do monstrous evil than nothing at all. I don't think I have the wrong end of the stick there.

Basil could have told me. Hume was a first-rate theologian. Good intellect and an even better man. He might have had the same adversary I wrestled every night. I liked him nearly as much as Soper. Heenan wouldn't have known. I found him something of a clodhopper, if he hadn't been such a Vatican operator, and I swear I could smell the usquebaugh on his breath. Runcie was a dear old boy with iron in the soul, too. Served in the Guards and got the same gong as me. Coggan was a cold fish but utterly without "side" and had no illusions about his capacity. As for the present incumbent, whenever I see him on the box I want to shout, "Get yourself a spine, man!"

WELL, TODAY, I have performed the part of this trip which was one of the covers. I gave the keynote speech at the formal Opening

Day of the overseas branch of a very famous English public school in Thailand. Extraordinary, really, despite all the historic connections. Harrow and Shrewsbury already have branches here, so I suppose it was only a matter of time. They can play the cricket match with Harrow. My speech was an absolute Pharasaical model of humbug and self-serving tommyrot. Mission, ideals, formation of character, the young are our real argosy etc., etc. The last came closest to the true point of the school which is strictly as a cash-cow for the charity-status institution back home (which will pay not a penny in tax). The purpose is to generate boodle, filthy lucre, moolah.

The Next Major Dramatist, in his role as former beak and very young member of the Board of Governors here, organised it. (It would have been just the thing for my chum Chula to have sat on, actually). I hardly dared look the NMD in the eye as he passed me my envelope. I can safely say that, unlike Mrs Leonowens or the young Bangkok drabs, I am a very highly-paid prostitute. "Uncle George and Professor Beezten would have been proud," he muttered. "Dear boy, they'd have puked," I replied with my most brilliant smile.

The deputy head, strapping English girl with a Dip Phys Ed from Crewe and Alsager (it could at least have been Loughborough), caught my gaze lingering too long on some winsome lad and had the nerve to wink at me. As I said, I never consummated with the late Dennis Anstruther, still less anyone else, so my conscience is clear. A naughty thought is not a deed. Certainly, I feel no shame. The unlikeliest chaps turn out to be rosy on both cheeks. The lad who won the Sword of Honour in my Sandhurst intake (not an unpleasant 18 months) was one of the finest young men I ever knew and as queer as a coot. Posthumous VC, that one. In general, the current hooh-hah in the Anglican and Episcopal Congregations – on just this dreary topic – appears to be the result of querulous American self-importance confronting elephantine African intransigence. Why can't sleeping dogs lie?

From the corner of my own eye I glimpsed the Head-to-be (and I really fear he is going to be as much of a disaster as Chevenix-Trench, though for different reasons) fortifying the cup that mildly depresses from his hip-flask. I have always preferred the old-fashioned term "drunkard". Alcoholic makes it sound like an achievement and alcoholism a branch of knowledge.

Then as we ourselves went in to tea, George's nephew (to be accurate great-nephew) said in that languid Eton way, "Oh, by the way, Victor, may I introduce you to . . ."

In front of us, also flaunting the languid poise, was a young half-caste Thai, English mother out of a well-known county family, stupendously wealthy and even grander Siamese father. I actually find the manner of effortless superiority quite insufferable (not just as a yellow stocking from the Hospital for clever but indigent boys). I've gone against my class interest and never voted anything other than Labour since shortly after the War. The whole notion of the Anglican Congregation merely being the Conservative party at prayer is one that is as grossly inaccurate as it is deeply offensive. Having said that, the last Labour government was an egregious disaster. So much for the younger generation.

Suez is generally perceived as our worst post-war foreign policy blunder but the fall-out was relatively short lived. Iraq will exercise its baneful effect for decades to come, not only abroad but at home. While the Pakis and Indians were doing revolting things to each other from '47 on (of which chopping each other up was only half) it was all very well and the British ruling-class could wrinkle its nose in collective disdain at the safe remove of several thousand miles. Now it's happening in Bradford and, for Pete's sake, on the hallowed old Tube, which was our refuge during the Blitz. Talk about the chickens coming home to roost.

We were blithely taken to war because the midshipman who found himself the captain of the good ship Britannia thought it a great opportunity to turn a Nelsonic blind eye to all the signals the evidence was giving. To change the metaphor, they found themselves playing an adventurous forward game but forgot to defend the home goal. They opened the floodgates to mass immigration and inflicted the present condition of cultural miscegenation upon us. I won't even start on the City and the Third Murderer from North Britain in charge of the piggy-bank. The Labour government betrayed its electorate and I shall never vote for them again.

The particular example of miscegenation George's nephew (a slimmer but still recognisable version of his great-uncle) was inflicting upon me was a type that has always scared the wits out of me. SOE was full of them.

"Delighted, Uncle Victor, if I may," he drawled. Damn his impertinence. I knew something of his personal history. He'd been in Pop with George's nephew. His English mother had been keen on marrying him off to a titled Irish girl who doted on her younger brother (four females in that family). Under the impression it would be an easy ride, this 13-year-old had wound up as the Thai lad's fag. For some trumped-up misdemeanour he'd given the little chap a caning that was still talked about years later. Left his backside in tatters and needed a hospital visit. All hushed-up, of course. Amazing how flexible the institutions of the English upper-class can be – the younger brother of the late King of Jordan personally carried a sidearm in a shoulder-holster and had a live-in Arab bodyguard throughout his teenage years at Harrow. Anyhow, that was the end of the Thai boy's English mama's marriage plans. Shades of *The Unbearable Bassington*.

I had seen straightaway he wasn't the slightest bit interested in gels. Takes one to know one. I recall the bit in Isherwood's autobiography where Auden is helping him bring in his German boyfriend on the boat-train. The weasel-faced immigration officer with the bright eyes peruses the German's private correspondence and says he would say these are the kind of letters someone would write to their sweetheart, not an employee. "Wouldn't you say so, sir?" It's Goodbye to Harwich for the German lad. Auden (as "Hugh Weston") says what makes it worse is that the weasel with the bright eyes was one of us.

The half-Thai lad was good enough to volunteer to me that the Siamese term for an individual of mixed race is Look Khreung (or half-child). I refrained from telling him, there and then, that they were the first and only words of Siamese I learned from a friend of mine of the local blood royal 60 years ago. I'll save that for later. The young fellow was certainly wholly one of us in Mistress Thatcher's sense. As I said, he reminded me of a couple of the more psychopathic SOE operatives I knew, the kind of upper-class Englishman who manages to be both effete and ruthless.

During my stint at Trinity Hall and Christ's in the awful winter of 62-63 I was dragged along to a flick by, of all people, the 18th century specialist Jolly Jack Plumb. On the way through the slush, we'd agreed that two more different centuries than our own periods (the 17th and 18th) had never existed in such close contiguity. The film in question, not an adornment to the Age of Reason, was *Mutiny on the Bounty*. The actor, Trevor Howard, who had skin as bad as Auden's, was Bligh while an American of smoulderingly rugged good looks, whose name I forget but it was Italianate, played Fletcher Christian. I take my hat off to him. He had that kind of suave menace down to a "T". He was more frightening than Bligh, as being less predictable and, when push came to shove, less trammelled. Those of us with a conscience so often are.

The "Delighted, Uncle Victor," and the follow-up, "It's an honour to meet the legend," was all pre-arranged eyewash between us for the benefit of George's nephew. Not only were we so deep in regular (or irregular) correspondence that we were virtually penpals, we'd already met. It was the Siamese half-blood who turned our "asset" in Pondok B (we currently have fingers in Pondoks A, E, G and Pesantren F). I think of this "asset" as well described – the Nancy Boy was a little ass. It was this young Look Khreung, too, who quite gratuitously manhandled the old scholar when I was present in Singapore. There was no need for that kind of thing, none at all. No doubt he got up to worse at the Black Holes of jails he helped run for the Yanks at Don Muang and north of Bangkok, where he was supposed to give the Arab militants "rendered" by the US a lot worse than the water treatment. (Which by the standards of Gestapo or Kempeitai, Mossad or Mullah, is relatively innocuous). As the Americans had no less than seven bomber bases in Thailand in the 1970s, pouring death and destruction upon the Vietnamese, I cannot now throw up my hands in horror at the thought that they still possess a couple of interrogation centres.

I know someone I'd like to stick in one. I have to say the Nancy Boy was absolutely useless. Not just gilding the lily but pulling the longbow. The Imam was much better value for hard fact. I got to the old chap by pointing out to him that *merdeka* for the South was never going to come through the means advocated by the group: rather it would delay it by turning the provinces into a version of Kashmir without the scenic mountains and mirroring lake. Both religious-secessionist, d'you see, like Aceh, not irredentist-secular like the origins of the First Iraq War or, basically, the Palestine issue which is susceptible to a political and territorial resolution but for Israeli obduracy. (And, in Arafat's time, Palestinian obduracy).

I'll give it to Mr Look Khreung, though, he immediately grasped the strategy of us "imploding" terrorist groups, splintering them and setting them against each other and the common criminal gangs. Worked like a dream in the Lebanon for us with the Iranian-sponsored kidnappings. Hats off to us for once. I have to say that, for a change, I do sing along to Mahler's tune that the little half-blood went well over the top, literally and figuratively, in his actions on this front. Then again his extreme measures seem to have worked. When in Rome . . .

Over tea and wads that would have disgraced a crookedly run NAAFI, George's nephew and I prated about the theatre (not my pond at all). He said he (*qua* dramatist) had it both ways: classic and modern. A play, or for that matter film or television script – screenplay was the word he used – could be made as luxuriantly literary as he wanted (not very) with page after page of italicised direction and elegant exegesis, or it could be spare as famine. What he liked (he said) about the form was the freedom it gave him. He far preferred the shorthand of cinematic jump and ellipsis and what he called, "Inception of sub-plot B at 22 per cent run-time and resolution at 101 per cent," to the laborious explanations of cause and effect, the mechanical links in canonical prose narratives, and the agonising over the stages of psychological development. Veridian harumphed – I mean, to me late James is modernist enough – and said you couldn't chuck the baby out with the bathwater. We then proceeded to compare late Alec with early Alec. He said early Alec was plot-propelled, while late Alec was character-drawn. The two engines worked to different effect and were completely irreconcilable as pulling in different directions. "You pays yer money and you takes yer choice," he said. "A twist in the plot violates and subverts character, whereas a descriptive stroll round a personality stymies a plot."

"Can't personality, can't traits be revealed in action?" I inquired mildly. "Old Joe Conrad and RLS were quite good at that. Graham always was, too."

"Greene!" shrieked the Next Big Thing. "Greene, that plotty, pedestrian, middlebrow hack! That humbug!"

Well, all English heads turned, but not American or Thai, the parents of most of the prospective pupils.

"Forster," I said equably, (George had probably told him about my silly little feud with Morgan over Philby and Co), "Forster talks of . . ." but the young fellow's dander was up. "For goodness sake, Victor," he said crossly, *Aspects of the Novel* was plonked in a jar with the older Dead Sea Scrolls, it's such an antique." For the next three minutes I beamed and nodded my way through my earful. Clearly theatrical London is a bit like the Forum of Caesar's day, everyone bristling with daggers in their back or looking for a pair of shoulder-blades in which to plant their own.

". . . I mean, not even all the craft Guinness or Olivier could have mustered at their peaks would bring life into Brenton's or Hare's waxworks," he declaimed, finally drawing half a breath.

Very swiftly my half-blood Terror inserted his own knife between the ribs. "How I wish Greene had written The Quiet Englishman," he mused.

"Not bad for an Oppidan," said George's nephew sheepishly and the rest of the afternoon passed quite pleasantly.

AFTER THAT one's passage could only be from the ridiculous to the sublime. Which is to say, the sublimely foolhardy. The turkey convention was held in, let me write this slowly, Nakhon si Talay, which I would describe as Llandudno with pawpaw trees. The idea, as at a jamboree, was to get close enough to the fire for a bit of ambulance (terrible pun beloved of Teddy) and actually meet, as it were, the local fire-brigade (as sinister a bunch of thugs as one could imagine and very much in the tradition of their predecessor death squads of the 1950s). All this without getting so close that one might get scorched like the moth. We were just south of Prachuap Khiri Khan, nowhere near even the fringe of the real south but nearly 300 km or so from the provinces in conflagration. Minimal security was actually safer as being less obtrusive, though Jerry T. was muttering into his moustache about the gratuitous idiocy of the whole thing the moment we alighted from the limousine. Actually, if I'd had to stick the pin in the map, it's exactly where I would have chosen as well. Mind you, knowing the ruthless little so-and-so (the Look Khreung, not Jerry) a little better now, one wonders whether one isn't the goat tethered for the tiger under his tree-hide.

We have not a single but a pair of other conventions overlaying our own one. The trade manual (unwritten) says, or used to say in my day, either stage things in a totally secluded, secret, and sanitised retreat or go for occlusion in blatancy with an intervening public layer. There are too many people coming from too many places for the former, so it's the latter but with, as I said, two layers of sandwich armour. The problem isn't the occasion, or its geographical situation, but me attending it at all. Rules are being broken. Merde should be acting as my cut-out but, then, he is generally acknowledged to be a liability, while the Nancy Boy – if not Omar, the old scholar – has never met me. Six of one and half a dozen of the other, but a regular operative would never be allowed his whiskers so far out of the burrow. I think London are in a quandary how to control me. I have never been a member of SIS. I am palpably ancient, have no official position, still less rank, but I personally recruited, as young men barely out of their teens, the chiefs of the chiefs of the present day chiefs. In other words, your grandfather fagged for me. How do you discipline such a Methuselah?

The filling of the present forum, as it were, is somewhat fresher than the gobstoppers and humbugs for sale in my ancient tuck-shop. It is constituted by a mixed bag or dolly-mixture of brighter security people, Foreign Service, the more dependable "house" journalists, academics, military attachés, consultants, analysts, frank spies, and a real living, breathing US Senator, all under the umbrella of a clearly "spook" think-tank funded by a very famous US Foundation. Surprised they were willing to get their fingers so muddy. The only similar event I'd ever been to – you may be surprised – was in Brussels in '53 where a young don from St John's, who'd mopped up in the Low Countries as a youthful intelligence officer in 45-46, made the calm but startling observation that every single Walloon and most of the Flemings in Belgium should have been shot for the filthy things they had done in cahoots with the Germans. He proceeded to prove his point cogently, to me at least. Nasty but unheralded bunch, the Belgians.

I had my work cut out to keep the air sweet between my own nasties, too. Blessed are the peacemakers for they shall inherit the feuds. Descending in the lift on the penultimate day, they were sniping away at each other for all they were worth. If George's nephew was bound by the protocols of the duel between gentlemen, this was the gutter. Only the presence of a delegate from one of our cover mummeries, or *trompe l'oeil*, stopped the spat from degenerating into something truly unpleasant. And this chap was clearly on his way to his room with his unwholesome pathic, who definitely qualified as one of Wilde's unkissables. The pair seemed as claustrophobic as poor Lillian the day she read of Dennis' death in the evening paper while she was riding the Bakerloo line in rush-hour.

The US Senator, by the by, was female. Real aura about her. Bright, hard, quick on the uptake, and looking 20 years younger than her age, thanks to vitamin pills and the knife. She wasn't the star turn as far as I was concerned. This was a very impressive Kiwi called Dee Kaye of whom I had been instantly suspicious as the latest flavour but slowly came round to recognising as the real thing and not ersatz Thompson, as so many of the Americans are.

I had begun my intervention, as I told you, with: "Lady and Gentlemen, why am I here? This profound existential question is for once susceptible of rapid answer . . ." I pointed out how the flashpoint names of today were to be found in the yellowed British dispatches of yesteryear. Jack Masters – neither his name nor *Bhowani Junction* stirred any recognition in the faces of these forty-somethings – had been stationed for several dreary months in Basra in 1943 during the first Anglo-Iraq War. Tora Bora appears as Tura-Bura in a first paragraph of Kipling's – a place of jagged menace – while the Pashtun appear as the Pathan. I quoted *Arithmetic on the Frontier*:

> *A scrimmage in a Border Station*
> *A canter down some dark defile*
> *Two thousand pounds of education*
> *Drops to a ten-rupee jezail.*

The lady senator's eyes misted for a moment as she thought of all those felled lieutenants, now, as in Vietnam, the most dangerous rank in the US Marines. I injected a moment of light relief when I pondered why villains in American dramatisations of the classics always spoke in English accents. On I went with selective force followed by indiscriminate pacification (as opposed to the usual situation of v.v.). I pointed out that the enemy body count, used as a gauge of success in Vietnam (more like a bloody talisman, really), would now be a reverse litmus test. A battalion commander would be successful over the long haul in direct proportion to the number of his men he had lost through hesitation to dial in the bombs, rather than the locals he had killed. (Collective intake of breath). Got less of a hand than I had expected. Never mind. At least they'd draw the line at fiddling with the engine of my jet.

Dee Kaye didn't immediately warm to me. He was one of those people whose appearance totally belies their character. Useful to them, confusing to us. Of Irish extraction, despite the Jewish-sounding surname, putty-complexioned, coarse-featured with a music-hall Paddy's snub nose, bow-legged, and thick-fingered, he appeared as full of subtlety and discrimination as a New South Wales butcher two sheets to the wind on a bender in King's Cross. Until he started talking.

This he didn't do to me, at first. It dawned on me. I had been sent to Coventry. I offered him the sugar-bowl. "No thanks, padre." Then, "I take it, can I, that you've never been responsible for the lives of men in battle?" After that, his broad back as he engaged in desultory conversation an ex-SAS major, currently making a killing, if that's the proper word, out of a close-in protection (e.g bodyguard) firm.

Jerry Trelawney, in whose bag of clubs the De Lisle had ridden on the plane, Brigadier Trelawney (tiny chap, resembled the actor who played Captain Mainwaring in the TV comedy about the Home Guard), J.M.M Trelawney who invented a new segmented police truncheon which both choked and struck with centrifugal force (regretfully rejected as too effective by half) and who had given fearsome lock and submission classes to us in SOE and later to the Customs and Excise, whispered in Kaye's ear.

A little later Dee came over. He had a cup of coffee for me. "I didn't sugar it, sir, on the assumption you preferred it bitter." All that with a straight face. Jerry had told him about the gong. I knew it straightaway. Unlike Runcie, I had the bar to go on the ribbon. Won it twice. Neither time, by the way, did I do anything special. Just that someone high-up happened to be watching. Gave my hand to a Geordie in a flaming Matilda turret the first time. "Felt like a lardy cake in the oven, sir," he said. (They should have given the medal to him for his coolness). For the bar on the ribbon, I threw a pile of horse-blankets and a tin bath-tub on top

334

of a rolling potato-masher. Very well, then, I did proceed to sit on the bucket. Got the shrapnel scars to prove it – no worse than an Eton thrashing.

I was a terrible shot with the sidearm. That ridiculous lanyard. Made one look like a cinema commissionaire. I must have discharged my Webley a grand total of nine times. I started by aiming to miss but stopped doing this when it resulted in a hit on an unfortunate German. "Good shot, boy-o!" exclaimed Lance-Corporal Jones – he of the 10,000 hexamine brew-ups – forgetting both profanity and correct forms of address to an officer in his surprise. Thereafter, I aimed to kill and never injured another German, thus completely reconciling the qualms of conscience with the claims of country.

By the end I was very sick of it. The waste, the criminal waste, of young life on all sides. George and Teddy always gave the impression of thinking I would have been a scholar anyway but only entered Holy Orders, as the accidental archdeacon as it were, because of personal revulsion from all the violence. Actually, Colvin in his quiet way was the more perceptive: I would always have been a priest. Becoming an historian was the fortuitous bit. I wanted to warn and alert – by precedent – the young whose elders had so carelessly thrown away the flowering promise of my own generation. I wanted to help the youthful part, practically as well as scholastically, and hope I will always extend my hand even – or especially – to those who are the least pleasant and lovely in their lives. Anyone can skulk in his scriptorium. The unlovely includes, for present purposes, Mahler whom I insisted should be invited to attend, even if only at the last moment as a tail-ender, though he did his very best to make me regret it, as I say, by his atrocious boorishness in the lift.

Dee – quite the opposite – did not take up my cordial invitation to address me as "Victor". For my part I refrained from calling him "Sonny". After all, he had retired at 37 as a Lieutenant-Colonel to open his consultancy in Washington.

Ten minutes into our conversation – rather more animated than his words with Major Fletcher Christian – I said to him, "So the very modern major-general, or even major, should forget about spit and polish and be half-assassin, half-anthropologist?"

He burst out laughing. "I've got the doctorate and the notches on my pencil to prove it."

Dee's catch-phrase, and it had become a "buzz-word" in certain circles, was the "Tangential Terrorist". He believed the most effective enlister to jihad at the local level – and the universal level was but a congeries of smaller theatres – was our own crudeness. It wasn't a question of greybeards going round instilling the righteousness of jihad into young and impressionable heads (though that certainly happened in the *madrassahs* and *pondoks*). Extremist outsiders – the Chechens, Saudis, Dagastanis, Syrians, and Yemenis fighting with the Taliban in Afghanistan, for instance – who had only stepped on stage shortly before the arrival of our own punitive columns (now airborne and not cart-mounted) were to us indistinguishable in costume and appearance from the less virulent indigenes. The locals had not particularly warmed to the outsiders – as the Iraqi Shias had not to the Sunni Wahhabis and al-Qaeda – but our bombs and rockets shoved them literally and figuratively into the same foxhole. And in foxholes there are no atheists. Dee said that, coming from rational and highly secularised intellectual traditions, most of his fellow analysts were reluctant to admit that religion itself – an abstract idea of God – was the motivator of insurgency and not appalling social and economic conditions. In his opinion, the leaderships were out and out fanatics whom no amount of reform and alleviation programmes could win over but that the rank and file could be susceptible. "It isn't a question of cut off the serpent's head and its body will die but cut off the body and the head will die."

I took advantage of the opportunity to point out something Teddy had never lost a chance to impress upon me: the Outlander less tolerant than the locals born into a particular history was not a phenomenon confined to the Islamists. The lunatic Israeli fringe comprised many Russians and Americans. The key to the pacification of the Middle East lay in a change of heart among the Jews of New York rather than Tel Aviv. This tribe, Teddy always said, was vicious, vituperative, vocal, and voted. No President could gain or hold office without pandering to them.

"That's certainly a major part of the problem," Dee admitted. "If you look hard at the detailed picture in Iraq or Afghanistan, and probably here as well, the loyalty of the Jihadist is to village and elders. Some of them might have been to Jeddah or Mecca or Kabul but the village is their world. Even if the broadening of their horizons means they can't comfortably fit into the life of the village any more, that's what they're really fighting for, just as a soldier doesn't give his life for his country, or his regiment, or even his platoon, but his mates in his section. We know he'll do that and you knew that before I was born, sir. The Mujaheedin fight globalisation but Jihad itself has been globalised. There's no return to the old life from that."

"You sound almost sorry for them!"

"You have to think like your enemy. You can't call a man who flies a plane into a building a coward. He's anything but that. If you're going to defeat them, you have to understand their motivation."

"The problem is empathy can turn into sympathy."

"You're quite right. I don't pity them, actually. I admire them. But it's also my job to destroy them."

"So you have no regrets about the two invasions?"

"I didn't say that! The whole notion of military adventurism in the Middle East, oil-grab or political reconstruction, is fricking delusional," Dee said. He paused fractionally. I was used to this with soldiers and the young. They became at ease with the Archdeacon and then suddenly a hole opened in front of them.

"When the provocation and the dog-collar are both large upon me," I said equably, "I intone the words Effingham Junction. One's gist is usually comprehended."

Following on from this, we both agreed we detested the macho ethos of the American forces – on the ground or aloft – that had wrought so much mischief. It was now I learned not to pronounce the word as macko. It is a perfectly revolting Latin concept; I think, authored by gauchos on the high pampas with bum (excuse the vulgarity) and *mate*, rather than baccy, on the mind when they weren't perforating each other's bowel wall with cold steel. Total lie, of course. Men find danger enervating, even emasculating, while women find its prospect – not its actuality – sexually exciting. The girls at Somerville were always up for a dare, while the men were far more cautious, even Dennis Anstruther who played fly-half for the Greyhounds. This was the only explanation I could subsequently muster for the attraction quite distinguished female barristers felt, in the days of yore, for hardened East End criminals and, latterly, for black men. I had been sufficiently unwise to broach

the subject to Teddy, regarding his niece, the Next Major Dramatist's one time affianced, now a QC and Recorder (they met at a
cocktails in my Embankment flat) when he (Teddy) succumbed to
one of those luxurious fits of choler where he would not cease to
heap verbal coals upon my innocuous head for quite five minutes.
That Christmas I received a Heavy Goods Vehicle plate from him
(the former Lord Lieutenant had been a Commoner in his year at
Balliol). It said: DRIVER HAS A LIMITED VIEW.

He (Teddy) always said my clients were not just totally incompetent and unaccountable as a body (while, as a paradox, intelligent
and responsible as individuals) but worse than useless. We were a
festering wound in the side of civil society. He thought we were a
laughing-stock to even the friendlies. Philby, Burgess, Maclean,
Blunt. Why stop there? Teddy said. Hollis, too, for certain. Maybe
even Wilson. Why on earth had he resigned? The addict of power
never voluntarily relinquishes it, even if conscious of going gaga.
I knew Wilson when he was at Jesus, down the Turl from Brecon.
I thought of it as Taff House (the wild Welsh there thought it great
fun to defecate in the baths of Exeter just across from them but
they never made it up to Brecon). George, fellow-economist of
Wilson's, would never be drawn but just smile knowingly. Incidentally, I disagreed with Teddy *re* Wilson, not about Hollis. Harold
might have been playing the two ends off against the middle but
would always have put himself first, never his boon Moscow pals
from Board of Trade days. He wore Gannex rather than Barbour,
which gnomic remark I will explain shortly. Oldfield was a more
baneful influence, by far. What he is now generally remembered
for is his penchant for the lowest kind of young man and his spectacular miscalculation in employing bank robbers in Ulster in the
1970s. But what I and the old Indo-China hands remember him for
are his misjudgments as head of station in Singapore, decades
previously. Credit where credit is due, he didn't tolerate fools like
Mahler very gladly and I bear him no grudge on account of dented
hubris there. However, our lopsided relationship with the Cousins
began there and then. His subservience to them in Asia was totally
gratuitous. The independence my generation had tried at some
personal cost to preserve against OSS was simply thrown away –
and when we were in a strong position over Malaya, too. It was
not as if we were the Frog Foreign Legion coming out of our

bunkers at Dien Bien Phu with our hands up in the air to a bunch of boys in black pyjamas. If he had stood up to Angleton more, the Cousins would have taken us less for granted in future years. It wasn't the Soviet bruin that had us in a mortal hug but the American grizzly. As to Oldfield's personal indiscretions, well, never mind . . . but as someone who might have been prone to the same but resisted them, I am probably more, rather than less, censorious than those who know immunity from the plague. "Rent" boys, indeed. I never thought that much of the Manchester history school, I can say with a sniff.

I now said to Dee, without a single snuffle, that the whole James Bond myth about the Russian bear was claptrap. I was always sorry it was Ian, rather than Peter, Fleming who had the idea of the 007 books. Peter was the one with the talent, though the impulsive young man hardened into the old curmudgeon. I met him briefly when he ran D Detachment in SE Asia towards the end of the war. This was supposed to be the local equivalent of the dirty tricks and deception outfit in Europe that planted documents on a drowned corpse, stating the D Day landings would take place near Calais. Whether I am correct in that supposition or not, the whole Bond-ian notion of the shaggy bear from Smersh was nonsense. The KGB agents I sat in on, far from being burly butter-balls, tended to be slightly built chaps, although with a compensating swagger about them that our lads entirely lacked. Perhaps I only got to see the three-quarters and not the scrum. Nevertheless, it is very easy to identify the British spy by a certain visible affectation of dress. Wander Whitehall lonely as a cloud. No daffodils especially evident but anyone in the country habitment of waxed green canvas and checked lining known as the Barbour coat will be a spy. I jest not. Any hostile foreign power or group – as Dee pointed out, we were armed to defend ourselves against bombers and tanks when the current threat is from an idea – wanting to degrade our gathering, analysing, and communications capacity should simply shoot everyone in SW1 sporting one of these garments. Dee laughed but, as I repeat, many a wolf slips by under the cover of sheepskin, or olive-green Ventile. The trainers were wasting their time on the anti-surveillance drills. Just follow the coat.

In fact, our trade has been "globalised", as Dee put it, as much as holy war has, as much as al-Qaeda has been franchised to regions, *pace* Borges, that have never seen a camel. Why should we be immune to the winds of change, we who are exposed to them as much as we expose them? The dirty work we used to undertake ourselves – the kind you need to deny the moment it's happened – has been contracted out to the most unsavoury rabble of international freebooters. Why mince words? Assassins and cut-throats. I was offered Croatians – *Croatians*, for heaven's sake – and an Israeli female masquerading as a Georgian to act as escorts and generally sterilise the particular pimple I seem to have squeezed on someone's flank. Their last stop, apparently, had been Port Harcourt where on SIS's behalf they'd neutralised (in entirety) a syndicate of Nigerian heroin smugglers considerably less dyed in the wool than they – the Croats – themselves. No thanks, no fear. It was not thus in my day. I got Jerry to go instead with me to Siam, which they seemed to think was to be seriously under-dressed for the event. Only the current "budgetary constraints", i.e. the notorious parsimony of HMG which is nothing new at all, enabled me to get away with what in extenuation I would merely own as minor temerariousness

A young Singaporean case-officer joined us with a propitiatory plate of Bourbons. They had been Dennis' favourite biscuit. I did wonder how on earth the organisers had contrived to serve us on Civil Service green glass crockery at the remove of 5,000 nautical miles. The young Chinese was an absolute charmer but behind him, not far behind, were thugs and floggers. They had close military ties to the Israelis. Our interests were in safe hands with them. It was no surprise to any of us that they cracked the fellow who gave up Hambali's whereabouts in Ayuttayah, just up the river from Bangkok. (I declined the offer of the rice-barge cruise from the hotel concierge, plausible cover though it would have been. I am not quite that long-suffering). What no one in the business believed was the mujahid in custody in Singapore escaping via the lavatory window on his way to court or whatever it was. I doubt his friends did, either, but saved everybody's time and trouble and cut his throat the minute he clocked in. We were a lot subtler with our chap or chapess, though the young half-Thai had no compunction at all about knocking off the trio of young thugs and leaving their corpses on the main road. I do find it a little harder to deal in this way with a human being but we're not in a clean trade, are we, my dear? The age-old argument between ends and means.

The Singaporean was accompanied by another, much older, Chinese who rejoiced in the name B.K. Napoleon Wong. He had original ideas that totally belied his years and appearance. He shook me up, in fact, and it's good to be shaken up, I mean, intellectually, of course, at advanced years. He said that the whole American sing-song about human rights in China was simply a – doomed – attempt to put a bridle on the awakening beast. The US has never given a fig about human rights abroad, Professor Wong said, and has always been happiest abetting the likes of Batista, Somoza, Marcos, Pinochet, Suharto, and Pahlavi, not to mention the House of Saud. China is a threat and the US would like to see it weakened, which is to say rendered less efficient. One way to do it would be to dilute central control and allow dissentient voices to question the Party's all-prevailing wisdom. He said the pattern of Chinese history was for brutal authoritarianism emanating from the capital or anarchy at the peripheries: you had the First Emperor or the Warring Kingdoms.

"Would you rather be hanged or shot?" said Dee. "Oh, Colonel Kaye," said Professor Wong, "they shoot you first, then hang you up for an example."

He then proceeded to say that, if the human rights refrain was the song, the diplomacy was the dance. According to him, China had complete control over both the Burmese generals and the North Korean dictator. They snapped their fingers in Peking and it was done in Rangoon and Pyongyang. When the North Koreans got stroppy about nuclear inspections, or sank Japanese or South Korean corvettes, or lobbed a few rounds of HE over the line, it meant China was displeased with the Americans or Japanese. Whenever the conditions under which the unfortunate young woman Ang San Suu Kyi (I think I've spelled that right) was held varied, that simply meant another phase in the dance between America and China had begun. If they let her out of the house, it was a carrot to America. He said the irony was exquisite – the US always bleating about rights and the Chinese, totally po-faced, advancing them for a week or so in Burma.

He said the real issue for the moment was over the currencies and trade but this really did lock the Americans and Chinese into a tango when they didn't like each other at all. "Like the Prince and the late Princess of Wales," I said mischievously. As an Irish Antipodean of presumably republican sympathies, Dee smirked.

Professor Wong's final pearl of wisdom was the impossibility, the total impossibility, of any kind of local Islamic hegemony in SE Asia, based on oil or press of numbers. "China," he said with a kind of gloomy pride, "will squash everyone in the area. Its domination of its environs and, by the last quarter of the century, the world, will be absolute. And if you thought the Americans were heavy-handed and short-sighted, God help you when it's us. The only counter-balance will be two billion Indians."

"Well, I come from the home of lost causes," I replied cheerfully, but refrained from quoting the blind Argie. I'll look Napoleon up in the *World of Learning* when I get back. Someone did say he'd achieved the Double First of being imprisoned by both Mao Tse-Tung *and* Chiang Kai Shek. And delivering the Trevelyan Lecture and speaking at Chatham House, if I have any influence of my own left.

Dee and I retired to a quiet spot to continue our own talk. At these kinds of do, the informal, impromptu part (like bumping into B.K. over char and biccies) is the most important, as with an undergraduate's education: the lectures in schools quite otiose, the tutorials less so in good hands, but the real donkey-work (as with the psycho-analyst's couch) done by the young themselves, sharpening their wits on each other in the JCR.

Dee and I found ourselves differing over the validity of the use of coercive methods in interrogation. I said I was against the use of torture. No need to catalogue the specific forms; depravity does not rule out ingenuity. We all know what different cultures have up their sleeves. I will confine myself to saying this particular sphere of human endeavour has not noticeably progressed since the late Middle Ages. I was sufficiently imprudent to state that sleep-deprivation, cold, disorientation techniques, simulated rages, false promises, and mock executions were permissible. There is the famous occasion where a hooded subject was threatened with the last thing he saw – a red-hot poker – but touched with an ice cube. A huge weal promptly formed on his skin. Probably the urban legend of the craft, as the Nancy Boy tried retelling the tale to me at an early stage of our correspondence.

Dec asked me where I drew the line. Did a beating-up resulting in a cut lip or bleeding nose constitute torture?

I said drawing the claret was not the criterion. The merest slap in the face was inexcusable ill-treatment and prohibited but the establishment of a state of chronic discomfort as opposed to the production of acute pain was legitimate. Dee countered that I put myself on a slippery slope; it was too vague for young inter-rogators under pressure to get results. He said even bright lamplight in the eyes should be disallowed. I pointed out that even on jury service, the members received a single thin sandwich at long intervals to concentrate their minds the better on returning a prompt verdict. He said this seemed to have been the idea of our own hosts as well! It was difficult to get a bad meal anywhere in Thailand but they had achieved this.

We discussed the, by now, hackneyed, hypothetical scenario where a terrorist knows where a nuclear/biological device is located which will go off within the hour. With the lives of thousands at stake, is torture justified in those circumstances? He reluctantly said, yes. I said it could be countenanced if the interrogator has inflicted upon himself exactly the same torture at the same moment. It would be a sacrifice and a duel – of wills. Dee smiled in polite bafflement – obviously thinking I was as crazy as . . . I don't know . . . Orde Wingate. He said my suggestion combined elements of Quixote, Christ, and Baron Masoch. I agreed, but did he have anything better to propose? My arrangement offered exact moral equivalence. He said only if both subjects had the same threshold of pain. One might feel it more keenly than the other. I said, yes, I certainly would but had no qualms about offering myself up. Dee said, "Well, that would be typical of your generation, Victor." That was the first and last time he called me by my name. I demanded a suggestion from him and he said, in that particular situation perhaps, inebriation could be induced or a suggestible condition attained with psychotropic drugs.

I retorted, "Well, that would be typical of your generation!"

We both agreed that torture as the norm degraded the society that used it and would have measurable coarsening consequences on civic life. We both noted the well-known paradox whereby the victim felt soiled after the ordeal and the torturer did not. I refrained from telling him about the harrowing wartime debrief I did on a very, very brave female operative of ours who was possibly Patient Zero in the medical taxonomy of this particular trauma. The way we left it was that Dee felt ill-treatment was never justified and I thought that, in one case in 10,000, it might be. My feeling is that he will come to my opinion when he is my age. I did not say this; it would have sounded patronising.

Shortly before we retired to our rooms – considerably more spartan than the metropolitan luxury to which I had become accustomed – Dee to do nothing more urgent than "field a call" (coming from Canberra he was not jet-lagged and as an Iraq veteran possessed cast-iron bowels) – he spoke to me of the forthcoming article he had placed in *Foreign Affairs*. This was entitled the Short Wash/No Rinse/Long Spin Cycle. Apparently this is a reference to the washing "machine". I wouldn't know. The last time I wrung my own socks was in 1945. My scout, Bill, looks after all that. In this article Dee writes of the primacy accorded to the propaganda war directed not against the enemy, who as a zealot is proof against our slings and arrows, but at the home electorates. This instead of the real and most important, but long-term, task of establishing sound governance in places like Iraq or Afghanistan and, also, our gallant allies Pakistan and Saudi Arabia.

I had the BBC World Service TV on in my room – reception rather less snowy, such are the ironies of the global village, than the Brecon SCR – when I saw the most revolting sight. Concurrent with our little shindig, the ASEAN heads of state were meeting in quite what dictatorship or quasi-democracy I never bothered to ascertain and still couldn't tell you. One thing I do know: however bog-standard the despotism, the luxury hotels would be of a standard higher than anything we could muster in London, though there's always something to be said for the faded elegance of the good old Randolph's tea-room, with a splendid view to boot of the Ashmolean. What I saw on the box wasn't exactly the Mona Lisa or even a Froggy water-colour – more like Hieronymus Bosch meets Mabel Lucie Attwell – but it was certainly the masterpiece of humbug encountered in my life and I've met some. (For starters, the dead Pope both Matthew Lumumba and I called the "Altar Ego"). The screen was filled with the countenance of a child ancient in days. Its short, androgynous hair could have been that of a boy or a girl. The eyes were closed in rapt contemplation. After a few seconds one realised, with a heave of the stomach, that it was someone's depraved idea of a mug transfigured by prayer. The camera moved, I suppose on the same principle as a box-brownie, backwards, and one saw as well as the face a pair of hands, the chubby fingers indeed interlaced in prayer like a bunch of rotten bananas. It was the face of a middle-aged dwarf, not a child. The eyes opened, as suddenly as a voodoo doll's. The lips moved but instead of the curses, imprecations, and satanic obscenities that would have been tolerable out spewed a litany of invocations to someone called "Lord" (not God, he wouldn't have been listening). It was an ASEAN "leader", caught not just between a rock and a hard place, not just with a hand in the till but on the phone, rigging elections. My briefing had included everything about the creature and its ill-aspected consort. After this paragon passed a whole procession of the area's political elite, nation by nation. Not the halt, the crooked, the lame in any physical sense but morally so. The vicious, the weak, the petulant, the pompous, the sly, the dishonest, the frankly murderous, and – even worse – the imperturbably bland. The midget came on again, clasping its hands and invoking God in its commonplace crimes. I thought of all the perfumes of Araby, I thought of Chaucer's Summoner.

Yes, it turned my none too delicate stomach. It made me ashamed to be a priest. It made me wonder if I would not have gone to the mountains and taken up a rifle – as so many priests did and do – had I the deep misfortune to be born into such a degraded society. It made me think for one tumultuous second that the zealots were right. Of course, our embassy people had to keep up the pretence of normality in their intercourse with these monsters though, as at a Vampire's ball, they no doubt sometimes looked in the mirror and saw only themselves.

In general, it seemed to be a matter of quantitative change securing an alteration in quality, too. Knock off two or three people and you are just a murderer. Steal a few hundred thousand and you remain a thief. Kill thousands and it's no longer murder; it's dignified as genocide. Eliminate a rival, or the brave individual who wishes to reform the whole shebang, and it's now assassination. Steal hundreds of millions and it has stopped being theft; it's corruption. Attain ripe years, maintain a façade of cultivation and dignity and, hey presto, from being a thug and thief you have transformed yourself into a distinguished Asian elder statesman. I suppose the truly tragic thing is not that these societies allow the wicked to practice their evil and flourish but that the otherwise unremarkable, or even virtuous, have to become debased and corrupt themselves in order to survive the quotidian round.

Dee had also been tuned to the same channel in his room. He saw from my face what had been going through my mind. "Yep," he said. We now proceeded to find common ground for the first time. We agreed that the cure had to be better than the disease, that the existing governments we were propping up were rotten to the core and doomed us to failure. Dee spoke of the need for honest government and moral credibility. Again, he thought that the hardcore jihad could not be converted or defeated by reform – they were driven by a wholly religious idea – but that the foot-soldiers, the local rank and file who gave them the strength of numbers, could actually be detached by what seemed very much the programme of Latin American Marxism in the hands of radical Jesuits.

"Any regime we put our weight behind must be built on three pillars," he said finally. "Legitimacy, transparency, honesty."

"In that case," I said, "the Americans had better start putting their own house in order!"

We were joined by the others for the film show. "Video Night in Nakhon Si Talay," said Dee, which got a laugh from the younger set. I have no idea what he was going on about. The actual films, *The Battle of Algiers* and *Queimada*, were simply splendid. I said so in Jerry's ear and was brusquely but justifiably hissed silent by that volatile little man. It was still difficult for me to remain so when I saw the protagonist of the last film was recognisably Fletcher Christian, now with a paunch and in genuine need of the wig he had donned for the mutineer's part years previously. I really must go to the cinema more often. Ludwig Wittgenstein never turned his nose up at the flicks, sometimes watching two a day.

As with our video night, the whole affair was much more pleasurable than I had anticipated. I must stop being so cynical and think more positively. I am full of years. I must enjoy my declining ones. I am glad I came, if only to appreciate more what we are in danger of taking for granted in England and to see the changes that have taken place in this area since I was last here, a busy lifetime ago.

This was a pleasant interlude but not exactly a meaningful part of my life. It was good to see people and sights that were far from routine. I doubt I shall leave the shores of England again. I still have things to do, projects as yet unwritten. The Bursar dropped some hints, as did the Regius Professor. The Wardenship could be mine. Brecon beckons . . .

2

Snooky

It was all to be so easy, so simple. You would have thought these people had force-shields, warp-fields all around them. In fact, Snooky just rapped, "Beam me up, Scotty!" and she was in to the control-room of the starship *Enterprise* already. Captain Kirk and Mr Spock, you see, wanted to take a cruise in the park's darkness, around the shrubbery, across the sand-traps, not through the glittering galaxies.

The "great prize" Shaykh had in mind for us – dynamiting a Hindu temple in Silom (yah, darlings, they deserved it doubly, both as *kafirs* and for their hideous garishness) – palled next to the lottery win two of the emails gave us.

By this I don't mean Vice Versa's communications to me of November 25 and December 12. These arrived *after* I'd confessed to Shaykh. Snooky was glad about that. I mean, she didn't come clean to her hero for the wrong reasons. She'd bared her breast for the best, not out of self-preservation, though, yah, she admits she looked up the word "manumission" on line.

It was the letters which Snooky "appends below" – and nothing pretty ever swings from there – that blew everything wide open. They arrived within two weeks of each other, V.V.'s first. It was never meant for Snooky's eyes but was from Vice Versa to the Look Khreung. You could see how it had happened. Vice Versa hadn't wanted to save it to draft for me to retrieve as usual, no way, but had clicked the Send box for it to go directly to the Look Khreung. Then autocomplete on our particular system had thrown up me, aka Ludorum, from the address book as the commonest correspondent under the letter 'L' and Vice Versa had clicked on the faint blue lettering. Off the email had gone in its entirety . . . to Snooky, the last person in the world Vice Versa wanted to read it. If his trackpad was half as skittish as mine had become, it would have been autonomous as a Ouija board. Out of habit again, Vice Versa must have clicked on Blind Carbon

Copy for the Look Khreung. Thus the Look Khreung, who would have been young enough to understand the ins and outs of rocketmail, would never know who the head recipient of the email was, as he would have done had he only been Carbon Copied-in. And he'd never find the email after Snooky trashed it in a hurry from the record of sent mails.

Those who live by the email shall die by the email.

I was only surprised Vice Versa hadn't done it long ago. It was easy enough for eagle-eyed kids to slip up and possibly inevitable for the absent-minded, sight-impaired, stiff-fingered old duffers of this world, including erudite old duffers with enviable vocabularies. When I looked at it closer, part of the text also gave signs of being produced by the beta version of a speech-recognition program like, say, the Serbian software DragoDiktat which Vice Versa had ineptly pasted in and sent off in panic, half-corrected, before it vanished into the cyber dimension and he had to do it all over again. He'd have been better off trusting his arthritic fingers. He had actually had a conversation while he was on the speech-to-text software, too, probably with his butler.

So, on I read with mounting horror but no disbelief. Imagine Snooky's lips forming a shocked "O" while her unplucked eyebrows rise into her fringe.

This was it:

TO: LUDORUM
CC: BLANK FIELD
BCC: LK-FLOREAT- 50/50, À VOUS
SUBJECT: GOOD RIDDANCE
DATE: 29/12/200-
FROM: VICE VERSA
YOUR MESSAGE HAS BEEN SUCCESSFULLY SENT

Yes, I, too, am looking forward to re-making your acquaintance. When next we meet, we shall have to comport ourselves before others as the most perfect strangers. There is, of course, nothing we could say in person that we could not commit – I was going to say to pen and paper – but I should say to the monitor-screen. We have had an unofficial, unprofessional, and thoroughly unconventional relation-ship, as I have done with our bugbear, the Nancy Boy. My corre-

spondence with the latter has flouted all recommended forms and protocols. Really, I require no cover, no escort, simply because my involvement in all this is so unlikely that no one could possibly guess it. Even I have to pinch myself sometimes. It would not even form the fabric of the most lurid penny dreadful. Why on earth would HMG have its thumb in the Thai pie? And by line of internet, too, at the remove of thousands of miles. All to the good. Official deniability is the name of the game. Monkey business as well as any other business process can be "outsourced" in this, the cyber-age. SIS has no Bangkok station. I have no line manager. What glorious freedoms the dinosaur-at-large enjoys! However, when we do have a private moment, I will shamelessly drop the name of a Siamese patriot I had the pleasure of befriending more than half a century ago. He was of even bluer blood than yourself.

I shall hie my old bones to Northern Thailand after arriving in Bangkok on January 4, then will return to the capital and perhaps proceed in a southerly direction thereafter. (Sorry to sound like P.C. Plod reading from his notebook before the magistrate; such notes, it was the opinion of a very dear friend of mine, when bailing out his foreign students before the bench, were almost always fictitious and sometimes even non-existent. The constable would be reading from the blankest and most unsullied of pages). And, yes, you were always right about the Nancy Boy, who was also reading from an empty book in contempt of ourselves. I freely own it.

Enter new paragraph break Exactly where the conference will be in Thailand has still not been made extant full stop Inefficiency rather than considerations of security comma one feels full stop. I am given to understand the short list includes Prachuap Khiri Khan, Khao Lak, Nakhon si Talay, Nakhon si Thammarat, Surat Thani, and Krabi. Open parentheses The placehyphennames mean nothing to me comma everything to you comma I am sure full stop close parentheses put the tea tray on the davenport please bill never mind the sugar basin spare your knees just sport the oak theres a good chap now where the dickins was I ah yes There will be some kind of cover mummery overlaying our own seminar. One might consider it a sacrificial coat of paint, not that one hopes anything will happen to the civilians. Of course, now it belatedly occurs to me: perhaps you yourself are the one charged with the organisational details. Or perhaps your dizzy seniority exceeds your years and it is delegated.

The Nancy Boy swore by return of post that Target T. is still alive and ditto the old scholar Omar upon whom you laid such rude hands in Singapore. I did ask if Target T., the enforcer, had ever fallen under a cloud of suspicion as I wished to know if your little ruse on the highway had succeeded. Three men were robbed of their lives to set the ground for that little gambit, however disreputable those lives were, so you can say it was my conscience speaking. If Target T., the enforcer, was never terminated, however suspicious the leader was of him, and if he has indeed survived, I think we should work on turning him and having him work with Omar. This might seem odd after having worked to secure his demise but in this line a certain flexibility is always required. I respectfully submit that in Target T.'s particular case blandishment would work better than threats or ill-treatment which might prove counter-productive on a battle-hardened veteran of the Afghan wars and, quite possibly now, Moro wars in Mindanao. I did ask the Nancy Boy if anyone had fallen out of favour recently as they could also be worked on.

Meanwhile, we all have to wait for the old scholar to report to us rather than risk contacting him. Let us give him eight weeks before we do that. Experience, usually the best educator, taught me that it would be a good idea to provide him with a "PIN" number, as in banking, together with a series of "alpha-numeric" codes to cover most eventualities – e.g. 1. Need for extrication and rescue (fallacious hopes for him, I'm afraid, but issued much in the same spirit as young pilots like Goering resented the non-issue of parachutes in the First World War as bad for morale). 2. Important information to impart. 3. Impending atrocity. 4. Need to meet etc. These codes would be secure, swift, and avoid the mendacious subjectivity that has ever characterised the Nancy Boy's reports. At that time I decided it would be better to keep the old scholar Omar in reserve, or as background music, while the Nancy Boy could, for the time being, be our prima donna, singing solo soprano. All Omar has to do is "text" a three or four character code on the mobile telephone, assuming he is capable of that – which is a large assumption, as I for one certainly couldn't.

It now occurs to me that should we succeed in recruiting another of the influential figures in this particular pondok we would have too many chiefs and not enough Indians. (That was certainly the case, if you recall, in Pesantren F). It might be expedient to unmask the

Nancy Boy in order to thicken the old scholar's cover and no better a person to do this exists than Omar himself, perhaps in conjunction with the enforcer, two words being better than one. As another sop to conscience – mine entirely – perhaps this could be arranged when the Nancy Boy is actually already sprung from the pondok, otherwise we are going to have as many corpses as the end of Hamlet.

Of course, you as the man on the spot shall have the final say. I merely say my own say. Were the Nancy Boy to come to a sticky end, mine would probably be crocodile tears. I did tell him in my last communication that you would require him to repair to Ayuttayah to formalise his setting at liberty. Whatever happens to him there, whether indefinite detention in your little holiday-camp with the full range of water-sports available, or an end to all his troubles, is your decision. It would certainly be convenient and far more secure to write an absolute finis to his doings. The problem is that, once let go, he's very much a loose-cannon on the deck. The innate loquacity and indiscretion of his type, allied to a certain amount of perfectly understandable resentment, could jeopardise the survival of better agents we recruit in the future. In this case, were we to allow him to continue on his merrie way, we would be responsible for several deaths rather than one. In a strictly Benthamite sense, the moral, as well as expedient, thing to do, might be to write a termination to his career in the form of block capitals. That is to say, capital punishment on the block. Personally, I am most reluctant to proceed to such extreme courses. If I say the ball is in your court, you will probably change the analogy and offer me Pilate's basin and towel. However, the ball is most definitely in your half and I will support absolutely whatever decision you make, thumbs up or thumbs down. It's going to be down, isn't it? If so, for the record, I ask you to think long and hard and remind you that the quality of mercy is not strained. Clemency is the prerogative of strength, not the excuse of weakness. For the record, too, I don't believe Merde's tale of you having the smugglers from the criminal syndicates decapitated in zealot-style and the heads placed on stakes to sow dissension between them and the insurgents. So, I trust in your judgment as I would Solomon's.

yours ever,
V.

YAH, SNOOKY PUT THAT in her pipe and smoked it. It wasn't V.V. who'd be the Look Khreung's for evermore. It would be Snooky. She was gonna be hung out to dry and I mean parched as pemmican. How perfectly spiffing, old beano.

THERE WAS ALSO AVRIL, dear Avril's, email. I cried when I read it. It had no practical effect on our planning. It only helped as confirmation, as a checksum, and as whittling down the likely alternatives. But Snooky will print it, even though Avril's unjustified reproaches made her tears run hot and bitter, for the reason it shows that, against all odds, there still exist kindness and loyalty in this fucked-up world:

TO: moviebuffs@1976siamssentinel.com
SUBJECT: NO SUBJECT
DATE: 4/1/200-
FROM: cruollootmonth@notmail.com

Snooky – I know you're there. I had a few bounce-backs but some have got through. I don't know where you are, or what you're up to, but I know you're in trouble. Deep trouble, darling. Double trouble, treble trouble. Choose the heading you like, I'm on your page now.
  The most horrible guy has been bugging me. It's a Eurasian guy; you used to call them Half Child. Snooky, he's scary. If I was talking to you, my voice would be trembling now. I know this address is safe and he won't get to this because it's the one you used for your fan mail. And you never used to get any! Yeah, don't think I didn't know you were writing them to yourself. They were complete inventions. Then showing them off in the news-room!
  He wants me to bring you out from wherever you are. Lure you. He thinks you don't want to see him. I think he's right. I never want to see him again. He's as cold and creepy as a lizard. Good looks but hard and merciless. My gaydar was going bing, bing, bing. Only a fag could treat a woman with such cold cruelty. No way a straight guy could. The gay pimps gave the girls the worst beatings in Montreal. (So, that'll be good for your self-esteem, huh?) He said they'd revoke my visa, not just the work visa, that I'd broken this law and that regulation when I was in the boiler-room. I've got it now. You called them Look Khreung.

He was waiting to get behind me in the queue at that Starbucks we always used to go to. I jumped a mile. "Hi, Avril," he said. "Caught any good movies lately? Snooky sends her love." When he started getting heavy and threatening me, it was actually less creepy. After the first shock wore off, my mind was whirring in top gear. I could see the edge of an Ubatihet Air *ticket* sticking out of the edge of his Moleskine notebook. I knew I had to do it there and then, while the coffee was still scalding, and I knocked the entire cup into his lap. While he was grabbing himself, I stole about a two second glance at the ticket. *Nakhon si Something or Other.*

His whole face went white with hate. I think he could kill without compunction. I'm sure he has.

What have you done, Snooks? It's not money-lenders putting the strong-arm on you, I can figure that out. Have you been dealing drugs big-time? Have you got compromising photos of someone powerful?

He said he could get me a job as stringer for the New York Mail and head of a Press Agency so big you wouldn't believe it, if I only co-operated a little. He said he would ensure your safety. Ha-ha.

Well, I won't. Co-operate, I mean. That was his prepared line. Of course, with the look that could kill on his face – that was totally unrehearsed – it wasn't very convincing.

Snooks, I don't know why I'm doing this for you. You're the most selfish person I know. Do you realise that? Would you ever stick your neck out for me? I doubt it, honeybunch. What have you ever done for me? Shut up, will you. I can just hear you coming out with that Ali MacGraw line, "Love means never having to say you're sorry."

Get away, honey, get away as far as you can. And I don't mean get high. Don't you ever go near Nakhon Thingamajig. Ayuttayah would be bad, too.

Your friend, your real friend,
Avril

P.S. Yeah, you can pay me back that 23,000 baht for this. No, seriously, if you need money, I can help. I'm always here for you, *tea ruck. Pie nigh?* No, whatever you do, don't tell me. *Choke dee.* You'll need it.

THE LAST EMAIL was more like – as Evelyn would put it in the elevator – a blast from the past. No, make that an effete sibilance. But that camp *coo-ee!* down the thin but infallible reed of POP 3 aggregated and auto-forwarded email opened all the otherwise sealed doors and impermeable air-locks to us, the marauding alien *juwae.*

TO: moviebuffs@1976siamssentinel.com
SUBJECT: PROPOSAL
DATE: 10/1/200-
FROM: dr.evelynB@arteneum.ac.edu.ph

Dear Miss K-.,

I hope this address will still find you. In case you've forgotten, we met in Bangkok at the prize-giving some three years ago. I'm the brother of Ainsley who was the chairman of judges who gave you the Critic's Award you so richly deserved. Not only did you deserve the bounty of the sponsor (a New Zealand bank, was it?) but perhaps also an Oscar for the well over the top, ham performance you gave when receiving the cheque from Ainsley. I was unable to locate you on Facebook, nor does your charming escort at the Bangkok prize-giving, April (or was it June? forgive the levity) have an account. Someone similar appears to be on Twitter but I could not be sure. I can certainly recommend both sites as doing wonders for your romantic life, as they have for mine. Unfortunately as I have lopped 30 years off my age and six inches off my terrible height, I cannot actually meet anyone in the real world. I have to address you formally – I don't feel I can presume to call you "Snoopy" as your companion on that day did. The lady appears to have had quite a miraculous escape at the Phuket discotheque bombing. One wonders who Prince Charming was who so providentially rescued the swooning – or, by her account, quite well-swooned already – damsel. She described him as tall, dashing, and handsome. The fact that he was thus in the manner of Ainsley, rather than swart and ill-favoured like myself, makes one wonder if he was not a figment of fevered fancy or just journalistic licence. Perhaps the kindest explanation is not female hysteria but the explosion causing a derangement of memory. The general opinion is that her reviews are a pale shadow of yours. Is this just a sabbatical from which you will return triumphant to the newspaper? Are you writing a book? It seems Tom, Dick, and Harriet (by which latter I mean the dreaded American housewife) are churning out first novels these days and getting paid millions for them. I'm not trying to butter you up in order to get you to accede to my forthcoming request (get on with it, Evelyn) but Ainsley rather thought, on the evidence of your reviews and the parodies, that you might have a gift for fiction.

I find myself presently at a conference in what might loosely be described as your part of the world. We have two – but actually it is three, as I will explain – separate conferences. The first, which I am personally participating in as a lapsed Catholic and the son of a demented mother with Parkinson's, is on the vexed issue of Euthanasia.

The second relates to Transgender Issues to which, it will come as no surprise at all, I am inviting you to contribute at rudely short notice. This is because one of the Transgendered delegates was inconsiderate enough to take an overdose of sleeping-pills in Geneva last week. Yes, dear, we could have doubled her up at both conferences, I know. (I trust this does not offend? I'm going to dither about deleting it now).

The third – and I really ought to be more discreet but so far from swearing me to silence they have not even had the courtesy to tell me they are jeopardising my hide – is a security think tank or, in Blunt language, as it were, a coven of spies and spooks. It purports to be a kind of forum for the more up-market part of the travel industry, with the whimsical but meaningful title "CATS and MICE", the latter acronym being the well-known one of Meetings, Incentives, Conventions, and Exhibitions and the former – occasion-originated, one feels – standing for Cruises, Alpine Adventures, Trekking, and Safaris. Such I garnered indirectly – at third hand, actually – from my youthful frenemy and fellow Postmeister (a whimsical Oxonian quiddity meaning Open Scholar) of five decades past at Morcom College. I trust the tale that follows is not going to prove too outlandishly alien for you. Even to me, it seems set in another world and from another time. A long, long time ago in a quadrangle far, far away . . .

Actually, come to think of it, I can almost imagine you reading your essays to the likes of V.H.H. Green or young Steven Lukes, clad in the long gown of the scholar, with nothing on underneath and those long legs modestly crossed. So bear with me, while I unravel an ancient history that has extended its overarching strands to this unlikely place today. The undergraduate rival and fellow scholar at Oxford that I mention above rejoiced in the name of "Merde" Mahler. A lanky, carrot-haired streak of malice, his only friends were the two non-public schoolboys in our year, Jakes Mendelhsson and Barry Parry. Mendelhsson, who had come to us from Newcastle Grammar School, was a martyr at a precocious age to Irritable Bowel Syndrome and was found dead from an accidental overdose of sleeping pills at 21 – naked but for a singlet – in bed, in his digs in Jericho, with a copy of Rex Warner's The Aerodrome in his cold hand. He was our Exhibitioner but no whit less bright than Mahler or, dare I say it, the dashing young Evelyn. The poor sod came from a very poor family and was reduced to working in a factory that made Canesten pessaries to earn some pocket-money in the Long Vac – the £60 Postmeistership and £40 Exhibition were in the nature of laurel leaves. His funeral was the saddest of the kind, thronged with young faces. The poor lad had barely begun life's journey and his terminus was hardly a Passchendaele. One of his Geordie set cracked up shortly before Finals – way before the days of LSD – and was taken away to the Warneford, babbling about Jakes not being dead at all but, like Merlin in his cave, living in a locked bag in a dayak longhouse in the jungles of Sabah from which he would be reincarnated, after the passage of two years, as a head-hunter. Mendelhsson's autopsy showed a heart problem from childhood rheumatic fever and nothing else unusual except a prodigious quantity of spinach between his teeth. You can see from this that I was actually one of the steadier types in my year!

Barry Parry, he of the wonderful name, was a very pleasant boy from Aberystwyth who ended up quite high in the British Council. Everyone liked him and he was a leading light at the Union, too; pleasantly voluble in that dithyrambic Welsh way. Well, a few months ago I heard on the grapevine from Barry – who managed on sheer niceness the difficult balancing act of remaining a lifelong friend of both mine and Merde's – that Mahler, The Shite, was grumbling in his bitter old way about being kept away from an event at this very place on this very date and I was able to put two and two together. (Parry tells me Merde lives like a king at a glorified marina in Langkawi that might have been transplanted from the South of France).

357

It was no secret to about six or seven of us that Mahler had been recruited by British Intelligence shortly before graduation. This was the standard form of induction in those dear, departed days. A personal connection of some kind, the right school and university necktie, and being the proper sort of chap sufficed. (Mahler was a Harrovian, or was it Winchester?) On the strength of his fifth proxime accessit *in a poetry prize (not the Newdigate, one hastens to add) he had wangled himself a joint invitation to tea from V.H.H. Green and Vicky Veridian. Both these Reverend gentlemen were notorious secret service recruiters at Oxford, although circumstantial evidence suggests they were better scholars than they were poetasters or spymasters. When we asked Mahler innocently in the JCR (Junior Common Room) what had transpired at tea, the callow youth that he was then clammed up with self-importance, thus raising my eyebrows from the very start. As I say, he was not a popular lad and he was once dumped by an Ainsley-led gang into the refreshing waters of the fountain on Mameluke Quad. I stayed aloof from the hearty japes – it was some-thing that usually happened to "aesthetes", amongst which number I am vain enough to classify myself, before the War. It was a nostalgic retro-moment, an attempt to recreate the 1930s, rather than an act of bullying and I think Mahler was in fact deeply, deeply flattered by the attention. Barry had a towel ready and bought him a cup of cocoa in the refectory. It was a different matter with an American – not a Rhodes Scholar – a few years older than the rest of us who was even more unpopular than Merde and widely reputed to be CIA. Barry and I joined the lynch party and we put him into the river. He was incapacitated, rigid as a pole, the while we carried him aloft and, unable to move a muscle, did rather give the game away as he snarled, "You fuckers better watch out, I'm trained to kill." The threat, or lurid admission, was greeted with a roar of laughter from us and a strange look by Mahler, who this time was also one of the dunking party.*

I will admit Merde possessed a useful, if unoriginal, intellect and did secure First Class honours but he then proceeded to "fail" the Foreign Office exam which a capable plodder like him should have passed with flying colours. I was coming out of the Richardson Quoin during my last week in the golden condition of undergraduate – the B.Litt was to be drabness itself – when I saw the back of a D. Phil. gown entering the rooms of our Senior Tutor, The Rev. Derek Koldov (who later became Bishop of Barchester). Three minutes later Merde trotted up the flight. Snoopy, it was too much for me. Yes, I richly deserve the ducking-stool. I crept up the creaky lino of the staircase and put my ear to the door. I distinctly but faintly heard the conversation, apparently between Mahler and Vicky Veridian, the latter clad in his Doctor's gown. (And, I hasten to add, a black corduroy suit underneath). When I applied to my ear one of the sherry schooners Derek's scout had left on the landing, perfunctorily rinsed at the buttery, I heard the conversation considerably less faintly. I swear the first words I heard Vicky V. say were, ". . . the equivalent of Hello, Sailor," followed by a burst of laughter from both Koldov and Mahler. (It took a bit to make Merde laugh; the only other time I recall was when Mendelhssohn came to a fancy-dress party as a fried egg). The gist of it was that Merde was to be inducted into MI6. I would have eavesdropped longer but at that point what I did unmistakably hear were the unsteady footsteps of Jock, Koldov's scout, returning to take in the sherry glasses. Well, I left with as much sang-froid as I could muster, only remarking to Jock at the bottom of the flight, "Could you ask him to lay in an amontillado that's a little less sweet?" By the time he reached the top of the stairs, poor Jock had probably forgotten all about me. I do believe Mahler's first task, just as a preliminary exercise without practical consequences, was to write reports on half a dozen of us in his year and submit them to Green, rather than Veridian. We included "homosexuals", an Indian Trotskyist, and a rather peachy young Trade Unionist who had transferred from Ruskin. Yes, alright, I climbed through Mahler's window when he was out. After I saw the impertinent remarks he had made about me, I felt no compunction whatsoever. Perhaps he felt he was treading in Kit Marlowe's undergraduate footsteps with Walsingham. If so, he was sorely mistaken. (Marlowe was a contemporary of Shakespeare; in fact, if you believe the wackier of Ainsley's pals, he was Shakespeare. Apologies if this is old hat to you).

After graduation, I baited Mahler (yes, I'm a vicious old queen) with only a half-certainty, about his real work as a spy for many a year. From his point of view, the joke wore increasingly thin, until one day he abruptly ceased all contact with me. That was tantamount to an admission. How can he – they – have been so inept, of such little nerve?

Many years later, Merde sent a mutual acquaintance of undergraduate days, once known as Dieter the Tart (for his sour wit, dear), *to ask me* en passant, *right at the end of a very pleasant half-day spent bicycling around a remote island in Hong Kong, why I thought Merde was in the secret service. The entire day – no, preceding year and a half – had been a softening-up process for this single elabor- ately casual question. This acquaintance was 1. a diplomat and 2. a dipso. He had "stalked" and "groomed" me as it were by email for some 18 months, having pretended to discover me again on the internet after the lapse of four decades before visiting Hong Kong. (Ainsley's chum, Kingers, that chain-smoking reprobate, had retained Ainsley as Distinguished Visiting Invigilator for a week, otherwise neither of us could have afforded to spend more than 36 hours in what is basically a shopping-mall writ large). I don't actually feel offended by Merde and Dieter's guilefulness, so much as outraged they should think I would be obtuse enough not to see through the whole shoddy but transparent subterfuge in seven seconds flat. Of course, I was actually privy to hard info as to The Shite's status, as well as the circumstantial clues and ear-to-the-door anecdote I have related to you here, but was smart enough not to show all my hand by passing it on to Dieter. "Is that all?" he asked in faint disappoint- ment as the ferry drew back into the Outlying Islands pier. I pissed myself laughing inside. (But I also have sufficient sense of respon- sibility to and, yes, affection for, the memory of the golden lads Mahler and I once were, to refrain from passing it on to you as well now! I can tell you the security leak dated from his most isolated days as an operative half-way up the arsehole of Asia in what was then known as British North Borneo and was . . . no, I won't, I won't . . .) I have to say the harsh reek of metabolising vodka was coming out of Dieter's pores all day but – somewhat more professional than Mahler – he still kept his nerve when it mattered. He was grey, bald, and pot-bellied. I remembered a slim, handsome, and amusing boy and wished that was the way I shall recall him. It won't be. He hasn't been in touch with me from that day to this which is not just a bit bloody obvious but very poor spookcraft, too.*

If Mahler had refrained from deceit and years ago had merely muttered a quiet word of confirmation and remonstrance into my shell-like, I would have desisted from the mockery. Of course, I would never out him publicly. That might put him in physical danger. Funnily enough, the mean-spirited bugger wouldn't hesitate to do that to us if it was in his smallest interest. I don't suppose any eyes other than our own are ever going to read this letter, or be interested in hacking our accounts, but should any of Merde's auld acquaintance ever come across this, they need to smile faintly to themselves and keep their traps firmly shut, especially in the presence of journalists. (Sorry, my dear). Once there are two lines, no, two words, in a gossip column, well, the genie is out of the bottle with a vengeance. I enjoin them to enjoy the joke, on their tods and in solitude, without compromising Merde and me. And, of course, whatever you do, not a word to April.

Basically, Mahler's nerve failed him and he showed himself well out of his depth in the wrong business. And this was dealing with poor old Evelyn, not the Bulgarian KGB with their lethal umbrellas. The Old Shite panicked and fell back on slyness, just as the Young Shite always did. They'd have been better off picking me or Ainsley back in 195- . In the end Mahler proved far more unreliable. He was a terrible bullshitter, barely dipped into the weekly reading lists, but his essays at tutes, if somewhat jerky, contrived a knowingness well beyond his years and non-existent erudition. I would imagine his reports to his superiors are semi-fiction and inflated in the same specious mode. Ainsley won the poetry prize, incidentally, by half-plagiarising some silver-age Georgian pseudo-de la Mare, while I was third proxime, call it bronze medallist. I suspect the old spymaster never approached us on the basis of the calumnies Merde poured into his ear over the tea and scones. I mean, one more public school queer in the British Secret Services wouldn't have hurt, would it. It'll all be history soon. At 74 (damn! I've let my own age out of the bag!) Mahler – known in his youth as Agent Orange after his coiffure – is long overdue for retirement.

Of course, you couldn't blow the cover even of a superannuated trog like Merde with impunity. The CIA and SIS, are, in my opinion, not that brilliant at protecting their publics, but damn good at harassing the individual citizen who crosses them, or refuses to oblige them. They remain as unaccountable as a serpent and twice as venomous. You'd find yourself landing at Changi with half a kilo of heroin in your checked baggage in no time at all. "Oh, do move with the times," Ainsley snorted. "You'd find cyber tracks leading to a kiddie porn site you never knew you'd owned."

"Oh, I'd just spill all the beans to the papers, then," I said. "I'm distinguished enough to place an article where I want, when I want."

"I think the problem is," opined Ainsley, in that intensely irritating and rather condescending way he has (you yourself got a dose of it at the prize-do), "not so much that they can ruin your life, which no one doubts they can do better than anyone, but that if your big mouth ever gets you into serious trouble in Asia with, say, the incongruous combination of the Burmese junta or Jemaah Islamiyah, it's Merde and his pals who will be charged with the thankless chore of extricating and protecting you. And they can be pardoned if they do it with something less than alacrity and enthusiasm."

Anyhow, theirs, the Cats and Mice, is the real event; we are just smoke and mirrors. I think someone half-way literate might be having a private joke as a well-known writer who visited parts neighbouring here, as well as corners of the globe even less salubrious, once described our secret service as the best travel-agency in the world. The whole thing, you as a film critic will agree, resembles that hilarious movie The Witches by Nick Roeg (like you, I adored his Performance with the divine young Mick Jagger and the butch aristo James Fox plunging downmarket as a South London gangster). You will recall, the witches, wearing latex facemasks to disguise their, well, witch-like proscesces, are at a convention in a luxury seaside hotel ostensibly in aid of the RSPCC (sic) but in fact to devour all the children in England after transmogrifying them into mice (real rodents, not acronyms). Saoul Bello (remember him? how couldn't you with a monicker like that) would say it is revolutions which devour their children. I don't have much (actually anything) to do with this last layer of the onion, so won't cry over it. The spooks here at this very moment – minus Merde, so far – run the whole gamut from hardy, erstwhile berobed mountain warriors to Canberra couch commandos and Potomac potatoes, with one of them well past pensionable age. I think of him as the Abominable Snowman or The Old Man of the Mountain. He's an FRS and FBA, so I overheard, and also wearing a dog-collar in the tradition of Veridian or Green which may or may not be cover, but hearing him expatiating in the coffee-lounge he appears to hold social and political views that would not go amiss at a BNP rally. Unfortunately, they are not wearing name badges on their lapels otherwise I could place him. It would be rather surprising if they were, I suppose. His face does seem familiar. Had they imposed the vow of omerta upon me, my lips would have been sealed. I do still feel a bit guilty about telling you, my dear, but if you come you are entitled to know and, really, the whole thing is so preposterously obvious. Trust a queer to blab (but this one won't betray his country).

I will end on a cheerful note, Snoopy. The Euthanasia topic I misheard first as Youth in Asia. This led to hilarious misunderstanding and double entendres on both sides. My opponent in this debate was a charming, open-minded and quite worldly priest – a newly ordained Jesuit, of course – so I was surprised my innocuous remarks on the subject of Youth in Asia appeared to inspire such consternation and dismay in him. When I began by saying we were talking of not millions but hundreds of millions of people whom we should strive our utmost, financially and by example, to help in the realisation of their goals, his face dropped the proverbial mile. "I think," he said nervously, "you are exaggerating the numbers involved."

ME: Quite the contrary, Father. I am rather underestimating.

FATHER X.: Whatever the numbers, even one is too many. We must put every possible obstacle in the way of these deluded people.

ME: We will start a formal programme and alert potential enrolees by all means possible – traditional print media, street-flyers, the usual social networking sites, and as this is, after all, a Third World Country, vans equipped with loudspeakers and posters. These are used by fruit-sellers, to advertise concerts, to notify demonstrators of political rallies, and we will not be embarrassed to use, like them, bright colours and cheerful music, to entice the young who are our targets. Every spare cent of national resources and whatever aid comes from overseas must be devoted to alerting candidates and their families to the possibility of an improvement to their situation and the bringing to an end of the misery and dissatisfaction of unfulfilled lives. We will educate and train them to this end. When I say Youth, I venture to suggest 12-years-old and above and, in special cases, from the age of seven. This would certainly appeal to the well-known motto of your Order, Father. We should provide centres where literature of self-help can be disseminated. Places where not just guidance but technical assistance is given. We can call them drop-out centres, even provide coffee and light refreshments to speed them on their way. To those unsure or shy because of their tender age, quiet *encouragement may be given that they may find the courage to take the momentous step. We could have completely new buildings constructed, either permanent structures of brick and mortar or temporary pre-fabs, or use schools on a 24 hour basis with special night sessions. There could be subsidies to despatch the very deserving overseas.*

FATHER X.: Dr. B-., I can hardly believe my ears.

ME: Priests, Father, even those so eminent as yourself, should not stand aloof but lead by example. Show them yourself how it's done. Let your own seminarians enrol first. I cannot imagine a worthier project for the Church to support. Let us give them at least the means. The rest is up to them.

FATHER X.: Good God, man.

In the end, of course, we got it straightened out. Ainsley doesn't believe me but I swear I have only touched up my account a bit.

We are at the Hotel Thalay in Nakhon si Talay and if I do not hear from you by email, still feel free just to drop by without warning. My mobile is . . .

Yours ever,
Evelyn B.

SHAYKH READ THE MEN'S EMAILS with a calm and imperturbable face. But Tariq said in a voice that quiverered with rage, "God Willing, I will show this *kafir* what my own young men can do . . . God Willing, we will burn these newly built Churches down around their ears."

"Er, no, Haji," Snooky said tentatively. "It's a pun or a homonym . . ."

"There are no homonyms in our ranks, eunuch," bellowed Tariq, contradicting himself in a single breath but Shaykh waved him silent. "Ahmed," he said, "the meaning of this? I cannot understand the way the Arts talk among themselves. I know all the individual words but not exactly what they mean when all put together. The chief of the Crusaders, the head of the snake, is here for us to cut off? You can work out where exactly he is?"

"Then, as usual, Shaykh, you comprehend the entirety. Yes, it is likely he is in Nakhon si Talay. Not to a certainty, but very probable."

"Put a number to that possibility."

"Ninety per cent."

"God is Great!" shouted Tariq. "We will attack tomorrow! If I join Imran in the garden of the martyrs, so much the better."

"Wait just a little, Haji," I said. "If we simply kill them, we waste half the opportunity. How much better to capture them. The fame of our *pondok* and our Caliphate would resound in the *ummah*, then."

"If God Wills, that would be the greatest of victories. But how?"

"Let me think a moment."

"But of course! You would like solitude? No? Then coffee for Ahmed! Sweetmeats!"

Snooky veritably purred and basked in the sunshine of Shaykh's attention and favour. That was sweeter than any coconut jelly or *pandan* blancmange. It didn't need too much thinking, in fact. I laid it out like I'd analyse one of Avril's unrequited crushes, always culminating in the advice, "Forget him." But this time Snooky's counsel would not be a negative.

First of all, how could we make absolutely sure who we wanted was where we thought he was? Easy. Tip off the Siamese police, who were as stupid as they were brutal, that there was a hit team after the important *farang* they were supposed to be protecting. Our observers in the six towns Vice Versa had mentioned would only have to look for the flurry of belated security around the hotel where an imminent terrorist atrocity was jeopardising the local police chief's promotion prospects. Avril's information, if you could trust her, and I did, I did, also narrowed the list of possible venues to just two towns.

The trouble with this was that, with all the Siamese wasps buzzing around, it made it that much more difficult to get at Snooky's nemesis. Better to make the small gamble that he was where, according to Evelyn and Avril, all the signs indicated he would be. You didn't have to invoke Game Theory for that.

How to get Vice Versa out of his safe place? First of all, I took a photo of Tariq reading yesterday's newspaper and sent it as attachment. It was ironic Vice Versa wanted proof a live man was still alive, while assuming the dead Umar was still of this world. Then I sent a text with the PIN code – located among Umar's scant effects – for "Meeting necessary." Umar had committed it to archaic

Jawi script which I could read but Shaykh and Tariq couldn't. We'd grab Vice Versa and any bodyguards on the way to the meeting. Back came a message stipulating Bangkok in a week for Umar and Ayuttayah three days later for Tariq. Snooky, as Umar, replied he had to make the meeting in the South, within an hour of the *pondok*, in order to preserve a convincing alibi.

No reply from Vice Versa. I had requested an immediate one on the grounds Umar was being sent to a "distant land". That brought a smile to my face. I had to figure Vice Versa didn't suspect anything. He just hadn't attained seniority, and presumably ripe years, by putting his head into nooses for no good reason. We had to do it another way. With Evelyn's invitation, Snooky could get into the conference and the hotel easily enough, see the lie of the gland, and get out without impediment. That was the reconnoitring and ground-breaking Shaykh and Tariq always insisted on. But how to winkle Vice Versa out into the open town?

It was actually Shaykh who put me on the path. I mean, not had the idea himself but prompted Snooky. Dirty tricks were not that noble man's department.

"God Willing, you find the enemy's weak point," he mused. He had just gestured for Snooky's coffee-glass to be filled a third time. "Then you can negate his strong ones. Ahmed, what are your thoughts on their, his, failings? How are they most easily ensnared? What do they covet most? What will they risk all for?"

"Let me see. Oh! Holy Shit! No, no. I mean, God is Great! Sorry! Sorry! Why didn't Snooky think of it? Honey-trap!"

Shaykh looked considerably disappointed. "God is Great, your suggestion is not. That was always Hassan's weak point and, to a lesser extent, of Umar. But an English gentleman, a milord. Are you sure the lustre of gold is what motivates them? This was not my father's experience with them."

"Ha! No, Shaykh. Honey-trap, not money-trap. Men will risk anything for . . . er . . . physical . . . sensual . . . gratification . . . you know . . ."

"Sex?" said Shaykh incredulously.

"Yes, Shaykh, sex. Remember Imam Umar – God have Mercy upon him – how he found the police Colonel's routine? Not everyone is as virtuous and unsullied as you. I rely on God."

"Ahmed, you have no idea how much your words please me.

But are you sure? The Communist boy was clean in this respect, clean as the mountain snow, where his uncle, the head of military intelligence, was black in his evil. He was a Arts but he would have no truck with the loose women. The foul and dirty police threw him out of this country, out of Siam. Do you know that? He who was clean and decent, when this country is a sewer of iniquities and whoredom for the foreigners. For speaking disrespectfully of your King."

"Shaykh?"

"I babble of things gone by. They cannot be revisited, even if I so wished, and I do not. Sex?"

"I rely on, um, God, Shaykh. In my experience all men, and most specially *farang*, will take the most foolish risks, sell their grandmothers and betray their friends and country for 15 minutes of lust. Even if it clearly leads to ruin. Education, experience, intelligence, power, responsibility, duty, nothing stands in the way of desire. It's as irresistible as the tsunami for the minutes it lasts. Then they awake and look around at the destruction surrounding them. Afterwards they might suffer remorse, but it will never stop them. This is man. Except for you, Shaykh. I rely on God. And Jefri."

"Well, from your mouth comes wisdom. God is Great. They called it the Greek Love. This was their Achilles toe. They would have been great but for this and their superstition. This was being the weakness of the Greeks."

"Also of the Yemenis," interjected Tariq sardonically, "if a ewe could not be found."

"Silence," said Shaykh. "Fools should be wise enough to know when the wise speak and when it is wise not to speak." Tariq grimaced but, by the time he had unravelled Shaykh's words, the latter had finished his next sentence. "Great were their achievements but God still would not relent and all their knowledge was but sin. Archimedes the Engineer, Pythagoras, Isosceles. Until the knowledge passed into our hands."

Also Alexander the Gay, Snooky thought but was certainly wise enough not to say. Instead she said aloud, "And Socrates, the one who was made to drink the poison juice because he corrupted the youth. His friends walked him round and round to make it circulate faster and speed his end."

"Did they now?" said Tariq. "What kind of fruit was the juice squeezed from?"

"Sophocles," said Shaykh dismissively, "was just a Arts. What do you expect? I rely on God. Practise as little guile as possible. Let it not take place while he is travelling. I would not like that." He went back to his calculations.

"Set it up, *koti*," said Tariq.

"Tuan?"

"You heard the Boss. Set up your honied mouse-trap."

JEFRI, SNOOKY, ISKANDER. The Three Musketeers. The Three Mujaheedin. The Three Stooges. Tariq and Shaykh to follow. No weapons, no weapons at all, other than well-sharpened knives. Too risky to convey past the checkpoints and roadblocks 200 plus miles North. Yah, Tariq was our Lethal Weapon. Shaykh wanted to turn the tables on the Crusaders. Do something only they normally got to do: extract information at leisure from captives under duress.

Evelyn's Trans-Gender debate I gave a miss, so to speak. I didn't exactly fit the bill any more. Evelyn actually reeled with shock when he finally accepted who I was. I said I'd do the second part of Euthanasia instead. He enthusiastically agreed. Afterwards he said, "Dull as ditchwater, sorry." He was correct. It was. In the right hands anything can be. Even Jihad lessons, under Haji Hassan.

There were a few Trannies still around as Snooky arrived. I think they were fixtures on this particular NGO circuit. Quite a few from Singapore and Manila and even one from England but no one I knew. Some nightmare creature called Chaylla was doing her version of Mata Hari's Dance of the Seven Veils when I passed them by. That is to say, it was transparent as an act of contrition and remorseful self-discrediting. On the whole they were so, so, drab. Coulda used a few make-up and wardrobe tips from The Gang.

If their drag left something to be desired, so did that of the spooks. Snooky now saw what Evelyn meant about the undercover coven. If you were in the loop, it was kinda . . . blindingly obvious. Of course, if you were just passing by, you wouldn't cotton in a million years. My cellphone, like everyone else's except the spooks, had been confiscated at the door for the duration but there were free computers everywhere.

Going down in the joint's Japanese elevator, from a company that had made fighter planes in its samurai past, and could still make the ears pop and the stomach lurch with the soaring and plunging of this glorified metal box suspended from its greasy cables, Snooky had her moment of epiphany that was puke-making rather than glorious.

On floor 7 (coming down from the roof garden and pool on 15 where I'd been having iced tea with Evelyn on his expenses) the door slid open with its usual vainglorious ping. This time it really was the augury of something dramatic. In stepped the Look Khreung, with a panther's sure but stealthy tread. (Wearing a black sleeveless clima-fit running tunic over tan cargo-pants sure helped). Oh, God, Snooky died three times then and there. Behind him was a nondescript, grey-haired, limping duffer. The Look Khreung was saying ". . . begin at Calais." He pressed the Mezzanine button. His companion replied, "You'll have to do a little better than that, if you're going to shock me. But I didn't like being called a Pharisee."

Nothing about the old man was the least remarkable, except for one thing. Average height, a little portly, a British voice that was quiet but relentless. But the eyes. That was the first thing you noticed. He was talking to the Look Khreung but not looking at him. The old man's gaze swept over Evelyn B., discarded him without interest as exactly what he amounted to, then looked at me. It was a casual encounter in a hotel elevator. The gaze was not unfriendly but all-enveloping. You felt all your foibles were immediately known but they had stopped being ridiculous. I knew at once he was a teacher, Imam Umar on pentathol, Hassan on mind-expanders. He was an inquisitor. He'd make you do the work. He wore the round collar of the Christian priest. He was with the Look Khreung.

Holy Shit! I knew who he was, how he figured in Snooky's life. The old man said, "Look, sign him over and you'll be rid. No need for extremities. Murd . . ."

"Well, that would be a fate worse than death, wouldn't it," replied the Look Khreung calmly. He began to turn. Avril had not recognised me. This hybrid monster might. It was his job to. I thought of leaping to open the elevator escape hatch – might have tried it on, if I'd had dear, dead Do-Ann's inches – of sticking a finger down my throat and vomiting on the floor but half a litre of tea and some mint leaves wouldn't really be revolting enough.

I grabbed Dr B. by the nuts and pushed my tongue down his throat. He made gagging sounds, not of lust but asphyxiation, and his desperation gave him the strength to spin me round as I hissed into his ear, "Let's do it."

The elevator stopped at the fifth floor and a very tall man with dyed red hair, the shade of which was decades too young for him, stepped into the lift.

"Well, talk of the devil," said the Look Khreung. "Better late than never."

"Just belt up, will you, you little cuff-link," retorted the newcomer.

"Now, now, children," said the Look Khreung's original companion before asking the newcomer if his room was comfortable.

I looked straight into the Look Khreung's eyes. I saw exactly the same expression in them as I had done aeons ago at our last meeting. Total disgust and contempt. But not a glimmer of recognition. He had no idea who I was, like Edmond Dantes in *The Count of Monte Cristo*.

Ping! The elevator arrived at Mezzanine. At that moment it was as good as the Third Moon of Klingon.

"Bloody queers. They're coming out of the woodwork today," observed the Look Khreung. "Place is swarming with them."

To me he said in Siamese, "Animal cunt."

"Takes one to know one, old fruit," said the red-haired man.

As the doors glided open, the Look Khreung said, "I don't much care for your tone, Marley. Don't forget, I am not your subordinate. And I'm certainly your social superior. You guested at the KCC. I was in the Hillingdon."

"Wouldn't the Piers . . ." said the red-haired man, only to be silenced with an abrupt, "That's absolutely enough, gentlemen. Desist," from the elderly man, my controller and cyber contact Vice Versa.

Shit, discussing assassination in calm voices in the elevator. At least Imran and Tariq always did it hot-hearted.

"By the way, old chap," said Dr. B. brightly to the red-haired man as the doors were closing, "written any good odes recently?"

"Pathetic as ever, Evelyn," the other replied, "but do persist in your deluded little fantasy. Regards from Barry and mine to Ainsley."

By ourselves again, Dr B. smiled knowingly at me. "Well, that was the wind of history buffeting one! The answer's, yes, I'd love to, but could you have a shave first? And you might like a bath?"

AT THE HALAL (as opposed to hotel) coffee-shop – a distinction as important as that between Euthanasia and Youth In Asia – my companions hung on my every word. Like God, coffee means different things to different folks; is served in ways that are not alike; fills different vessels, usually the unlikeliest and humblest, with heat but not light, before the coldness of death; keeps those ministered-to alert, preparatory to oblivion; is on the lips before it quickens the heart; is frequently fortified with alien spirit and is acrid in essence before it is smoothed with the milk of kindness for the faint-hearted. Oh, yah, and so dark and cloudy it's impossible to see what's at the bottom of it. Would Snooky share these refreshing thoughts? She knew much, much better than that.

Tariq said, "Are you sure, eunuch, are you sure?"

"I rely on God," I answered. Clearly, this was not sufficient for Tariq. He scowled.

Jefri said levelly, "It doesn't matter. It doesn't have to be exact. God Willing, we may find out afterwards. Or not. But a blow struck in the dark can be as effective as any other." He shrugged when I looked at him in surprise. Mostly, people grow into responsibility. Jefri was the opposite. He had developed into someone more formidable by learning not to care.

Shaykh said, "Condition Green, God Willing."

Snooky said, "I think he is not so interested in girls, don't ask me why."

With a leer that for once went unreprimanded, Tariq said, "Find a pretty boy, then. But it won't be you any more."

NO, IT WASN'T. It was Air Fun. She'd always been the most masculine in the gang. I mean, gay as shit (and there's nothing gayer than a turd) but hovering between common faggotry and true transvestism. She'd finally come down on the side of being a boy, a divine boy, of course, camp as Liberace, who took it in every orifice, but still a lad, however cute.

"I thought you'd go that way, kid sista," I told her that was now

371

him on the SIM she had never changed (one thing at least unaltered). I told her (sorry, old habits die hard) a white lie – oh, yah, a very, very grey, grubby one. We were gonna fix the blackhearts who'd killed Do-Ann.

"Best thing I heard in years, Snooks," she trilled into her Nokia, the one she'd kicked out of the hands of the gurgling Japanese on the Sukhumvit pavement years ago.

"It's given great service," she corroborated to me over a cup of piss-warm *halal* coffee. "Your friend's cute by the way." Iskander blushed. I'd never seen someone quite so dark manage it but he did, he did. Tariq's eye popped out of his head. "Uh-uh, uh-uh, Haji," I remonstrated in English, funnily enough always the language of obedience where Tariq was concerned, "we need her."

"Him," said Air Fun proudly. "What's with the pirate look? Today it's fashionable in the modern South?"

Tariq grimaced with fury but had the discipline to sit there and take it.

"Er, Snooks, how about some uppers for Roger? My piles are killing me after the coach."

"Who the fuck's Roger? I told you to come alone."

"I am. My English boyfriend gave me the name."

"No promises, but I'll see what I can do."

"No big deal."

"*My pen wry.* By the way, if your English is so good, what's a Nancy Boy?"

"It's a *katoey*."

"Thought so!"

Snooky knew her man, and I don't mean Air Fun. Vice Versa was kind of an Evelyn B. bound by an honour code he would not flout. He was a teacher. He wanted to impart, he wanted to help. He was a killer, he was a healer, he was a shaman who could go either way. He was also a stylist, old style. I could hear him, sure, but it was like hearing Shakespeare or beautiful oratory through a thick wall from way back beyond in the Mansion of English.

That evening Shaykh would say, "Use his goodness against him."

"Shaykh?"

He struck Snooky violently on the shoulder and turned away. "I throw myself on the Mercy of the Compassionate, the Lenient. I have become as bad as the Indonesians."

But hours before that exchange, I said to Air Fun, "Smoke a pill and a half of Mad Mix. He'll mistake the speed for quick wits. But try and look straighter, willya. Take these."

"These" were a reasonably current Thai-language copy of *National Geographic* with diagrams of early human migration patterns on the cover, an older English-language issue with photos of treasures from King Tut's tomb, a Thai-English dictionary, and a translation of Hamlet – the most convincing artefacts of cross-cultural aspiration that could be dug up in the backstreets of Nakhon si Talay on a drizzly Sunday afternoon. Air Fun laboriously spelled out the name of Shakespeare's tragic hero, phonetically rendered into Siamese. "It's breakfast, no? We have stuffed Thai omelet."

"No," I said emphatically, sticking not one but six gel pens into Air Fun's shirt pocket. Then I had a stroke of genius. Haji Hassan's pince-nez, which had wound up in my possession. Haji had tried appropriating my red shades but I'd won in the end. Yah, they could have been designed for a flighty young gay looking for a touch of grave cool.

"Mm, can I keep these Snooky? They make me look rich."

"Cretin! They're to make you look less stupid than you really are. OK – here's the line. You work part-time as a tour-guide to Malaysians to put yourself through night school. You wanna be a secondary school teacher. You've been studying English. You like the teachings of Yaisu Christ but are still a Buddhist for now . . ."

"Yes, I do. I mean the teachings of Yaisu. He was very *chai dee*, very kind. He said the poor will become rich."

". . . so thou shalt not pick his pocket. But sit close. No physical contact, not even the knee. No hanky-pank at any time. Never anything improper – we'll lose him if you do that. But let him feel your breath when he bends over to look at the magazine . . ."

"Okey-doke. Got a tic-tac? Braces breath, you know."

"I don't know, actually. Other than that you can get a nose and a boob job for the price of three wires on your front teeth. OK. Now behave and go learn your lines."

"I can't really believe he was the one behind Do-Ann dying."

"He wasn't. He'll lead us to the ones who were."

"Whatever. The *farang* call these eye-rings 'scepticals', y'know. I had an English boyfriend for a while."

"Yah, you fucking told me ten times. And spectacles is the word you're looking for, Air Fun."

"Hey, these eye-rings are plain glass. I mean, they don't do anything."

"Oh." Now I knew. Hassan had worn them as an affectation. He'd probably seen every face I'd pulled and certainly every gesture I'd made in his Arabic class.

Tariq had been sitting in on this exchange, it being beneath Shaykh's dignity to spy. Hassan or Umar would have been more suitable but there was no longer the luxury of choice. Tariq's head had been going back and forth like the spectators at a tennis match between a pair of those statuesque Russian girls all the Gang would have liked to be (after Yah Royal Heinous Diana, Princess of Wales). If Air Fun and I had been batting a clod of shit backwards and forwards, Tariq could not have looked more disgusted. "I'll see this *koti* out, *koti*," he sneered as only he could sneer. Later, when I was shoving 1,000 baht notes into Air Fun's politely reluctant fist at the bus-station (a waste of time and money, as Air Fun's throttled corpse would be last off the coach at the terminal in Thonburi), Air Fun would say, "He's horrible."

"Who? Not the English teacher?"

"No, *he's* just like Yaisu. He's a good man. I meant, Mr Black Heart. Your friend Jack Sa-pallow with the eyepatch. He just shoved his monster into me and put his hand over my mouth. I'm still bleeding from the haemorrhoids. It was worse than the Nigerian. I could hardly breathe, not that I was worried about that so much as my bum."

"*What?*"

Poor Air Fun. His last word to me would be, *"doot"*, the Siamese for asshole.

ON THE other hand Vice Versa's first words were, "You look better than I had imagined." They were intended for me but addressed to Jefri. It took a few seconds for Snooky to work out what had happened. The old man with the piercing eyes had mistaken little Jefri for me. As the old *farang* had a large bump on his forehead and a bleeding nose, this was disappointing but understandable.

Jefri had yet to add sphinx-like imperturbability – or, like Shaykh, Chinese inscrutability – to his armoury of leadership traits, so for his part he was a little surprised to be singled out (bearing in mind, Vice Versa's arms were secured by Tariq and he was facing Shaykh at his most focussed). In fact, Shaykh was so focussed he was in danger of setting the warehouse on fire.

"I told you not to hurt him," he reprimanded the Juniors.

"We didn't, Shaykh," Iskander said. "He jumped on to Irwan's motorbike and got away. I've never seen anyone take corners so fast. It was only the children crossing who made him swerve and hit the post."

The old *farang* was quick now, too. He immediately perceived Jefri hadn't understood him and began to look around for other possibles. His glance went straight over me; in fact, he wasted as little time on me as he did on Tariq.

I said, "Me, Tuan. It's me, sir."

"You!" he exclaimed. "But .. ,"

"Yah," I admitted. "I'm a little the worse for wear. Snooky's had a hard time."

"God is Great!" Shaykh exclaimed. "By the intervention of Mighty Allah, Ahmed turned from the path of apostasy to that of righteousness. He confounded your slyness and your scheming. He preferred the line of straightness. As for Tariq, he never wavered."

"Well, I think I know who you are," said the old *farang* – and the calmness of his words was a contrast to his injuries and the indignity of his position. (Snooky has never pitied, but rather always secretly despised, the bleeding). "And, of course, you would know all about betraying your salt, or at least your father would."

"You dog!" shouted Tariq, driving the old man's face into the table.

"You," said Shaykh in a calm and dangerous voice, "are a liar and slander a brave and upright man. God Willing, if he had been here he could have answered you himself. As it is, you put a knife into the heart of his son."

"God is Great! Here's the other one," announced a Junior, now rising through the ranks of the *pondok* much as Jefri had done.

"The other one" was a man as old as the priest, but considerably smaller. Totally bald, with a toothbrush moustache, he reminded me of a comedy character in some British farce of the 1950s out of the Ealing Pinewood studio (Snooky always wondered where that was; she will never visit it now). From a bag of golf-clubs, the Junior pulled out a little rifle, reminiscent of a Portuguese blunderbuss from a four-hour Siamese historical epic.

"Secure him in the corner," said Tariq, "we'll host the guest of honour first, as they do in Afghanistan." Tariq was too stupid to know, still less use, the *double entendre*. The double-tap pistol volley was more his line. But the old *farang* was not to know this and to his credit he did not show a flicker of emotion at the prospect of what happened to prize captives in the Pamir Mountains. " 'Lo, Jerry. Sorry to see you here. Got us into a pretty pickle, I'm afraid, and you did warn me. I'm an idiot. Very unprofessional."

"Surprised we're not trussed up in two separate pots over the same fire. Don't blame yourself, Victor. It's fine by me. It's a cleaner way than the prostate I was telling you about. I think they got me with an electrical stun-gun in the bunker on the reverse slope of the tee. Probably stood my four hairs to attention and taken years off my age."

"Nothing wrong with old Carruthers, I see."

Tariq brought matters to an end by punching the bald old coot squarely in the face. The man collapsed into unconsciousness without a word or groan. Snooky was knocked out, too. She'd only ever seen good-looking young guys exhibiting bravado like this, on celluloid.

"Why you take this sudden interest in us all of a sudden?" Shaykh asked. "You are being the MI Sixes, I think?" Snooky didn't know whether to laugh or cry. She didn't know where or who she was, or who she owed what to, but she knew she'd heard one of the worst lines she'd ever heard.

"Thinking would be a new experience for you," said the old man, whom I now knew was called Victor. "Do try it."

"God have mercy upon you," said Tariq, "because his Mujaheedin will not."

"I," said Shaykh calmly, "am an engineer and you are just a foolish Arts. You are the lightweight. I am a mathematician but I cannot count the Followers of God we shall make here."

"Well, I'll call you Godfrey, then. Yes, Godfrey the Adder, if you're so fond of arithmetic. You have the temerity to justify your evil in the name of God. Any God? You are free of any trace of God, Godfrey."

"Islam is submission," said someone in English. To my immense surprise, it was Jefri. "Submission, Tuan, to the Will of God."

"In submission," said Shaykh, "we find freedom, but not in submission to the Siamese. Not for these brave fighters. They will never submit to the yoke of Bangkok."

They all smiled, the non-submitters, Snooky rather more wanly than everyone else. She had never heard Shaykh talk like this before. It had all been Caliphate until now.

"Is the freedom to be ruled by a corrupt band of your own worth blowing the limbs off little more than children? Maiming the innocent? Disfiguring the uninvolved? The IRA thought that game wasn't worth the candle in the end, all but the lunatic fringe, but then you do look loony to me."

"Any suffering by the *kafirs* and even Muslims is a cost of nothing compared with carrying out the Will of God. It is a zero sum. I can look on any number of torn bodies."

"Then you are nothing but unalloyed, distilled, quintessential evil. But even you cannot attain that condition and still remain human. That distinction belongs to the devil – whose work you are carrying out."

"Why is it that dropping bombs from above while sitting comfortably in a machine is moral and the brave martyr who sees his victims' faces and dies with them is a coward and evil? Why is the delivery system being the defining of morality? Is a backpack so evil in itself?"

"Ha!" shouted Tariq. "You are silent now!"

"There is," said Victor, looking at the young Mujaheedin, "justice on both sides. You who were born here and are dispossessed by the Siamese. But think of the Siamese who were born here, worked the land, watered it with the sweat of their brows. Do they not have a just claim, too? There are two rights, not two wrongs. And two wrongs do not make a right, however warped your calculations."

"If," said Shaykh, "you took this boy's," pointing to Iskander's, "cellphone and gave it to your son and he passed it to his cousin, would it make it any less the original owner's and you and your descendants anything more than thieves?"

Snooky applauded despite herself and the others joined her,

though – for sure – Tariq was the only one who understood. She remembered it as a favourite riposte of Shaykh's.

"We, the warriors of God, are just and clean. We are righteous. You call us essential oil of evil but we are clean. You are dirty – you came to sodomise that, that . . . thing, neither man nor woman."

Victor flushed with anger. "I did no such thing."

"You are a dissolute. Your crimes rise in their stench to the nostrils of God. You came to practise your abominations on that *koti* and you were ensnared by your sins."

"That assumption says more about you than it does about me. I wished to assist the boy in his aspirations, as simple as that. I had no ulterior motives. I have never, ever, taken advantage of anyone who was a pupil, to whom I was *in loco parentis*."

"You *loko*, OK," leered Tariq who had picked up a few words of Chabocano dialect in Mindanao, mostly – as you may surmise – those descriptions addressed directly to his own person.

"You are a shameless liar and, God Willing, I have the measure of you," said Shaykh levelly. "You tell us now of your spying on us, what you know, and who else you have suborned and led astray from the path of righteousness. Umar, I know of. Have you recruited the *Group 453* or the *Mourners of Haji Tulong?*" asked Shaykh, naming respectively a criminal syndicate running a protection-racket / gun-for-hire operation and the second largest group after the *RCK* fighting for an independent Sultanate of Patani, autonomous of Malaysia.

Victor grinned, he actually grinned. "You think you're as wily as a waggon-load of monkeys, don't you, but you know even less than I do and what I know isn't worth knowing."

"We will be the judges of that, Crusader," said Tariq.

"You are going to do me harm, I know that, but you are wasting your time. I am an old man, long retired from the fray."

"You will tell us many things. Now you are the monkey."

"I despise your wiles, your lies – to yourself and to others – the deception practised upon me. I am not perfect but I am not a trickster. If I ever admired one of your countrymen, it was Zia, for his honesty and bravery. He would have wasted no time shooting the lot of you."

"Zia?" said Tariq, astonished. "In that case, I am going to grant you a clean death – after you have spoken."

378

"Well, as your leader Godfrey the Adder would say, it's the thought that counts. Thank you so very much."

Shaykh now said, "You shall also find me direct, if you do not try to dupe me. Your real name, who you report to, how much you know about us, how you plan to hurt us, how much do the Siamese know? Answer these questions."

Victor opened his mouth but at that moment the earth moved. Or rather the little recumbent character-actor came to life like a force of nature from his simulated unconsciousness. He turned out to be an actor, after all. I still don't know exactly how he did it and Snooky talks as one who saw and did questionable things – not star-ships on fire around the rings of Orion or the C2 rays lighting up the Battenberg Gate, like the android in Bladerunner, but Ladyboy vs Farang on Beach Road 1 when victory lay not always with the strong and sturdy over the slim and simpering but where the smooth and svelte routinely overcame the macho and the muscled. The little *farang* with the toothbrush bristles under his nose ankle-tapped mighty Tariq, wrapped his skinny legs round the burly arms of our warrior, extending them as if nailed to the floor-planks, and with careful palms snapped his neck like dry cane.

"Crucifix restraint and neck-crank, class," he said. "The legs provide the vice, the hips the torque."

Frankly, if Archangel Jibreel had descended and done *Singin' in the Rain* we could not have been more shocked.

I don't know how long passed before Shaykh grabbed the fat rifle. Several seconds, for the bald little man did not rush his words, just as his movements had been smoothly unhurried. Shaykh pointed the gun at him and pulled the trigger to no effect. He pulled something, shoved it back, there was a click, nothing more. No thunderous bang, such as even the little revolvers could produce, but Jefri fell backwards without a word, blood welling through the chest of his spotless gown. Iskander seized the tubby little weapon from his master, cocked the bolt, fired with no more than a click and a neat hole appeared in the *farang*'s forehead. Behind was a different story. The back of the man's head flew off; hair, scalp, blood, brain-tissue, bone-shards splattered against the wall like a mud-ball.

"Oh, my son, my son," cried Shaykh, lifting the dying Jefri in his arms. At that moment Snooky envied Jefri. "Oh, my son, my weak eyes have killed you. Oh, God, Oh, God, have mercy."

Victor said, "God forgive you and me. I wish I was sorrier."

Shaykh's lips moved soundlessly. He really did resemble The Fly, trying to communicate with his wife. He found his voice. "Kill him," he said. "Let there be one less."

"Interrogate, Shaykh?"

"No. Eliminate."

"Wait!" Iskander called. "Jefri is saying something."

Shaykh put his ear to Jefri's mouth. Only the new bubbles in the blood showed Snooky that Jefri was trying to speak. Snooky coughed. There was her own blood on her fingers but she knew she had not been touched by the quiet, lethal little rifle. She was as doomed as Jefri; what was rebelling in her bloodstream was slowly but surely bringing her to him.

"Youth tube," said Shaykh. "What does he mean?"

"YouTube," said Iskander. "He wants us to stream it there."

"No. A thousand times, no. Not for *kafirs* to gloat."

"Not Jefri, Shaykh," a Junior said. "We have no record of it. We will show the world justice. You called it equivalence, the reckoning. We will kill the old *farang* on YouTube. He is the responsible. If he had not been here, the rifle would also not have been here to kill Jefri. We will punish him for this! God is Great, Shaykh! We will show the world."

Shaykh's lack of demurral was his assent. The Juniors needed no encouragement. Six, seven, nine gizmos appeared from beneath the gowns, the older Iskander's neither the priciest nor the fanciest. Iskander looked more appalled than Shaykh at this display of high-tech contraband from the grey area between *haram* and *halal*.

"God is Great! Jefri has gone!" said the Junior.

"May God be well-pleased with him," said Shaykh as we all followed on his heels in pursuit of the time-honoured phrase ". . . *well-pleased with him.*" As the chorus died, five or six pairs of young arms pinioned Victor to his chair, while Iskander levelled a camera-phone with a Carl Zeiss lens.

"Ahmed," insisted Shaykh. "God Willing, Ahmed. He tried to dupe and befoul Ahmed. To Ahmed the glory."

The rifle was placed in Snooky's hands which were neither willing nor unwilling but just clumsy.

"Young man, for what it is worth, I grant you my personal forgiveness for what you are about to do. O, Almighty God, I commend my soul to thee and to you I consecrate my life, with all its infirmity and weakness. *Sic transit gloria mundi*. In the end it was but *vanitas*. Thy Will be done."

Snooky raised the rifle, looking down the barrel the same way as she had lain on top of the huge black sewage pipes bridging the river when she and Jefri had been young in another world.

Those eyes, that gaze of Vice Versa, of Victor. It was steady, steady, like the sun, not flickering like a star. Snooky was mesmerised by it. She could not move her index, her trigger finger. It was paralysed. But she could glimpse Iskander hand his camphone to the youngest *juwae*. Snooky felt Iskander's bony hip against hers. His left hand supported her own left under the wide barrel, his right fingers overlay hers, the index on top of her trigger finger. His hot breath played on her cheek. He had clearly lunched on curry and, yes, banana. He whispered, "You're gonna be a star, Ahmed." As his finger was pressing down on hers, as urgently as any loins had ever imposed themselves against her buttocks, Victor beamed. He said, "Get a wriggle on, will you? I haven't got all day."

Frantically, Snooky shouted, "Cut, cut! It's a spoiler! Blooper, blooper!" but it was too late. Iskander's finger in the superior position would have its way. Click went the rifle and Victor's life was over. He had upstaged us. He would never, ever, figure on YouTube.

TWELVE HOURS later. It might as well be 12 years later. It might as well be 12 x 12 = 144 years later, one gross years in the future. Snooky feels stranger than she has ever felt. It's the beginning of the end. The sickness is taking control. She will do a double milkshake of Nubain and Ice, all shaken together into a potent froth. No, make hers a triple. Call it the poor man's speedball. Shaykh has given her permission. "God wills that any means that get the job done are *halal*. For the martyr to achieve his purpose nothing should be considered *haram*."

In a few hours we have to bury Jefri and Tariq. It must be done before sundown. Iskander knows a quiet spot, a secret plot, in the middle of a palm-oil plantation.

"What shall we do with the bodies of the old *kafirs*?" asks the rising Junior.

"Cut their heads off and place them between their legs," suggests another. "Tuan Tariq would have liked that."

Jefri would not, thinks Snooky. The *pondok* is going the way Tariq would have wanted, the way Shaykh doesn't want. Snooky says, "Ahmed has an idea."

Shaykh looks attentively at her. Currently, she is Shaykh's favourite, which is kinda dangerous, a short-lived glory. Shaykh, she knows, is grooming her for a purpose. "We will use their corpses, or at least that of the clever one, Victor, for our own purposes. We will use their bodies to kill others."

"Rig them, God Willing, with explosives?" asks Iskander.

"No," says Snooky. "We will use him to get into the building. We will put him in a wheelchair, no, better the golf-cart you caught his friend in, and under it will be the device. He will be the admission ticket." Yah, thinks Snooky. Victor will be my Trojan-horse. He will be El Cid strapped dead to his stallion, leading the charge, but not against the Muslims this time. He will be the corpse of Kagemusha, inspiring the samurai. He will not have the last word. This is what is truly important.

"But we have to bury Jefri and the Haji," a Junior remonstrates indignantly. "There is not enough time."

"Shh. Don't contradict Tuan Ahmed," another rebukes him. Snooky smiles radiantly at the Juniors. She says, "This is for later, some time later. Only God could build the Caliphate in a day."

All regard her. There is a horrible, truly horrible, unspoken question in the air. "Salt," says Snooky, "dry ice. *My me bun ha*. No problem," she translates for Shaykh.

"This is *haram*," says one of Imam Umar's old pupils. "Even if they are *kafirs*." He wrinkles his short nose in disgust and is not the only one.

"It is not good," says Shaykh. Now all eyes turn to him, as they should. Snooky's disappointment is short-lived. Why did she ever doubt him? "Dry ice," Shaykh informs the Juniors, "is a bad expression. It is not exact, it is not scientific. It is a Arts expression. It is poetic and poetry belongs to God. Ice is frozen water, which is a liquid and liquid, by definition, cannot be dry. Dry ice is actually gas. It is carbon dioxide or the CO_2 which, yes, is frozen, but is not being ice and it is so cold it burns, producing by paradox the effect of heat."

"We call ice 'hard water' in our language, Shaykh," pipes up another Junior. Snooky thinks, but does not say, Shaykh would rather have heavy water. A pregnant silence follows. After a while it dawns on even the most sceptical that Shaykh is backing Tuan Katoey, Khun Snooky.

"Iskander," commands Snooky, "help Ahmed." She is feeling queasy but not from the projected task she describes. "Strip them. Then pack rock salt round their bodies. After that the, um, chunks of frozen gas. Get it from Cold Store supermarket – their ice-cream department. We have a *juwae* there. Then they will not rot."

"God Willing," says a Junior.

All this is a diversion for Snooky. It postpones, defers the reality of having to accept Jefri's death as real. At length it sets in, slowly at first, seeping into the bones like the misty cold of a mountain night in Mindanao which in the tropics, of course, is something paradoxical and unexpected as the purposeless demise of Jefri, Jefri the (potentially) Great. Snooky thinks her heart will break. But not if she does a double Valium on top of the Ice 'n Nubain shake she injected. Perhaps Shaykh and Dr Pinky Chomapnooj Cheuan together could calculate what of life remains to her. Not much, is the layman's answer. She goes to her Macbook to send an email. What she has in mind is the Look Khreung and Mad Dog Chon, the animal of a politician's son who killed Do-Ann. Of course, it won't be coming from Victor's address but she will embed a reason for that in the text. Maybe the old guy could forget a password. Confidently, she presses the power button. Clicking and crunching ensue, as of amyloid plaques, dancing and entwining and knotting and entangling into clumps and thickets in the brains of the senile demented. (The ranks of whom Snooky will never join, thanks be to God). On the blue screen of the hitherto trustworthy Mac a giant question mark flashes. Yah, yah, triple yah, indeed, thinks Snooky. She should get one tattooed on her dick, her hated dick. She goes to – who else – Shaykh. Shaykh is doubtful.

"If one could ask too much of Allah, you are asking too much," he says. "Risk and reward. You risk all for a small increment. We can kill all of these dangerous people, there now in one place together, all the eggs in one basket, but they could escape while you try to add two more eggs, small eggs to the basket."

Snooky is still silly enough to think she would like two very small eggs herself.

"Risk Theory," Shaykh says eagerly. "You are hearing of that, Ahmed? The *kafir* generals consult it, too."

Snooky says, "Whatever, Shaykh. God Willing, I mean. These two men left alive are important. They are now our most dangerous enemies here. The others, the *farang*, cannot harm us, however powerful they are overseas. Only these two can know to come after you and the *pondok* when Ahmed is gone."

She is not actually lying to her hero, is she? She is just embellishing the truth as she will decorate her face with make-up for her last performance. She is almost disappointed, nearly disillusioned, when Shaykh's expression changes to one of consternation and he says, "May God be well-pleased with you when he sees your face, Ahmed. That is good, I had not thought of that. But how will you bring them? The honeycomb again?"

Snooky wonders what Allah will think when He sees her face. "Easy, Shaykh. I was going to send email, but now I see the phone of the one who killed Haji Tariq lying on your table, it occurs to me that they do not need to hear a voice on the phone. I will send text, an SMS. That is even better than email as coming from a specific source – that particular phone number. They will assume it is from the pair of old *farang*."

"God Willing, can you imitate them so closely?"

"Shaykh, Ahmed has spent his entire life mimicking something he is not. In my written words I can be them. I can be them absolutely."

Shaykh's face darkens. Why? For once Snooky's strange attributes can help the Jihad. At that moment a Junior shrieks, "God is Great! Tuan Tariq has returned from Paradise!"

"*Alhumdulillah!*" screams the former protégé of Imam Umar, thanking God presumably on the basis that, if the Imam wanted no truck with Tariq in this world, he would want none in the next, either. Like Frankenstein, in lurches Tariq. One arm dangles by his side, useless, the arm without the hook. His head is craned at a strange angle, like a particularly bad case of cricked neck from a strange pillow. All that is missing is the bolt through the temple. He gives vent to strange, monster-like grunts. Snooky understands he is in pain. "Ahmed," she says, "has just the thing for you, Haji." Yah, 2g of Nubain in the outer quadrant of the left buttock.

Tariq's eyes glaze as the hypodermic goes in. He sighs in relief. "But, heroin, Ahmed?" he manages.

"Nubain, Haji," Snooky tells him with more than a hint of smugness. "Thanks be to God. Man-made chemical, not from the poppy, but similar, ah . . ."

". . . molecular structure," supplies Shaykh.

"Ahh," groans a blissful Tariq, "it feels just like heroin. I am no longer in hell – I praise God – but in the clouds."

Snooky's jaw drops but Shaykh takes no notice and she keeps quiet. No one has thought to ask her how she came to possess the stuff, though she would say the Moro medics gifted it to her in Mindanao.

She sends the SMS – oh, so easy for Snooky. There's method acting and there's method texting. She will pretend to be . . . not necessarily Victor, or Vice Versa, as he was, but the black and white old timer Noel Coward. He will do as Snooky's ventriloquist's puppet spewing green ectoplasm. Coward, something Victor was not, though Noel in Snooky's gaydar screen was almost certainly a friend of Mrs King's.

"PURSUANT to our exchange of pleasantries in the lift," inputs Snooky, *"oblige me by having that young gangster Chon brought down from the North by mane force if necessary. Attend upon our arrival in the hotel carpark at six-ish. Pray don't disappoint. Gerry sprained an ankle exiting a bunker on the golf course and is in a stupor of morphine in the buggy. I'll be with him. Doesn't know his ass from his elbow. Pippin, pippin, old fruit."*

Barely three minutes later the Look Khreung's reply. He'd swallowed line, hook, and sinker, as they say:

"Oh, I'll be waiting for you, alright, my Cox's."

SNOOKY has her last dispositions to make. She is not gloomy; she is cheerful, she is gayer than she has been since . . . maybe the last time they threw her into the swimming-pool after the hotel press-conference. Attention, that's the thing for us. A TV's fantasy is to be on the TV. Usually, the attention came with disapproval, tinged, or frankly hostile. How pleasant now that it should come with respect, admiration even. This is gonna be the greatest performance of Snooky's life; unfortunately, one without the possibility of an encore or a second take. Pity she won't be there for the grand finale. Tariq is talking about somewhere called Yookay. At first Snooky thought he was talking about Ukraine – all the Pattaya mafia come from there. Now she realises he meant England. The dynamite for Snooky's swansong is coming south from Burma. Much safer than bringing it north from Yala. They won't expect it from that direction. Snooky's not sure but she thinks one of the Pattani gangs were intermediaries – they know the Burmese Colonels from their speed pill business.

They say I won't feel a thing. It's too fast. I'll just see a white, clean light. Then I'll be in a cool garden, with tinkling streams, among the *houris*. "Maybe Ahmed can be one of them, he'd like that," says Iskander, out of earshot of Tariq and his mighty leathern slipper. Well, I know I certainly won't feel a thing. I'll be high as a kite, won't Snooky.

Snooky bathes, shaves for the last time. Oh, those days when it was only her dizzy legs. She makes her martyrdom video, the most recent movie sub-genre: noir and verité combined. She is star, director, screenwriter, voice-over, and, as in her tyro days, caption-writer combined. She makes Iskander do three takes but the first was the best. Snooky, you see, always was a lousy actor. Avril always knew when she was lying.

Tariq comes to pay his last respects to Ahmed. Snooky gives him a *wai* with her battered, but, once upon a time, nightly Ponds-creamed, hands. She doesn't suppose she can find anywhere selling stick-on falsie nails in this dump of a town. Her old foe the Cyclops holds out his paw. Snooky assumes it is a generous conciliatory handshake but as she reaches out he takes her own hand and plants his hairy lip upon it. Nothing creepy, just a specimen of gallantry from an unexpected source.

"Go with God, Ahmed," he says. "The Boss knows he can rely on you. See him now."

Shaykh's stern face wears a rare smile. "Rejoice, Ahmed," he says. "God has given you a great work."

"Shaykh, I know," Snooky replies. "I was weak but now I am

strong. I have nothing to live for but now I can turn what little is left of my life to account."

"God Willing," says Shaykh. "God always willing. Your courage and resolve are equal to the bravest martyr. It is just that the integer from which the subtrahand is taken is smaller."

"*What, Shaykh?*"

"No matter. *My pen wry,* as you would say. Those who follow Arts usually have no knowledge of science. It is not your failing alone."

"I am weak in myself, Shaykh, but I am strong in the cause of the Caliphate. I rely on God."

"That I know. I have the measure of you. I know what you amount to. I count upon you. Do not take it amiss that you should be accompanied by mentors. I trust your resolve but there is a certain procedure we all have to follow, leaders and led alike."

"Shaykh, there is no need. I am willing. I will kill those who killed my friends."

"Yes, Jefri was indeed a brother to you. You must feel his loss the most among us."

"Not just Jefri, Shaykh. My sister."

"They, too? I was not aware. God is Great! I was not aware. Then your revenge will be doubly sweet. Believe me, Ahmed. I do not doubt you, but you will still have an escort. Iskander, Tariq, the important others. Think of them not as jailers or coercers but as an escort. You may need them to penetrate the screen of the Siamese or to put you out of your pain, should there be a malfunction. Had you thought of that?"

"Pain, Shaykh, is not going to be a concern."

"God Willing, Ahmed."

"Even without . . . Yes, Shaykh. I rely on God."

"I need to send all of them with you, Ahmed. Only I will remain. They will all go, as the evenings of our lives depart. Do you wish to serve me, Ahmed? Then do this for your Shaykh."

"Tuan."

Snooky withdraws. She hefts not one, not two, but three of the Nubain ampoules. They are the size, shape, and colour of the plastic capsules in hollow German chocolate eggs, the kind with toys inside. A lavish serving of ice for this milkshake, too. Will Snooky even be able to stand? The tiniest prick. Not into the thumb web this final time but the luxury of mainline into the brachial. Snooky will vapourise. There'll be nothing left to autopsy. Only her head. She knows that. That's typical. She'll take extra special care of her face now. As much care with her make-up as she is currently taking with fixing the dope. And she'll dress as what she is – a woman. She'll tell Shaykh and Tariq that's part of the subterfuge, to get her closer. Her and the two old dead *farang* in the golf-buggy, rolling along like a waggon of the Old West into the sunset. Her and Victor, together at last, like two jaggedly-shaped pieces of a jigsaw puzzle, which defy all expectations by clicking seamlessly together in the end. Snooky will be smiling, smiling the Siamese smile, the Indonesian beam, grinning like the cat that got the milk. And it won't be just deceptive, simply to allay suspicion and get in close. No, it'll be how Snooky truly feels. With its silver canopy and the dry ice fuming, the buggy'll look like a gigantic bong of meth. Yah, it's gonna be a smash hit. Travelling at walking speed in the buggy, it's still gonna be a bigger impact than the highest of high-speed crashes Steve McQueen ever did. And Snooky is a heroine. Heroes crash. Hero on heroine.

To Live and To Die in Nakhon si Talay.

Timetoshootupaah.

imshinyimpure.